THE BILLIONAIRE'S BABY

L. STEELE

1

Karina

"Gah, you're a frustrating man, Wolfgang." The radio announcer groans. "You know that?"

"Exactly why you like me." Wolfgang chuckles. "And Ivy?" There's a pause when, I swear, I can imagine him leaning in closer to her. "The name's Wolfe."

"Errm," Ivy clears her throat over the airwaves, "so that's our favorite TV trope, brought to life by Wolfe and me…which sounds like something out of Red Riding Wood."

"Hood." Wolfe chuckles.

"That's what I said." Ivy huffs. "Red Riding Hood. So, as I was saying, that's our favorite TV trope. Can you guess what it is? This is Ivy—"

"—And Wolfe," the male announcer interjects.

"And we are so very pleased to be guest hosting the Evening Show on your fave, Smile London FM. Email us, call us…and let us know—"

I lean forward and shut off the car radio. What a couple of twerps those two are. Firstly, the attraction between them is off the charts. Secondly, they have no idea about it and are clearly dancing around it, all but punching each other in the face with the force of the tension building between them. Thirdly…well…if they don't sort it out, they are going to blow up on the show in front of everyone. No doubt, smack each other in the face before smacking each other on the lips. Ha! I snort aloud. Good to know my sense of humor is somewhat alive… Especially considering I have to spend the evening evaluating and repairing security on the boat of Mr. Full-of-Himself-Douchecanoe, aka Arpad f'ing Beauchamp.

A man whose demeanor is every bit as pompous as his name. Yeah, he comes from old money, la-dee-dah. Like I care. But to see him stomp around with that giant stick up his ass, you'd think he's conscious of his status every single second of his life. Which, he probably is. Which is why he'd ordered me to get to his boat and fix the security camera on it that he claims has stopped working before he sets off to whichever island it is he is sailing off to next.

A camera, which had been set up by someone else before I came on board as his security consultant.

Some of us have to spend the evening working; others party till dawn, then sail off into the sunrise. Of course. Admittedly, he and the rest of the Seven pay me a lot… Like a l-o-t; enough for me to leave my life in LA and move to London to ensure that their security detail is top notch.

The Seven had been kidnapped as pre-teens by the Mafia. They had been rescued, but not before it had left them with a burning need to get even with the perpetrators of the incident. It also means that the men are ever vigilant about the Mafia attacking them or their loved ones. That's why they had asked me to increase the security on them and their families. Add to that, the fact that most of the Seven had recently met and married the women of their dreams... And it means I have a shitload of people to protect, from a security standpoint.

Which means… Yeah, I have never been busier. From finding the right talent to add to my team, to constantly upgrading the security details for the ceremonies when any of them decide to get married—the latest being Damian, the rock star who married his almost-nanny and produced a single that knocked the socks off of every single critic and countdown chart.

So, I can't complain. My bank account is happy…which means I should be happy. Only I am not.

I am not one to rest on my laurels, not one to bask in my success… I know what I want next—a family of my own. Good news is, I am already working on it.

In fact, I have a date tomorrow night to fire the first salvo in that direction. No pun intended. I snort aloud. I just have to get through this last chore on my list and then I can get some rest—and god knows, I need it—and be ready to get started on this latest project.

I ease the car into the parking lot of St. Katherine Docks, then grab my bag—which, while being stylish enough to take to a party, is also spacious enough to hold my emergency tools—and head down the line of gleaming vessels. Trust London's wealthiest to bag a spot in the center of London to park their toys. I search for one yacht in particular… What had he called it?

Heartbeat. A weirdly sentimental name for someone who is known as Killer… Not because he kills in real life, but for the killing he makes as an Angel Investor in Silicon Valley. Yep, that's how Arpad f'ing Beauchamp makes his money.

Investing in those who have the ideas but not the financial where-withal to bring them to fruition. He has a knack for spotting talent, I'll give him that…. And that's all I'll ever concede, and definitely not to his face.

The man has a mean streak a mile wide, if any of our brief interactions are any indication. Rumor has it, he doesn't even spare the women he dates… But then, the kind of women he prefers are known for their taste in men who take charge in the bedroom… And push things beyond the point of comfort. Good thing I am not one of them.

I prefer my men amenable and my food spicy. See, the thing with food? It never lets you down. Finding the best restaurants in town and eating out is a particular fancy of mine. Table for one, please. Oh yeah, nothing like the silence of my own company to unwind in the evenings. I am not lonely, just alone. And there is a difference between those two words, right?

I reach *Heartbeat* and clamber overboard, then walk over to the cabin and key in the password. Letting myself in, I glance around and press what I think is the light switch. Bingo. The door clicks shut behind me as I glance around the space. Whoa, this is a yacht? More like a floating mansion. It had seemed reasonably sized from the outside, but in here… Wow! I walk down the steps to the sunken living room. Plush leather seats span one entire side, with a coffee table in the center, and a flat screen on the opposite wall. I walk through to a galley that has an island table, but only one chair. Huh? That's weird. Doesn't he entertain on the boat? Bet he does, so what's with the lone chair?

On the other hand, the gleaming kitchen equipment is more what I expected. It's top-of-the-line and would rival any five-star hotel, I am sure. Not that Mr. Alphahole, here, would ever deign to step into a kitchen. He probably travels with an entire crew to fetch and carry for him. Bet he spends his time jerking off to porno that he watches on that screen as he shoves his hand down his pants and… Please… Argh! Don't go there.

I walk past the kitchen and push the sliding doors apart to find— OMG! A complete, fully-furnished, massive bedroom. Complete with a super king-size bed that takes up almost all of the center of the room. On the far end is a door that, I assume, leads to the bathroom. There's a set of mirrored doors beside it that must lead to a walk-in closet? Clearly, he's spared no expense in doing up this space. Everything is gorgeously designed, if space efficient.

On the other side of the cabin is a narrow freestanding table, and on it, a neat coil of what looks like… A rope? How weird. I move closer, then reach out and brush my fingers across the cord. It's soft to the touch, almost sensual, the material reddish in color, with sparks of gold flecked through it. I bring it to my nose and sniff. An edgy, almost nutty scent tugs at my nostrils. My core clenches. Wow, what the hell does he use this for anyway?

I step back, glance around the room, take in the massive, sliding glass doors. Beyond them is the view of the now-darkening water, rays of sunlight from the setting sun painting the sky a smoldering red and orange.

I stare at the bed again… *Leave, turn and leave, right now.* Come on, surely, a sniff won't hurt? Besides, there are no cameras in the bedroom. At least, there were none indicated on the security detail for this boat I'd inherited from the previous agency… So he'll never find out, right?

I cross the floor, walk around the bed and run my hands across the pillow. Soft… Egyptian cotton, thread count innumerable, no doubt.

Only the best for the asshole, after all. I lean over, bury my nose in the pillow... Don't judge.

Notes of bergamot and cloves, and something dark, musky, edgy — something dangerous — envelops me. I'm instantly wet. *What the hell?*

How can his scent turn me on so? And when I loathe the man? And his attitude, and the way he thinks he can boss me around, and expect me to drop everything and prioritize him above everything else. A shiver runs down my spine. Only my sense of hate getting the better of me, of course.

That's why my stomach flutters. That is the *only* reason my heart beats so fast in my chest. Shit, now I am turning myself on, and that will not do. Not when I have work to do. I pivot, then retrace my steps toward the cabin, and head for the captain's area. There, at the extreme right, I pull up the controls for the security cameras.

I get to work fixing the controls...and am done in fifteen minutes. There, that was easy. It took more time to drive here through the late evening traffic.

I stretch and yawn, suddenly overwhelmingly tired. It's been a long day, long week, long year, actually, setting up business in this city. But I am in a good place, confident my business is going to do well. I pack up my tools, head for the door, then hesitate.

Should I? Why not? It shouldn't matter. I pivot and head back toward the bedroom, then glance out the large window and admire the spectacle. So damn beautiful. If only I had someone to hold my hand while I enjoy it. Nah, doesn't matter. I have me...don't I? And my love for yoga. The only way I know how to unwind. I roll my shoulders, and my muscles protest. Shit, I am too tense.

I place my handbag on the bed stand, then raise my arms high above me. The skirt of my dress pulls tight against my thighs. This won't do. It's why I hate wearing dresses. Damn. I pull off the dress, drape it over the foot of the bed, then kick off my heels and walk over to the center of the room.

I face the window of the yacht, then raise my hands again, bring them down, flow down onto my hands and the tips of my feet, then push up into a downward facing dog. I hold the pose for a few seconds, until my hamstrings burn, my biceps stretch, give. I rock back and forth, then swoop up, back to downward facing dog, then jump forward, straighten. Take a breath in and out, then repeat the process.

By the time I'm done with my routine, my muscles are limber, sweat

beads my forehead. I wipe it off, then stretch and yawn. A pleasant
tiredness buzzes in my blood.

Yeah, I could rest for a little while, then get out of here.

Hold on, bad idea. *Honestly, are you actually thinking of staying on here
for more time than is absolutely essential?*

I reach for my dress then stop, glance at the bed. It looks so comfortable. I yawn again. Coming down from a yoga routine always relaxes me
so much. My limbs grow heavy, my eyelids seem to be weighted down,
and I can barely keep them open. I could nap in the car, of course...but
it's almost dark and that doesn't sound safe. And I know it's not safe to
drive home without catching a few minutes of shut-eye.... I sneak a peek
at the bed again; it looks so comfortable.

Just a short nap. That can't hurt... Can it? It'll rejuvenate me
enough for the ride home which, again, I am in no condition to navigate
when I am this exhausted.

I slip into the bed and draw the covers up to my chin. His dark scent
wraps around me. Goosebumps flare on my skin. It's as if I am
surrounded by him, as if he's cocooned me with his body, and he's all
around me, with me, in this bed. Should I set an alarm on my phone to
wake up? Nah, I'll be fine. It's only a quick nap, after all.

Besides Arpad a-hole isn't going to come back before the morning,
and I'll be long gone by then...

A delicious warmth envelops me and I close my eyes.

A rumbling creeps into my consciousness and I push it away. I press my
cheek into the soft pillow, draw in that scent of bergamot and cloves. His
scent. Mmm. A languid heaviness tugs at my limbs. My muscles relax and
I drift off again. Until a loud creak tears through the silence in my mind. I
jackknife up to sitting position, my heart pounding in my chest. My pulse
rate ratchets up. I strain to see through the darkness. Where the hell am I?

That's when the entire room seems to tilt. I scream and slide off the
bed. I hit the ground on my ass, roll over to hit the glass wall of the
cabin. I turn and press my nose into the transparent barrier and stare
out. Darkness, broken only by the white-tipped foam that crashes
against the side. I gasp, then scramble back until I hit the bed. The boat!
I am on the boat, which is no longer harbored. It's at sea, with me on it.

The entire yacht creaks again, the walls seem to groan, the boat lurches up, and I hold onto the edge of the bed, anchor myself, as it seems to grunt and screech like it's possessed, then straightens. Silence, for a second. The hair on the back of my neck rises, I smell the ozone in the air, then the boat groans, and hurtles down.

The momentum carries me forward toward the wall of the cabin.

I throw out my hand, manage to grab the edge of the bed, hold on as the boat seems suspended in space, before it hits something — the water I presume? — with a crash. The sound echoes in my ears, reverberates down my spine. Then the vessel tilts in the opposite direction. I glance out the glass wall and scream again. Water. So much water, I am surrounded by a wall of water. What the hell is happening? How did the boat get here? I hit the ground on all fours, crawling my way up to the door. Grabbing the handle, I pull myself up, then twist the knob open. I lurch forward as the entire boat goes into another incline. Damn it. I race forward, throw myself onto the couch in the living room and hold on until the boat rightens again. Then cross the living room, up the steps toward the captain's cabin.

That's when I see the man silhouetted against the wheel. He's wearing shorts that cling to his tight ass. And what an ass it is. The fabric outlines the indentation on each side, only to stretch across the girth. The waistband shows off his inverted V figure and his back… I gulp. The planes of his back flex and buck as he grips the wheel of the boat, widens his stance, and leans into the next wave. The next wave… What the — ? It's a huge, huge wave. A behemoth of a WAVE. I glance up and cry out, for he's driving the boat straight up the crest of a monster of a wall of water. There's a crash of thunder, then lightning flickers beyond the boat and I gasp again. An entire sea of darkness, capped by furious white tips, and in the foreground, his massive shoulders that bunch and knot as he grapples with the wheel, holds the boat on course.

Another clap of thunder in the distance, and the alphahole — for it is him, Arpad f'ing A'hole, the bloody owner of this boat, my crazy-ass employer, my frigging boss, who's driving this boat straight into the storm.

He throws back his head and laughs. What the hell? Is he crazy? Does he have a death wish or something? I stomp forward to ask him just that, when the boat groans and begins to slide back, taking me with it. My legs seem to go out from under me. I scream as I hit the decking and roll back. The boat pitches and I am thrown against the wall. Darkness envelops me.

When I open my eyes again, I am back in the bed, in the bedroom of the boat, the sheets pulled up to my chin. Huh? Was it all a dream? I sit up and pain slices through my forehead. I groan, fall back against the pillows.

"Take it easy." A low voice rumbles across the space. I glance over to meet familiar grey-blue eyes.

"You?" I cough. "What the hell are you doing here?"

"It's my boat?" He leans forward and my gaze takes in his bare chest, the sculpted six-...no, eight-pack? Nah...not possible. No one has an eight-pack, do they?

"Enjoying the view?"

I tip my chin up, meet his gaze.

"I've seen better," I lie.

He chuckles. "You must be feeling better. Though, I admit, I preferred it when you were flat on your back in my bed, naked."

I peek under the sheet. "What the hell?" I gasp, "Where are my underclothes?"

"Had to take them off, since you bled all over them from your head wound."

I touch my forehead, and the pain flashes behind my eyes. "Ow," I moan.

"Let me see that." He leans over me and his scent intensifies. His chest planes ripple and his biceps bunch as he reaches across.

I pull away. "It's fine," I grumble, "it's just a bump. It's not bleeding."

"I won't hurt you," he rumbles.

Why don't I believe you?

"Unless you want me to..." His lips twist, "Do you want me to, hurt you, my little stowaway?"

"What?" I scowl, "Of course, not."

"Then why are you here?"

2

——————

Arpad

"Not by choice." She tips her chin up. "Trust me, I'd rather be a million miles away."

I grin. "And yet, here you are."

"I came in to check the security cameras—which are working now, by the way. The next thing I know, I am waking up to the apocalypse." She scowls. "What the hell were you doing driving the yacht into a storm?"

"What the hell are you doing on my boat?"

She reddens. "I checked the camera—which is functional, by the way—you can thank me later—" She tosses her hair and winces. "After which, uh, I guess I was too tired, and decided to work out?"

"Work out?" I drum my fingers on my bicep. "Exactly how did you decide you were going to work out."

"I was tense, and decided I need to do a quick yoga session."

"Hmm." I rub my chin, trying to understand this. "So, you decided to do a quick yoga workout, dressed in…" I glance at her dress laid out at the bottom of the bed.

"No, I took off the dress," she mutters.

I tilt my head. "Good thing. I don't like that color on you anyway."
She gapes, "You don't?"

I shake my head. "Black doesn't do you justice. You're such a fiery personality, you need to wear red."

"Red?" she murmurs.

"Yep," I bend over her and lean in enough to share my breath with hers, "it brings out the highlights in your hair."

"Oh." Her pupils dilate and her breathing goes ragged. She inches closer, close enough for her breasts to graze my chest. And damn it, I'm instantly hard.

I straighten and she blinks, as if coming out of a trance. I can't stop the smirk that curls my lips. "Your heels," I murmur, "you took them off as well?"

"What?" She straightens, then glances around her, "Sorry, what did you say?"

"Your stilettos," I point to where I'd placed her footwear by the side.

"Right," she swallows, "of course, I took them off."

"And then you proceeded to work out in my cabin?"

"It was just a basic routine with few stretching poses." She blinks rapidly, "You know, like downward facing dog?"

Oh baby, I'd love to downward dog you. The thought of having her balanced on her hands and toes, butt in the air...tits thrust out as she arches into the pose... I clear my throat. *Jesus, is it hot in here or what?* I widen my stance. "So, you came into my cabin, where you shouldn't have been in the first place, did a quick workout, then crawled into my bed?"

She wrings her fingers together in front of her.

I stare at her.

She flushes. "In my defense, I wanted to find out if the living quarters were secure or if you needed a camera or something here as well so —"

I hold up my hand, "Hold on, back up. So, you came into my bedroom to check if there were cameras...and then what? You decided to stay on?"

"Not really." She hunches her shoulders. "I came in here and it was so calm, I decided to do my yoga routine. Then, the bed was so inviting, and I was so tired, and I might have uh, decided to take a nap..."

"A nap?"

She nods. "Yeah, stupid idea, but I was exhausted and I didn't think you'd be back for a while," she mumbles, "and besides, you owe me for coming in and fixing your security camera, on what should have been an evening off."

"Had plans, huh?"

"Kind of." She sits up. "Shit, what time is it?"

I raise my shoulder, "Beats me."

"Where's my phone?" She glances round the space. "Please, please I need my phone."

"Phone?"

"So, I can check the time." She spots her bag on the table, and her features light up. "Can you get me my bag?"

"Why?"

She scowls at me, "So I can get my phone from it, you ass."

"Get it yourself," I drawl, then drop into the chair and lean back for good measure.

"I don't have any clothes on."

"So?"

She gapes. "You're a complete alphahole, you know that?"

"I'll take that as a compliment." I smirk.

"Oh, F off." She pulls the sheet up and around her shoulders, then swings her legs over, and hitching up the sheet, walks over to the table. Still holding the cover, she manages to grab her bag, unzip it and pull out her phone. "What the hell?" she yelps. "It's almost 10 am."

"It is." I tip back my chair, watch her as she waves her phone in the air.

"Turn this boat around."

"No."

"I have to get back."

"Too late."

"You don't understand," she snarls. "I have somewhere I need to be."

"So do I." I scratch my chest and her gaze drops there. She swallows. I drag my hand down to my waist and her breathing grows shallow. Hmm, interesting. Apparently, little Miss Perfect here is not as impervious to my presence as she'd like me to believe.

"Don't do that," she mutters.

"What?"

"That entire showing-off-your-torso thing."

"Was I?"

"You were, and you know it." She tips her chin up. "I demand that you get back to land right now."

"It's that important, huh?" I frown at her.

She tosses her hair back from her face. "Of course, it is. That's what I've been trying to tell you all this while."

"Why don't you tell me what made you get that tattoo, first?"

She scowls, "What tattoo?"

"How many tattoos do you have?" I smirk.

She opens her mouth, and I raise my hand. "Yes, I saw it, when I took off your underwear. Deal with it."

Color smears her cheeks.

"You're a piece of work, you know that?"

I chuckle, "That's not the answer to my question."

She tugs up the sheet then, purses her lips. I wait as she seems to consider her options. "So, if I tell you the rationale behind the tattoo, you'll take me back to land?"

I shrug.

She glowers at me, then snaps back her shoulders. "The line you saw that I had tattooed... It's from my favorite poet."

If you but knew the flames that burn in me which I attempt to beat down with my reason.

I recite it at the same time as her.

"You know the poem?" She frowns.

"Pushkin." I nod. "I know who wrote it. I want to know why you have it tattooed on your back." I hadn't missed the cursive written on one side of her spine; it was beautiful, evocative and unexpected... And yet, exactly the kind of verse I'd expect her to love. Deep, intense, yet fiery and passionate. It is so much Karina, that I have to find out more about it. "Well?" I lift one eyebrow. "Why did you get it?"

She draws in a breath, then glances away. "Because I was so rebellious as a kid and it got me into so much trouble. I got it to remind myself that it's okay to pick my battles. I don't have to win everything. Just the important ones, you know?"

I stare at her. "You don't like to lose," I mutter, and she tips up her chin.

"Neither do you," she states.

"Which leaves us at a stalemate."

"Which leaves you on the yacht, and me back on land," she insists.

"No," I drawl.

"What?" Her features tighten. "You promised to take me back."

"I did no such thing."

"B... but..." she stutters, "you said...."

"No, I didn't." I waggle my finger at her.

"You...you liar," she chokes out.

"Wrong—" I swallow down the chuckle that bubbles up. Karina—angry, all flashing eyes, and glowing skin. My god, the adrenaline from the chance to spar with her is better than the thrill of closing a killer deal in Silicon Valley. "I didn't say anything. You asked if I would take you back if you told me about the tattoo. I shrugged and you assumed that meant yes." I pretend to yawn. "You need to pay more attention to the details, doll."

She walks over to the side-table near the bed, places her phone on it, then swivels to stand over me. "What the hell is wrong with you?" she demands.

"What's wrong is that you are naked in my bedroom and I haven't touched you yet."

She frowns. "Don't try to intimidate me, you ass."

"Oh, you'll know when I'm trying to intimidate you, Stowie."

"Stowie?" She blinks. "I have a name, you know."

I look her up and down, "I'm not in the habit of remembering the names of my hired help.

"Hired help?" she splutters. "How dare you?" She launches herself at me, and hits my chest with such force that the impact knocks me and the chair over.

I land on my back; my head connects with the hard floor and her knee connects with my stomach. "Uff," the breath rushes out of me. She scrambles to get away, and I grab her around the waist, flip her over onto the ground and lean over her. "There... Much better," I mutter.

"Let me go." She makes that little snarling sound at the back of her throat again. How cute.

"Now, now, is that any way to thank your savior?"

"Savior?" She huffs, "More like a kidnapper."

"If the title fits." I raise my shoulders. "I did patch you up, and put you to bed."

"So?" She snorts.

"And saved you from being lost at sea in a storm."

"You were saving your own hide, you… You complete tosser."

"Apparently, living in London has improved your insults, at least."

"It's done nothing for your attitude, you bastard."

I click my tongue, "I think I need to wash out your mouth." I stare at her lips. "Or maybe I should shut you up another way, hmm?"

"Don't you dare." Her golden eyes blaze at me.

"You have no idea what I am going to do."

"Don't I?" she mutters. "You were thinking of kissing me."

"Hmm." I lower my face until my nose bumps hers, "Now that you mention it…" I hold her gaze and the gold of her irises deepen to a burnt amber. "Fucking beautiful," I mutter.

She blinks. "You don't have to flatter me."

I take in her features, the slope of her creamy shoulder, the shape of her curves so soft and under me. "The first thing you should know about me," I growl, "is that I never lie."

"What's the second?"

"I never back away from a challenge."

She purses her lips. "I am not challenging you."

"Hmm, I could have sworn that's what your earlier words sounded like."

"I was simply asking you to turn the yacht back and drop me off."

"Can't, babe."

Her gaze narrows. "You don't understand. I need to be back by 5 pm."

"Hot date?"

She glances away, then back at me. "Something like that," she mutters. "It's just...someone I have to see."

My gut twists and something hot stabs at my chest. "Drop him," I command.

"What?"

"Whoever it is, you're not meeting him again."

She opens and shuts her mouth, "You're completely off your rocker."

Tell me about it. Why the hell do I care who she's going to see? It's not like I have a claim on her. Still, when I'd tucked her into my bed, something had felt right about it. And not just that she had her eyes closed, and wasn't glaring at me like she wanted to rip my head off, which is her natural response whenever she sees me. So why the hell am I still holding her down, with my hips between her legs, my groin flush against hers, my chest wearing the imprint of those beautiful breasts?

"Stay with me, for the next thirty days," I snap.

"What?"

"That's how long this trip is for."

"You're joking."

"Told you, I never joke."

"Get off of me." She slaps at my shoulder.

"Not until you give me your answer."

"Then my answer is no."

"Refuse me and I'll strip the contract for the security details for the Seven from your company."

"You can't do that." Her features twist, "You wouldn't dare do that. I'll take you to court."

"Don't dare me, Stowie."

"Don't call me that."

"What would you prefer?"

"My name, for one, you ass. You can call me Karina. On the other hand," she pushes up against me, "don't call me at all."

"I prefer Stowie." I take in her flushed features, the pulse beating at her throat. "So what do you say? Do we have a deal?"

"No."

"I am not letting you up unless you agree."

"What is this? Compulsion?"

"Coercion." I allow my lips to kick up in a smirk. "Or would you prefer seduction?" I lower my gaze to her lips. "Will you taste as sweet as you smell or will you be as prickly as your demeanor, hmm?"

"You'll never find that out." She makes a noise deep in her throat, and the sound travels straight down my spine. My groin hardens. Bet if I look down, I'll see the crotch of my pants tented. She must sense it, or rather, feel the thick length jab into her stomach, for her gaze widens. She gulps, the sound audible in the silence.

"Thirty days," I stare at her parted lips, "during which we explore this chemistry between us. Then we can go back to our individual lives as if nothing happened."

"Thirty days." Her tongue darts out. "That's it? And we both walk away?"

"Seven-hundred and twenty hours to explore each other." I peer into her face. "That's forty-three-thousand two-hundred minutes to give into the attraction between us and find out exactly what it holds."

She blinks, then shakes her head. "You mean we shag each other, don't you?"

"Not giving it names, babe. Why don't we let nature take its course?" I glance up into her eyes. "With a little help from us, of course."

Something passes across her face, an expression I can't quite discern. "What?" I scowl, "What is it?"

"Thirty days." She nods. "I'll agree, but I have a condition of my own."

3

———————

Karina

"You're not exactly in a position to add stipulations," he rumbles.

His big body holds me down, the weight of his hips on mine not altogether unpleasant… Okay, so it's delicious, actually, having him pin me down like this. The heat from his big body surrounds me in a cocoon of intimacy. The strength of his dominance slams into my chest, holds me in place. A moan tumbles from my lips and his gaze drops to my mouth again. "Where were we?" he asks.

"I have a condition," I insist.

He frowns, "I don't take kindly to negotiations."

"Not a negotiation. It's a…" I bite the inside of my cheek, "a way to leverage the situation for the benefit of both of us."

"Oh?" He tilts his head. "Now you're talking."

Of course, the a-hole billionaire businessman needs to be spoken to in the language he understands. No problem. I got this then.

"I want something out of this, uh, association."

"You're getting your company."

"I already have that," I point out.

"You're ensuring the survival of your enterprise and your employees."

I fight the urge to roll my eyes. "I want more," I press. "Surely, you understand that, don't you—capitalizing on any given situation to ensure you optimize your return?"

"Hmm." He swipes back a strand of hair that's stuck to my cheek. "What is it you want?"

"A child."

He stares. "Excuse me?"

"You heard me," I retort. "Thanks to you, I am going to miss a crucial appointment this evening, where I was going to have an intrauterine insemination."

"A what?" He blinks.

"An IUI," I explain, "where I would have been inseminated artificially with sperm from a donor."

"A donor?"

I nod. "I've been on fertility medication to stimulate my egg production. My peak ovulation window is this evening, and if I don't get there in time, all of my work will go to waste."

"Hold on." He shakes his head. "You had an appointment this evening, to inseminate yourself with some man's sperm—"

"Not some man, someone I chose after careful screening."

"Right." He nods. "And now, since you can't do that, you want me to —" He seems at a loss for words, and honestly, the spectacle of this confident alphahole at a loss for words, is more than funny. I can't stop the chuckle that escapes me.

"Weren't expecting that, huh?" I mutter. "Surprise," I sing out.

"So, you want me to stand in for your sperm donor?"

"Damn, you're bright." I widen my gaze in mock surprise. "So, what do you say?"

"To what?" He scowls.

"To donating your sperm to my cause, of course… Only, you'd do it the old-fashioned way."

"So unprotected sex, huh?" he rumbles. "Resulting in possible offspring?"

"It's known to happen," I deadpan. "So, what do you say?"

"Huh." He glances down at our position, then springs up to his feet, as if he can't wait to put distance between us.

Ha, knew it. Nothing like talking about real stuff like family or kids

or, god forbid, the L word to have an alphahole backtrack and give you
a wide berth. Jeez, I should have used this conversation earlier. It
would have saved me so much time.

I wrap the sheet more securely around me, then try to stand up. My
feet entangle with the bloody sheet, and I fall back. "Bugger." I huff.
Yep, I'm American, but damn, if I don't love using the British insults.
They have a certain *Je ne sais quoi* about them, don't you think?

"Let me." He holds out a hand, and I stare at it.

"Take it," he mutters. "After what you told me, I am not likely to
jump on you—not that I would have earlier either—but trust me, until
this…whatever this insane conversation between us is sorted out, I am
not likely to...you know…" He frowns down at me as if still not
comprehending what we'd discussed thus far. Typical male attitude.
Instead of trying to talk it out, pretend the problem doesn't exist in the
first place.

I grab his hand and he hauls me to my feet, then abruptly releases
me. He retreats and it's as if he's sucked out all of the heat in the room
with him. I tug the covers under my arms, then fix my gaze on him. "So?
What do you think?"

"What do I think?" He drags his fingers through his hair. "I am not
ready to have children."

"You don't need to take responsibility for the kid."

He turns on me. "It's my sperm," he points out. "That's *if* I decide to
donate sperm the old-fashioned way and shag you, which I haven't
agreed to yet."

"Thought that's what you suggested?"

"That was before." He draws in a breath. "Look, this is all a bit
sudden."

He pats the pockets of his shorts, then frowns. He glances around
the room, walks over to the bedstand, snatches up a pack of cigarettes
from the drawer. He pulls out a cigarette, places it in between his lips,
but doesn't light it.

"You smoke?"

He drops the pack back on the bedstand. "I'm trying to quit."

"You'd have to if you wanted anything to do with the child."

He levels a dirty look at me and I raise my hands. "I mean, that's the
point I'm trying to make. You wouldn't have to change anything if you
didn't have anything to do with the kid. I'd take care of him or her. In
fact, I'd insist you don't have any relationship with them."

"Hey," he protests, "you're acting as if I would be a bad influence on the kid."

"Wouldn't you?"

"Of course, not." He draws himself up to his full height. "I'd be a bloody good father."

"Of course, you would," I say in a soothing voice. "In this instance, though, I would have sole custody of the child, since this is all my idea. You'd sign away your rights to the child after conception, so your only role would be limited to that of—"

"The sperm donor."

"Exactly." I nod, "You only have to show up, uh, do the deed during the time we are together. Then we part, and hopefully, by then, I am pregnant."

"With my child," he snaps in a low voice. "*My*. Child."

The hair on the back of my neck rises. Okay, this isn't going as I'd intended. I'd broached the conversation because I really didn't want to miss the opportunity when my eggs are ripe for fertilizing, and I had thought he wouldn't have a problem with it. After all, I am still offering him what he wanted in the bargain—the chance to sleep with me. Only it isn't completely without strings— Okay so maybe it is a bit of a surprise to spring on the man, but still, come on. Surely it isn't a big deal to him. Is it?

"Well, technically," I venture, "it would be my child once you sign the rights over."

He frowns.

"See? There'd be no responsibility, no ties to bind you. You'd have fun in the creation process and then you'd walk away."

He moves the unlit cigarette to the other corner of his mouth.

"Just how you like it, right?" I tilt my head, "You can continue to play the field, continue with your merry lifestyle, piloting this yacht around the world, whenever you want, wherever you want, at the drop of a hat."

He growls low in his throat, and the sound chafes across my skin. All of my nerve endings seem to fire at once.

"Do I, uh, take that as a yes?"

"Yes." He folds his hands over his chest, then glares at me. "On one condition."

"What's that?" I frown. "What other condition could you possibly have for this situation?"

"Marry me."

Arpad

"What?" She gapes. "Marry you? Why the hell would I do that?"

"Hold on," I protest. "Marrying me wouldn't be as bad as you're making it out to be."

"It would be worse," she mumbles under her breath. "And why would I do that, anyway?"

"Ah, why wouldn't you do that?" I stare at her. *What's wrong with this woman?* "There are many women out there who would have loved to hear that proposal from me, I'll have you know."

"Well, then marry them."

"I want to marry you," I insist.

Her cheeks flush. "No way." She shakes her head. "This is not happening."

"Relax, it would be a fake marriage," I assure her. "We'd just pretend to be married for the time it takes to meet my family."

"Meet your family?" Her gaze widens. In surprise? Horror? "I'd rather dive off this boat right now."

"Hey," I scowl, "they aren't that bad." I draw in a breath, "Okay, so they aren't the easiest either… Hell, what family is? Which is precisely why I need you with me when I go to visit them."

"Why the hell do you need backup?" She looks me up and down. "You seem like you could manage almost anything and anyone on your own."

"You haven't met my family." I roll my shoulders. "They are, shall we say, quite full-on."

"All the more reason that I am not the right person for this. I am no good with situations of the, uh, emotional kind. Why do you think I opted for artificial insemination?"

"Because you couldn't find a man who wanted you enough to start a family with you?"

She pales; her breath hitches. "You know what? Forget it. This entire thing is a bad idea. It's best we keep our distance from each other for the time that we are on this boat." She marches past me. Something glimmers on her cheek.

Aw, hell, is she crying? Something hot stabs at my chest. I swoop down and grip her arm, "Hey, I'm sorry. I didn't mean that."

"Of course, you did." She stares down at where I've locked my fingers around her. "Let me go."

"No."

"You don't want to fight me," she says in a low voice. "I run my own security agency. I have learned more than my share of self-defense skills, enough to take on men far more dangerous than you."

"Now, you're daring me, and you know I can never back down from a challenge."

"Is that right?" She lifts her gaze to my face. "We'll see, shall we?" She yanks on my grasp; I tighten my hold. She feints, locks her leg around mine in a seamless move and tugs. I throw my arms around her, press her close as she kicks my legs out from under me.

The world tilts and I hit the floor of the cabin with a resounding thud as the back of my head connects with the hardboard. The breath whooshes out of me; pain slices down my spine.

"Let go of me, you oaf." She struggles in my hold. The covers slip down to bare her luscious breasts.

I take in the pink areolae, the beaded nipples that seem to pebble further under my scrutiny.

"Avert your eyes, you mofo." She smacks my head.

"Ow," I gasp out a pained breath even as I squeeze my arms around her, and haul her to my chest.

"Dammit, unhand me." She pushes her knee into my groin and I groan.

"What the hell? If you keep that up, I won't be able to father any children, Stowie."

"Aargh." She punches my shoulder. "I," she punches the side of my face, "hate," punch, "that," punch, "name."

"What the fuck?" I growl, then scissor my legs around her, flip her over so she's once more on her back. The sheet she's draped around herself tightens further. She wriggles about, tries to free herself, and I lean more of my weight on her, imprisoning her under me.

"You big bully," she fumes, then lashes out with her arm. I duck, only to grab her arm and twist it above her head. She throws a punch with the other, and I catch her wrist and pull it up, then shackle both her wrists with my palm.

"Much better." I take in her flushed features. At least, the color has returned to her face. "Now where were we?"

"Nowhere," she growls. Her eyes flare; her dark hair falls across her forehead. She's fucking gorgeous and beautiful and so vital. I want a piece of that; something… Someone so alive that she could fire up the dark corners of my life.

"Wrong answer," I retort. "Care to try again?"

"Oh, sod off." She blows the hair off of her face. "So easy for you to use your strength to overpower me, huh?"

"I use everything I have at my disposal." I hold her gaze, "Including you."

She makes that sound of anger deep in her throat that fucking cuts me off at the knees.

"Jesus," I growl. "Why the hell did you have to be so… so irresistible?"

"Speak for yourself," she mutters. "Let me off this boat."

"No."

"I need to get back," she insists.

"There's no need for that, considering everything is settled."

"Nothing is settled." She yanks at her hands and I tighten my grip. "Except that you are officially out of your friggin' mind."

"Maybe," I whisper. "Maybe not. All this off-the-charts chemistry between us, you gotta admit, it's best put to good use."

"And I told you what I want out of it." She glowers.

"So did I."

"It's unacceptable to me," she snaps. "I am not marrying you."

"It's a pretend marriage."

"Oh." She blinks, then firms her lips. "I'd still have to put up with your presence."

"You'll have to do more than that if you want to get pregnant by me." I stare into her eyes and she swallows.

"*That*…would be different."

"How?"

"It would be working toward a bigger goal."

I can't stop myself from leaning into her further. My hardness stabs into her belly. "You have no idea how true that is."

"Argh," she makes a gagging sound, "you're so full of yourself."

"And you can be full of me too."

Her cheeks redden. "Jesus, that's a terrible pun."

"Welcome to my part of the woods, Sparks." Okay, now that…nickname… That wasn't intentional…but I have to admit, it does fit her better.

Her golden eyes flare. She opens her mouth and I click my tongue. "No more arguing. You pose as my pretend, newly-wedded wife on my annual trip home to visit my family, and I'll be more than happy to impregnate you."

"It's not that simple. It's not like I can get pregnant in one shot." She snorts. "Pun intended."

"Oh, I intend to keep trying as many times as needed, and a few times more for good measure," I promise.

"For the duration of this trip, you mean?" she corrects me.

I frown. "Yes, that's what I mean. Next thirty days, you and me, Sparks, and as much of my semen as you can hold. What do you say?"

"Fine," she mutters, "but it doesn't mean I have to like you."

"Fine," I reply, "but it does mean that I get to kiss you, and do with you as I please."

"Wait, what?" She opens her mouth. "What do you mean?" She begins to struggle under me. "You bastard, I should have known you'd have something filthy and underhanded hidden up your sleeve."

"So, are you turning down this offer?"

She balls her fists. "Don't tempt me."

"So, you're accepting this agreement?"

"I don't really have a choice, do I?"

"That's not an answer." I peer into her face. "Yes or no, Sparks?"

She draws in a breath, glances around the space. Then she exhales heavily and says, "Fine, you have me. Okay, I need this—"

I lower my head to hers.

4

———

Karina

He holds his lips close to mine, so close that I breathe in his air. So close that the heat of his body surrounds me, cocoons me. So close that I can hear his heart thud in his chest. Smell the salt of the sea mixed with that primal, dark maleness of him, the thing that had attracted me from the moment I'd seen him, a year ago in LA.

I'd walked into the conference room of my office, the sun had poured in through the windows, too bright, as always, in LA. The rays had framed this tall figure that had seemed to fill my entire line of sight. The light behind him had thrown his face into shadow while high-lighting the rest of his magnificent physique.

The fitted formal shirt had stretched across his chest, only to be tucked into the waistband of his slacks that had molded to his thighs. He'd taken a step forward and the muscles of his legs had uncoiled. A primitive fear had gripped me then. This man—he was trouble. If he came closer, I'd be sucked into his presence, his larger-than-life persona that dominated the room and sucked the oxygen from the space. Then he'd walked out of the light and the full impact of his blue-grey gaze had smashed into my chest. I swear, I'd forgotten how to breathe… My lungs had burned; my stomach had bottomed out. My knees had buckled under me and I'd had to hold onto the back of the chair in front of me to keep myself upright. He'd stared at me, no hint of any emotion on his face. He'd looked me up and down with an expression I can only describe as cold and calculating.

"Karina?" He'd spoken my name and the deep timber of his voice had rolled down my spine, coiled in my belly, and heat had pooled between my legs. That's when I'd known that I had to stay away from him. Keep as much distance as possible between me and his overpowering presence, the way he'd eaten me up with his gaze, had glared at me and peered into my soul as if he'd gleaned my secrets.

"Karina…" he whispers my name against my mouth and all of my senses pop to life; my pulse begins to race. I shove at his shoulders, and this time, he rolls off of me. Then rises to his feet. He holds out his hand to help me up; I ignore it.

I secure the sheet under my arms, then push myself up to standing position.

He peruses my features, his gaze intense. Heat sears my skin; my pulse pounds at my temples. There's no denying there's something between us. Shit, is that going to complicate the situation? Only if I let it. Which I am not going to do. Of course, not. I have more sense than to let that happen... Right?

I clear my throat, "you mentioned you could do anything you like with me?"

"Does that bother you?"

Yes.

Yes.

No. I scoff. "Nothing you do could possibly shock me."

"No?"

"It's what I'd expect from you, needing props to enhance your performance in bed."

"Is that what you think?" He laughs and his entire face lights up. His grey-blue eyes seem to glow with some kind of inner joke, one I am obviously not privy to.

"Why don't you enlighten me then?"

He shakes his head. "What would be the fun in that? Why can't you simply let the events unfold, take things as they come?"

"Is that what you do?" I frown. "Let things come to you?"

He looks me up and down. "After all, you did come to me."

"After you insisted that I check the camera on your yacht."

"Were you doing anything better?"

"Anything else would have been better than having to be here."

He clicks his tongue. "That's why you decided to stow away and fall asleep in my bed?"

I redden, then jut out my chin. "I was tired," I snap.

"So am I." He drags his fingers through his hair. "I don't want to fight with you, Sparks, much as it is refreshing as a form of foreplay—"

"Hold on." I fold my arms across my chest. "Is that what you think this is?"

"Are you denying that the attraction between us makes you antsy? That it doesn't make you want to throw yourself at me, and tear my clothes off, and jump me right now? That, as we speak, you're not undressing me, wondering what I have on below these?" He hooks his finger in the waistband of his shorts, and of course, my gaze darts to his crotch, at the trail of hair that disappears, at the tent in his crotch that he makes no pretense of hiding.

"I am not admitting to anything," I mutter.

"You will; it's only a matter of time." He smirks.

"Keep dreaming," I scoff.

"What makes you think I haven't been?"

"Huh?" I stare at him. "What do you mean?"

"Unlike you, I don't fight my instincts. Since the moment I laid eyes on you, I knew this day would arrive, when I'd have you with me, on my boat, in my bedroom…" he leans in close enough for his nose to bump mine, "at my mercy."

"Everything I'm doing is of my mercy." I tip up my chin.

"That's what I like about you." He chuckles. "That's what attracted me to you in the first place. The fact that you want to come out the winner in any situation. In that sense, we are very alike."

"I am nothing like you." I swipe my hair over my shoulder. "I am not the one taking unfair advantage of the situation I find myself in."

"Is that right?" He raises his arm and I flinch. He tucks a strand of hair behind my ear, "Keep telling yourself so and you'll still not believe it."

He peers into my eyes and I hold his gaze, stare into those deep fathomless eyes of his. "On the other hand, I agree that I need to make the most of this situation I find myself in. I want a child, the timing is right, and I could do worse for a father."

"Are you admitting that your genes and mine together could make for an extraordinary offspring?" He smirks.

"Any child of mine would be incredible," I glance up at the ceiling, "and yeah, you'll do for a father."

He laughs, then cups my cheek. "And I changed my mind. I want some rights."

"What?" I blink. "What do you mean?"

"Visitation rights, babe."

"I already told you I get sole custody of the child."

"And I am telling you now that I want visitation rights."

My heart begins to thud. This is going completely wrong. This isn't what I wanted. My child...belongs only to me. I am going to bring him or her up on my own.

"No," I snarl. "No way."

"Think about it." He raises his hand. "Don't turn it down so quickly."

"I don't want you in my child's life." I flatten my lips. "I don't need to think about it."

"You sure that you want to waste the opportunity you've been given of actually becoming pregnant? And all because of your own ego."

"My ego?" I gape. "Look who's talking. Only the most full-of-himself a-hole that I've ever met."

"At your service." He straightens. "I don't make any pretenses about who I am. I like control, I like challenges, and I never turn down a dare."

"Is that why you like to chase storms?"

He straightens and I have to tilt my head further back to meet his gaze.

"Clearly, you have a death wish," I allow my lips to twist. "or maybe you like to challenge the elements?"

His gaze intensifies, his nostrils flare, and he clenches his fists at his sides. "What's it to you?" he finally growls. "You're still here, and so is this boat."

"Is that what you do when you disappear on one of your sailing trips?" *Shut up, already. What are you trying to do, push him? Goad him into losing his temper? Why can't you simply walk away from this entire deal anyway, huh?*

"You have no idea what you're talking about," he barks.

"Oh?" I swallow down the dryness in my throat. "Enlighten me then."

"You haven't earned the right to that yet." He steps back and the heat of his body recedes. A chill grips me. I rub my fingers down my arm. Shit, why the hell do I already miss his proximity?

"Make up your mind about what you want. It's in your hands now." He looks me up and down. "Meanwhile, I'm going to take a shower."

Turning, he heads for the bath.

5

Arpad

I shove down my shorts and toss them aside. What the hell was I thinking, asking for visitation rights? And the kid is not even here. I mean, she isn't even pregnant and I am planning out some kind of future for us. Is that why I'd proposed the mock marriage, as a way to keep her close?

No… That much was true… I need to get my grandmother off my back about my family life, or lack of… And this is too good an opportunity to squander. Besides, what could be better than spending 30 days with the woman who's intrigued me since I'd first lain eyes on her. Fuck her, get her out of my system, and use her to divert my family's attentions. It's a perfect plan.

So why the hell are the visitation rights so important? The thought of her pregnant with my child, having one of my own… Something that had never occurred to me, not until she'd raised the topic. And no way, would I walk away from her if she became pregnant as a result of our possible liaison. Hold on…

A child? A fake marriage? Actually tying myself down to another in some form? Holy hell, how the fuck had my thinking changed so completely, and in a matter of minutes? I should have left her in my bed and walked away, but of course, I hadn't been able to resist watching her sleep. And when I'd undressed her earlier… Not that I would have taken advantage of her when she was asleep, but hell, I am man enough to appreciate the creamy flesh of her tits, the impossibly small waist, the rounded hips, the smooth thighs, and the sweet flesh between them.

The blood rushes to my groin. I can't stop the groan that grumbles up my chest. I've been sporting a hard-on since. Oh, I'd covered her up and walked away, but I hadn't been able to leave the room after that. And then I had to complicate it all. I flick on the shower and step under the spray. The steam from the shower rises up and I drag my fingers through my hair, pull it back from my face.

What the hell am I doing, even considering some kind of future between us? And why am I not repulsed by it? In fact, it feels… Different, new… Something to look forward to. Is that how bored I've grown with my life? Not even setting out on my yacht to sail off on another adventure holds the same appeal.

Just a phase. That's all it is. Just until I find the next takeover to occupy myself. Another storm to chase and conquer. She had been right about that, as well. How had she guessed my motivations so quickly?

Only the Seven know of my penchant of challenging the elements. I plot my trips carefully, to ensure I run through the eye of at least one storm; though the one last night had been just a spot of heavy weather. The real storm is still a few days off and that's where I am headed. With her on board, though, I need to change my route fast. Putting myself at risk is one thing…but her… No… I can't put her in jeopardy. Not in that way.

I reach forward to turn off the shower, when cool air touches my back. The door to the shower cubicle opens behind me, and before I can turn, she's slipped in front of me, straight in the path of the shower.

I stiffen. "What are you —"

"Shh." She reaches up to place a finger on my lips. "You get one hour per week in visitation rights."

I take in her bare shoulders, the curves of her gorgeous breasts, the flare of her bare hips. The water flows between her legs and droplets glisten above the cleft of her pussy.

My mouth dries; my fingers tingle to touch her.

I reach for her and she prompts me, "What do you say?"

I drag my gaze up to peer into her features. "It's not enough." I frown. "One day per week." I drag my fingers across my chest and her gaze drops there; her pupils dilate.

"Two hours," she whispers. "Please." She opens her mouth to speak and I shake my head. I squeeze her shoulders so she drops to her knees in front of me.

"Show me how much you want this deal."

She stares up at me, her eyelashes spiked from the water. Her dark hair sticks to her forehead, and ripples down her back. She draws in a breath and the tops of her tits tremble. Fuck me, but I want to grab those sweet globes and squeeze them. "Do it, Sparks," I order.

She sets her jaw, curves her fingers into fists at her sides. Her gaze narrows and color smears her cheeks. My cock instantly lengthens… This woman—her fire will be my undoing.

"Don't keep me waiting," I growl.

"Don't talk to me like that."

"I'll do anything I want to you for the next thirty days, and you'll take it."

"No." She rises up and I push her down again, and hold there. "Tick-tock, babe. You only have a few more hours when you are at your most fertile. You need this more than me."

"*This* isn't going to help me get pregnant, asshole," she growls.

"Alphahole." I peel back my lips and she glowers back.

"Last chance," I snap. "Take me in your mouth or—"

She reaches up, curls her fingers around the base of my cock and wraps her lips around the head.

She holds my gaze as she licks around the rim. My stomach muscles clench. She presses her other palm to my thigh for balance and her touch sets off flickers of lust in my groin. She squeezes the fingers of her other hand around the base of my shaft and I widen my stance to support myself better.

She bobs her head, takes me in further, and I can't stop the groan that rips from me. I dig my fingers into her hair, watch as more of the length of my cock disappears inside her mouth. She swallows and heat sears up my spine.

"Bloody hell." I cup the back of her head, pull her back, until I am balanced at the edge of her mouth. She stares up at me, her golden eyes daring me. She licks around the head of my dick, then releases the base of my dick to cup my balls. She squeezes and my adrenaline spikes. Fire laces my nerves and my groin tightens. I pull her forward so my cock slides down her throat. She gags; saliva drools from her lips and combines with the water from her shower.

"You're so bloody hot, Sparks," I growl. "I am going to take your mouth."

6

Karina

Blowjob, huh? I am going to suck his soul through his cock. I am going to blow him so hard he's going to see stars for days. At least, that had been my intention... Until he takes control. With him, there's no giving… Arpad f'ing Beauchamp always takes and takes… He tugs on my hair and pulls me away, "Breathe through your nose," he orders.

I draw in a breath, then another. He nods, then thrusts me forward so his cock hits the back of my throat again. He pulls back, then forward, again and again. His cock fills my mouth, my throat, the soft skin curved around the steel of his shaft. He digs his fingers into my hair and tugs. Pinpricks of pleasure sear my scalp.

Moisture pools between my legs and it's not from the shower. I reach down to touch myself and he snaps, "Not until I let you."

I stare up at him, at the water that clings to his shoulders, the marks of some kind of friction burns now faded against his skin, the tendons of his throat that stand out in relief under his skin. His jaw tics, as he continues to tug me forward and back, and forward. My teeth graze across his shaft and he hisses. "Fuck." He slaps his other hand against the shower wall as if to keep his balance. He widens his stance, looms over me as I dig my fingertips into his thigh, continue to massage his balls with the other. "Bloody hell." His thighs twitch, his upper body shudders as his chest rises and falls. "I'm going to come," he growls, right before his balls contract and he shoots his load. The salty taste of his cum fills my palate, overflows down my chin as he seems to come and come. I swallow and his entire body shudders. He pulls out, only to haul me up to my toes. He closes his mouth around mine, drinks from me, sucks on my tongue and ravishes my mouth. My core clenches and my knees threaten to give way. Without breaking the kiss, he bends, grabs me under my thighs and hauls me up and against the wall.

He nudges his dick against my opening and I shiver. He pulls me to him and thrusts into me in one smooth move. Too much, too full, he stretches my channel, crammed into me with such precision that it feels like we are two halves of a puzzle. There's so much of him, surely, he'll consume me. He'll split me open and I won't be able to resist him. I want him, want this… This…crazy hunger that tears at my gut, that crawls inside me, urging me to thrust my breasts up and into his chest. I lock my ankles around him, fold my arms around his neck and try to hold on as he begins to fuck me in earnest. The planes of his back flex; his hips contract as he pulls out, then plunges deep into me. I can't stop the howl that rips up my chest, but he swallows it. He cradles my head with his big palm, then he continues to plow into me again and again. My entire body jolts with the momentum. My tailbone smacks into the wall and pain sweeps up my spine. I moan and the sound coils in my core. His length throbs inside as he holds me pinned to the wall. "Arpad," I groan, "Goddam you."

He pulls out once more, then tips his hips forward and nails me with such force that my entire body jerks. Tendrils of pleasure curl in my core, I throw back my head and groan, "Ohmygod." My eyelids flutter down.

"Look at me, Sparks."

I snap my eyes open and stare into the depths of those grey-blue eyes.

"I am going to fuck you now."

"Wh… what?" I stutter.

He bares his teeth, in that primal look I am coming to classify as an *Arpad special.* He brings his fingers down and rubs his thumb into my swollen nub. Shockwaves course through me. My pulse rate ratchets up and my blood pounds so hard in my chest that I am sure I am going to black out any moment.

"Don't you dare," he growls. "Stay with me."

He holds my gaze, then he tilts his hips and drills into me again. He sinks so deep inside me that I am sure he's cleaved me in half. "Ah!" I throw back my head and connect with his palm.

"Eyes on me, Sparks."

I crack open my eyes, stare into his blue-grey ones which seem to have turned almost colorless. A nerve throbs at his temple.

He lowers his hand to curve his fingers around the nape of my neck. "Come," he growls, and the orgasm sweeps up my spine, shatters behind my eyes. Flashes of light consume me as I scream. He fits his lips to mine, absorbs every last sound. The climax fades away and I slump into him. He pulls out of me, then reaches behind me to shut off the shower. He carries me out of the cubicle, and lowers me to my feet.

I press into him and he holds me with one big arm around my waist. He reaches for a towel, wipes me down, slides it about his big body then throws it in the direction of the laundry basket. He swoops me up in his arms, carries me back to the bed, and tucks me in.

I crack my eyes open, drag my gaze down to his semi-erect cock. How the hell had he come so much and still not gone flaccid? "You didn't come inside me?" I mumble. "Why didn't you? It would have been the perfect time."

"Not yet." He circles his thumb across the edge of my lips. "I need you to be completely rested for what I have in mind."

He straightens and I am about to ask him what he's talking about. That's when he turns to go and I see the marks on his back. Had he been whipped? The lines crisscross his skin, turning his back into a patchwork of scars. My guts twist. Shit, that must have hurt a lot.

"Ari," I call out, "what happened to you?"

He pauses at the door, then glances over his shoulder. "You haven't earned the right to find out about that yet."

I open my mouth again and he shakes his head. "Sleep. You are going to need it."

Turning, he leaves.

How annoying. He could share a little more of himself. Not that I had done anything of that sort, or intend to let him closer. Still, he could open himself a little more about what had happened. After all, he could well be the father of my child… Not yet, considering he hasn't come inside of me. Why didn't he, though? How the hell had he restrained himself so? Why the hell is he holding back? I have to find out… Right after this nap. Darkness engulfs me and I close my eyes.

When I awake, the light radiates through the sliding doors. I grab my phone, check the time, then blow out a breath. It's only noon.

There's still time for him to shag me. In actual fact, I'll still be fertile in the next few days... Now, if only I can figure out why he didn't come inside me earlier.

I sit up and glance about the space. I spot the glass of water on the bedstand and down it. The muted thrum of the boat's engines rolls through the space as I swing my legs over and stand. My thighs protest. A sensation of him between my legs... Of how he'd pounded into me, how he'd kissed me. I touch my lips and wince. Hell, I feel raw all over. Like he fucked me hard… Which he did and didn't, and damnit, where is that jerk anyway? I need some answers. I glance around and find my handbag on the table. The coil of rope on the table is gone. Huh? Was it displaced when the boat hit the storm?

Where the hell are my clothes?

I glance around, then stalk over to the closet, pull it open. There are a few T-shirts, jeans, one set of formal wear, hung in one corner. I search for a pair of sweats, but can't find any. How strange.

I settle for a pair of his jeans, tying them at the waist with a belt — because that's the only way they'd stay up — then shrug into a sweat-shirt. Of course, I am swimming in the clothes, but at least, I am covered. I roll up the sleeves of the sweatshirt, then pulling on a pair of thick socks, head out and into the living room. I walk up the small flight of steps to the captain's cabin and find him at the wheel.

He's changed into a pair of jeans and a sweatshirt that defines the breadth of his shoulders. He's so big that he blocks out the light that pours in from the windshield in front. His hair curls around his collar. His feet, clad in worn boots, are planted firmly on the floor. He seems at peace, more so than any other time I've seen him.

"You like being at sea."

"It's the only place where I feel free."

"Were you restrained a lot as a child?"

He freezes, doesn't reply for a few seconds. "What do you mean?" he finally asks.

"Were you disciplined a lot? Maybe you were sent to boarding school and found it stifling—?"

"I went to a day school with the rest of the Seven."

"Oh." I swallow. "Was that where you guys were—" I hesitate.

"Kidnapped from?" he drawls. "You can say it. We survived the ordeal. It made us who we are today."

"And what's that?" I scoff, "Ruthless, obnoxious, too confident..."

"Focused, goal-oriented, not hesitant to go after what we want..." He looks me up and down. "I rest my case."

"You didn't come after me," I protest.

"No, you came to me." He nods.

I stare at him. I mean, he is right, in a way. "It was a mistake, my being aboard this boat when you left the dock. You know that, right?"

"Or maybe a Freudian slip?" He curls his lip. "Maybe you wanted to stow away, maybe you wanted to be found out by me, and maybe you wanted to spend time with me."

"Maybe I did want you to be my sperm donor..."

"Did you?"

"I admit, there is something here," I wave at the space between us, "but most of the time, I want to slap your face."

"Getting kinky, are we?"

I scoff, "Only you would enjoy that."

"Don't be so sure you wouldn't."

"Don't you dare." I fold my fingers at my side.

"Don't challenge me." His features harden. "For the next thirty days, you do what I ask, no questions."

"Yeah, yeah," I mutter. "So, what's next? You going to throw me down and fuck me?"

"Don't be crude." He smirks. "And by the way, my clothes look good on you."

I shiver. His clothes. I am wearing them, and while it is out of necessity, it seems more intimate than I care for the situation to be. "It's temporary," I mutter. "What did you do with my clothes?"

"You won't need them anymore."

"Wait, what?" I blink. "What do you mean?"

"You wear what I allow you to, for the next—"

"Thirty days, yeah, yeah." I throw up my hands. "You sound like a broken record."

"Calm down." He presses a few buttons on the dash, then slaps a lever in place. "There, that should do to keep the boat on course for a while."

Which is more than I can say about my life right now.

He turns to face me, "Are you hungry?"

7

Karina

Twenty minutes later he places a plate of French Toast on the table in the galley.

"Breakfast for lunch?" I ask.

"Are you complaining?"

"No, actually, this is my favorite dish." I glance up at him, "I could eat it all day."

"I'll keep that in mind."

Alphahole being nice to me? I scan his features but his expression seems sincere enough. Hmph. I stare down, take in the perfectly presented plate.

Damn, he's even dusted powdered sugar on the French Toast. For someone who's an obnoxious grumpy-pants, he's gone to great efforts to prepare this meal for me. Fine, fine, so he can cook. So what? Doesn't make him more appealing. Of course, not.

He seats himself at the lone chair, then proceeds to uncork a bottle of champagne. The liquid fizzes out.

"What are we celebrating?"

"You, us… The start of a beautiful relationship?"

"Nothing beautiful about it so far," I snort, before turning it into a cough.

"What's that?" He smirks. "You say something?"

"Me?" I widen my gaze, "Of course, not. Just admiring your presentation of the food. I had no idea you could cook."

"I had no idea you couldn't."

I frown, "How do you know that?"

"Lucky guess?" He pours out a glass of champagne, then holds it up to me. "To us."

I don't respond. I watch as he takes a sip, then nods in approval. "Want a taste?"

I shake my head. "I am not…drinking."

He blinks, then comprehension fills his face, "Because you're uh…"

I nod, "Yeah, because I'm readying my body for a possible pregnancy."

He takes one more sip, then places the glass aside. "I won't either, then."

Huh? I stare. "You don't have to… I mean, you can…" I shake my head. "Why would you do something like that?"

He frowns down at the plate of food, then back up at me, "Seems the right thing to do. After all, I am one-half of the equation here… At least, for the next—" he stops and chuckles, "few days.'

"Good save," I mutter. "Is that food for me?" I jerk my chin toward the plate.

"It's for us."

"I don't see a chair for me."

"I never have company on this boat."

"You mean you've never…"

"Never had a woman on board," he confirms. "You are the first."

"Not sure how I feel about that." I walk over to the table, reach for the sole fork and knife he's placed there. He slaps away my hand.

"Ouch." I shake out my fingers. "What was that for?"

"No eating until I feed you."

"What?" I exclaim. "This is complete bullshit. Don't tell me you have no other cutlery."

"This is it," he confirms to me. "I don't carry any extra weight aboard this ship."

Except for me, apparently.

He pats his lap, "Come here, Sparks."

I stare at him. "And if I won't?"

"Where will you go?" He glances about the space. "We are at sea, in case you've forgotten."

Not likely.

"Come on," he lowers his voice to a hush, "be a good girl now."

I set my jaw. Hate being called that. Good girl, huh?

He cuts himself a piece of the French Toast and eats it. "Mmm." He licks his lips. "Sure you don't want to share?"

My stomach rumbles. He cuts another slice, then forks it up, and offers it to me. "Go on, you know you want to."

"Only if I can feed myself."

"Not happening."

I fold my hands about my waist.

"If not for yourself, then think of the child you want to conceive. You need all the nutrients you can get for that, don't you?"

I pale. "Bastard."

He blows out a breath. "This is getting tiresome. Apparently, you still haven't committed to our agreement."

I have and I haven't. I mean he's definitely the best candidate for my plan to have a child of my own. If only I weren't this attracted to him. Or if I weren't actually looking forward to sleeping with him...

Hell... This isn't supposed to be remotely enjoyable. Not something I should be looking forward to... But the thought of those fingers on my skin again, those lips on mine, the rasp of his whiskers across my inner thighs as he swipes his tongue up toward my core... A shiver runs down my spine. My toes curl. No doubt, he is virile enough that I'll be pregnant by the end of the week... But what will I have given up by then? And it isn't about the fact that I'll see him afterward, accompany him when he visits his parents, or the possible visitation rights that he wants... Which, by the way, I have no intention of granting him...

It is...the fact that I will not come out of this entire encounter unscathed. Our interaction in the shower had confirmed to me what I already knew... The man will seduce me, bulldoze through any barriers I may have built, and imprint himself on my body, my soul...my emotions... No way, am I going to let him do that. I need to find a way to protect myself. I need to...be compliant to what he wants, pretend to give in, while I guard that part of me deep inside that belongs only to me. If he thinks I am giving him anything more than my body, he is so wrong. The only way out is to beat him at his own game.

"Fine," I mutter, "have it your way." I brush past the table and plonk myself on his lap.

He frowns at me, then reaches down to scoop up some of the food. "Open," he holds the fork to my mouth. I part my lips and he feeds me. I curl my tongue around the tines and lick up every last remnant of the morsel.

His eyelids grow heavy as he watches me chew, then swallow.

He holds up another forkful to me, and another, follows my every move closely. I wriggle around to make myself more comfortable in his lap, and my thigh brushes the hard column at the crotch of his jeans.

"Oh." I freeze.

"Surprised?" He holds out another forkful to me.

"I'm more unsure why you didn't allow yourself to come inside me earlier," I mumble.

"Patience, Sparks." His lips curl. "I plan to take my time with you, savor your every curve, lick your skin, taste your cunt, spank your butt and suck on your nipples, until you come from the sensations."

I swallow.

"That…uh, that sounds uncomfortable."

"Oh, trust me, I am going to make you very uncomfortable."

"You…you are?"

He nods."

"Make no mistake, I am going to worship you. I am going to dominate you. I want more than sex with you." He leans in closer until his eyelashes brush mine. "I am going to make art with you—dirty, filthy, impossibly screwed-up, emotionally moving art, that's going to consume you and me, and by the end, you won't know where you begin and where I end."

Heat blooms between my legs; I squeeze my thighs together.

"And what happened earlier in the shower?" I force out the words through cracked lips.

"Just an appetizer." His smile widens, "I am going to swallow all of you, Sparks. And by the time you realize it, it will be too late. I won't stop until you're a part of me, until I am imprinted in every cell of your body. That's what you agreed to and I intend for you to honor this understanding."

My throat closes and my nipples harden to pinpoints of pain. Bloody hell, if he can turn me on with just his words, how will it feel when he goes through with what he has in his mind?

"That's only for the duration of our arrangement, isn't it?"

His forehead creases.

"Tick-tock, Alphahole." I curve my lips. "You are wasting time already. Or maybe you are better at threats than actual action, huh? Maybe...." I close the distance even further until my lips almost touch his, "maybe your threats don't measure up to what you can actually deliver, huh?"

Arpad

What the hell? Why is she provoking me? Her pupils dilate, her breath hitches, and if I glance down, I have no doubt that I'll see her nipples outlined against the fabric of my sweatshirt.

"It won't work," I drawl.

"What?"

"Your less-than-effective attempt at getting a reaction from me. No one forces me, of course. Least of all, you, Sparks."

"Is that your opinion?"

"It's my experience." I grab her waist, then lift her up and plant her on her feet. She squeaks.

"Take it off," I growl.

"What?" She frowns.

I jerk my chin at her clothes, "Those are mine."

"I don't have anything else to wear."

I glare at her.

"You expect me to be naked?"

"You challenged me. You lost the right to wear clothes."

"Have you lost your mind?" She gapes. "This is the twenty-first century. You don't get to treat me like...like..."

"My possession?" I kick up my lips. "Oh, but you are sweetheart. You're on my yacht, where my word is final."

She opens and closes her mouth. "This is ridiculous."

"Is it?" I fold my arms across my chest. "Strip," I snap, "or I'll make you do it."

Her cheeks tinge red, and the pulse at the base of her neck speeds up. She reaches down, grabs the hem of the sweatshirt and pulls it up and off of her. Her breasts capture my gaze instantly. Creamy with pink areolas and dark nipples that stick up at me. My fingers tingle and the blood rushes to my groin. I stare down at the jeans that hang low on her waist. "Take them off, but first your socks."

She bends to slip off her socks, then unknots the belt. She slips her fingers under the waistband and pushes them down to reveal the length of her thighs; her tiny waist, the flare of those beautiful hips that I'd had under my fingers not too long ago. I draw in a breath, can't take my gaze off that gorgeous smooth-shaven pussy that I want to suck on; right before I thrust my tongue inside her and eat her out until she comes again. My groin hardens. A bead of sweat drips down my temple.

I ball my fingers at my sides, watch as she kicks off her jeans.

She plants her hands on her hips, tips up her chin and meets my gaze. "Enough?"

"Not really."

I circle the air with my fingers and her nostrils flare. Her golden eyes blaze at me. She draws in a breath and I shake my head. "You need me more than I need you, babe. Remember, you need me to pump you up with my cum before the end of the day.

"You're so damn crude," she splutters.

"It's the truth."

"Fine. Fine." She spins around on her heels, then faces me. "Happy?"

"Once more, and slowly."

She grits her teeth. A chuckle boils up and I press my lips closed. Wouldn't do to tell her just how adorable I find her right about now.

"Do it," I snap instead. She stares at me then pivots on her heel. By the time she's done a full circle, goosebumps pepper her skin.

"You're cold."

"Of course, I'm cold, you ass. I'm naked and it's the middle of winter, and we are out on the godforsaken sea."

"That won't do." I click my tongue. "I think it's best I warm you up."

I step forward and she skitters back.

"Do I scare you?"

"Of course, not," she scoffs. "In my line of work, I've seen all kinds. Especially egomaniacs, who think they own the world, are a dime a dozen.'

"You've never met someone like me, I promise."

"Oh?"

"I don't think… I actually *do* own everything I see right now, including you."

"So you keep saying." She purses her lips. "Except, you haven't delivered on your promise yet."

"Eager to have me inside you? Do you want me to fuck you right here on the table, Sparks?"

She swallows; her gaze darts to the table then back to my face.

"Is that what you're going to do?"

I tilt my head, pretend to consider it. "No."

"Then what?"

"I am going to tie you up, first."

"What?"

I bend my knees, thrust my face into hers, "Run, Sparks. The longer you evade me, the easier I'll go on you."

"Are you serious?"

"Go," I snap.

She turns, then dashes out of the galley. I follow her at a leisurely pace, as she races down the steps, across the living room, to the door that leads out to the upper deck.

"What the fuck?" My heart slams into my ribcage. I race forward, reach the door to the deck in time to see her disappear under the waves.

"No fucking way," I roar. "What have you done?"

I run back to the cabin, drop the sea anchor to limit the progress of the yacht; then race back to the deck, toe off my sneakers, and dive in after her.

I hit the water and the impact shudders through me. The cold overpowers me, flash-freezes me from head to toe for a second. I dive down into the depths, then open my eyes. Where the hell is she? Why the hell did she do this? This woman... Wait until I get my hands on her.

I catch a glimpse of white from the corner of my eye. I swim through the darkened water toward it, when something grabs my ankle. My pulse rate ratchets up. I glance down to find it's her. She yanks me down. I reach for her. She evades me, pulls me down with a sharp tug. I lose my equilibrium, descend further. By the time I find my balance and swim upward, she's far above me. Of course, the woman swims like a fish and when I get ahold of her... Adrenaline laces my blood. I kick my legs, propel forward, up through the depths. I reach her as she breaks the surface. I swim after her, swoop forward to grab her, miss. She pulls forward. I put on a burst of speed and grab her ankle as she reaches the yacht.

"Let me go," she pants. She kicks out at me.

I duck to avoid her, then yank her to me, "What the hell were you thinking?" I yell.

"I wanted to get away from you," she gasps.

"So you jump overboard?"

"Seemed like the thing to do." She tosses her head.

"You're in so much trouble." I thrust my face into hers. "Get on the boat."

"Oh, fuck you."

"Oh, I'm going to do that too," I growl. "But first, I am going to whip your arse for what you did."

8

Karina

"Ow, you asshole, let go of me." I strain from my position where I am sprawled across the bastard's lap.

He'd shoved me onto the boat, climbed on after me, then dragged me inside the yacht. He'd held onto me as I'd shivered in his grasp, while he hauled anchor, and pressed a few buttons. The boat had restarted, he'd pulled a lever, then he'd turned me over on his knee.

"W...wait," I stutter through the trembling that grips me, and it's because I am chilled to the bone. Honestly, that's all it is. "Don't you... n...n...eed to steer the boat or something?"

"Auto-pilot," he bites out.

"I... I'm...cold." I try to pull away from him. "I think I need a hot shower.

"I have a better way to warm you up." He drags me back onto his lap, before his palm connects with my left asscheek.

"What the hell are you doing?" I yell.

"I've gone easy on you so far. I should have known you'd take advantage of my good nature."

"Good nature?" I shove the hair back from my face, "You don't have a bloody good-natured bone in your entire body."

"If that were true, I would have let you drown. Instead, here I am, trying to pound some sense into you."

He spanks my right butt cheek, then the left again.

"Ow, that hurts, you bastard."

"Say you're sorry for what you did," he demands.

"No," I snap. "You told me you'd go easier on me the longer I could evade you."

"So you decided to put yourself at risk?"

"It's my life, you…you…complete cock. I'll do with it what I want."

"Wrong answer. Your life belongs to me, for the duration of the arrangement, and I forbid you to do anything that will jeopardize it. You understand?"

He spanks me with such force that my entire body jerks.

"Say you understand."

"I do," I howl. "Okay, I understand."

"Good."

He smacks me once more across my butt and I scream.

"What the fuck? Why did you do that?"

"Just insurance."

"Stop," I beg. "No more, please."

Tears prick the backs of my eyes. Seriously? I can't be crying. Not now. I'd refused to bend to him; I'd been right in that… Though diving into the water? That had been spur of the moment, and probably stupid, to say the least.

"It's all your fault," I huff. "You are so bloody high-handed, it makes me want to defy you."

He cups my burning asscheek, massages the pain into my skin. I shiver. Only because I'm cold. It's nothing to do with how warm his palm feels against my skin. Nothing to do with how wet I am between my legs. And no, it's not due to the dunking I just took.

Another shudder grips my shoulders.

He pauses, then straightens to his feet and throws me over his shoulder.

"Hey," I protest, staring at his very hard, very hot backside. Jesus, why the hell does he have to be in such good shape? I reach down to pinch his ass, and he clicks his tongue.

"Don't," he growls, "not unless you want the favor returned."

The skin on my backside twinges in reaction. Nope, no way, can I deal with any more of his attentions on my posterior. Not right now.

He hauls me into the bathroom, turns on the shower and dumps me under it. I turn into the hot water, then wince when my backside protests.

The cubicle door shuts, and he steps in behind me. "Don't hog all the water," he commands.

He pours shampoo into his hand, washes the sea water out of my hair, then turns me around and begins to soap me.

"Hey," I grab his wrist, "what the hell are you doing?"

"Taking care of my property." He glares at me, and I shiver. "Lower your hands to your sides," he orders.

Only when my fingers touch my thighs do I realize I've obeyed him. *Jerk.*

He washes every part of my body—my hips, my thighs, between my legs—with clinical precision. He squats down, then raises one foot onto his thigh. I hold onto his shoulder for support as he cleans between my toes, brushes across the underside of my feet.

A giggle bursts from my throat.

He glances up at me. "Ticklish, huh?"

I purse my lips.

He repeats the action with my other foot, as I try desperately not to laugh, then rises up and begins to wash his hair with the motions of a man who's done so almost every day of his life.

I pour out some of the liquid soap, then rub it across his pecs, down his cut abs, across his thighs. I soap between his legs and his shaft throbs in my grasp.

I glance up to find him staring down at me.

I hold his gaze, move aside to allow the water to wash off the soap from his groin. Then I sink to my knees. Without breaking eye contact, I take him inside my mouth.

"Hell." His knees seem to buckle; he digs his fingers into my hair and tugs. Goosebumps rise on my skin. I bob my head, take him in and his cock hits the back of my throat.

His gaze intensifies. His nostrils flare. He pulls out, then hauls me to my feet, reaches behind me to shut off the shower.

"I wanted to—"

"You'll do as I say—no more, no less. You get me?"

"Yes…" For some reason I want to say 'master,' but no way, am I going to give him the satisfaction of that.

He walks out of the shower cubicle, holds out a towel. I step into it and he rubs me down. Once more, he takes his time and pays special attention to my breasts, my hips, my thighs. He pats down the flesh between my legs and I shudder.

He tosses the towel aside, grabs a fresh one and dries himself off. Then he hauls me up in his arms.

"I can walk," I protest.

"Something I intend to remedy."

"Wh…what do you mean?" My belly flutters and moisture laces my core.

He smirks down at me. "You'll see."

He stalks outside, lowers me to the floor half-way between the bed and the door. "Stay," he commands, then walks over to the bed and seats himself. Legs wide, his already hard cock juts up against his stomach.

He jerks his chin, "Crawl to me."

"What?" I stare at him. "No."

"Look outside," he orders.

I glance through the glass windows to find the sunrays lengthening. It's approaching 5pm. I know because I'd checked my phone earlier.

"How many hours do you have left in your ovulation window?"

Bastard. So that's why he hasn't put his dick inside me yet? He wants to wait until he makes me submit? We'll see.

I glare at him and he glances down at the floor, then back at me.

"Do it," he says.

I sink to my knees, then lower my palms to the floor and crawl across the floor. When I reach him, I pause, then tip my head up.

"Good girl."

I flush. Why the hell do his compliments mean so much?

He reaches for the first aid kit I only now notice on the bed-stand. He pulls out some cotton, dabs on some antiseptic, then proceeds to dab at the bump on my forehead which, honestly, I'd forgotten all about until he'd brought my attention back to it.

I try to pull away and he grunts, "Hold still."

He pinches my chin so I don't have a choice but to obey. He cleans the wound, pastes on a fresh plaster, then leans back to survey his handiwork.

"Not so hard, was it?" he grunts.

"Why are you doing this?" I mutter.

"Shh," he notches his knuckle under my chin, leans down and brushes his lips over mine. "You don't get to talk, Sparks. Not until I give you permission."

I scowl. "I am not so sure I like this agreement."

He peers into my eyes. "Want to cancel it, then?"

I swallow, stare at him.

"Giving up so soon?" He curls his lips. "Didn't take you for a quitter."

I'm not. I firm my lips. Besides, I've come this far, and I am so close to my goal. So close to getting what I want—a chance at a baby of my own.

"Want to call it off?" he asks.

I shake my head.

"So, you'll do as I say?"

I nod.

"Good, close your eyes."

9

Karina

I close my eyes, and instantly, all of my other senses come into focus. That dark masculine scent of his magnifies; the force of his dominance crashes into my chest, pins me down and holds me in place. My nerve endings thrum. Every part of me is focused on him…The slide of his feet on the wooden floor, the warmth from his body as it envelopes me.

I sense his gaze raking over my features, my breasts, the flesh between my legs. Can't stop the blush that rises to my cheeks.

"You're beautiful," he rumbles.

That hard voice rolls down my front, coils low in my belly as he, no doubt, intended.

I sense him rise to his feet, turn my head to follow as he steps past me.

I must have made a sound or he must sense my discomfort, for he presses his hand into my shoulder. "I'll be right back."

And damn, if his touch isn't reassuring?

I track his footsteps across the floor, then the sound of the closet door opening. The rustle of fabric, the whisper of something else…

Something soft that slithers against his skin. The hair on the nape of my neck rises.

His footsteps approach; he pauses behind me. I shiver. Somehow, even with my eyes closed, I am aware of how he must tower over me, how he must glance down at me, how at his mercy I am right now.

A soft cloth wraps over my eyes.

I whimper.

"Shh," his warm breath grazes my ear, "I'll take good care of you."

That's what I'm afraid of.

He knots the cloth behind my head, then places his palm on the flat of my back. He urges me to place my cheek onto the mattress.

I sense rather than hear the slither of something. A rope, maybe?

"What are you doing?" I stutter.

"I won't hurt you.'

Won't you?

His breathing is steady as he slides what I assume to be a knot up each of my arms and around my shoulder. He cinches the rope at my back over my spine, then slides it up and round my biceps.

"You alright?"

I swallow.

"Nod, if you are."

I nod.

"Does it feel okay?"

I draw in a breath. It feels strange. It feels...not bad. It feels restrictive, but not in a bad way. I nod.

His actions seem to speed up as he knots the rope again at my back, then slides two more knots up my arms to above my elbows.

He leans in and presses a kiss to the back of my neck, "Okay?"

I nod.

"How does that feel?"

Strange, but not as much as I would have expected. It's actually freeing… Like I don't have to do anything but follow the sensations as he ties me up. *OMG, he's tying me up! What the hell is he going to do to me after?* My heart begins to thud and my pulse quickens. I draw in a breath, but I can't seem to get enough air.

"Hey." He wraps his arms around me, and pulls me up against his chest. "You okay?"

I shake my head vigorously. *No, no… Jeez, this isn't what I signed up for.*

Give me the cold impersonal touch of the technician who slides the sperm into my uterus.

He tucks my head under his chin, tightens his hold about my body. The hard warmth of him sinks into my blood. The planes of his chest dig into my back. The pain is almost a comfort.

"Shh." He lowers his head, presses his cheek into mine. "You're safe, I promise. I'll never let anyone harm you."

But who will keep me safe from you?

Bloody hell, stop with that line of thought. Alphahole, here, is simply screwing with my head. Mean one moment, soft the next, and this entire tying me up thing… Bet it's simply to signal to me that he is the dominant one in this relationship. To flout his ownership, no doubt. Doesn't mean anything. A shudder grips me. I set my jaw, take a fortifying breath.

"Ready to resume?" he asks.

I straighten my shoulders. I can do this. I can match him step for step. I nod.

"You're fucking perfect." He presses a hard kiss to the corner of my mouth. A flush ripples over my skin. He moves away and I lean in his direction.

He chuckles. "Soon. First I want to ensure you're relaxed."

Relaxed? He's kidding right? How am I supposed to relax when I'm all bound up?

He continues to knot the rope at my back, then slide the knots—

"They're called wings." He says as he tugs on the ropes that slide up each arm.

He tugs the center of the binding that sits in a heavy chain down my spine.

"How does it feel now?"

I tilt my head. *Not sure really.*

"Would you like it tighter?

Yes.

Yes.

No. I shake my head.

"Okay, maybe next time?"

Keep dreaming.

He continues placing the knots against my spine, then finally, pulls my wrists together at my back. He places my palms together and whispers the top around my palms. He knots and tugs, then sits back. "Beautiful."

The reverence in his voice makes me blink behind my blindfold.

He guides me up to my feet, then hoists me up onto the bed, on my knees. He presses down on my upper back and I bend over and press my cheek into the mattress. He grips my thighs and pries them apart. Cool air hits my center. I shudder. My breathing grows more shallow. I am painfully conscious of where I am — on his yacht, in the middle of nowhere, away from anyone I could reach for help, and bound and blindfolded with my ass up in the air. My core clenches, moisture pools between my legs. I swallow and wait… Wait.

"You're gorgeous." His low voice shudders up my spine. I press my palms together, and damnit, if he hasn't orchestrated it so that I seem to be praying to him… Begging him… Pleading to him... For what?

He grips my hips on either side, his palms so big, so warm that surely, each fingerprint is burned into my flesh.

Something nudges at the opening of my slit and I stiffen.

"Shh." He massages the curve of my waist. "Relax." He stays right there, with the head of his cock teasing the opening of my entrance. I draw in a breath, another, force my shoulder muscles to unwind. I am not giving in to this man, not that easily. I will not allow him to over-whelm me. I push my cheek further into the mattress, widen my knees further.

He slips inside me, and a shudder of heat ripples up my spine.

He pulls out, then rubs his dick across my pussy, and again. My belly flip-flops. My thigh muscles shudder. He drags his cock up the valley between my butt cheeks, teases my back hole. I clench my butt. *No.* I shake my head. *Don't you dare.*

"You're going to ask me to take you there one day. You know that, right?"

I snort, then cry out when he thrusts into my melting channel in one smooth move. Goddamn him, how does he always find a way to surprise me?

He stays there, his throbbing length buried inside of me, stretching me, allowing me to adjust. As if that were possible? How can he fill me up so? How can he be so bloody big?

He bends over, and the warmth of him sears my back. He wraps my hair around his palm, tugs my head up and toward him. He presses his mouth to mine. "Give in to me," he whispers.

No! I shake my head.

He straightens and pulls out in one smooth move, only to thrust into me with such force that my entire body jolts. The bed frame protests. He plunges in and out of me, in and out.

He releases his hold on my hair, only to squeeze my butt with just enough force that I squeeze my inner muscles around him

A groan rumbles from him. "You're so hot, so tight. You feel incredible, Sparks."

He propels his hips forward and impales me, hits that spot deep inside me again and again with such precision that I gasp. The climax sweeps up my thighs, my spine... Explodes behind my eyes with enough force that I throw my head back and scream as I fall apart. He continues to thrust in and out, then wraps his fingers around my neck. He bends over me, kisses me on my lips once, then whispers, "I am going to fuck you now."

Wait, what? What the hell is he talking about?

He pulls out, then impales me in one long, smooth stroke that fills me up completely. I can't stop the moan that spills from my lips. He begins to pound into me, fucking me as he'd promised. With every stroke his balls hit my sensitized clit. Each time he sinks into me, ripples of heat shoot up my spine. My knees tremble and my toes curl. I can't come again, not so soon, surely not.

He tightens his grip around my neck, enough that my lungs begin to burn. Spots of darkness creep in along the sides of my vision. He tilts his hips and buries himself inside me with such force that I can feel every ridge and bump of his shaft.

A trembling grips me. He releases his hold around my neck, allowing the oxygen to rush to my lungs. He leans over, and commands, "Come," and I shatter as he comes inside me.

10

Arpad

I watch her sleep, her eyelashes dark against her cheeks. Her lips are parted. Her hair in tangles from how I'd wrapped it around my palm and tugged. She'd climaxed again, and watching her fall apart on my cock had been the sweetest thing ever. I'd unbound her right after, pulled her up the bed and into my arms. She'd fallen asleep with her head on my chest, her arm flung around my waist. I'd wanted to drift with her, but the thought that she could possibly, very soon, carry my child… A hot sensation stabs at my chest. Somehow, this is not what I had bargained for when I had set out on this trip. Or when I had proposed that she accompany me on my trip home as my pretend wife. I hadn't expected to feel…this pull…this need to take care of her. This need to push her away, yet make her climax again.

I slide out from under her, pick up the rope from the floor and fold it into a figure eight. I place it on the coffee table, slip on my jeans, and walk to the cabin of the ship.

I pick up the satellite phone and dial.

"Mr. Beauchamp?" Edward answers the phone. "Where are you calling from this time?"

"I'm on my way to Lille in France to see my family."

"Don't you like your alone time on these trips? To what do I owe this pleasure?"

"Considering four of the Seven have seen fit to tie the knot and Baron's unreachable…well…"

"You mean I was your last option?"

"Currently, my only option."

"Don't tell me," his sigh is loud over the waves, "woman trouble, huh?"

"What makes you say that?"

"It's the only time you Seven want a sounding board… That, or when you want to get married."

"About that," I cough.

"No," Edward begins to laugh, "don't tell me. Not you too, Arpad? What the hell is happening to you guys?"

"There's nothing like that," I assure him.

He only laughs harder.

I pull the phone away from my ear and stare at it. What the fuck is wrong with him?

"Come on, man," I bark down the receiver, "get a grip."

"Fine." He chokes down a chuckle, then seems to compose himself. "So, what's up with you and Karina?"

"What the fuck do you mean by me and Karina?"

"Aw, come on. You don't think the sparks between you two have gone unnoticed by the rest of us, do you?"

"What sparks?"

"Really?" He scoffs, "You're going to deny that there's something between the two of you."

"I would have if you'd asked me a few hours ago."

"What do you mean?"

"She's with me."

"What?" he exclaims. "On the boat?"

"It's a bloody expensive yacht," I growl.

"Hmm."

"What do you mean by that?" I frown.

"You could always turn around and drop her off, couldn't you?"

"I was too far from shore by the time I found out about her presence."

"So, you're taking her along for this trip?"

"Taking her to meet the family."

"A bit premature, isn't it?" He chuckles again.

"Stop cackling," I mutter, then rub the back of my neck. "She's agreed to pose as my wife."

"Wife?"

"Fake wife."

"Right."

"Why do you sound like you don't believe this?" I complain.

"If you only knew the number of conversations I've had with each of the four who got hitched." He pauses and I can sense him shaking his head. "They each insisted there was nothing to it, yet they all ended up married. Not that I am complaining. I, for one, happen to think marriage is a gift from God."

"Right."

"You don't believe me?"

"Not here to debate the merits and demerits of the institution." I scowl. "And I called to speak to Edward my friend, not Edward the priest."

There's silence, then Edward replies, "Not that the two can be differentiated from each other."

"Come on, man, I could do with a second opinion."

"None needed, you're in love," he declares.

I swear, "Thought you, at least, were beyond that childish stuff."

"Think what the others found with their women is childish?"

I blink. "They were exceptions. Lucky bastards, who connected with the right woman at the right time."

"And here you are, on a boat, with the woman you've worshiped from afar—"

"Worshipped?"

"—but never had the balls to tell her how you feel about her."

"Now, hold on." I plant my phone on my other ear. "That's a bit harsh, don't you think? Considering she's been a thorn in my side all this time."

"No kidding. You guys have had it bad for each other since you first met."

"Yeah, we can't stand the sight of each other."

"And yet, you didn't throw her off your boat."

"Not like I could have dumped her out in the middle of nowhere."

"Instead, you're passing the time how?"

"Uh, she wants me to father a child with her."

"What—?" he shouts. "And you're telling this to me… A priest?"

"And my friend."

"You know what I'm going to advise you then?"

"To marry her?" I venture

"Or walk away from her."

"I don't know..." I ponder my choices.

He blows out a breath. "So how can I help you then?"

"Is it wrong for me to want to be a part of this child's life?"

"Assuming a child does result from your relationship, you mean?" he reminds me.

How strange, I've been so very sure that I'll have her pregnant very soon. I shake my head, "Yes, exactly."

"I'd expect no less from you."

"Hmm." I squeeze the bridge of my nose.

"You don't sound convinced."

"I am a bit confused," I mutter. "And don't ever tell the rest of the Seven I admitted to that."

"Your secrets are safe with me.'

"Did Baron confide in you too?"

"Huh?" I hear his surprise across the phone line. "Why do you ask that?"

"Only because all of us tend to confide in you."

"It's natural, since I am a priest."

"And a billionaire."

"My money's in a trust, which supports various charities."

"That's noble of you, Father."

"We're not talking about me, though," he reminds me.

"True." I rub the back of my neck. "So, what should I do?"

"Nothing."

"That's your advice?" I growl. "To stay put—"

"And let nature take its course."

"Meaning?"

"Even when you think you're doing nothing, forces beyond your control are at work."

"Is that your belief?"

"It's the way life is."

"Damn, I hate how fatalistic you sound."

"All I'm asking is that you trust the process."

"You mean trust in God?" I mutter.

"You said it," he says lightly.

"Hmm." I roll my shoulders. "So, go ahead with this plan, take her home to see the family?"

"If your instinct says that's right."

"Thanks, Father," I grumble. "Good talk."

"You did all the talking." He laughs.

"Yeah, that's what I mean. How is it that you manage to say so much without saying much at all?"

"It's an art. One I've had time to perfect."

"Of all of us, you were always the most slippery."

"Why, because I forged my own path?"

"Because—" The screen in front of me beeps with an incoming weather forecast. I glance at it, then speak into the phone. "It's because you were the most courageous of all of us."

"You mean the weakest, right?" he replies. "After all, I'm the one who renounced the world and took the easy way out."

"What you did was no mean feat. You dug into yourself, found what your conscience demanded of you and pursued it. Only question is, did it work?"

His sigh is heavy. "I'll let you know when I know."

The computer screen in front of me beeps again, "Before I go, there's one more thing. Can you call Karina's second-in-command and let her know that she's taking a few days off and can't be reached? Meredith—" I refer to our assistant, "has all the information you need."

"Okay." I sense Edward nod down the phone. "Remember what I said? Follow your instinct."

I disconnect the phone call, glance down at the weather report again. "Fuck me."

A sound behind me has me swinging around.

I scowl, "What are you doing here?"

11

Karina

"Jesus, you're touchy today." I hold up my hands, "See, no weapons. I am no threat."

"Snooping on me, huh?" He smirks, "Did you miss me?" He looks me up and down, takes in the T-shirt—*his* T-shirt—I'd pulled on before I'd wandered over.

"Of course, not." I scowl back. "I was simply curious."

I nod toward the computer screen he'd been looking at, "Everything okay there?"

He glances back at the screen, "It will be."

"What's that supposed to mean?" I walk over and peer around him at the screen. "What's that?" I point to the concentric circles splayed over blotches of red and green.

"The weather forecast."

"Huh." The images on the screen blip and change. "It's like no forecast I have seen before."

He chuckles. "I'd be surprised if it were. These here are files from the Numerical Weather Prediction programs."

"What does that mean?"

"It's raw weather forecast data, that helps me plan ahead."

"How's that?"

"It allows me to look at the overall pattern being shown by the files, rather than the wind at points." He scans my features, "Does that make sense?"

"It gives you the big picture?"

He nods. "It's the raw prediction with nothing added and nothing taken away, which allows me to be in control of what factors I should consider on top of this standard information."

"What other factors would you consider?"

"I tend to use this app," he nods toward another screen, "to share how the fronts and wind systems are developing over time. It's a three-step approach, effectively." He gestures with his hand, "You have the coastal waters on the English side first. So, I would look at what sort of acceleration I'll be getting there and consider the tide. Then I'll look at some other coast-specific forecasts to see if that is predicting any sort of thermal enhancement. Then, the further offshore you get, the more the accuracy of these files," he taps at the screen I'd first seen, "increases. So, I'd be focusing on them and what I expect to come in, based on what has been developing out there. When I get to the other side of the Channel, I would, once again, look at high-resolution files, compare them with a coastal waters forecast, or something similar for that side, to see if they are matching what the weather prediction files suggest and what I expect."

I stare at his face.

"What?" He scowls.

"It's the first time I've seen you this excited about something other than—"

"You?" He smirks.

"Making money?"

"That ol' chestnut." He studies me. "You shouldn't always go by appearances."

"I could say the same."

"Touché" He tilts his head. "No mistaking you for what you are."

"Which is?"

"A strong, confident woman, who knows what she wants and doesn't hesitate to go after it."

"And yet, here I am."

"Exactly," he agrees. "You saw a good deal and grabbed it with both hands."

"Hmm." Is it though? Is it what it appears to be on the face of it? What happens if... When I get pregnant? Can I do this on my own? Will he stick to his end of the bargain? Do I want him to?

"You're overthinking this." He says this while glancing, once more, at the screen. "Take each day as it comes, Sparks. Don't jump ahead."

"Is that what you're doing?"

He straightens, then turns to me, takes in my appearance. His eyelids grow heavy. "I'm deciding what to do to you next."

A shiver runs down my spine and my thighs clench. "About that," I clear my throat, "you could have warned me."

"What would the fun be in that."

"When you practice Shibari—"

"Kinbaku."

"What?" I scowl.

"Shibari in Japanese means to tie."

"Isn't that what you did?"

"While Kinbaku translates to tying tightly or tying deeply." He raises one eyebrow. "It describes a practice where connection between the *nawashi,* that is the rope artist, and the *dorei, i.*e. the slave or rope bottom, are important."

"Are you calling me your slave?" I mutter. "I'm not sure I like that—"

"—Yet." He grabs my waist and hoists me up.

I squeak, then wrap my arms around his waist. "What are you doing?"

"How long does your fertile phase last, you said?"

"Umm," I swallow, "technically, the peak was a few hours before my appointment yesterday, but I am sure the days following would count too."

"Let's feed you first."

He carries me across to the galley, lowers me onto the chair, then pours me some orange juice from the open pack.

"How much have you got stocked away?"

"Enough for one person on this trip."

He walks over to the stove and busies himself, chopping vegetables.

"What do you do when you're not sailing?"

"What do you do when you're not running your security business?" he retorts.

My company. My employees. Shit, I haven't thought of them since I got on the boat. When was the last time I went through an entire twenty-four hours without stressing about my responsibilities? When was the last time I took my eyes off my goals, huh?

He adds butter to the skillet, then casts me a sideways glance, "Where did you go to?"

"Nowhere."

"I must not be doing a good job if your mind is elsewhere." He smirks.

"You're full of shit," I mumble.

"And you need to submit to me," he declares.

I spit out the orange juice and he chuckles.

"Some warning please?" I choke out. "I haven't had my breakfast."

"So, it's fine to get kinky with you after you've eaten?" He shoots me a glance over his shoulder.

"The rope play was all well and good," I glower at him, "but I'm not doing it again."

"Oh?" He peruses my features. "Not only will you be my rope bottom, but you are going to enjoy it."

"Says who?" I frown.

He turns off the flame on the stove then turns and glares at me, and my pulse flutters. Moisture laces my core. Oh, hell, what is it about his dominant ways that gets me all hot and bothered inside?

I tip up my chin, and he jerks his chin to the ground. "On your knees," he orders.

"What the hell?" I gape. "Is this one of your stupid mind games?"

"Do it," he commands.

"And if I don't?"

"You don't want to know."

"Try me." I sniff. "You and your stupid threats."

He moves so quickly, I gasp. The next second he's seated on the chair and I am bent over his knee… Again. For a man his size, how the hell does he move that fast?

"Count to ten—" His gravelly voice shudders down my spine.

"What?"

He pulls up the T-shirt so it's bunched around my neck, and his palm connects with my naked backside.

I squeal. "What the—?"

He spanks me again. "Wrong response."

"Wait—"

He slaps my ass a third time. I shudder, dig my core into his thighs. His palm connects with my ass again and I wheeze. "Why are you—?"

"The more you delay starting the count, the more I get to spank you, Sparks."

"This is so not fair," I burst out, and he flattens his palm across my butt. He massages my skin and the pain sinks into my blood. My core clenches again. "Arpad, what the hell are you doing?"

He drags his fingers across the flesh between my legs and I groan. "Start counting."

He squeezes my ass with enough force that I yelp, "Fine, fine."

He slaps the curve of my flesh and I squeak, "One."

He spanks me again.

"Two," I huff.

Slap.

"Three."

Slap.

"Four."

Slap.

"Five," I wail.

He doesn't stop after that until he's reached nine, each of his slaps punctuated by my counting. By the time he's done, I'm shaking, tears running down my face. I blink them away. At least, I didn't give him the satisfaction of yelling or protesting. If he thought he was going to make me submit this way, he has another think coming.

He swipes his fingers between my legs and a shiver runs up my spine.

"You're wet already," there's a note of wonder in his voice, "and I haven't even begun."

"I am done here." I strain against his hold and he leans his weight across my back, effectively holding me in place.

"We're not done until I say we are."

I turn my head to stare at him, "You're so...so..."

"Irresistible?"

"Full of yourself."

"And you like me that way."

"Ha." I shake the hair out of my eyes. "Keep deluding yourself."

"You're the one denying your need to give in to me."

"Keep dreaming, buster," I growl.

"Oh, I'm gonna do more than that." He raises his hand again. "I'm going to withhold your orgasms until you behave."

His palm connects with my ass with such force that my entire body jerks forward.

"Ten," I snarl, then clamp my lips together. I will not cry out. Will not allow him the satisfaction of finding out how much he's hurting me and turning me on. *No, no, no.* I squeeze my thighs together. Curl my fingers into fists and squeeze my eyes as he slaps me again.

"Give in to me, Sparks," he rubs his palm across the burning skin of my arse, "and everything will be okay."

"Nothing will be okay," I grit out through clenched teeth, "and I am not going to—" He presses his lips to the curve of my butt and I shiver. He licks the abraded skin he'd just smacked and a groan spills from my lips. Damn it… The contrast between the pain and this tenderness… It's too much.

"Arpad," I breathe.

"Hmm." He presses little kisses up the curve of my spine, while he slides his fingers between my legs again. He slides one finger inside of me and I gasp. He adds a second and a third, then begins to work them in and out of me.

I shudder and he pushes aside my hair, then tugs down the T-shirt to kiss the nape of my neck. Goosebumps pop on my skin. Oh, my goodness, how can the touch of his lips on my skin be so…everything? He licks around the shell of my ear, then sucks on my earlobe. My toes curl. I clench down on his fingers and a groan sounds from above me. "You're so hot, so wet, Sparks."

He presses his lips against the side of my neck, then bites down gently. I buck in his hold and he straightens, then folds his fingers around my nape. I shiver. His grasp is both dominating and soothing…somehow. He slides his hand down, presses his palm to the small of my back, and warmth pools between my legs. He scissors his fingers inside of me, then twists, and I gasp. Tremors begin at my toes then spiral up my legs.

That's when he pulls his fingers out.

12

Arpad

Her shoulders bunch, her thighs spasm, the sweet scent of her arousal fills the air, and damn it, but I don't want to stop. I want to turn her over, bury my face in her pussy and suck on her clit, lick her lower lips and bite on that swollen flesh until she comes all over my face. But… I will not. The hard column between my legs protests. That's when I know I need to get her off of me, need to put distance between us for a little while… Just until she's learned her lesson. I lick her cum off my fingers then swing her off my lap to place her in front of me.

Her knees buckle and I hold her until she finds her balance.

"What are you doing?" She gasps as I tug the T-shirt, *my* T-shirt, down about her knees.

"This looks better on you; you should keep it."

"What?" She gapes as I straighten and brush past her to the stove. I flick on the flame under the skillet.

"Arpad," she snarls, "what the hell are you playing at?"

"Not playing, just teaching you how to behave." I add the vegetables to the skillet, then crack the eggs into the bowl and whisk them.

"I'm not a bloody pet," she snaps.

Adorable. I can't stop the smile that tugs at my lips. "No, you're more than that." I pour the egg mixture into the skillet.

"You could have fooled me," she mutters.

"Doesn't mean I don't need to tame you." I glance over my shoulder.

She folds her arms around her waist, draws herself up to her full height. "I need to call my office and make sure everything is okay."

"It is."

She gapes at me. "How do you know? Did you—" she pauses, scans my face. "You didn't." Her cheeks redden. "You did not get in touch with my team and tell them where I am."

"Someone had to do it, so they wouldn't get alarmed, considering you were," I look her up and down, "otherwise occupied." I smirk.

Her cheeks grow fiery, then she curls her fingers into fists. "So help me, Arpad, if you messed with my company and my employees—"

"Relax, Sparks," I drawl, "I had Edward pass on the message to your second in command that you were taking a few days off and couldn't be reached."

"Right." Her shoulders sag, then she tosses her head. "I'm never not reachable." She sniffs.

"You need some time off. Isn't too much stress a deterrent to conceiving?"

Her features freeze. "You bastard," she snarls.

"It's true, isn't it?" I tilt my head, "You want to get pregnant. I am happy to oblige. In fact, I am doing everything in my power to ensure that our joined mission is successful."

"You sound so sincere," she stares at my face, "I almost believe you."

"That's because I am." I turn back and pop the bread into the toaster. "I have your best interests at heart, Sparks."

She scoffs, "Sure, you do. That's why you tied me up, huh?"

"It's part of our agreement." I turn to glare at her.

"It's not what I agreed to."

"You agreed to submit to anything I want," I point out.

"This," she waves her hand in the air, "this isn't what I expected."

"You concurred." I tilt my head.

"You could have warned me." She holds my gaze.

I survey her flushed features. "Fair enough." I place the spatula to the side, turn off the flame under the skillet and cover it. "I won't tie you again until you ask." I prowl over to her. "And ask, you will, I promise."

Her pupils dilate.

She bites down on her lower lip and my gaze drops to her mouth. Pink lips, swollen from where she's been worrying it between her teeth.

I reach out, drag my thumb across the puffy flesh.

She shivers, then steps back, "Stop that."

"You don't get to dictate this arrangement."

She throws up her hands, "Hello, this is about me getting pregnant, isn't it? So clearly, I need to get a say. Besides, left to you, I'm not even sure you're going to copulate with me."

"Copulate?" I blink. "Did you say copulate?"

"It seems more official than using the F word," she mutters. "In this situation, I mean. After all, we have an arrangement, right?"

I stare at her, and she folds her arms across her chest. "Look," she draws in a breath, "I'm trying to figure out what the hell you want from me, okay?"

"That's where you are going wrong." I tuck a strand of hair behind her ears. "You don't need to overthink this. Just surrender yourself to me for the next few days."

"Surrender?" She stares up at me. "You're asking me to put myself in your hands."

"What do you have to lose, hmm?"

"My control?" she snaps back.

"Would that be so bad?"

"You don't understand." She rubs her fingers across her arms. "I've never gone a day without working. Not in a long time. I've devoted every second of my working time to building my business, and now, out of the blue, you tell me to switch off."

"It's good for you to occasionally pull back."

"You mean slack off?"

"I mean gain perspective." I take in her agitated features, the way she shuffles her feet, then twists her fingers together in front of her. "Something you could do with," I add.

"Now you're accusing me of what? Being too close to my business?"

"All I am saying," I shove my hands into the pockets of my jeans, "is that you need to take some time to breathe, to recalibrate, and give your body and emotions a chance to readjust to this new reality you want."

"Which is?" She frowns.

"A child."

"Yes, of course. I know that." She huffs. "All of this is about me having a kid, isn't it?"

"I get that." I peer into her face. "Your wanting a child? I get that, loud and clear. What I don't understand is how, if you are so career-oriented, you are going to have time to bring one up?"

"I'd, uh, I'd prioritize the baby, of course," she purses her lips, "if I get pregnant."

"*When* you get pregnant," I correct her, "you'll have to rearrange your entire life around the child. You can't be this focused on your career. If all you think about is your job, how will you make the space in your life for a kid?"

She rakes her fingers through her hair, "I'd, uh, I'd manage."

"Will you?" I fold my arms across my chest. "It seems to me, you haven't really thought through the dynamics of how you're going to raise a child."

"Oh?" She draws herself up to her full height. "And you know everything about childcare, huh?"

I do, because I wasn't prioritized when I was young, but she doesn't need to know that.

"Are you going to elaborate on the details for me?" She huffs.

"No, I am giving you the space you need to think things through." I lean forward on the balls of my feet. "Being away from your job and your daily life is the perfect opportunity for you to process the issues. You'll be surprised how much clarity you get with distance."

"Is that what you're doing?" She glances around the space. "Putting distance?"

I chuckle, "Now you're reading too much into my statement."

"But that is what you're doing, aren't you?" She searches my features. "You're running."

"Next, you'll tell me it's because of the incident, where I was kidnapped as a kid, that I like to spend time away from the world and on my own, sailing around the world."

"Don't you?"

I roll my shoulders. "No."

"No?" Her forehead wrinkles. "Then why do you—?"

"Prefer the company of the waves to the city?"

"And your friends."

"The Seven." I nod. "I keep in touch with them via regular calls. Besides, the frequency with which they have been getting married, I've seen them more in the past few months than I have since right after the incident."

"You guys supported each other a lot during that time?"

I rub the back of my neck. "More like, used each other as punching bags.'

"You mean sounding boards?"

"Punching bags." I widen my stance. "Put seven boys who've been through an emotional and physical rollercoaster, not to mention impending puberty which has all of us in a tizzy, and the last thing we want to do is talk."

"Ah," she nods, "and how did your families react to what happened?"

I set my jaw. "The incident was hard on mine. But they supported me. They were there for me, when I needed them most."

"You're close to them?" Her eyes brighten with interest.

"Close enough," I mutter. "It was a relief, in a way, when my father moved back to Lille. Not that I didn't enjoy having him in London, but it put too much pressure on me to stay in touch, visit him. This way, I have my space, and whenever I need to see him or my grandmother, I just hop across the pond."

"You're lucky to have them so close." She drops into the chair, then crosses her legs. The slim line of her thigh beckons. My fingers tingle. Only when my thigh grazes the chair, do I realize that I've followed her.

I bend down, tuck a strand of hair behind her ear.

Her breath catches. She parts her lips.

Something electric springs between us and the hair on the nape of my neck rises. Bloody hell. This chemistry between us has been there from day one, when she'd spilled her chai tea latte all over my slacks. One side of my lips kicks up and she frowns.

"What's so funny?"

"Just thinking about how we met."

"You were an obnoxious, self-obsessed businessman, intent on having his own way."

I smirk.

"And only you'd take that as a compliment." She sighs.

"Only you'd go toe-to-toe with me, from the moment we set eyes on each other.

"Doesn't happen often, huh?"

"Never," I confess.

"I'm glad I didn't make it easy for you." Her lips curve.

"Oh, but by the time I'm done, you'll be on your back, on your front, on your hands and knees, upside down with your mouth open," I lower my face to hers, until her scent sinks into my blood, "ready and willing and waiting to service me. Asking me to tie you up and take you any way, every way I want, begging for the orgasm that I, and only I, can grant you, you feel me?"

Her breath hitches, her pupils dilate until there's only a circle of color around the outside, then she slaps me.

13

Karina

His head snaps back with the impact. His gaze narrows, his nostrils flare, his hand swoops out, and I squeak when he wraps his fingers around my neck. "You know what attracted me the first time I saw you?"

"Wh…what?"

"Your fire. Your attitude that you didn't give a toss about anything, that you could take on the strongest challenge and overcome it."

"And…now?" I swallow.

"Now, I think it's that very outlook that's going to get you into so much trouble."

I flick out my tongue to lick my lips and his gaze drops to my mouth.

"Do that again and all bets are off." He releases me so suddenly that I crash into the back of the chair.

"I won't forget this, Sparks," he adds. "I am going to repay it with interest. That, I promise you."

The ding of the toaster interrupts the silence. I jump and his lips curl. He straightens, then walks over to rescue the toast. He slides them onto the plate with the omelet, then walks over to place it on the table in front of me.

He jerks his chin and I frown. He tilts his head and I rise to my feet. He sinks down, then pulls me onto his lap.

"What the hell?" I protest. "What are you doing?"

"Feeding you before I fuck you."

My skin tingles. Jesus, this man has a filthy tongue…and a filthier mouth. The things he'd done to me with that mouth earlier. I wriggle around in his lap and the hard column in his pants jabs in between my asscheeks.

"Keep that up and I'll lay you out on the table and eat you instead."

Moisture laces my core and I squeeze my thighs together. "That was a terrible line," I scoff.

"So why are you turned on?" He leans over to scoop up some of the food then holds it to my mouth, "Open."

I flatten my lips together, and he chuckles. "You're cute when you're annoyed."

"I'm not annoyed, I—"

He slides the food inside my mouth. I lick the food off the fork tines and his gaze intensifies. "Careful," his voice rumbles up his chest, "you're testing my patience."

"Wasn't aware you had any." I chew the food and swallow. The flavors linger in my mouth. "This is good." I frown at the food, then up at him.

"Why are you surprised?"

"Just thought you, with your billionaire lifestyle…."

"Billionaire lifestyle—?" He forks up more of the food, offers it to me. I wrap my lips around the fork, and once more, the buttery taste of the eggs underlined with the fragrant notes of basil, seeps into my consciousness. "It's really good." I say with my mouth half-full.

"I cook better than most people."

I blink, then laugh, "Of course, you do."

"It's the truth." He feeds me a few more mouthfuls of the omelet along with the toast.

I open my mouth, and he bypasses me. Instead, he wraps his succulent lips around the fork tines and licks it clean.

My belly flutters, my mouth waters, and trust me, it's not only for the food.

He reaches for the food, offers it to me again. I lean forward, and this time, he brings it to his mouth.

"Hey," I protest as he repeats the previous action; this time he seems to curl his tongue around the fork even longer.

I should look away, should get up and walk out and... Go where? It's a freakin' boat. And I'm trapped here with him. And we have a deal, for better or worse. He's promised to give me what I need most. The price I have to pay for it is not that much, in the larger scheme of things. If anyone can get me pregnant quickly, surely it is this very virile a-hole of a man, right?

He reaches for the remaining food on the plate and I wrap my fingers around his wrist.

He freezes.

I trail my fingers across his knuckles and goosebumps dot his skin.

Huh. Imagine that. Apparently, alphahole, here, isn't impervious to my charms, either. I slide the fork from his grasp, scoop up the last piece of food from the plate. I turn and hold it up to his mouth. "Open," I murmur.

He parts his lips and I slide the fork between them. He swirls his tongue around the tines and my core clenches. He curls his fingers around my wrist, moves my hand down. He squeezes and the fork slips from my fingers to clatter onto the table.

The sound ricochets between us as he leans in closer, closer. He places his lips right in front of mine. The heat from his big body enfolds me, sinks into my blood. The scent of him — bergamot and edgy dark-ness goes straight to my head.

His gaze holds mine. Those blue irises lighten until they seem almost transparent. A mirror that reflects back some of the sensations I am feeling right now. Lust, need, a gnawing emptiness that spills from my core.

"I am going to kiss you now." His breath sears my mouth.

I lean in closer, until my lips almost touch his. Until there's only a hair's breadth of space between us. No, not even that. Less than that, actually.

He stays that way for a beat, another. My hairline prickles; my toes curl. This anticipation... It's w-a-a-y sexier than anything I've ever experienced. My throat closes and my breath comes in small pants.

"Ari," I whisper, and his gaze intensifies.

"Say that again."

"Arpad."

"No what you called me earlier."

"Ari?"

His lips kick up, "I like the sound of my name from your lips."

"Does anyone else call you that?"

He shakes his head.

"That'll be our secret, huh?"

"Here's another." His smile broadens. "I've fancied you since I first laid eyes on you."

I chuckle, "I thought you were angry with me."

"I was."

I wrinkle my forehead. "I don't understand."

"Somehow, you got under my skin. You made me want to haul you close and ravish you. And this feeling of being so near the edge, of not knowing why I felt what I did, of not wanting to let you go until I found out why I was having this reaction to you… It made me feel—"

"Uncomfortable?"

"Out of control." He says simultaneously. "It made me want to push you away and keep you close at the same time."

I take in the sincerity of his gaze, the depths in those grey-blue eyes of his which invite me to trust him, to drown in them. "It's why you had the Seven offer me the contract for the security of your businesses?"

He doesn't blink, and if I hadn't been looking for it, I might have missed the twitch in his left eye.

"That's it, isn't it?" I lean back to put distance between us. I am still in the circle of his arms, but whatever. "It was you who was behind my getting this contract. You did it, knowing if I accepted it, I'd have to move to London."

His jaw tics, "Are you accusing me of wanting you near me?"

"I am saying that you manipulated my career, so you could have me in a place where you could control me."

"You're getting ahead of yourself."

"And you're delusional if you think your over-the-top, interfering ways are going to win you any favors with me." I jump up and he drags me right back down into his lap.

"I'm not done with you."

"Oh, but I'm done with you."

"We're just getting started, Sparks. Remember, you need my cum inside you."

"Maybe I don't care anymore. Maybe I'll simply miss this window, then inseminate myself with the sperm of another man."

His jaw hardens. A nerve throbs at his temple. He glares at me and that hint of meanness that I've become so familiar with reveals itself in his eyes.

I swallow and my nerve-endings jangle. *Don't poke the beast. What the hell do you think you're doing?* And when have I ever backed down from a challenge, huh?

"Actually, I think I need to find another man. Someone who doesn't impose stupid conditions and who'd be more than happy to fuck me and—"

He swoops out his hand and curls his fingers around my throat. "What did you say?"

"I said I need to find someone else to sleep with—"

His grasp tightens. I try to draw in a breath and my lungs burn.

"What are you doing?" I cough, grab at his wrist as he thrusts his face into mine, then licks his tongue up my cheek.

"Don't talk about another man when you're with me," he growls against my skin. The vibrations sink into my blood, span my chest, then dip straight down to the flesh between my legs. I can't stop the panting sound that spills from my throat.

"Nod, if you understand."

Yes.

Yes.

I shake my head.

"What a little liar you are. And just when I thought we were getting along so well."

"Oh, bugger off," I choke out the words and his eyes gleam.

He loosens his grasp only to lower his head. He bites down on my lower lip and my breath catches. He presses little kisses down my chin, my neck, then fastens his mouth over the fabric surrounding my nipple, and bites down. I feel the tug all the way down to my core.

"Stop," I gasp. "Stop that."

He brings his other hand up to massage my other breast and, honestly, my insides liquify. The warmth of his fingers on my flesh, the scent of him lapping at my nostrils, the heat from his big body that surrounds me, and presses down on my chest, to pin me in place. He raises his head to nuzzle at the curve of where my shoulder meets my neck. I shiver and pinpricks of pleasure dance across my skin. He's not even trying really hard and I am turned on. When it comes to him, I can't resist the allure of how my body responds to his touch.

He releases his hold on my nape, only to bury his fingers in my hair. He tugs and I bare my neck. "Look at you, all ready for the taking."

"I'm not," I grit out through clenched teeth.

"So, you don't want your orgasm?"

That's not what I said. I clamp my lips together, refuse to groan when he buries his nose at the base of my throat and draws in a long breath. The hard column in his pants throbs against the curve of my butt, and my stomach flip-flops. Jesus, how can I resist him when I am completely engulfed by his presence?

He licks the skin between my clavicles and a moan spills from my lips. He presses little kisses down to the valley between my breasts and heat flushes my skin. He tugs down the collar of the T-shirt, then laves my nipple with his tongue. Moisture pools between my legs. My eyelids flutter shut. Oh, my god, this is crazy. How can he make me come apart, so quickly?

"You're more responsive than any ship has ever been to my touch."

I snap open my eyelids. "Did you just compare me to a boat?"

"It was a compliment." He turns his attention back to my other breast, then curls his tongue around my nipple. He sucks on it and my fingers tremble. Jesus, it's as if all my erogenous zones are connected to parts of me in a way I didn't think was possible at all.

"Only you," I gasp out, "would turn around the meaning of the words to suit your needs."

"And I thought this was all about fulfilling your needs."

He slides his hand between my thighs and I tremble.

"Thought so." He raises his head and smirks. "You're ready for me. Admit it."

"No."

He peels back his lips and his teeth glint against his tanned skin. He releases his hold on me, only to shove the utensils on the table aside. Then he grabs my waist and hoists me onto the table.

"Hey," I squeak.

He plants his big palm in the center of my chest and applies pressure. The world tilts. The next moment I am on my back, on the flat surface, staring up at the ceiling of the boat.

He wedges his shoulder between my legs, forcing them apart. Cool air hits my exposed skin a second before he grips my ankles and places them over each of his shoulders.

I glance down to find him peering up with a wicked look on his face.

"Wha—" I clear my throat, "what are you doing?"

"Eating the rest of my lunch."

14

Arpad

I swipe my tongue up her pussy lips and she moans. I slide my tongue inside her channel, grip her thighs and spread them apart even further. She thrusts her hips up and into my face, and that sweet scent of her arousal goes to my head. I weave my tongue in and out of her, then slip my fingers in between her arsecheeks. She freezes, and I lick her clit, circle the swollen nub with my tongue. Her thighs tremble. She buries her fingers in my hair and tugs. The pain heads straight to my groin. Hell. My cock lengthens in my pants. I slide my other hand up her smooth skin and squeeze her nipple. She shudders, then locks her thighs around my head as I suck on her pussy, then close my mouth around her clit and draw it in between my lips. Her entire body bucks. A groan bleeds from her, and my balls harden. I raise my head, then rise over her, to fasten my lips to her mouth. The taste of her lips combined with that of her cum, sends the blood rushing to my groin. I pull back, stare into her flushed features, her wide eyes, the tendrils of hair stuck to her brow.

"Jesus, you're gorgeous." Something hot coils in my chest. I plant my elbows on the table and bracket her in. "Why the hell did it have to be you?" I frown at her.

She stares back at me, her golden eyes wide, beseeching.

I reach down, release my cock, then position it against her entrance. I thrust into her and she gasps. Her mouth opens and closes. I bend, fit my lips to hers, slide my tongue inside her mouth at the same time that I pull back and impale her in one long, smooth move. Her entire body jerks. The table creaks. I begin to fuck her in earnest, plunging up and into her. A groan trembles up her throat; I swallow it, dig my fingers into the curve of her hip and hold her as I continue to move in and out of her. In and out. I wind the strands of her hair around my palm and tug. She moans, then flings her arms around my shoulders, digs her fingernails into my back with enough force that pain shivers down my spine. My balls tighten and my shaft thickens inside of her. I pull all the way out, stay poised at the rim of her channel. She pushes her pelvis up, and I tear my lips from hers. "Tell me you want me."

She firms her lips.

"Say it," I order.

She pouts, then reaches down between us. I slap her hand away. "You don't get to touch." I snap. "Not unless I allow you."

"And when is that?"

"When you admit that it wasn't an accident that you stowed away on my boat."

She stares. "You're crazy."

"I am only just beginning to understand what's between us."

"What's that?"

"You're infatuated with me."

"What?" She gapes.

"It's true. Don't deny it. In fact, your subconscious had picked me out as the father of your to-be child, even before you realized it."

Her gaze narrows. "You're doing this purposely, aren't you?"

"What?"

"Trying to make me angry?"

"I won't deny that having you livid at me is a turn on."

"That's why you're accusing me of some utter bullshit?"

"Is it?" I drag the crown of my cock up her pussy lips and her eyes dilate. "Tell me you need this. Tell me you can't wait for me to fuck you, to bury myself inside your hungry, melting pussy and shag you so hard that you'll feel me inside of you for days."

Her breathing grows ragged and she moans, "Fuck you, Ari."

"I will. All you have to do is give me what I want." I reach down, sink my thumb inside her arsehole and her back bows off the table.

"Jesus," she pants. Sweat beads on her upper lip. She digs her fingers into my hair and yanks me close to her. "Damn you," she snarls. "Damn the day I set eyes on you."

"Say it," I growl.

"Fine." She heaves out a breath. "I want you," she swallows, "I want you to make me orgasm. I want you to fuck me until—"

I propel my hips forward and impale her in one long, smooth stroke. Her eyes roll back in her head and she tightens her grip on my hair. Fire sizzles down my spine, warming my blood. My pulse begins to thud at my temples. "Look at me," I growl.

She mumbles under her breath.

"Eyes on me, Sparks."

She opens her heavy eyelids, then holds my gaze as I pull back then sink into her, burying myself to the hilt. She parts her lips and a tear runs down from the corner of her eye. I bend my head and slurp it up. Then without taking my eyes off of her, I thrust in and out, in and out. She holds onto me, moving with me, holding herself open to the battering I am subjecting her to. She meets me thrust for thrust, pushing up to accept me, as I plunge into her, again and again.

A shudder grips her and color smears her cheeks. "I am going to—"

"Come with me," I command as I pull out, all the way out, then lunge forward until my balls slap against her arse.

She throws her head back, and shatters. The ripples of her climax shudder up her body, her pussy clenches around my dick, and that's when I come deep inside her. My orgasm seems to go on and on, until I slump over her body.

We stay that way, skin slick with sweat, her fingers entangled in my hair. Her body shakes under me and warmth spreads against my shoulder. I pull back, then glance down to find her crying.

My heart stutters and my skin suddenly feels too tight for the rest of me, "What's wrong?" I pat at her hair, not sure what to do. Jesus, bringing a woman to fulfillment? That I can do, but a weeping woman…? How the hell am I going to calm her down? "Sparks?" I cup her face, "Did I hurt you?"

She only cries harder.

I pull out of her and straighten. She throws her arm over her eyes.

Why is she trying to hide from me? I scoop her up and into my lap. She buries her head in my shoulder and continues to sob. Shit, this isn't good. Why the hell is she still weeping? I rock her, run my fingers through her hair, try to calm her. We stay that way for a few more seconds until her crying slows down.

"Feeling better? I ask.

She sniffles, then rubs her hand across her face. "Let me go," she hisses.

"What?" I glance down at her in confusion.

She pushes against me and I raise my arms. She slips off my lap, almost falls on her arse, then straightens. She heads out of the galley area and toward the bedroom.

"Karina, stop." I jump up to my feet and follow her, through the bedroom and into to the bathroom. She closes the door and I hear the snick of the lock.

"Karina," I bang on the door, "let me in."

"Go away." Her voice reaches me—brittle, angry, hurting. Why is she hurting?

"What is it? What happened?" I place my ear against the door. "At least, tell me what's wrong."

"Nothing's wrong, I..." She turns on the shower, which drowns out the rest of her statement. *Aargh!* I dig my fingers into my hair and pull on it. "Open the damn door." I slam my fist into the wooden barrier. "Open, right the fuck now, or I swear, when I get my hands on you, I'll make you pay."

The shower shuts off. There's silence, a beat. Another.

Then, her voice barely audible through the door, she asks, "How?"

Huh? "What do you mean?"

"How will you make me pay?"

<h1 style="text-align:center">15</h1>

Karina

Is that all you've got to say for yourself after falling apart in his arms? Jesus, that orgasm… It was more than that… It was a seismic wave of epic proportions that carried me higher and higher, then fell away, leaving me to crash to earth. Had I blacked out for a second there? Maybe. I'd never come this hard before. In fact, I'd come with more vengeance than the last time when he'd tied me up; and I'd thought that first time had been intense. Ha, I should have known better.

Every time he fucks me, it will only solidify the connection between us. It is going to tie me to him, going to churn my guts inside out and spit me out, and I won't be able to do anything about it. Hell, I don't want to stop it. As soon as he glances at me, I'm all but ready to throw myself at his feet and beg him to take me.

This…is not how I'd envisioned this association of ours progressing. I am not the kind of person who loses control… Not when my father had treated me like one of the boys and forced me to run ten miles every morning.

Not when I'd stood up to him and proven that I could successfully run my own business. I'd proven to the world that I could take care of myself without anyone's help.

So, why the hell had I fallen apart when this bastard of a man, who has no idea about me or where I come from or what I've been through, had put his hands on me—and his cock inside of me?

I wipe my arm across my face. It was only sex—until it wasn't. Every encounter with that man is turning out to be far more intense than I'd expected. At this rate, I am going to walk away with a child... But without my heart. I cannot fall for this guy, no way.

"What did you say?" He raps on the door again.

I unlock it and swing it open. "I said," I tip up my chin, "how do you plan to make me pay?"

He peruses my features, then frowns. "What was that about?"

"You first." I fold my arms over my chest.

"I don't answer to anyone."

I snort. "With that attitude, it's a wonder you've had any success in business."

"Or maybe it's because of this very attitude, that I am willing to take the kinds of risks no one else will."

"Is that what I am? A risk?"

"You're an investment, an asset, make no mistake about that, Sparks. An easy way for me to get my family off my back about my bachelor status. And if I get a few free fucks along the way—"

Only when my hand connects with his face again, do I realize I've closed the distance between us. For the second time, his head snaps back, and the imprints of my fingers stand out against his face.

His eyes gleam and his nostrils flare. He cracks his neck and a thrill of fear slithers down my spine.

He takes a step forward.

I skitter back. "I... I'm sorry." My voice wavers. Hell, that won't do. I can't allow him to see how this mean angry side of him scares me, and turns me on. Shit, why am I behaving in such a stereotypical manner? Just because he is a dominant son of a bitch, doesn't mean I have to connect with my inner submissive, right? Wait... What? Inner submissive? What the hell? I am used to being in charge—at home, at work... And no rich, prick alphahole is going to take that from me.

He prowls toward me and I dig my heels into the ground. *Don't give in. Don't allow him to overpower me.* "You...You deserved it, though. How dare you insult me that way? How dare you act like...like I am your property, like you own me, like you can command me to do anything you want."

"Oh?" His lips twitch. He drums his fingers on his chest, as he looks me up and down. "Are you telling me you didn't give me that right once you agreed to this partnership?"

"Partnership?" I scoff. "More like a one-way street, where your word is law."

"See?" He drags his thumb across that plump lower lip of his, "You do get it, after all. I knew you were clever, Sparks. Knew I'd made the right choice all along.'

"You…" I gape at him, then snap my jaws shut. "*You* made the choice? *I* was the one who proposed that you father my child."

He grins and I stiffen. Damn it, I walked into that. Somehow, everything I tell him gets twisted around to suit his own needs. No way, am I going to let him get away with it this time. I am going to show him that I am not like his other women. He cannot simply walk all over me.

I grab the hem of my—okay technically *his* —shirt then pull it up and off.

His chest muscles go solid. He freezes in place. The twin orbs of fire that are his eyes seem to blaze, a blue flame, the hottest of all. He rakes his gaze down my breasts, down my stomach to my smoothly shaved pussy—I did it for myself, just so you know. I like to feel good in my skin and taking care of my body is an essential part of my regimen.

I jut out my hip, prop my hand on it, then watch as he approaches me.

He sinks to his knees, stares straight at my core. And my thighs tremble. "Jesus." His hot breath sears my center.

Goosebumps pepper my skin. He pushes his face into my core, and inhales. And the sheer intimacy of the moment, the animalistic way that he hums under his breath, that he stares at my center with adoration, is more than I can bear. Sweat beads my upper lip and my thigh muscles tremble. I fold my fingers at my sides, don't move as he blows on my heated, throbbing pussy.

"Damnit," I swear aloud, and his lips kick up.

"Want me to make you come again, huh?" He smirks.

"How about I make you come instead?"

He glances up at me, then shakes his head, "You don't get to call the shots, sweetheart. Have you forgotten that?"

"It was simply a suggestion." I flutter my eyelashes at him, and his breathing speeds up. Oh, this could be fun, after all. I slide my fingers down to strum my pussy lips and he tracks my movements. I part my legs, slide my fingers inside my cunt and a fat drop of cum trickles down my inner thigh. He licks his lips, lowers his head and slurps it up.

Goosebumps pop on my skin. Bloody hell, did he just do that? The carnal nature of this man overpowers all other aspects of him. Perhaps, I had underestimated him, huh? Perhaps he's not as easy to control as I'd thought, after all? Had I been wrong in that spontaneous suggestion that he become my sperm donor? I try to slide back, but he places his big palms on either side of my hips and holds me in place.

"Don't move," he commands.

And simply because he said that, because he asked me to obey him, again, I shuffle back. His grasp tightens, his fingertips digging into my hipbones with enough pressure that I yelp.

He glances up. "Shh," he admonishes me. "Watch me as I eat out your pussy."

That's when a loud beeping sound cuts through the silence.

16

Arpad

The beeping sound cuts through the lust-filled haze in my head. I freeze.

Her gaze widens. "What's that?" she asks as it dies out.

I rise to my feet. My heart begins to race, but I school all emotion from my face. "Get dressed," I order.

"What?" She folds her arms in front of her. Her beautiful tits thrust out as she draws herself up to her full height... Which still means she only comes to the level of my chest. "Don't tell me what to do."

"This is not a drill, babe," I growl. "Wear your clothes, and your boots."

"I don't have any, remember?"

Well, crap. Of course, she doesn't. "Follow me." I turn around and stalk to the door. I pause and glare at her over my shoulder, "You coming, or what?"

The beeping starts again. "Suit yourself, but don't blame me if you're caught out in the open sea without any clothes on."

"What?" The color drains from her face. "What do you mean?"

I draw in a breath, force myself to calm down. "Nothing." I jerk my chin, "Just put on some clothes and come to the cabin."

"No," she crosses over to me, and grabs my arm, "don't treat me like a stupid female who needs to be mollycoddled. I've been running my company since I was eighteen. I've seen lots of hostile takeovers, employees who tried to ruin my company by stealing from me… You name it, I've faced it and emerged unscathed—"

"But have you faced the fury of Mother Nature?"

She blinks. "What?"

"That's a storm warning." The beeping ratchets up in intensity. "Shit." I turn and hurry into the room. Pulling on boots, and a sweatshirt, I head for the closet door at the far end. I grab hold of a handful of clothes, then a pair of shoes and throw it on the bed. "Help yourself," I tell her.

She walks over to the clothes, picks up the jeans and the sweatshirt. "They're your size," she says accusingly.

"That's because they're my clothes. Sorry they don't fit your sense of style," I growl.

She hesitates.

"It's either that or you go without clothes," I point out.

The beeping increases in pitch, and she jumps. I head out the door, and to the closet in the living room with the survival gear. I grab a life jacket shrug into it, then turn to find she's right behind me. She's rolled up the legs of the jeans almost in half so I can see the over-sized boots, and the sweatshirt cloaks her like a tent, but at least, she's covered—in my clothes. A hot sensation coils in my stomach.

I slap the other life jacket to her chest. "Wear it," I command.

She sets her jaw, but shrugs into it. Good.

I head for the cabin, shut off the beeping instrument, then check my weather coordinates, and swear aloud.

"What's wrong?" Her voice sounds right behind and I want to tell her to leave, but hell, if there is no time for that.

"Storm's headed for us," I grit out through clenched teeth.

"But we just passed one last night."

"That, sweetheart, was a rainstorm."

"A… rainstorm?" She gulps.

"Idle sport, the kind I wouldn't hesitate to take on with my eyes closed."

"And this…this is—"

"A category 3 which, if you weren't on board, I wouldn't hesitate to face head on, but since I do care about your sweet little ass, I am going to have to find a way to steer around it."

"So, I was right then, you like to drive your boat straight into rough weather?"

"You could say it's a specialization of mine."

I take in the progression of the storm…which is too rapid for me to outrun. Even at top speed, there is no way we can beat it. I can only think of one way out… But I have to be sure. I begin to plot out the coordinates on the map as she leans around me to peer at the screen.

"You do realize how crazy that sounds, right?" She moves closer and her scent intensifies. My cock twitches in response, and damn it, why is it, that even trying to figure out how to save our lives, I am so aware of how completely edible she is?

"What's crazy, is that you are still here trying to distract me while I plot a course to get us to safety."

"What are you going to do?"

"Find a place to take shelter until the storm blows over."

"And how long will that take?"

"Hours, days…"

"Days?" She scowls, "I'm assuming those days are part of the thirty days I have to spend with you?"

"No."

"No?" Her eyes widen.

A chuckle breaks free and I turn it into a cough.

"It's not part of the deal," I reiterate. "You'll simply have to put it down to time invested in your attempts to have a baby. Not to mention, time invested in saving your life."

"Aargh," she makes a noise deep in her throat, "this cannot be happening. As it is, I'm regretting having made this deal with you, and now you're telling me I'm going to have to spend more time with you?"

"More time to ensure that you get pregnant…unless," I jerk my head in her direction "you're already with child?"

A strange sensation flutters in my chest. A child. My child. With Karina—the woman who'd entranced me from the first day I'd laid eyes on her; the sassy spitfire who'd never hesitated to go up against me. How would a baby we created look? Would she have her golden eyes, my dark hair, her pert nose, my stubborn jaw? A little girl…or boy… Either is good… Ideally, twins. Shit, that means we'd have multiplied by two overnight. We? Did I just think of myself in the plural there?

She pales, "You…you don't think I'm already…?"

"Well, if the right sperm found its way up your Fallopian tube and fertilized an egg, then —"

"Stop," she holds up her hand, "I know how it works, you ass."

"So why do you look like you're going to faint?"

"Just… It's too sudden."

"What were you expecting, anyway?" I frown, as she sways. "You okay?"

"Yes." She shakes her head.

"Is that a 'no' or a 'yes'?"

"Don't you have to focus on taking shelter from the storm?" She folds her arms around her waist, then stares past me at the sea ahead. The waves seem calm, nothing out of the ordinary, but I am not fooled. I know how quickly the weather can change. I glance at the weather data, then consult the map.

"Well," she insists, "what are you going to do?"

"Why don't you leave that to me, huh?"

"What, so you can play the big macho male who can shelter the woman —"

"His woman."

"I'm not yours."

"And yet, you may be carrying my child."

"Don't go getting all possessive on me now. We had a deal remember? I get custody of the child, if there is a child at all, and you get visitation rights."

"For the next 30 days you are mine."

"I don't recall agreeing to anything of the sort."

"Are you denying that you willingly acquiesced to pose as my wife, for the duration of this time?"

She throws up her hand, "Yes, but that doesn't mean —"

That's when the first wave hits the yacht.

17

Karina

One second, the water is serene. The next, a swell hits the boat. The vessel pitches to the side and I scream. My feet seem to go out from under me and I stagger. My heart races and my pulse pounds. The ground comes up to meet me; the next instant, I am pulled up and against his hard chest. His scent, bergamot laced with the salt of the sea, fills my nostrils. His heart thuds against my cheek, or more likely, it's mine, since he's wearing a vest.

"You okay?" His voice rumbles and the vibrations surround me, cocoon me. I turn my nose into the material of the life jacket across his chest. I stay there for a beat, another. I don't want to let go. I wrap my arms around his waist, and he blows out a breath. He pulls me into his side, then behind him. "Hold on." His voice sounds from somewhere above me, "I need to steer us out of the way of the rough weather and toward our hurricane hole."

I turn my cheek into his back, and I am not ashamed to say that I follow his instructions, for once. I lock my arms around him.

"Hurricane hole?" I clear my throat, "What's that?"

"We need to find port, but not just any port will do. It needs to have high cliffs or mountains surrounding it.

"To shelter from the storm?"

"That's right." He turns the boat a steep right. "And I know just the place."

I close my eyes, not because I am tired, not even because I am afraid —okay, maybe I am, a tiny bit apprehensive. Okay, a little more than that. I am a city girl. I've lived in crowded metropolises all my life, and I enjoy the rush, the traffic, the ability to drive my car wherever I want. It means I am in control. I can steer my way. I can see where I am going, get my bearings. But this… Surrounded by waves that seem to get bigger with every passing second, this…pitching of the boat as it climbs up yet another wave, only to slide down the other side, then scale the next swell… My stomach churns and my breath catches in my throat. *I am not afraid. I am not.* I squeeze my eyes tightly.

He squeezes my hand, the one which has a death-grip on his life jacket, as we speak.

"Not long now," he reassures me.

I nod, want to say something in reply, but honestly, my throat is dry. The boat climbs up a wave, slowly…slowly…like the ascent up a roller-coaster —that first part, when you know they are simply setting you up, taking you higher and higher —then a pause, and the boat seems to hurtle down. Another scream boils up, and I bite the inside of my cheek to contain it. I am a strong, career-driven woman, who has built my life to be exactly the way I want —that's why I am still single at thirty.

Gah. Stop that. Now's not the time to think about the mistakes of the past. As my life coach had mentioned, you do what is right for you in the moment and it is the right decision, always. And yes, I have a life coach. Cliché, I know, but it seemed the best way to visualize the kind of life I want —a career, a family, and a man… Okay, I had hoped for a man, but honestly, after the kinds I'd met in my twenties… Not that there was anything wrong with them, but none of them had what I was looking for —that kind of animalistic attraction combined with sensitivity; a mixture of dominance and the ability to give me enough space to find myself… Know what I mean? Well, that was until Arpad… And he… Well, our very first encounter had been enough to convince me that I certainly didn't want him in my life.

I have no time for men who think they own the world and any woman they meet, and insist on taking charge. A car can't have two drivers, right? And I am the driver in my life. So, what the hell am I doing clinging to his broad back while he steers the yacht?

I loosen my grip, just as a screeching sound fills my ears and the boat seems to go into freefall. My heart pounds in my throat and a low moan escapes my lips. I lock my arms more tightly around his waist, squeeze my eyes shut as the boat hits the bottom of the wave-valley with a thump, then begins the journey all over again, and again. I lose count of the number of times the boat rises and falls. With each descent, my stomach plummets. With each ascent, my heartbeat seems to fill my ears. Sweat beads my palms while a ball of panic bubbles in my chest, and grows bigger, wider, until it seems to fill all of me. I plaster myself to him, squeeze my eyes shut, draw in one breath, then another, then block out the sound of the wind, the waves that scream and try to get to us, the creak of the boat, the groan of the various components of the vessel as they resist the elements, and try to hold on. I cling to him with all of my strength.

Hours pass… Or maybe they are just minutes. I must have dozed off… How could I? In the middle of that storm? Is it because I'd felt so safe with him? Because I knew he wouldn't let anything happen to me? That I could be in the middle of a world gone crazy and he'd still protect me? My protector. My savior. Mine.

"Karina?" His voice reaches me and I shrug it off.

"Sparks?" Warmth seeps up my arm from where he's dragging his knuckles up the side of my forearm. He grips both of my hands in his and squeezes. "Time to wake up."

"Wh…what?" I flicker open my eyelids and stare at the scene through the large windshield in front of me. We seem to have docked at a wooden jetty that juts out on a calm sea. On either side, we are surrounded by mountains. Clearly, we are in some kind of inlet shelter. Exactly the kind that would protect us from the elements.

Beyond that, a pebbled beach stretches up to a line of trees. "Where…where are we?"

"We have to go." He tugs on my wrists and I lower my hands. When I step back, my knees buckle. He turns and grasps my shoulders. "You all right?" His blue gaze takes in my features. My stomach flip-flops again. A warmth spans my chest, then slides down to my core.

"Karina?" His voice is impatient. "How many do you see?" He holds up two fingers.

"Two," I mutter, "and yeah, I am fine. Just a little shaky."

"Understandable." His forehead furrows. "We were lucky we managed to get here before the storm hit, but we need to get off the boat."

He walks out of the cockpit and into the living area, heading to the closet at the far end. He pulls out a backpack—already packed, by the look of it—and heaves it over his shoulder. Then he swings the strap of a gun—a gun?—over his other shoulder.

"What's that for?" I nod toward it as he walks back and grabs his mobile phone and charger from the counter.

"It's a flare gun." He grips my hand and pulls me out of the door of the cockpit and onto the deck. He bends, grabs the bowline and swings it out and onto the pillar that protrudes from the jetty. With a tug, he secures it, his movements smooth.

I watch as he steps off the boat and onto the jetty. He holds out his hand, "Come on."

I hesitate.

A gust of wind blows over me and whips my hair back from my face. "Karina, come on," he orders. "Jump, I'll catch you."

I glance down at his outstretched palms, then up to his face.

I swallow, not sure why my heart is racing, why it feels like if I take this step, I'll lose myself forever. Why the hell am I being so fanciful, huh? I measure the distance between the boat and the jetty, then spring forward. He plucks me from the air, his hands warm and solid against my waist. Placing me on the ground, he grabs my hand, then turns and sets a brisk pace up the jetty with me in tow. The flare gun is hooked over his other shoulder as we head across the sand.

"The gun," I clear my throat, "do you think you'll need it?"

"Probably not." He forges forward through the gathering darkness. "But it's best to be prepared."

"Ah."

He casts me a sideways glance. "You don't have to worry. I'll take care of you."

That's exactly what I'm worried about. I am not used to feeling this helpless, this dependent on another person. And somehow, we've ended up here on an island, just the two of us…and… "Where are we anyway?" I take in my surroundings—the pebbled beach beneath our feet, the waves crashing on the shore behind us. The wind picks up and buffets us. I lean into it, trying to push my way forward. His grip firms and he pulls me along. Clearly, the breeze is no deterrent for him. "How did you find this island?"

"I own it."

Of course, he does. Considering I am the security consultant for his business, you'd have thought I'd know about it. Apparently, not. How many other secrets does this man have, huh? I take another step, stumble—because, of course, the shoes are too big for me—and he rights me. Then, the first drops of rain hit me. He speeds up. "Come on, let's get inside before we get drenched."

I allow him to haul me away from the beach, up the flat grassy slope and through the tree line. We walk fast until we reach a clearing. There, in the middle of the space, is a single-story structure with sloping roofs and large windows.

We walk up the pebbled path to the door. He releases my hand, then places his palm on a flattened board next to the doorway. Nothing happens for a second, then the door swings open.

18

Arpad

I step in through the doorway, then feel around for the switch on the wall. My fingers hit it and light floods the space.

I walk through the living room, past the circular settee that faces the fireplace, and to the table pushed up against the big window.

Behind me, I hear the door snick shut. I place my bag on the table, turn to find her standing on the rug in the middle of the room.

"It's a little bare, huh?" She sweeps her gaze about the place.

"I like it that way. It's my place to get away from the rest of the world and be myself, a kind of hideaway. Besides, as long as the water and electricity work, we should be fine." I shift my weight between my feet, "Of course, it's not like we had a choice. Better to be stuck here out of the path of the storm —"

She snickers, "Relax, Ari, I was kidding."

Right.

She holds out both of her hands, "This is pretty luxurious for an out-of-the-way getaway cabin."

"Chalet." I correct her.

She turns to me, "Chalet?"

"That—" I gesture behind me, "the kind of space you find on a yacht is a cabin. I prefer to call this," I jerk my chin toward the structure in front of us, "a chalet."

"Of course, you do." She takes in the space, "Nothing rustic about it, huh?"

"I don't stint on creature comforts."

"I'm with you there." She half smiles. "I mean, life is short. Why not enjoy the best of everything it can offer along the way?"

"Apparently, we agree on something." I grin.

"What a shocker." She rolls her eyes. "Speaking of, how many rooms do you have here?"

"Why don't you explore, while I start a fire?"

"Fire?" She glances at the fireplace. "How are you going to do that?"

"Umm, with wood?"

"Where are you going to get the wood from?"

I flex my biceps. "I'm going to chop it of course."

Her jaw drops. "Really?"

I snort, "Of course, not. I have a caretaker from the mainland who comes by every few weeks to make sure everything is in working order. He also stocks the wood in the shed adjacent to the house."

"Oh."

"You almost look disappointed." I chuckle.

"Kind of." She rubs her nose. "The image of you stripped to the waist, chopping wood as you sweat, had a kind of appeal…"

I raise my eyebrow.

"—for all of one second," she adds hastily.

I smirk. "It's fine to share your fantasies. In fact," I tilt my head, "I very much want you to share your fantasies."

"No fantasies."

"Aww, come on, don't hold out on me now, especially since we were finally having a real conversation—"

"Not." She tips up her chin, and walks toward the open plan kitchen that adjoins the room. She takes in the oven, the coffee maker, the counter that separates it from the living room. She opens the refrigerator and whistles, "You weren't kidding about the caretaker. This place is stocked. If I didn't know better, I'd think you had anticipated coming here…" Her voice trails off. She closes the refrigerator and turns to me. "You hadn't, right?" She tilts her head.

"What are you asking?"

"You didn't engineer all this to get me here on an island away from everybody and—"

"At my mercy?"

She swallows.

"And if I had?"

She twirls a lock of hair around her finger. "Then I'd have to wonder why you went to all the effort." She frowns. "Although, not even you could have anticipated the storm," she laughs nervously, "right?"

"Right."

I shrug out of the lifejacket, then walk over to the closet by the doorway and hang it there. I proceed to remove my shoes and put them aside. When I straighten, she's still watching me. "Your shoes." I point toward them, "You're tracking mud across the place."

"Oh." She clomps over to me, then toes off her shoes. The wind bangs against the door and she shivers.

"You cold? Want to take a shower?"

"Yeah, sure."

"Straight through to the bedroom."

She nods, then walks inside.

I head to my backpack, and pull out the things I'd managed to pack before our hasty departure. Spare clothes, extra flares, a torch, a rope… I lay them on the table.

"What's the rope for?"

I turn to see her eyeing me from the doorway.

"What do you think it's for?" I ask.

She juts out her hip and props her hand on it. "You seriously weren't thinking about…"

I tilt my head, "About—?"

"Never mind." She walks back inside. I hear the bathroom door close, then open again.

Wait for it.

Wait for it.

She flounces out and into the living room. "There's no latch on the bathroom."

My lips begin to quirk, and I turn away to hide my smile. "I tend to be alone when I am here," I reply, then walk over to the kitchen, top off the coffee maker and switch it on.

The sound of the percolator fills the empty space.

"Still." She huffs, "Whoever doesn't have a latch on the bathroom door?"

"Be thankful I am allowing you to keep your clothes on," I drawl.

"What's that supposed to mean?" She throws up her hands, "Jesus, Arpad. Can you stop with the riddle-like answers and tell me what the hell your game is?"

"Game?" I turn, then lean a hip against the work top. "No game, babe. We ran into a storm. I made sure we got to shelter before it caught us."

"Somehow, I don't believe you."

"Somehow, I don't care."

"Somehow…" she shuffles her feet, "I can't get past the idea that you orchestrated all this."

"So you've said before."

"I mean, if you wanted to shag me, all you had to do is ask."

"And you'd have agreed?"

She shakes her head.

"I rest my case." I tilt my head, "I suggest you better get that shower in before it's time."

"Time?" She frowns. "Time for what?"

"Time for me to fuck you, of course."

"What the—?" she blinks. "You didn't just—" She shakes her head. "You can't just throw those words out like that."

"You mean, I can't declare my intent? After all, isn't that what you want? For me to fill you with my cum?"

Her cheeks redden. "You're being filthy just to upset me."

"You have it all wrong."

"I do?"

I nod, "I am being filthy because I know it turns you on."

"Oh, bugger off." She twirls a strand of her hair around her finger, a sure sign that she's nervous. Funny, how I know her gestures so well.

"Are you denying you like my talking dirty to you?"

"That's exactly what I am saying," she states.

"So, if I come over there and pull off your pants, and stuff my fingers inside your cunt, you won't be wet?"

She shudders, her pupils dilate and she twists her fingers together in front of her. "You wouldn't dare."

I tilt my head.

"Shit, I didn't mean it that way."

I take a step forward and she backs away. "I mean, yeah, I am turned on, but it doesn't have anything to do with you."

"No?" I prowl toward her and she stumbles back, until her hip brushes against the settee.

"No," she mumbles, "it's my hormones. It's, uh, what I have been taking to amp up my egg production. It makes me more sensitive, you know, and moody and edgy and—" I reach her, and she flinches.

I bend my knees, peer into her flushed features. "It's not good for you, whatever drugs you are on to stimulate egg production."

"And you know that how?"

"Anything artificial that forces your body to go against its natural rhythm can't be healthy."

"Let me be the judge of that."

"In fact, you are going to stop taking these drugs."

"No."

"Yes." I whisper my knuckles across her cheek. "At least, for the time we are together. I want you to be as nature intended you to be."

"And what's that?" she chokes out. "A woman whose biological clock is ticking down? Someone who's older than any of the girls you've dated before?"

"What are you talking about? You are far more beautiful, inside and out, than any woman I have met before. As for your biological clock, you're what, twenty-two?"

"Thanks for humoring me. I'm twenty-nine."

"I'm thirty-one." I raise my shoulder, "Age is just a number."

"Spoken like a man," she mutters. "Anyway, I can't believe I let that slip." She flattens her lips, "What the hell is wrong with me?" She squeezes her eyes shut. "How could I blurt that out? Why is it that when I am with you, I am not able to control what I say?"

"Maybe because I make you nervous?"

"Maybe it's because I loathe your presence."

"Do you?" I wrap my fingers around the nape of her neck. "Do you hate me, Sparks?"

She tips up her chin and stares into my eyes. "No," she holds my gaze, "I don't have any feelings for you."

"I, on the other hand, can't wait to show you how it can be when you put your trust in me."

"Trust?" She frowns.

"We may have fucked a few times, but you weren't there with me, Sparks."

"Of course, I was."

"You resisted me every step of the way."

"That's how I am." She raises her shoulders. "I am not a shrinking violet. I don't need to be protected and coddled. I stand up for myself, don't hesitate to go head-to-head with people who cross my path."

"Thank god for that." I pinch her chin, then press my thumb to her lower lip. "It's why I want you, Sparks. I know I can be myself with you, and while it may surprise you, you won't back down. I know you'll meet me every step of the way. You'll challenge me, annoy me, question my commands. It's what makes you so...attractive."

"Because I am a challenge?"

"Because I can't wait to have you fall apart over and over again. Because I can only hope to piece you back together in a way that makes sense for both of us. Because," I lean in close enough for my lips to ghost hers, "I want to be there when you subsume yourself in me and find out exactly what you've been missing all these years."

"You want to tame me?"

"I want to give you a chance to forget about the outside world. I want you to trust me to take you to the kind of heights where you won't remember anything else outside of you, me, our joined cum, our wet skin slapping against each other, your breathless sighs, your moans, your pants, your sweat-drenched tits, your reddened arse after I've spanked you enough times that even a gentle touch on your behind sends spirals of delight through your pussy."

She draws in a breath.

"Will you allow me that?"

Her pupils dilate, she licks her lips, lowers her gaze to my mouth and stares for a long second. Then she firms her lips. "No," she mumbles, "I don't think so. The deal was for you to impregnate me and me to pose as your wife. Doesn't mean I have to enjoy it."

"Too bad." I straighten. "I intend to wring pleasure from you anyway."

Karina

With that pronouncement, he'd turned back to the table and whatever it was he'd been doing earlier. I'd flounced back into the bathroom, shut the door behind me, and stood under the hot shower for a long time. What the hell is he up to? Why do I get the feeling I am in over my head?

Have I been played? Surely, not. I've known Arpad since LA. We have friends in common—Jace, for one, who is a friend of the Seven. It was Jace who'd first suggested that I take on the security for the Seven, and Arpad had backed him up. So why do I get the feeling that it had been Arpad's idea all along? It would be just like him to manipulate the events so it felt like the suggestion hadn't been his. And then, the messages to my phone, and getting me on the boat... There is no way he could have envisaged my falling asleep on his boat... And yet, here I am... Marooned with him, on a bloody island.

It seems like something out of a movie, except this is my life. My future he is playing with. And for what? Because he had an itch he needed to scratch? Men like him always think they can get what they want. Well, too bad. He has gone up against the wrong woman this time. I am going to keep up my side of the bargain and ensure that he delivers on his. But more than that... No way, am I giving him anything more. Definitely not my trust... Absolutely not my heart. No way, am I going to allow myself to fall for him.

I switch off the shower, step out and dry myself. I stare at the clothes I'd been wearing in disgust. No way, am I going to wear those again. I step out to find a bathrobe laid out for me. Huh? I glance at the bedroom door, then turn my back on it and manage to slip on the bathrobe before I pull off the towel.

I gather my soiled clothes and walk out to find him in the kitchen. He's changed into another pair of jeans and a T-shirt. His hair is mussed up like he's been running his hands through it. Of course, he has an extra set of clothes here. How often does he come here anyway?

The scent of something cooking fills the air. My stomach grumbles, loudly. He looks around at me, then points to a door on the other side of the kitchen. "Washing machine's through there."

I walk through, add my clothes to the ones already in there, and run the machine. By the time I step back into the kitchen, he's laid the table for two. He places a bowl of stew in front of each of the two seats. He pulls out a chair for me to sit, then walks around to the other chair where he sits facing me. He gestures to the food, "Eat."

I dig into it and the hearty taste of potatoes and onions laced with rosemary explodes on my tongue. "It's good." I lick my lips. "Did you put this together from scratch?"

He chuckles. "Not even my talents stretch that far." He wipes his mouth with the back of his hand, "I had my favorite chef cook it then freeze it and send it over."

I chew, swallow, then stare up at him, "You don't compromise when it comes to food."

"Why would I?" He shoves the stew into his mouth, chews as he holds my gaze.

"Just because you have money doesn't mean you have taste, and when it comes to food, you'd be surprised how many people compromise on ingredients. Not because they can't afford it… Or okay, sometimes it's also that, but more often, because they don't care enough about what they put in their bodies. I mean, we are what we eat, right?"

"And that's why I don't want you taking the fertility drugs." He arches an eyebrow at me, and I flush.

"Fine, fine," I grumble, "but we're not talking about the same thing here."

"Aren't we?" He stares at me.

I blow out a breath. "Deciding what food you put in your mouth is a choice."

"So is deciding what drugs you subject your body to."

I throw up my hands, "I had no other option. I wanted a kid, and I had no time to find a man. All of my waking moments were spent building up the company."

"That's something you care about a lot?"

I nod. "My father started the firm, and when I took over from him, I was determined to make it a success."

"You're close to your family?"

I purse my lips. "As much as my father would tolerate it."

He frowns. "What do you mean?"

"He was in the military when I was a kid. He left when I was ten but the ways of the army stuck with him. He was very strict, very firm… And brought me up the same way as my brothers."

"How many siblings do you have?"

I hold up my hand.

"Five?" he asks.

I nod.

"Five brothers?"

I nod again.

"All older than you?"

"Yep."

He raises an eyebrow, "Should I be worried about them landing on my door ready to beat me up or something?"

I stare at him, then glance away. If he only knew. "No," I shake my head. "When I turned eighteen, I had a choice. Join the very lucrative family enterprise that my father started after he left the army; or use the money my mother left me to grow my own business."

"You opted for the latter?"

I nod. "I took over the security agency which was part of the family business but which I could run independent of them. I had no wish to be associated with the family venture."

"Why is that?"

I glance at him, then away. "It wasn't to my liking."

"Why?" He frowns. "What is it they do?"

"Oh, you know," I raise my shoulders, "import, export, that kind of thing."

"But you weren't interested in it?" There's a strange look in his eyes.

"No," I stare down at my plate, "I didn't want to be involved in it."

"You didn't?" His jaw firms and his features grow hard. How weird. What is he upset about now?

I shake my head. "I wanted to do something of my own, get out from under the protective gaze of my family. You know what I mean?"

He stares at me, then finally nods.

"I wanted to branch out on my own," I explain.

"Why a security company?"

"Why not?" I raise my shoulders. "I'd heard so much about my father's experiences in the army, and much of it stayed with me. And unlike other girls, I wasn't drawn to the more feminine things in life. I didn't want to become a dancer or a singer or..."

"Yoga instructor?" He tilts his head.

"Now that?" I half smile, "I could see myself doing that. But I love yoga too much... It's too personal to turn it into a job, if you know what I mean."

"It's like sailing for me." He glances about the space. "It's in my blood; it's my passion. I'd never want to make it a livelihood for me."

I blink. Wow, we are talking. Like, really talking. And damn, if I don't like the man under the alphaholish exterior.

"How's the head wound?" He points to my forehead.

I'd taken off the plaster earlier and the wound had already scabbed over. "It doesn't hurt anymore," I say truthfully.

He reaches over, touches the site of the wound, and I flinch.

"You said it doesn't hurt."

"It doesn't," I mumble. "You surprised me, is all."

I pick up my spoon and dip it into the stew again. "My mother died when I was eighteen." I stare into the mixture in my bowl. "That's when my father had a heart attack. My eldest brother took on a leading role in the family business, and I decided to branch out on my own."

"I'm sorry about your mother." His voice is earnest.

"Thank you." I place my hands in my lap. Even after all these years, it isn't easy to talk about her passing. I hadn't considered how much of a rock she was in my life until I realized that I'd never see her again. I tug on my hair, then wrap a strand around my finger.

"Mine died not long after the incident." He glances down at his bowl, then back at me, "But you knew that already."

I nod. As their security consultant, I was privy to the details of the personal lives of all of the Seven. Still, Arpad sharing that part of his past with me? It means something.

"You miss her?" I ask softly.

"Every single day." His expression grows bleak. "I often wonder how the seven of us would have turned out if the incident hadn't marred us."

"It also united the lot of you, made you all friends for life."

He grimaces, "More like uneasy passengers on a boat where each of us has to pull our weight behind the paddles to keep afloat."

"I can't figure you guys out." I frown. "Sometimes I am sure you can't live without each other. Other times it seems you hate each other."

"More often, it's a little of both." He smirks, "And you? So, you weren't tempted to join the family business at all?"

Something in his voice makes me peruse his features. "No," I shake my head, "I want nothing to do with it."

His gaze narrows. "You sure about that?"

"Of course, I am." I frown at him. "Why do you ask?"

"Relax." He laughs. "All I meant was, it must have been difficult for your family to let you go, and then, it wouldn't have been easy to run a company on your own. But you didn't stop until you made it a success."

My cheeks flush. "Thanks." I busy myself looking into the depths of my stew... Or what is left of it. It really had tasted yummy, or maybe, I'd just been hungry.

"And you?" I ask. "Is this your life then?" I wave my hand in the air. "Footloose, fancy free, and able to do what you want, when you want?"

"That's the power of passive income." His lips curl. "My money's busy earning more money for me, while I am here with you, sheltering from a storm."

"You're deflecting."

"What was your question?"

"Doesn't matter." I scoop up the last of the stew and finish it off. "I was simply trying to have a conversation. If you'd rather I not speak, you simply have to say so."

There's silence. He blows out a breath, "The incident," he says. "You know about it, obviously?"

"You asked me to investigate the perpetrators, remember?" I point out.

He nods, then takes a bite of his stew before glancing up at me. "It's what brought the Seven of us together. We'd known each other before that...but that occurrence ensured we'd have a common background, unique to just us." He leans back in his chair. "It changed our lives forever. One second, we were average—well, as average as you could get with the kind of money most of our parents had—but still, we'd been preteens with the usual problems—football practice, videogames, and sneaking off to use our remote-controlled planes to spy on girls... The next... We'd been imprisoned in a basement without knowing if we could make it out alive."

"It affected all of you in different ways. I get it."

"Do you, though?" He holds my gaze. "You were eighteen when you had to grow up. We were preteens... All except Damian, who, at sixteen, was the oldest..."

A chill runs down my spine. "You were all very young."

He nods. "And then we weren't." He places his elbows on the table, then joins the tips of his fingers together. "Isn't it strange that, despite your best efforts, we've never managed to track down the brains behind the operation?"

I stiffen. "Are you faulting my capabilities?"

He tilts his head. "It was merely an observation; one professional to another."

I take in the earnest look on his face. Should I believe him? No reason not to, right? I nod, "Fine." I blow out a breath, then rise to my feet and begin to pace. "It's not for lack of trying. But every lead I've followed has turned out to be wrong, every clue I've unearthed seems to lead to a dead end. I've had my best operatives on the job, but nothing has come to light."

"Whoever they were, they are too well-hidden, probably in broad daylight, where you can't tell them apart from an average person."

"Exactly." I turn to him, "That's the point. They are probably not hiding at all, which makes it even more difficult to find out who they were."

"You wouldn't think the Mafia would be that clever."

I chuckle, "You'd be surprised. The Mafia no longer conforms to the stereotypes of men you see on screen. Their businesses are no longer limited to those that are illegal. In fact, many of them run their corporations like any average CEO would, employ people who probably don't even know the background of their employers, or that the work they do helps hide the illegal origins of the capital that built the company, and oftentimes, continues to build the company."

"You have a thorough knowledge, then, of the inner workings of their organization."

"They happen to be a peculiar fascination of mine," I prop my hands on my hips, "especially after—"

His eyebrows draw down, "After?"

"After the Seven contracted me to find out everything possible about the men behind the incident, of course."

"Of course." His lips firm. "Not that you've made much progress—"

I open my mouth and he raises his hand. "Not that I fault you for that, either. It's a tough case to crack. I get it. Not something that's easy for someone like you to handle."

"What the—?" I open and shut my mouth. "You're joking, right?"

He yawns, then gets to his feet. "Just calling it as it is, babe. It's understandable though."

"It is?"

He nods. "You being a woman and this being a man's business, after all. It can be a little too complex, not to mention, dangerous, for you to track down the Mafia."

"Of all the chauvinistic things to say—"

"Save it." He scratches his jaw. "In fact, it's probably good you haven't managed to find them."

My heart begins to race; adrenaline laces my blood. Just when I thought we were actually having a proper conversation, he had to go and say something that completely wrecked whatever truce we had found. "And why is that?" I ask.

"You'd have only gotten yourself into trouble, and then guess who'd have needed to come after you and save you?"

"Not you." I draw myself up to my full height. "In fact, let's forget we ever had a deal. After what you just said, you'd be the last person I'd choose to be the father of my child."

He clicks his tongue, "Not so fast. You are posing as my fake wife when we head over to meet my family, and I am holding you to that."

"And what if I didn't want to do that? What if… I refuse?"

He closes the distance between us, and the heat of his body thrums around me, and coils between my legs. He glares down at me with those burning blue eyes of his and I shiver. "I don't take kindly to a people reneging on their agreements." He peels back his lips and his teeth glint against his dark skin. For the first time, a sliver of fear licks at my nerves. I am alone with him, on his island, and no one knows we are together. Even my employees think I am away on vacation. As do my friends. I wouldn't be missed for a long time. By the time anyone got concerned, it would be too late. By then, he'd have, no doubt, carried out whatever plan it is he has in mind.

"What are you planning to do?" My voice cracks, and I clear my throat. *Don't show him how afraid you are. Don't.* I tip up my chin and his lips kick up.

"Isn't that clear?"

"No."

"Before we leave here, I am going to have you begging me to bury my dick in your pretty little pussy, to bring you to fulfillment and put you out of your misery. You are going to plead with me to fill you up with my cum, to ensure that I've impregnated you with my child. You are going to beseech me to complete what I started."

"No." I firm my lips.

"Yup." He reaches out, scoops up something from my chin and sucks on his finger. A thrill suffuses my skin. Damn it, and after he'd insulted me… Why the hell do I find his filthy words and his actions meant to subjugate me, so…so…much of a turn on?

"I don't give in easily," I warn.

His grin widens. "Neither do I."

"So, this is it, then? A stalemate?"

"Call it a challenge." He draws himself up to his full height and his wide shoulders seem to block out the rest of the room, "One I don't intend to lose."

19

Arpad

What the hell had I been thinking, throwing all those clues out at her? The last thing I need is for her to be suspicious about my intentions.

I turn over on my side in the bed… The big bed, in which I am sleeping alone. She'd opted to take the couch in the living room…and I hadn't offered her the bed. Damn it, I should have, but she'd made me so mad, I'd stalked out of the kitchen and headed here. And she hadn't followed. I'd heard her retreat to the living room, then the light had gone out a little later.

And she hadn't taken any covers or pillows, either. How the hell is she sleeping without something to keep her warm?

The wind slams into the windows and the panes rattle. It hadn't rained much yet…but clearly, the storm had hit not far off. Another gust hits the chalet and the entire structure seems to rock. I sit up, shove off my covers, then swing my legs onto the floor and stand up. I stalk into the living room. The fire I'd started earlier has died down and the room is freezing. I cross over to her huddled form on the couch.

She's in a fetal position, her arms around a cushion, another cushion under her head. She pulled on her now-dry clothes from the wash, including her socks, and it looks like she tried to use the robe as a blanket, so there's that. As I watch, she shivers, then pulls her knees closer to her chest.

The wind howls outside and she mutters something under her breath. I freeze, hold my breath as she subsides into slumber again. The light from the window dances across her face, highlighting the hollows under her cheekbones. She really is skinny, except for her tits, of course. My fingers tingle. As if she senses my gaze, she moves onto her back and the cushion falls from her grasp.

There's a flash of lightning, then the roll of thunder in the distance. Rain begins to pelt the windows, contrasting with the silence in the room. The fact that I've been standing here in my underwear staring down at her…for at least ten minutes now. Shit. I drag my fingers through my hair. *What the hell is wrong with me?* Why can't I seem to keep away from her? Awake or asleep, she holds so much power over me… If she only knew.

Her chest rises and falls, and her body twitches. Her breathing deepens. I turn to leave, then turn back to her. My feet thud on the wooden floor and cold seeps into my skin. Fuck this. No way, can I leave her here in this unheated room, and without anything to keep her warm. I place my arms under her and scoop her up. She stirs, murmurs something I don't catch, then curls into my chest and falls asleep again. Warmth pools in my chest. My belly tightens. She's so damn light…so tiny… When she's awake, her persona is so prickly, so full of fire, I often forget she's half my size in weight…and barely comes to the level of my chest.

To think, she's been on her own since she turned eighteen… And forged her success in a business that is notoriously dominated by men… And macho men, at that. I shake my head. The woman has a spine of steel. Something like pride grips me. Hell, she is a fighter, a worthy opponent, the possible mother of my child.

I stumble, then right myself, glance down at her features. She doesn't stir.

Why the hell do my thoughts always head in the direction of her possible pregnancy? Why does the thought of having a family not seem like such a stretch suddenly? Everything I want is here in my arms… All I have to do is reach out and grasp it. Except, she wouldn't see it that way, would she?

She is hellbent on having this kid by herself. What is that about anyway? She is only twenty-nine… There is more than enough time for her to meet someone and— I tighten my grasp on her, and she stirs. I pause, wait until she settles, then walk with her in my arms into the bedroom. I place her on my side of the bed, then slip in beside her and pull the covers up over both of us.

The sweet scent of her crowds me and my cock throbs. I glance toward her, take in her parted lips, her flushed features and know this was a bad idea. Hell, I'm the one who threw down the gauntlet, and told her I'd wait until she begged me before I took her. I intend to stick to my promise. Doesn't mean I have to keep away from her though, right?

I apply enough pressure on her shoulder to turn her over to her side, then I tug her close and spoon her.

20

Karina

Heat curls around me, sinks into my skin. I curve my back, thrust closer into the warmth. Mmm. So comfortable. I rub my cheek against the pillow, twine my fingers around his…his? I snap my eyes open, and find that, indeed, I have my fingers entangled with thicker, longer, darker digits… Which are attached to an arm that's thick and veiny, with dark hair that peppers the skin. I gulp, angle my body, only to realize the heat at my back is courtesy of the long, broad body that presses flush into me. I wiggle my butt and something stabs between my asscheeks. I swallow. I know that length. Am intimately acquainted with the girth, the thickness, the way that width of his had impaled me and brought me to fulfillment. My core clenches and moisture trickles down from between my thighs. Gah, I only have to think about how he'd taken me and I am melting…melting.

I try to move and find I'm pinned down by his thick arm that rests on the curve of my hip. His fingers are splayed across my stomach… across my naked stomach, for my shirt has helpfully ridden up to give him access. Just as my channel had expanded to sheath his cock.

Gah, get your mind out of the gutter, woman. Though you can't blame me for where my thoughts are straying, considering alphahole, here, is wrapped around me tighter than a boa constrictor around its prey. Not that I am prey, or that he is a snake. Okay, maybe he is... Especially that thing between his legs, which is one massive python. Ugh... That's it. I need to get out of this bed. I thrust one foot out of the blanket and the cold instantly grabs me. I shiver, push another foot out, try to slide out from under his arm, when his grasp tightens about me.

"Where are you going?"

His voice rumbles across my back.

I shiver... This time, from that chafing, gnawing sensation that curls in my belly.

"I...ah...have to pee."

"Liar." He hauls me against his large chest, settles me with my head tucked under his chin, his arms wrapped around me again. The contours of his body follow my curves, with his knees folded up against the back of mine. If there is heaven on this earth, surely, it is here, next to him, surrounded by his scent, wrapped up in his presence, which pins me down, and against him — No, that's his massive forearms, which he's wrapped around me. I wiggle my butt and am rewarded by the throb of the part of him that's very much awake and happy to be nestled in the valley between my butt cheeks.

"Umm, Ari?"

"Hmm?"

"I think... I really need to get out of bed."

"I can control myself, if you can."

"What?"

"I know that you sense this," he angles his hips just right, and his thickness slides up against me, "but it's just morning wood."

"Then why do you have your arms wrapped around me like it is going out of fashion."

"Keeping you warm, babe."

I shiver at the endearment. Bet the a-hole is half asleep. That's the only reason he sounds so warm and cuddly... Correction, he is very warm.... And most definitely, massively cuddly, emphasis on the 'massive.' I squeeze my eyes shut. Can't stop myself from heading down that path of thinking, huh?

"Surely you can think of a better excuse," I grumble.

"Is that what you think?"

"Isn't it?" I toss my head, or try to, because I can't move... I literally can't budge with how the alphahole is wrapped around me.

"Okay then." He releases me, pulls away, and the cold instantly seeps in. What the—? How is that possible? Did I get used to the proximity of his body heat so very quickly? I mean, we've barely spent the night together, and already, I miss being held by him.

"On the other hand," I mutter, "maybe there's no hurry for me to leave here."

"What's that?" he drawls.

"I mean, you can go back to doing uh—whatever it was—"

"Can't hear you, babe."

I hear the laughter in his voice, and I pout.

"I know you do, you ass. Just get back here and assume the position of, uh... You know—"

"Spooning," he rumbles from above me. "That's the technical term you're looking for, I believe?"

My toes curl. Just the thought of him fitting his body to mine again... OMG. My throat closes. I slide my arms down between my legs, both to keep warm, but also so I can push up against my empty core.

"Say the word, darlin'.

I sigh.

"Go on. How difficult can it be, hmm?"

His tone dips to a hush—the honey to my chai tea, the cream to my coffee, the ice to my vodka... You get the picture?

I blow out a breath, then mumble, "Please."

"Couldn't hear you."

What the hell? Why is he drawing this out in such an agonizing manner? "Fine." I turn to face him. "Spoon me."

My gaze clashes with his, holds.

His chest rises and falls.

His arm is folded under his head, and his biceps bulge... And damn it, why does that look so bloody hot? It's not like I haven't seen naked men before... But somehow, the beauty of his angular face, the puffy lips, the square jaw, the skin of his cheeks, still flushed from his nights' sleep, the tousled hair... Jesus, it's too much.

I lower my gaze, take in the planes of his chest, the sheet that dips low down on his hips, the hair that arrows down to his happy place... Okay, my happy place. *No, no, no. What am I thinking?*

"What are you thinking?" His voice is low and oh, so sexy, with that just-woken-up rasp, combined with that authoritative edge that's inherent in everything he says and does.

My toes curl and my core trembles, I open my mouth and close it again. Do I dare tell him? Do I? And hand the power over to him?

"What do you want?" His tone is steady as he stares into my eyes, and oh my, that's hot.

"I… I," I stutter, "I…"

"Say it," he snaps.

"I want you to shag me."

21

———————

Arpad

"Shag you or spoon you?" My lips twist. I don't stop the satisfied smile that curls my mouth.

"Can you…uh, do both?"

"I aim to oblige."

I swoop down and gather her close. Her pupils dilate. I press my lips to her forehead, to her upturned nose, to those rosebud lips. She opens her mouth and I deepen the kiss. I sweep my tongue over hers, suck on it. She moans deep inside, thrusts her breasts into my chest. I draw her hips flush against mine. My cock nestles in the warmth between her legs and she gasps. I kiss her again, once, twice, then lean back. I lower the zipper of the jeans she's wearing, tug it off, then pull the sweatshirt up and over her head.

"Turn over," I rasp.

She blinks once, then rolls over onto her side.

I shove down my boxers, kick them aside then grasp my dick and pump it once. I tug her close, until my shaft is once more nestled along the dent between her butt cheeks, then bring my hand up to cup her breast. I squeeze her nipple and she shudders. I slide my other hand under her, then palm her other breast. She wriggles her hips against me, pushes back. "Ari," she whines.

"Shh." I bring my palm up to her mouth, slide my thumb in between her lips. She sucks on it and I feel the pull all the way down to the tip of my cock.

I trail my fingers down to her core, strum her pussy lips, and she arches back, and into me, chasing that release that only I can give her. I slide my fingers inside her sopping wet channel, and she moans deep in her throat. I add a third finger, then a fourth, then curl them inside her. Her entire body jerks. She turns her head toward me, reaches up to kiss my mouth. I pull back.

I hold her heavy-lidded gaze as I begin to fuck her with my fingers. Her shoulders shudder, as her breasts heave, the pulse at the base of her throat beating in a rapid tempo. I lower my mouth to her throat and suck on her skin. She shivers, digs her fingers in my hair and coaxes me lower.

"What do you need?" I ask, "Tell me, Sparks."

"My tits," she gasps, "squeeze my nipples plea—"

I bring my hand up and twist her nipple between my thumb and forefinger. She gasps, then wriggles her hips and pushes her entire body back and into mine. "Shh," I bring my face up to hers, "I know what you want."

"You…you do?"

I nod. "And I'm going to give it to you."

I pull my fingers out of her, then slide my cum-soaked digit inside her arsehole.

She freezes. "Ari." Her gaze widens. "Wha…what are you doing?"

"Making sure you are ready for me."

"Not there."

"There." I nod.

"I… I'm not…" she swallows, "I mean, I can't. I don't want to."

"You will."

"But—"

I lower my head to hers, close my mouth around hers and kiss her. She hesitates, then opens her lips, allows me to sweep my tongue inside as I slide another cum-coated finger inside her.

She stiffens again and I continue to kiss her. "Open for me, babe." I share my breath with her, suck on her tongue as I bring down my other hand to play with her core. I grind my heel into her clit and a groan tumbles up her throat. I swallow it down, tilt my head to kiss her deeper, then slide a third finger inside her ass.

She shudders, her body tautens, and I cup her pussy, then guide two fingers inside her wet channel. "Oh," she sighs as I begin to work my fingers in and out of her. In and out. She lowers her hand to curl her fingers around my wrist. I pull my fingers out of her backhole, then grab my dick and position it at her back channel.

"Look at me," I command, and she raises her gaze to mine.

I nudge my dick into her back entrance and she stiffens.

I work my fingers in and out of her pussy, add a third finger then curl my digits. Her eyes roll back in her head and that's when I ease inside her puckered hole.

She moans. Digs her fingers into my wrist, brings her other arm up and curls it around my shoulder. "Ohmygod, it's…it's too much, too full. It's—"

"Not enough."

I bend and close my mouth around the curve of where her shoulder meets her neck. She gasps, then clenches around my dick. A growl rips from me. I lick the reddened flesh, then bring my hand up to cup her breast again. I weave my fingers in and out of her pussy, in and out. I thrust my fingers deep inside her and she throws her head back. "Oh, my god." Her body bucks, a trembling starts up her legs, her stomach, flows up her breasts and her shoulders. She gasps, "I'm going to—"

"Come." I command, and she shatters all over my fingers. Her body slumps, and I ease my dick in further.

She draws in a breath. "Oh, Ari—" she moans under her breath.

"Tell me how it feels," I order.

"It feels…full…like weirdly full, and yet…it's not…" she swallows, "not as unpleasant as I thought."

I cup my fingers around her swollen pussy, bring my other hand up to toy with her nipple. "Your tits, Sparks, they're beautiful, and your sweet little cunt, it's the prettiest little hole I have ever seen." She moans, relaxes further and I slip inside her fully.

She groans; so do I.

"Bloody hell, you're so damn tight, darlin'." I grit my teeth, and stay…stay where I am, allow her to adjust to my presence. "I never did think I was an arse kind of guy, but with you, it seems I can't let any hole of yours go unoccupied."

A whine tumbles from her lips, she clenches down on my cock, and goosebumps rise on my skin. I bring my hand up and wrap my fingers around her neck. "Look at me, babe."

Her eyelids flutter, then she focusses her dilated gaze on mine. "Ari," she whispers, "please…"

"I know." I begin to move in and out of her, as sweat slides down my back. I pull out, then ease inside her again and again. She curves her back, thrusts her hips up and takes all of me inside.

"Babe," I swallow, "you're killing me. This…this.. It's fuckin' hot." I ease my digits inside her pussy and she parts her legs, holding herself open at an angle that allows me to sink inside her. She arches up and into me, "Oh, Ari, that's too much, that's…soo good."

You're telling me? "Don't take your gaze off of me," I snap.

She flutters her eyelids as I keep the tempo—in and out, in and out. I thrust into her with enough force that my balls slap against the back of her arse.

I guide my fingers inside her melting pussy, then propel my hips forward and thrust into her once more. Her shoulders shudder, her entire body jolts. "Please, I need to, I have to—"

"Come for me, Sparks," I growl, and she cries out as she shatters.

22

———————

Karina

Yes, that's me. I had come not once, but twice, in quick succession, and one of those times had been with him in my ass. OMFG! What the hell is that about? How had I allowed him there…where no one else had gone before? Stop with that. Now I am quoting *Star Trek*? Clearly, I am delirious. Or close to it. Yeah, a couple of well-timed orgasms can do that to a girl.

I float down to earth and become aware that he's still inside me, and he hasn't come. He's hard, like really thick and throbbing inside of me. "Ari?" I whisper, and he pulls out of me, slides his fingers from me at the same time. I'm suddenly empty. My pussy clenches down, on where his digits had been and I feel empty, strangely bereft, as he sits up, throws the cover off and slips out of bed.

He turns and stalks over to the ensuite. I take in the powerful thigh muscles that contract with each step. The tight glutes, the scars of what had to be some kind of burns…or chafing that crisscross his back.

"Arpad," I gasp, then sit up as he prowls into the bathroom and shuts the door behind him. What the hell? I walk over, hear him moving around, then the sound of grunting, the wet slap of flesh against flesh.

What the hell? Is he jerking off in there? And after he fucked me in the ass? What the hell is that all about?

I shove open the door and walk in to find him in the shower cubicle, dick in one hand, the other slapped against the wall. I watch his face in profile as he grunts, as he screws up his features, the tendons of his throat stretching as he swipes his hand from the base of his dick to the crown again and again. His movements are hard, brisk, unlike how I would have grasped him. No way would I have the strength, the almost cruel grip he has on his shaft as he continues to pump, up and down, and again.

I should look away, give the man his privacy… But what the hell? He'd been inside of me, and for some reason, he hadn't wanted to come… Which still doesn't make any sense to me. His shoulders heave and his chest planes flex as he drags his fist up his cock.

And somehow, I find myself moving toward him.

I step into the space between him and the shower wall, slip my hand around his, tip my chin up to meet his gaze, and stroke him with my fingers about his. His breathing grows ragged, color smears his cheeks, then with a low groan he comes, all over my breasts, my chest.

He continues to stroke himself, emptying out the rest of his cum on me. Then, still holding his dick in one hand, he rubs his cum into my skin, around my nipples, down my belly, in between my legs. And somehow, it's as if he's marking his territory. His actions are both crude and a turn-on, at the same time. Why is it that every filthy thing he does is so…primal, so sexy? It's as if the mask he's worn to face the world has been stripped off here, in a cabin in the middle of the sea. And we are only a man and a woman, trapped in a fight to survive… Not just the elements, but also each other.

He lowers his hands to his sides, then reaches behind me to turn on the shower. He turns me around, so the water pours over me. He scoops up some soap and washes me. His movements are quick and thorough. He washes my hair as well, then himself, before rinsing off the soap.

When he's done, he flicks off the shower. Then steps out to wrap a towel around himself. He hands one over to me, then turns and leaves the bathroom. Huh. What happened? Why did he go all silent?

And after he'd taken my ass… And honestly, while it'd hurt… It had been intense. I could have sworn it had brought the two of us closer together… At least, so I'd thought. But apparently, it'd had a completely different effect on him.

I dry myself off, wrap the towel and walk out to find he's gone. Instead, he's laid out another sweatshirt and a fresh pair of his jeans. I slip into the clothes, then glance around. I need something to cinch around my waist so the jeans won't fall down, but what? I open the closet and aha! I find what I'm looking for.

I grab the rope from the shelf, tie it around my middle and over my sweatshirt. It nips in at my waist and holds up the boxers.

Awesome. There's no mirror to see how I look, but doesn't matter. At least, I don't feel naked. I pull on the socks he's laid out. So, not the most glamorous of get-ups, but at least I am warm. Besides, the sweatshirt smells of detergent and is laced with that dark, edgy scent which is unmistakably his. It feels like I am wearing him... Not. Well, not quite, considering how quickly he'd pulled out of me and left.

I walk out and into the living room to find the space warm. A fire crackles in the hearth. Outside, it's still raining, but in here, it's warm and cozy. Only, I am not fooled. Whatever had taken place between us... is far from comfortable. And I don't mean the sex...which was mind-blowing, despite the surprise of what he'd pulled on me. But hey, I'm no prude. I'd been curious to try anal... I wince as my butt spasms in response to the thought. Okay, so maybe not that soon again... But the experience had been mind-blowing, to say the least. And if the opportunity arises to do it again with this alphahole... I confess that I am game.

I head to the kitchen, and find him, once again, by the cooking range. He's pulled on a sweatshirt, and pair of jeans; his feet are bare. Apparently, he doesn't feel the cold. How could he, when the man radiates warmth like he has an built-in furnace or something? Besides, bare feet on this hot-as-F asshole... Uh, not complaining. They are strangely sexy, I'll readily admit.

He stirs the contents of a pan as I close the distance toward him.

When he doesn't acknowledge me, I sit down at the table. He pours out the mixture into two bowls, adds a dash of cinnamon, then places the oatmeal in front of me. He brings his bowl to the table, along with a container of sugar, which he places between us.

He spoons up his oatmeal, slides it into his mouth. He curls his tongue around the spoon and my core spasms. Moisture pools between my legs. What the hell? Why does the act of watching him eat, turn me on? Every muscle in my body is tense. All of my senses are honed in on him, all of my pores open and ready and willing to be touched by him.

"So that's your game?" I burst out.

"Game?" He raises his gaze and the heat in his blue-grey eyes blazes. "There's no game, here, Sparks."

"Then what was that?"

"What?"

I gape at him. Does he want me to spell it out? Seriously? Is that the kind of man he is? I frown. Not possible. My impression of him can't be that far off. Not when my instincts say otherwise. And well… I make a living with my instincts. They're the one thing I can depend on when nothing else makes sense. "Why are you so angry?" I cup my chin in my hand. "Why did you leave me like that on the bed?"

"Why not?" He spoons up more of the oatmeal, swallows. "You should eat yours before it grows cold."

I glance down at my bowl, then wince, "I don't like oatmeal, I'm afraid."

He jerks his chin, "Taste it, at least."

I blow out a breath, then dip my spoon into the creamy mixture, and bring it to my mouth. The scent of cinnamon fills my nostrils. I taste it and the nutty taste of oats pop on my palate.

I must have made a noise of appreciation for his lips kick up. "Good huh?"

"How the hell do you turn an ordinary meal into such an…"

"Foodgasm?"

I frown, "I was going to say experience."

His grin broadens. "I'll let this one go."

"Wasn't aware we were keeping score?"

"There's no score, sugar, because you are no match for me."

"What?" I snap my lips together. "Say that again?"

He dips his spoon back into the mixture, then brings it up to his mouth, chews, swallows. Then trains his gaze on me, "You are not in my league, babe. Why don't you just drop it."

I stare at him. "If by that you mean, I couldn't possibly be as much of an ass as you, you're right.""

He shrugs.

"I don't understand why you have to be this uncouth, so rude… so…"

"Impolite?" he helpfully supplies.

"That too. I was going more for plebeian."

He winces, "Not that word; anything but that." He places his spoon back in his bowl. "But the rest? It comes naturally to me."

"I think it's all an act."

"Oh?"

I nod, then drop my spoon back in my bowl with a clatter, "I think you felt something when you were, uh…"

"Fucking your arse?" he offers.

"Exactly," I stab my finger at him, "and you said that just for effect, knowing it would sound filthy enough to make me blush."

"Whatever." He stretches, then yawns. "Your theories don't interest me, babe."

"Stop that." I slap my palm on the table and the bowls jump. The sugar spills over the side of the container. I stare at the mess, then up at him, "Don't hide what you're feeling, Arpad."

He scratches his jaw, schools his features into that expression of lazy disinterest which is so much a part of him, and which I hate, and which I want to tear off to expose the man I'd sensed earlier, when he'd made love to me. And it had been that, no matter how much he wants to call it something else. There had been a depth of connection between us that I hadn't expected. "Why are you hellbent on reducing everything between us to something without emotion? Something contractual?"

"Because it is." He rises to his feet, then leans across the table until he looms over me. "That's all this is, babe, an arrangement. Don't you forget it. Don't go looking for meaning in what was simply a fuck… An above-average fuck, I'll give you that, but when this is over, we'll both walk away, having gotten what we want."

"You sure?"

He jerks his chin.

"That's all you want this to be, an exchange of what the other needs?"

That's all it is," he affirms.

"Fine." I jump up to my feet.

"Fine." He straightens to his full height, so I have to tilt my head back, then further back, to meet that blazing blue gaze. In their depths, something flickers, then fades away.

"Make yourself comfortable, I'm going to get more wood for the fire." Turning, he stalks off.

23

Arpad

That's me, walking away from a woman when I could have been inside of her, taking her, fucking her... Not loving her... What the hell am I thinking?

This is Karina, the woman I have been attracted to from the moment I saw her... It's the reason I am here with her, after all. Hell, I'd give her anything she wants.

Including a child? Shit. I drag my fingers through my hair... Now, that is something I had not factored in. A kid? A family? The kind of life I know I am not meant for. And yet, when she'd asked me to impregnate her... No way, could I have refused her. If she is going to carry anyone's child, it will be mine. As for walking away from her... Well, if...when she gets pregnant... We'll cross that bridge when we get to it.

I pull on my socks and boots. I grab additional ropes and head out of the chalet. The wind buffets me and I lean into the breeze as I walk down toward the jetty. I check on the yacht, making sure the dock lines are secure.

Once I am satisfied, I walk uphill, turning away from the chalet toward the building at the edge of the slope.

I shut the door and the wind instantly cuts out. Wiping my boots on the mat inside the door, I pull the satellite phone from my pocket and dial.

"Mr. Beauchamp?" Edward comes on the line, "Where are you?"

"In a chalet, on an island, somewhere between the UK and France."

"Ah, your favorite place to go when you want to run away from the world."

"What makes you say that?" I frown.

"Because that's where you went the last time the memories got too much for you."

"Fucking memories." I roll my shoulders. "You'd think as time passes, it would get easier, but it doesn't."

"Not all hurt fades with time," Edward replies. "Some of them burrow under your skin and make themselves at home, and then they become a part of you, something you don't want to let go anymore, because you're dependent on them. In a way, your identity is linked with the story and if you let go of it, you don't know who you are anymore."

"Is that your personal experience?"

"It's my…observation."

"Is that how it is for you?" I push the point.

Edward blows out a breath. "It hasn't been easy to move on from what happened. In some ways, I never will. After all, it's an experience that's shaped what I've become. But," he pauses, considering, "but I've come to realize that freedom is what you do with what's been done to you. Know what I mean?"

"Is that what you're doing, Ed? Finding yourself in what you have now become?"

Silence, a beat, then he says, "Maybe I didn't have a choice."

"What do you mean?" I frown. "All of us had choices… Maybe not in what happened to us, but whatever we did afterwards. We each took our lives in our own hands, remember? The one thing we swore to each other was that we'd never hesitate in going after what we wanted."

"Maybe this is what I wanted." He lowers his tone, "And what about you, Arpad. Is this what you want?"

"What are you talking about?"

"There's a reason you planned it this way."

"Planned it?" I frown.

"Having Karina on the boat when the storm hit so you could have time alone with her, away from the world. In fact, the way I see it," Edward continues, "you created your own liminal space."

"Sorry, you'll have to explain that to me, Father."

"You know what it is, Beauchamp." Edward's voice is impatient. "I'm talking about a space that is on a threshold of many possibilities. You ensured that the two of you are in a position to let go of the past for a period of time. You freed up all notions of space and time, allowing yourself the eventuality of a future together."

"You drunk, Father?"

"Now, now." He clicks his tongue, "Clearly, I touched a nerve, which is why you are resorting to personal insults."

"You're right." I begin to pace. "I honestly had no idea what I was getting into when I asked her to get on the boat and fix the security cameras. Maybe my subconscious had hoped she'd stay on for the duration of my trip… But hell, if I planned all of this… Well, not fully…"

"Aha," Edward snorts, "so you do admit that you wanted time with her."

"It may have crossed my mind, yes." I rub my jaw. "And okay, I did prepare for the eventuality that she'd one day be on the boat with me, but the storm and being holed up here… Nope, not that."

"Your mind is a powerful tool. When you truly want something, it can manifest it for you."

"And how's that working for you? What have you manifested lately, Father?"

"A reality that I'll have to live with for the rest of my life."

"You could change it," I point out.

"Could I?" he mutters. "The only way to avoid regret is to say yes to opportunity, after all, so yeah, you may be right."

"You talk in riddles, Ed." I bark out a laugh. "And yet, you often make more sense than anyone else I know."

"That's me," Edward's voice is bitter, "I can help others see the way, but my own way is not that simple to spot."

"Isn't that the truth?" I roll my neck. "And by the way, that entire regret versus opportunity thing… I hope you meant it for yourself."

"Maybe…" I sense him shrug over the waves, "maybe not. But this conversation is about you. So, what are you going to do next?"

"I…—" I hear a noise behind me, see her standing inside the door, "I have to go." I disconnect, and turn as she makes her way over.

"What are you wearing?" I take in the sweatshirt, the rope tied around her waist that outlines her hourglass figure, a reminder of how good she'd looked when I'd bound her, how beautiful she'd look if I were to tear her clothes off, then tie her up and suspend her, with her legs wide open before I take her.

"These are the clothes you left out for me."

"No, I didn't." I gesture to the rope about her waist.

"You mean this?" She dances her fingers over the rope. "I found it in the closet. I needed to find a way to hold up your jeans."

She blinks rapidly at me, "You don't mind, do you?"

My fingers tingle to reach out and yank the rope off of her, then tear off the rest of her clothes, before I bind her again and… *Stop with that. You bind her one more time, and you won't be able to walk away from her.* Weird, where are these thoughts coming from? I've never had such an emotional reaction to any woman before. Hell.

"Who were you talking to?"

"Edward."

She glances at my phone, "Think I can use it to call my team?"

"Do you want to call your team?"

She rolls a strand of her hair around her fingers. "No, strangely not." She shakes her hair back from her shoulders. "I don't miss the daily routine as much as I thought I would."

"Perhaps you were ready for a break?"

She glances around the small shed, "What's this place?"

I watch as she takes in the hard point in the ceiling, the mat below it, the ropes folded into figure eights that line up one wall, the other paraphernalia I use in my art on the table that stands against the opposite wall.

"Oh," she gulps, "so this is where you bring your women?"

I fold my arms over my chest and widen my stance. "There's only ever been one woman here, and that's you."

24

Karina

My heart begins to race, my pulse pounds, and my throat closes. I stare at him, trying to understand what he's saying. "So, no one else has been here before me?"

"Only me."

"And you've never brought anyone else to this island?"

"Told you I haven't." He tilts his head. "This is my personal space, where I go when I need a place to retreat and think."

"And you practice your rope tricks while you are…contemplating, the meaning of life and the universe?" I walk toward the wall, drag my fingers across the edge of a rope—which is strangely soft to the touch. "What is this made of?"

"Hemp." His voice is so close that I stiffen. How had I not heard him approach? "It holds knots well and is pliant against the skin."

"Oh." My stomach clenches. He hadn't said a word of anything that was faintly erotic and yet my mind had interpreted it as such.

"And this one." He reaches toward another folded pile, and strokes his fingers over it. "This one is stronger. I use it for the uplines."

"Uplines?"

"The ropes that I run through the harness on the person I am tying and then use it to suspend her from the hard point." He jerks his chin toward the ceiling.

"Her?" I turn to him. "Do you have someone you, uh—work with when you practice?"

"A few." He turns to me. "Why?" He scans my features. "You jealous?"

Yes.

Yes.

"Of course, not." I rub my hands down my forearms. "So, if you don't bring anyone here, how do you practice?"

"I have a space in my apartment in London that I use specifically for this."

"So why do you have this set-up here?" I jerk my chin toward the ropes.

"Why do you think?"

I scowl, "Because..."

He tilts his head.

"Because, uh, you believe in being prepared?"

His lips curl.

"Of course, you do." I draw myself up to my full height. "Fascinating as this conversation has been, I guess I'd better return to the chalet." I walk toward the door and open it, only for a gust of wind to blow me back. Rain whips over me and my fingers slip on the door handle, which is wrenched out of my grasp. The door slams shut. I stumble back, certain to fall, except warm hands grip my shoulders and righten me.

"You okay?"

I nod, a little too shaken for my own liking. I am not someone who leans on others. I've never allowed myself to slow down, not even after I decided to go it alone to have a child. The one constant in my life has been my career, the company I've worked so hard at building. Somewhere along the way, my identity had gotten fused with that of my work.

But just a day with this guy, and it's as if my feminine side has awakened in full force. Something about his strength makes me want to rely on him. He makes me secure in a way no one else ever has, and isn't that a laugh? This grumpy billionaire, with a penchant for tying up his women, is the one man I can't stop thinking of.

"I'm fine." I twist my shoulders and he releases me. "Guess the storm finally hit." I walk toward the window and stare outside. Rain whips across the pane and I can barely see through to the sea that I know is not far away.

"Is the yacht safe?"

"It's shielded from the worst of the winds by the hills that surround us and I went down to check on it earlier."

"Right." I shuffle my feet. Heat sears my back and I know he's come up to stand behind me now. "Sure is coming down outside." My voice shakes and I fold my fingers together in front of me. *Get it together, what's wrong with you?* He's just a man. So what, if he has a kinky streak a mile wide and I am standing in what is clearly his dungeon of pain... Or pleasure... Or both. "Maybe... Maybe, we should try and make a run for it to the main house?"

"Why? Do I make you nervous?" His voice rumbles from some-where above me and I shiver.

"N...no. It's just... I'm cold." A shiver runs down my spine, to back up my words.

"I can keep you warm."

"Not why I came here," I protest.

"Why did you come, then?"

I stiffen.

"Why are you here, Karina?"

No more Sparks, then? Why the hell do I already miss his nickname for me? And, I still don't understand what happened earlier. Why did he walk away from me? His retreat is written in bold print, reflected in every nuance of his.

"I... I'm not sure," I answer honestly. "I guess I didn't want to be alone."

"Is that all it is?" His voice sounds almost disappointed.

I turn and glance at him from the corner of my eyes, "Yes... That's all."

"Guess we'd better get back then."

Oh, okay, so that's how it's going to be? I mean, what had I expected? That he'd jump me again? Because I'd stumbled upon his den of sin? When he'd made it abundantly clear that there could be no real connection between us.

"Guess we should." I fold my arms around my waist.

He turns, heads for the door.

"Wait," I call out, and he pauses. "There was something else, actually."

"Oh?"

"You didn't come inside me this morning. I think you need to rectify it."

He freezes. "Excuse me?"

"Part of the deal is for you to get me pregnant." I glance away, then back at him, "Afraid you're not doing a great job of it, considering I am still in my fertile phase and you didn't fuck me last night."

His muscles tense and his jaw tics. He curls his fingers into fists and glares at me. "You want me to fuck you?"

I nod.

"Here?"

I look around, pretend I don't understand. "What's wrong with this space?"

He peruses my features, then turns around to face me completely. "Why don't you come out and say what's on your mind?"

"I already did."

"But you haven't told me everything, have you?" He takes a step forward and I draw myself up to my full height.

"I… I'm not sure what you mean."

"You followed me here because you were curious about what I was up to. You want to find out more about my penchant for tying up my women." He closes the distance between us and my belly ties itself up in knots—okay not knots… Bad comparison… My palms begin to sweat, despite the fact that it's freezing in here. "In fact, you wondered how it would be if you were to find yourself at my mercy again... My fingers on your skin, my breath on your cheek... As I truss you up, then string you up... Ready and open and willing for me," he bends his knees and thrusts his face into mine, "as I give you the chance to become one with the rope, to retreat from the world and all of its responsibilities. A safe space, where you can let go of all of your inhibitions, and connect with your feminine self."

Moisture pools in my core, and I chafe my thighs together. "I didn't think anything of the sort," I insist.

"You sure?"

No.

No.

"Yes," I nod.

"So, you want me to simply turn you around and push you up against the window and take you with no preparation, then?"

My throat closes and my pussy clenches. *Jesus, what's wrong with me?* Why does his uncompromising stance, his complete dominance, his lack of finesse when it comes to talking about us... Why does it sound so bloody appealing?"

"If I said yes...?" I swallow.

"Then I am sorry to say, the answer is no."

"What?"

"I have another idea on how to pass the time."

25

Arpad

"This is your big idea?"

She stares down at the board between us on the table in the living room.

I've lit the fire, thanks to the wood I'd hauled in from the pile in the small shed on the other side of the house. Not that I am lacking in space or anything. After all, the entire island is mine. Which is why it always feels bizarre to talk about geographical boundaries in relation to this structure, know what I mean?

But I digress... I'd built the fire, then decided the best course of action would be to keep my hands to myself and away from her. Not that I don't want her. On the contrary, clearly, I am fast becoming obsessed with her, and if I allow myself to take her one more time... It will be very difficult to walk away from her. Which is a bloody inconvenience, considering I promised her I would impregnate her. I needed a little time to think this through, hence... I reach for the letters on the rack, then lay them out on the board.

FOOL

. . .

Yep, that's me, all right. I'd thought I would trap her into an arrangement and use it to, somehow, get to the truth of who was behind the incident… But, somehow, all that has become secondary to this connection that has sprung up between us. Something I need time to process—Ha! Me—the man who doesn't think twice about navigating headlong into a storm… I need to evaluate my options here.

Falling for her is out of the question. So how am I going to fuck her, fulfill my end of the contract, and still, walk away without being trapped further? See what's happening here? I am the one being lured into an ambush, thanks to this green-eyed sprite who chews on her fingernail while she contemplates the letters in front of her.

"Your turn," I prompt.

She huffs, "Fine, fine. Give me a moment here."

"Do you want me to help?" I reach over and she holds her rack of letters away.

"Hey, stop that."

"Hey, just trying to help." I hold my hands up in front of me.

She scowls, then places the rack carefully in front of her on the table, "How old is this board anyway? I mean, who plays scrabble anymore?"

"I did, with my parents."

"Hmm."

She contemplates her letters, some more. "Tell me about them."

I stare at her.

"What?" she says without raising her gaze. "We're going to meet your family. Surely, I should know something about my fake future in-laws?"

"Right." I drag my fingers across my chin. My whiskers are getting itchy. Damn, if I don't need a shave. But for some reason I couldn't find my razor. Apparently the place wasn't as well stocked as I'd thought.

"You mentioned that your father moved back to Lille?" She raises her gaze to mine. "But you and your family lived in London?"

"Yeah, that's where my brother and I grew up. My father worked in the city."

"And you followed in his footsteps?"

"Not directly." I scowl down at the board. What the hell is taking her so long? Is she one of those people who analyzes every move before they make it?

I drum my fingers on the table, "Why don't you play as we speak?"

"Why don't you speak as we play?"

"I'll tell you more after you play."

"I'll play if you tell me more."

I lean back in my chair. "This is not a negotiation, sugar."

"Isn't it? Sure seems that way, considering you're not coming through on your side of the bargain."

"We still have time, don't we?" I glance toward the window where the rain is coming down in sheets outside. "After all, how long does your fertility window last?"

"Forty-eight hours," she snaps. "That's the most I am probably fertile post ovulation."

"That gives us...until, the end of tonight?"

"Exactly. So, if I were you, I'd get with the program." She lays out her words on the board between us.

C
  H
  I
  F O O L
  D

"You're kidding me," I growl.

"More like, you're the one who's been kidding me."

"Is that right?" I glare at her and she pales. She flips her hair over her shoulder, then begins to play with one of her locks.

"I mean, how hard can it be to, as you said earlier, turn me over and take me without—"

I hold up my hand, "Think very carefully about what you're going to say next."

"Without..." she hesitates, "Uh, without..."

"Hold on a second, doll. Let me play my word." I place my letters on the board.

. . .

C

H

I

FOOL

DIRTY

Her gaze widens, "How the hell did you manage that?"

"Now, your turn."

I replenish my letters as she contemplates her move.

"So, you were saying…?" I prompt.

"What?"

"Complete your statement, Sparks."

"I was going to say, how hard can it be to turn me over and take me without—" she raises her gaze to mine, "preparation?"

I rise to my feet so quickly that she blinks. I prowl around to stand behind her chair.

"What…what are you doing?" She shudders.

"Go on, mull over your move, sweetheart."

She turns her head to glance at me, and I jerk my chin, "Get up."

"What?"

"Stand up, babe," I urge her.

She rises to her feet, gaze still on me, and I click my tongue. "Eyes forward."

"You like to hear your own voice, don't you? I should get you a T-shirt with those words printed on it: eyes—" I spank her butt and she squeaks, "forward."

"Exactly."

I palm the curve of her arse and she shudders.

"Does everything have to be a kinky maneuver with you?" She huffs.

"Why? Are you complaining? It's not like you prefer vanilla, yourself."

"How do you know?" She half turns to frown at me.

"Don't," I warn her and she frowns.

I squeeze her butt cheek and she swallows. I jerk my chin toward the front and she faces forward again.

Unable to help herself, she asks, "Did you have me watched? Is that how you know so much about my preferences?"

Actually, no, but it's not a bad idea. It's something I should have done, something I am going to rectify right away, given how, despite my best efforts, I can't keep my hands off of her.

"Just a lucky guess." I plant both of my palms on either side of her butt then pull her back so she connects with my crotch.

"Oh," she lower's her head, "how can you be so hard, so quickly?"

"How could I not be hard?" I counter. "I've been sporting a boner since you walked in on me in the shed, wrapped up in my rope."

She wriggles her butt, moves back further, and my cock stabs in between her arsecheeks. Why the hell is she still wearing so many clothes?

I glance around for something—anything—to help me in my quest. There. "Don't move." I tap her shoulder, then prowl around and over to the kitchen counter. I grab a knife and turn.

She pales. "What are you going to do with that?"

I tilt my head, then stalk back to her. She turns her head and I curve my fingers around her neck, "Told you to stay with your gaze forward, didn't I?"

"But—"

I slide the knife under the coils of rope, then flick my wrist. The blade slices through the strands, and the cord falls away.

I raise her sweatshirt, tug down the jeans, then stare at the curve of her creamy butt. "Bloody hell," I growl, "how could I have missed looking at this sight in such a short period of time?"

"Ar…Arpad?" Her voice wavers. "What are you going to do?"

"I am going to fuck you now."

26

Karina

That's what I want, isn't it? For him to lose control and take me, despite the fact that I know he wants to bind me first. Isn't that why I had used the rope to bind myself? Yes, so it had also been functional, but subconsciously it was about taunting him, teasing him, trying to get a rise out of him, and damn, if I haven't succeeded.

He nudges my hair over one shoulder and cool air hits my nape. I shiver, grip the edge of the table and wait… Wait for his next move.

"It's your turn."

"What?"

"You're up next to play, Sparks."

"Fuck that," I swear aloud.

"Now, now," he chuckles, "don't be rude."

"Fuck you," I swear under my breath, and he laughs. The asshole actually laughs. I turn, and once more, he wraps his fingers around my nape, coercing me to stay facing forward.

"Focus, babe," he drawls. "Play your word, or do I need to help you with that?"

"Oh, bugger off."

He spanks my butt and my body jolts. The table shakes and a letter falls off the rack in front of me.

"Pick that up," he growls. I hesitate, and he snaps, "Don't disobey me."

"Fine, fine." I straighten the letter, stare at the board. "What's this, disciplining through Scrabble? Are words your kink or something?"

He chuckles, "Or something."

He slides his hand around to cup my pussy and my entire body goes on alert. My stomach clenches and my thighs spasm. I force myself to stay calm… *Don't move*… Don't say or do anything that's going to make him draw out this crazy touchy-feely approach he has going.

He kicks my legs apart and I shiver, dig my heels into the ground, with my feet wide apart and wait… wait…

He slips a finger inside my channel. I shiver.

He adds a second, then a third, and does that thing he does so well. He curves his fingers, grazing the walls of my sensitive core, and a groan bleeds out of me.

I hear the rasp of a zipper being lowered, then he pulls his fingers out of me, only to grab my hips and pull me back, positioning me, ready to impale me. Moisture beads my center. Ugh, I'm so empty, so ready… What the hell is wrong with me? I've never been this…needy for some-one… No, not someone… For him. It's Arpad… The alphahole who is going to turn my world upside down.

He is going to impregnate me and then I'll have a miniature image of him to look at every day and I'll never forget him. I'll spend the rest of my life wondering how the hell it would have been if there had been something real between us, if I had acknowledged my attraction for him, if I had thrown caution to the wind for the first time and grabbed at the chance of a future with him.

The crown of his dick nudges against the opening of my slit and I gasp.

"Your play, sugar."

I stare at the board, the letters that fade in and out in front of my eyes.

Then place the letters on the table.

C M
 H A

I R
F O O L R
D I R T Y
M
E

The muscles of his thighs go rock hard, as he tilts his hips forward and breaches me. My body jolts and the table shudders. The letters, though, stay where they are.

"What's that?" he growls. "What do you mean?"

"I mean…" I shudder as he pulls out of me, and stays poised at my entrance again, "let's do it for re —"

He plunges inside me with enough force that his balls slap against the backs of my thighs.

"—al," I scream.

The letters move on the board, displaced, disoriented, words blown to their components, like I've been, since I met him.

I groan as he bottoms out inside me. "Arpad," I gasp, "please… please…don't stop."

He presses his palm into the small of my back and applies just enough pressure. I lower my cheek down to the board, grip the edge of the table with my fingers.

"Fucking gorgeous."

He grabs my hips and begins to fuck me in earnest. In and out, with long, smooth strokes that have his length embedded in me, hitting that spot deep inside that he always seems to find with unerring precision.

I've got to say, getting pregnant this way beats the cold sterile procedure I had planned. I mean, this is, by far, the best sex I've had in my life… I'm not going to get this from anyone else… Not the expert way he maneuvers my body to just the right angle so he can, once more, sink inside of me, fill me, stretch me, cram me with his length that is so delicious, so beautiful, a work of art…

And I am, clearly, having an out-of-body experience. I've never had such an inherently spiritual episode before, not even with all of the yoga I've practiced. Hell, I'd happily hold any position he places me in… Just as long as he continues to fuck me, shag me, wring that next orgasm from me, which is approaching with the kind of rush that resembles when I do a headstand and the blood flows to my head…

"Ah!" He slams into me once more and my climax sweeps over me. It explodes behind my eyes, and I shudder, grip the table so tightly that my fingers hurt, my thighs tremble, my toes curl, every muscle in my body tenses… Then the orgasm ebbs away and I collapse.

Above me, he continues to pound into me again and again. Then finally, he growls out, his body tenses, and with a jerk of his cock, he comes inside me. He stays that way, entrenched in me. Aftershocks grip me, my pussy clenches around his dick, which I swear is still semi-erect. How the hell is that possible? He lowers his head and I feel the whisper of something against the top of my head.

He presses little kisses down my eyebrow, my cheek, the edge of my lips. I shiver. This… This habit of his, this half-kiss, is surely my undoing?

He licks my lips, then whispers, "Yes."

I peer up at him, "What…? What do you mean?"

"Yes," his lips curve up, "yes, I'll marry you, for real."

27

Arpad

"Et tu, Brutus?" Edward drawls across the phone line.

Yep. After I'd agreed to marry her… Fucking hell, I'd agreed to marry her… Yeah, take a breath, ol' chap. Get it together. So, after I'd agreed to marry her for real, I'd pulled out of her, then dressed, and made a quick exit. Not caring that it was raining outside, I'd pulled on my jacket and beat a hasty retreat to the shed.

Me… The man known for his cut-throat maneuvers when it comes to snapping up the best bets in Silicon Valley, I had raced out of that chalet like my tail was on fire… Not literally, but metaphorically. Jesus, I am in so much trouble. I need to talk to someone… Yep, like a fucking pussy, I call Edward tell him what happened. Not all of the details, of course. Just that I had agreed to her proposal.

"Now, that's not very charitable of you, Father," I grumble. "I swear, I didn't mean for it to end up this way."

"You mean with you ready to take a trip down to the altar?" He snickers.

"Hey, aren't you supposed to be happy for me, in your professional capacity?" I frown.

"In my professional capacity, I will not dissuade you from what you think is right for you… Just as long as it is right for you."

"You're speaking in riddles again, Father."

"Come now, that's my forte." A new voice cuts in.

"Saint?" I grimace. "What the hell are you doing there?"

"Not just him," Damian's voice sounds across the line.

"You too?" I glower.

"Oh, did I forget to tell you, that I patched in the others while you were sharing your saga with us?" Edward chimes in.

"Saga?" I snap. "What the hell, Father? Sorry, didn't mean to swear there. No wait…" I shake my head, "actually, I did mean to swear. Considering I trusted you enough to call you for your advice—"

"A bit for that isn't it, considering you decided to get married to her?"

"Hey," I protest, "Saint did the same, didn't he—?"

"Bloody hell," Saint swears aloud, "will you guys stop holding me up as a shining example of everything done right? Not that things didn't work out for me, but there's a crucial difference between my situation and yours."

"What's that?"

"I fell in love with Victoria as soon as I saw her."

"And as soon as I saw Julia, I knew she was the one," Damian declares.

"You mean I'm not in love with Karina?"

"You're fixated on her," Weston drawls, "but you sure you're in love with her?"

"Anyone else want to venture their opinion?" I growl. "Or have you jokers had your say?"

The barking of a dog sounds, then Sinclair comes on the line, "Sorry, chaps, Max insisted he add his thoughts on the matter."

"Brilliant, that's all I need—Sterling's mutt's point of view." I crack my neck. "I suppose you'll want to give your two bits worth on my love life, or lack thereof?"

"I don't know man," Sinclair muses, "from where I am, it's all clear."

"It is?"

I sense him nod at the other end of the line. "Sure," he replies. "You decided to lay this elaborate plan so you could keep her close. Then, you decided to get her onto your boat, which is more home to you than anything on land. Then you pushed it further by shoving your boat into the path of a storm, decided to take shelter, and then the inevitable happens and you realize you are losing control, so when she throws you a lifeline, you take it. You say yes to marrying her, and all because you've been a pussy all along. You tie it up all in bloody knots, because underneath it all, you feel something for her. But you don't want to admit it to yourself, let alone to her."

I squeeze the bridge of my nose. "That's some crazy shit theory you've come up with," I mutter. " In fact, I am not sure about what you say half the time."

"That's such a lame excuse, Beauchamp." Saint barks out a laugh.

"And what makes you such an expert on the topic?"

"Oh, let's see. It's because I married the woman of my dreams, and I have a kid on the way, and let's face it, I still haven't lost my edge when it comes to making tough decisions."

"Which is what?" I frown.

"That you need to tell her the truth."

"Which is."

"That you love her, which is why you manipulated her to move across the pond, then gave her the business of the Seven so you could keep her close. Now you're carrying out the ultimate in possessive acts by marrying her."

I wince. "And when I tell her... How do you think that's going to go down with her?"

"I don't know," Saint chuckles, "best case, she'll be pissed off at you."

My palms begin to sweat. "And the worst?" I clear my throat. "What would be the worst case?"

There's silence, then Saint says, "She'd leave you?"

I grimace. That's what I am afraid of. And it's not just my ego which would be hurt by that... Which, face it, it would, but that's not the only thing stopping me from telling her everything. *If she leaves me, I won't be able to protect her.*

My heart begins to race; my pulse rate ratchets up. Of course, what he's saying is true, although he doesn't know the half of it. I should let her know that I know about her background. That I know that she's connected to the Bratva. But a part of me wants her to trust me enough for her to confide in me. But then, I haven't told her all of my secrets either.

"You're right." I clench and unclench my fist. "I need to be upfront with her. Without that, whatever connection is between us, it doesn't stand a chance."

"Bloody hell," Damian barks out a laugh, "is that Mr. Take-risks-and-play-with-his-life Beauchamp actually agreeing to a rational approach?"

Fuck, if it isn't.

"Don't get your panties in a twist," I growl.

"Don't put your horses in front of the cart, Arpad," Edward warns me.

"What's that supposed to mean?"

"I mean, take it easy. Don't force the topic. Lead with your instinct on this one."

"You're telling me, Father." I rise to my feet. "I am the king of instinct. It's thanks to this very instinct that I have been able to sniff out and fund enough startups, thanks to which, I have enough passive income to not have to work for the rest of my life."

"All of which were ultimately decisions you made with your head. When it comes to your heart, though…it's another matter altogether."

"Not that you'll ever have to deal with that," I retort.

Silence for a beat, another, then I swear aloud. "Bloody hell, I didn't mean it that way, Father."

"Sure, you did." Edward's voice is tight.

"That was low," I insist. "Didn't mean to hit you where it would hurt the most."

"You were being honest." Edward's voice is low, "And it's true. Matters of the heart are out of my purview. There's space for love for only one in my heart...and that's the Lord above."

"Right." I drag my fingers through my hair. "Guess there's no other way but for me to face this…head-on, huh?"

"You got this," Weston exclaims. "Just rip it off like a band aid, you know?"

"Face this like a man, you dickwad," Sterling drawls.

"Eyes on the prize, you shitstain," Damian adds.

"Don't all of you get complimentary all at once." Why is it that when we get together, we somehow, lapse right back to being twelve and pre-pubescent wankers again?

"You don't have anything to lose, do you?" Saint, that asswipe, adds his two pennies' worth.

Yeah, I have nothing to lose… Except for my sanity, and my balls…

God help me. Not only has she ensured that I'll never want to fuck another woman, but hell, if I don't want to be inside her already again. This entire thing is turning out to be a nightmare. Perhaps I should have turned the yacht around after all, and dropped her off at port, huh?

And then what? I'd have always wondered how it could have been. Hell, it's not like me to overthink my actions… Not when it comes to business, and certainly not when it came to facing down storms.

"What-bloody-ever," I growl. "Thanks for nothing, you guys." I disconnect, then head toward the chalet.

I am used to living life on the edge. Surely, I can manage one tiny woman with attitude, huh?

28

Karina

What the hell? He did it again. He'd accepted my proposal. He'd agreed to marry me. This time, I'm sure he'll cut and run. I mean, why the hell would he agree to something like that? Surely, he is going to back out, right? Except, I don't think so. Shit, why did I propose that? Clearly, when I am with him, I can't think straight.

After the asshole had pulled out and left… I'd straightened my clothes, then the scrabble board. Then put away the stupid board game. I'd hyperventilated on what had just taken place, had been glad that he'd decided to head out and give me a chance to compose myself. And clearly, the only thing that's going to help me when I get so stressed is yoga.

So here I am, flowing into the most basic, yet most challenging pose of all.

On my hands and knees, I position my wrists under my shoulders and my knees under my hips. Stretch my elbows and relax my upper back. Spread my fingers wide and press firmly through my palms, exhale as I tuck my toes and lift my knees off the floor.

Reach my pelvis up toward the ceiling, then draw in my tailbone, and gently begin to straighten my legs, bring my body into the shape of an "A."

Press down and lift through my pelvis. As I lengthen my spine, I lift my tail bone up toward the ceiling. Then press down equally through my heels and the palms of my hands.

Engage my quadriceps.

Align my ears with my upper arms. Relax my head, gaze toward my navel.

Hold… Hold… Hold for one, two, three… My hamstrings elongate, my biceps tremble... S*hit. Focus, on how your palms dig into the rug* — Yeah, I chose the place before the fire because it's the warmest spot in the room, not to mention, the rug is thick enough to shield my knees when I need to push down on them to rise up... And continue to count, four, five, six. *Stop grimacing. That's not the point of yoga. Don't forget to breathe, in-out-in.*

I exhale as I gently bend my knees and come back to my hands and knees. A bead of sweat trickles down my spine. The hair on the back of my neck rises. I glance up to find him at the breakfast counter. He leans a hip against the edge, then crosses one leg over the other.

"Why did you stop?" he rumbles.

I scowl, then shift to a kneeling position.

"Why don't you join me?"

"No thanks."

"Worried you can't replicate the position?

"Baby, the only position I want to replicate is you under me, over me, reverse-cowgirl me, face-off with me —"

"Stop," I plead.

"—as I corkscrew you. Hell, I could even do the Om with you, or we could snow-angel together —"

"Enough," I scowl at him, "so you know your sexual positions."

"We don't need to go that far." He prowls over to me, "Why don't you do the plow, or the cobra or hell, the bridge position?"

"You know about them?"

"I know they are yoga positions that make for very gratifying sex." He smirks.

"Fine, fine," I huff, "you've made your point. And by the way, you're evading the topic."

"What topic?"

"The yoga poses." I tilt up my chin. "Bet you can't keep up with me."

"Is that a dare?"

He walks over to stand in front of me, and since I am still on my knees, it means I am at eye level with his crotch… Which is tented, and the shape of his length is clearly outlined by the fabric of his jeans.

"Don't you ever wear sweats?"

"Sweats?" His lips curl as if it's a dirty word.

I lean my head back to meet his gaze. "Yeah, you know, the loose pants with an elastic drawstring that men wear at home, because they're comfortable?"

He stares back at me.

"Right. Of course, not. It doesn't go with your image, now does it?"

"And what image would that be?"

"That tight-assed, stick-up-your-butt, grumpy-pants, alphahole who hates everything about the world around him."

"That's accurate." He folds his arms over his chest. "And for your information, I prefer jeans to sweats." He tilts his head. "Of course, if you want to see me in them, I'd be happy to oblige, especially since it allows for easy access." His grin widens. "Is that why you asked me about my preference in clothes? You want to make it easy for you to cop a feel, huh?"

"Argh." I make a gagging sound. "Why does our every conversation lead back to sex?"

"Because, you want to get pregnant?" he reminds me.

I sniff, then lower myself to plank position. "Stop trying to distract me and join in."

"I could beat you at yoga, any day."

"Really?" I bite the inside of my cheek. "Let's see you keep up, Romeo."

He drops down into plank position next to me. His movements are fluid; his biceps bulge and his shoulders flex. My throat dries and I almost lose my balance. *Shit, get your head back in the game. Focus, focus.*

I rise up to side plank. He follows, his breathing not even speeding up

Bloody ballache, need to up the ante now.

I move to all fours in the tabletop position. He follows. Then I place my knees under my hips and my hands under my shoulders.

I draw my shoulder blades together. Raise my right arm and left leg, keeping my shoulders and hips parallel to the floor. I tuck my chin into my chest to gaze down at the floor.

He follows, manages to get into position, only to fall over. He tries again, fails. Growls aloud, glances at me, and copies my position. Manages to hold it for a few seconds, then collapses, sweat gleaming on his forehead. "Bloody hell," he swears, "how the hell could it be that difficult?"

I hold the position for a few seconds more, then lower back down to the starting position. "Not as easy as it looks, huh?" I curve my lips and smile sweetly at him. "Want to try again?" I sit back on my heels.

"Yes," he nods, "but not yoga." He waggles his eyebrows, as he rises to his feet. "How about you continue your practice while I watch?"

"How about you sod off?" I rise to my feet and turn toward the bedroom, then squeak when his fingers tighten around my wrist.

"Not so fast, babe."

I turn to stare at him. "Yes?" I school all expression from my face.

"I told you to continue your practice, didn't I?"

"What if I don't want to?"

"Too bad." He raises a shoulder. "You will do as I say."

"A-n-d, there he is." I sniff. "The man who must have his way in all things."

"Yep," he nods, "you've definitely sussed me out, babe."

"Oh, go to hell." I tug my arm, which he still has a hold of, and his grasp tightens.

"Don't challenge me babe."

"Or what?" I retort. "You've already fucked me, and spanked me. Hell, you've already agreed to marry me, so what else can you do to me?"

He bends his knees, then pushes his face into mine, "Want to find out?"

No.

No.

"Y…yes." Argh, why is my voice so shaky. I clear my throat, "Bring it on."

He releases me, "Run."

"What?"

"Five." He holds up five fingers.

"What are you doing? Is it a countdown?"

His lip curls.

Of course, it's a countdown. *Why the hell are you asking dumb questions of this asshole?* Why the hell should I run anyway, huh? I purse my lips, stare at him.

"Four." He folds his thumb.

My heart hammers in my throat, my fingers tremble, and I curl them into fists at my sides. "This is not funny," I gripe.

"Three." Only three of his digits remain upright.

I gulp.

"This your kind of kink, then? It's not enough to tie up women, you prefer to chase them first?"

His smile widens, and damn him, but it's not nice. No, it's downright predatory of him to do so. My stomach flip-flops and my core clenches. So why the hell am I turned on?

"Two." He wiggles his two fingers.

Bastard.

"One." Only one finger is now upright, his middle finger.

"Time's up." He lunges forward.

I shriek, then swerve around him and race to the door. My pulse pounds at my wrists, at my temples; adrenaline laces my blood. I twist the handle of the door, tear it open and race out into the rain.

"Stop." I hear his voice a second before the wind swoops over me. I stumble, then brace myself and run in the opposite direction of the shed. Oh, no way, am I going to his torture chamber, where, no doubt, he can't wait to practice his craft on me. Only saving grace?

He hasn't brought another woman to the island and tied her up there. How many others has he tied up before me? It would have to be a significant number for him to reach the level of expertise he's at now. Something hot stabs at my chest… Not jealousy. No way. What the hell do I care who he practices his kink with? And will it stop once we were married? Was he serious when he agreed? And honestly, what had possessed me to ask the question?

I run uphill, not able to see more than a couple of feet in front of me. Shit, it really is bucketing down. Maybe this wasn't a good idea. But what the hell? He'd pissed me off with his stupid challenge, and of course, I had fallen for it and taken off. Not that I could have stayed there and allowed him to jump me either. My thighs spasm… And it's not from the thought of him throwing me down and spreading my legs and burying himself inside of me either. Nope. Get a grip, woman. This is the man who's chasing you through a storm on an island in the middle of nowhere. Do you realize how crazy that sounds?

I hear something above the sound of the wind and the rain. I shake my hair out of my eyes, risk a quick glance over my shoulder. Of course,

I can't see anything, considering the rain seems to have just notched up in intensity. My clothes are plastered to my body, a gust of wind slams into me, and I am almost blown back. I dig my heels into the ground for purchase, then lean into the breeze and force myself to take another step. And another.

"Karina!'

I hear his voice call out before the wind drowns it out again.

I increase my pace, cover more ground. More rain lashes against my face. Damn it. I wipe the water from my eyes, put one leg in front of the other. *Keep moving. Don't stop.* Somehow it seems imperative that I win this round. When did it become a competition, huh? This was supposed to have been easy, him rolling on top and thrusting into me and impregnating me... None of which has gone according to plan. I should have known better than to engage with him... Why the hell did I have to fall asleep in his bed in the first place, huh?

"Karina, stop."

I snort under my breath. There he is again, telling me what to do. Damn him and his dominant ways. I power through the wall of water which seems to have sprung up in front of me.

"Karina! Look out! There's a—"

I place my foot forward, encounter emptiness. I pitch forward.

29

Arpad

Her scream rips through my eardrums. My heart stutters. My pulse begins to race. Adrenaline pours into my blood. I lunge forward through the rain, up the slope and throw myself forward. I hit the edge of the slope, arm flung out, fingers grasping against emptiness. My throat dries. Where the hell is she? "Karina!"

The wind rips my voice into shreds. I swallow and peer through the wall of water. The ground gives under me and I scramble back. "Fuck!" I swear aloud, grip the edge of the crumbling slope, stare through the gathering darkness. "Karina, where are you?"

There's a sound… Is that her? Did I hear something?

"Karina, is that you? Answer me," I command.

"Ari?" Her voice is weak, and so low that I'm sure I must be mistaken.

"Karina?" I yell out, "Where the fuck are you?"

"Can't you stop swearing for one second?" She coughs, and this time I hear her clearly. Fuck, she's close. Why can't I see her?

I crawl forward on my stomach, and the edge of the slope crumbles again. "Fuck." I need to brace myself against something, but what? I glance around, spot a tree a few feet away. "Fuckin' fuck." I am going to have to go back to get something to help me with this.

"Karina?"

"Yeah?" She answers promptly, so that's something.

"You hurt? Are you okay?"

"My ankle's sprained." She coughs again. "I am just cold and wet."

"That's an understatement," I grumble.

"Wow," she gasps, "so you and I agree on something, huh?"

"The only thing we are in agreement on is that I am going to tan your hide when I finally get to you."

"It's all your fault anyway," she calls out. "If you hadn't initiated your stupid sex games—"

"It wasn't a sex game… It was just a way of keeping you on your toes."

"And why would you need to do that?"

"Do you really want to have this conversation now?"

"Is there a better time?"

"You stealing my dialogue?" I frown as I stare down in the direction of her voice and make out a ledge. The breath rushes out of me. Okay, fine, so at least, she's not far away.

"You alphaholes don't have the prerogative for always being in the lead," she yells back.

"Ha, when it comes to you, woman, I doubt I can stay ahead for too long," I reply.

"OMG, I can't believe you are being nice to me." She coughs again and my stomach twists. She can't stay out here for too long.

Thunder crashes in the distance, then lightning flickers and I see her on the ground, not six feet below, not too far… But not very close either.

"I am going to have to go back and get a hold of some rope so I can haul you up." I project my voice in her direction.

"Ha," she scoffs, "any excuse to truss me up, eh?"

"We could have skipped all this if you had asked me to tie you up when you came to the shed."

"You mean your room of pain?"

"Was it painful when I tied you up the first time?" I frown.

She hesitates.

"Tell me, Sparks, did I hurt you then?"

"No," I sense her shake her head, "it was different, that's all."

"Good different or bad different?"

"It wasn't bad. Actually, I think I liked it."

"You did?"

"Yeah." She coughs again and I frown. "Hold that thought, will you? I'll head out and be right back in a few minutes."

She doesn't reply.

"Karina? You okay?"

Silence, for a beat, another. "Yeah," she finally replies and her voice sounds weaker.

"Hang in there, Sparks. I promise, I won't take too long."

"If I'd known it only takes my falling off a cliff for you to go all sensitive and protective..."

"I've always been protective of you, Karina. You know that."

She doesn't reply.

"I'll be back before you know it."

I turn to leave when she calls out, "Ari?"

I pause. "Yeah, babe?"

"Get the rope that you'd have used to tie me anyway."

"You got it, babe." I lower my head, shield my face against the elements, then continue down the slope.

The same rope? She wants me to use the rope that I already picked out for her. How the hell could she know that? Is she that perceptive, that she'd clocked my peculiarities already? Or was it a lucky guess?

What a woman she is. I'd been sure she was going to tell me to hurry back, or that she was too cold, or that she couldn't last out there much longer, but hell, if she hadn't surprised me again. She's so tiny, so delicate, I often forget her looks are misleading. My woman has a spine of steel. She's a survivor. She's had to be, to have gotten this far on her own. But never again, will she need to do everything on her own. At least, for as long as I am with her, I am going to make sure she never has to do anything by herself. She'll have me as her back up and...

Hold on a bloody second. What the hell am I doing, building these plans with her...knowing that...she isn't being honest with me, that she is hiding her true identity? I shake my head. There are too many conflicting threads of thought here. I need to prioritize. Focus on one thing at a time. And for now, that is getting her back to safety.

I reach the chalet, tear open the door, then pound through the living room and into the bedroom. I open the closet, grab the rope that I had set aside for her, then snatch up two more of my strongest ones, just in case.

I am out and racing up the hill in minutes. The wind slams into me, pushing me back, and I have to double over to make progress. By the time I reach the top of the slope, I am panting. I loop the ropes around my arm, then drop down and crawl to the edge on my stomach.

"Karina?" I call out, and the wind once more tears the words out of my mouth. "Babe, you there?"

No reply.

Shit, shit, shit. Am I too late? Where the hell is she? "Sparks, where the fuck are you? If you don't reply in another second, I swear, I am coming down there, and when I do, I am going to spank your arse so hard that —"

"Yeah, yeah." Her voice reaches me. She coughs, then seems to gather herself together. "I know how much you like my ass, but if you don't pull me up first, I'm afraid it's going to have frozen and fallen off."

My shoulders slump. Whew, she's still there. Of course, she is. Where the hell would she have gone?

"Watch out for the rope, okay?"

I pull out the first coil of rope, make a lasso out of it, then throw it in her direction.

"Did you get it?"

"What?"

"The rope."

"Did you throw it?"

Fuck. I retrieve the rope, then aim the lasso in the direction of her voice and spring it at her.

"Did you see that?"

"Nope."

"Bloody fuck."

"Don't you know any other swear words? The F bomb is sooo passé."

"Ah, but nothing else quite encapsulates how I am feeling right now."

She chuckles, "Don't tell me that Arpad Alphahole is short of swear words?"

I pull back the rope, wipe my face on my sleeve. *Focus, focus.* "Sure, if swear words are what you want to hear right now, then how about... Wanker, twat, bollocks, arsebadger, jizzcock,"

She laughs, "You're taking the piss now."

"That too."

I throw the lasso at her, and feel it tauten. "Did you catch it?"

"Yes," she gasps, "OMG, I have it."

"Hold onto it, walk toward my voice."

There's a pause before I hear her swear loudly.

"Careful," I caution, "don't hurt yourself, babe."

My heart begins to thud and my throat closes. I tie the end of the rope to the other hank of rope I brought. Then I wind it around my middle, fasten it with enough knots. There, that should hold now. I lower myself to the ground and stretch-out with my head hanging over the edge.

I peer through the pouring rain. Where the hell is she?

"Can you see the edge of the cliff?"

"Not yet."

"Stretch out your hand, slowly… Tell me when you can feel the edge."

The rope vibrates as she moves forward. "Oh, I am there now."

"Okay, wind the rope around your middle. Let me know when you have secured it."

There's silence, except for the wind and the pelting rain, as she does so. The rope dances as some of the slack is taken up, then the length tautens again. "I'm ready."

"I'm going to haul you up."

"Okay."

"Are you able to use your good leg to balance against the wall, if needed?"

"Yes," she calls back, "I… I think so. I'll try."

"Good girl."

I begin to haul her up. My biceps feel it, my shoulders protest, I'm pulled forward by the weight of her body, and she screams out, "Ari!"

"It's fine." I blow out a breath. Still stretched out on my front I dig my toes into the ground for purchase. I tighten my muscles, wind the rope around my palms and haul.

My entire body tenses and my shoulders feel like they are being pulled out their sockets. Pain grips my chest and my back. I grit my teeth, continue to pull her up, slowly, slowly. "You… okay?" I huff out.

"Yes…" her voice is closer. She sounds weak, but at least, she is not panicking.

"You're doing so well, darling. I swear, it will all be over before you know it. Just a few more seconds, baby. That's all; hold on…" I continue to haul her up toward me. The rope abrades my skin, the rain drips down my forehead and I blink it out of my eyes.

The wind blows and the rope sways.

"Ari," she screams, and she's so close now.

"I have you, babe." I firm my lips, draw in another breath and yank upward; her head appears above the edge of the precipice. Finally. Fuck. It's as if I am seeing a newborn enter the world for a first time.

Warmth flushes my chest. Adrenaline pumps through my veins and I draw on every single reserve of strength left inside of me. I flex my muscles, then dig my feet into the ground and heave. Her entire body slides up and over the precipice. I wrap my arms about her, haul her close, and collapse with her on top of me.

30

Karina

Heat cocoons me, his arms shelter me, the scent of his maleness—the essence of pheromones and dark edginess that is so Arpad—envelops me. The breath rushes out of me, and only then, do I realize how tense I've been all along. My legs tremble, I raise my arm—or at least try to, for I find I can't move. My fingers tremble, my muscles turn to jelly. A shudder wracks me, and another. Pressure builds behind my eyes, moisture clings to my cheeks, and it's not just from the rain. My shoulders heave and I press my face into his hard chest and allow the tears to flow.

"Shh." He rocks me, runs his fingers down my hair, winds his arm around me, holds me close. "I got you, babe. I got you, and I'm never letting you go again."

I only cry harder, the pent-up pressure from finding myself on his boat, and then trying to resist him and failing, wanting to be tied up by him and not wanting him to know, the sheer intense connection between us, which had made the times we'd come together so much more potent; all of it seems to come to a head, there in his arms, on the top of a peak, on an island in the middle of the English Channel.

"Jesus, Sparks, you're breaking my heart," his voice whispers in my ear.

I lean back, tilt my chin up. "Kiss me," I sob. "Please Ari, kiss m —"

He lowers his head and closes his mouth over mine. And the kiss is anything but gentle. He thrusts his tongue inside my mouth and takes and takes, and shares his breath. I press myself closer to him, push my breasts into his chest. I lean into him and part my lips and allow him to fuck my mouth with his tongue.

The kiss seems to go on and on. I lose myself in the softness of his lips, the hard demand of his tongue as he swipes it across my teeth. He winds his fingers around my knotted hair and tugs. Pain slithers down my scalp. I moan deep in my throat. I am alive. I am here in his arms, with him. I tear my mouth from his, stare into his face, "Tie me up again and fuck me."

He stares into my eyes as if taken aback, then chuckles. "This is why I can't resist you. You always surprise me, Sparks."

"I…do?"

He nods.

The sun filters through the clouds and I blink.

"Well look at that." He glances up at the sky. "The storm blew over."

I stare about me, and sure enough, the rain has faded away as quickly as it had started. The pale orb of the sun lights up the bottom of the clouds with a silvery lining.

He rises to his feet with me in his arms. I glance down to find that the rope which winds around me is also wrapped around his waist. "We're connected," I mutter.

"Eh?" He strides down the slope, his long legs eating up the distance.

"The rope," I swallow, "I am wearing it and so are you."

"Imagine that." He shakes his head. "Never thought I'd see the day when I'd be entangled in my own rope."

"I'm also very muddy."

"I prefer you dirtied up, Sparks." He chuckles.

It's a strange feeling… To be carried. It makes me feel cherished, cared for, like I could lean on him. Something I haven't done since…

I had been a small child and my father had wiped my tears after I had engaged in a particularly bad fight with the school bully…who had been much bigger than me. He had been called to school that day and my principal had had a word with him. My father had been disappointed in my behavior, yet he'd also comforted me.

He'd told me that I need to choose my battles wisely, for I could never hope to win all of them, but I could minimize the risk of failure by deciding which challenges to go after.

And since meeting Arpad… My subconscious has decided that he is the biggest challenge of them all. I haven't known what to make of it… Clearly, the disagreements between us, resulting mainly because of his heavy-handedness, have made me think that I hate him… But all along, it has been a precursor for the attraction between us. And something more… This sense that we, somehow, fit together. Two parts of a puzzle, whose big picture I still can't see... But there is this need to find out what it might turn out to be.

So, I press myself as close to him as I can, allow myself the decadence of luxuriating in his strength, his solidity, the utter masculinity that resides in every angle of his body, the thud-thud-thud of his heart against my cheek as I close my eyes and drift off.

"Sparks?"

"Hmm."

"I need to get you out of these wet clothes." His voice rumbles around me, the heat of his body a siren's call. I turn, lean toward the source of the warmth and he chuckles.

"Just need to ease this shirt off you, okay?"

I crack open my eyes to find he's doing just that. He slides the shirt off one shoulder, then the other. Goosebumps erupt across my skin. The world tilts and I turn my head to find he's carrying me into the shower cubicle. He lowers my feet to the ground, then supports me as he turns the shower on. The hot water is a shock and I sneeze once, twice.

"Shit, hope you're not going to catch a cold, sweetheart."

Sweetheart," I mumble, my eyelids so heavy I can barely keep them open. "You called me darling earlier, then baby…" I murmur under my breath.

"You have a preference?"

"All of them… All the time." I close my eyes and relax against his big body as the hot water soothes me.

I must have dozed off again, for when I come to next, it's dark. I rub my cheek into the soft pillow, glance around the bedroom. The rugs on the floor, the door to the closet in the corner, the table with the two chairs pushed up against the window…. Right, guess I must have fallen asleep during the shower and Arpad had put me to bed again. I glance down and find I'm wearing another of his T-shirts. The material is soft. Not because of being washed too often; it's just the quality of what he wears. I bring my arm to my nose and sniff. The scent of detergent and Arpad fills my senses. My stomach rumbles and I realize I am hungry. Guess I must have recovered if my body wants to be fed so insistently. I swing my legs over the edge of the bed, and stand. My ankle protests. I lean my weight on it and find it holds. Okay. Good. I limp to the door, open it and walk through into the kitchen.

His back is to me. Once again, he's wearing a new pair of jeans with a sweatshirt. Over one shoulder is a kitchen towel. As I watch, he bends over the skillet where he's stirring something, then raises the wooden spoon to his mouth and tastes something. The biceps of his arm bulge, the planes of his back bend and dip in an all too familiar symmetry. My toes curl. I drink in the sight of his narrow waist, the tight arse, the powerful corded thighs that flow down to meet strong hamstrings and his feet... His gorgeous feet are bare again.

"You don't like wearing socks?" My voice comes out rusty and I clear my throat.

He turns and surveys me from head to toe. "What are you doing out of bed?" He scowls.

"I was hungry..."

"Get back under the covers. I'll bring you food."

"But," I frown, "I feel fine."

"You look wrecked."

"Oh," I pat my cheeks, smooth the hair from my face, "thanks for that."

I purse my lips, and he sighs, "You always look beautiful, no matter what time of the day or night... You know that, right?"

Blood rushes to my face. "Right."

He jerks his chin toward the bedroom, "Go on, get back under the covers. I'll bring you something to eat."

I hesitate and he glares at me. "Don't disobey me."

"A-n-d he's back," I blow out a breath, "alphahole of the fucking century."

His gaze intensifies. "Don't fuck with me, Sparks."

"What happened to all the endearments?" I fold my arms around my waist, "You were going all baby this and honey that with me..."

"Honey?" He frowns. "How bourgeois do you think I am? Besides, you're fine now, aren't you?"

"So, you said those things because you thought I was in danger?" I scowl.

"Obviously." He raises a shoulder. "You didn't think I actually meant them, did you?"

My mouth drops open. "Jesus, you're a piece of work, you know that?"

"I don't care what you think about me, as long as you get back to bed."

"And if I don't?" I set my jaw.

He turns off the flame under the skillet, places the wooden spoon aside and covers the dish. Then he flicks the dish cloth from his shoulder and turns to face me, "Do you want me to come there?"

I swallow and my stomach twists. Pinpricks of heat flicker down my spine. Damn it, why does the threat from him turn me on so?

"And if I said yes?"

"Are you saying yes?" He takes a step forward and I shuffle back.

He moves toward me and I hold up my hand, "N…no… I mean, yes. I mean, forget it, I am heading back."

I limp my way to the bedroom. Why do I let him get under my skin so? Why can't I simply stay out of his way? Why do I keep giving him the opportunity to put me in my place? And why the hell does he have to be so rude to me? Especially after showing me his tender side? I am not going to cry now, no way. I sidle into bed, pull up the covers, then glance up when he walks into the room. He has a tray with a bowl of something that smells absolutely delicious. He places the tray on the table by the window, then comes over to me. "Sit up," he growls.

I stare at him, and he tilts his head. "Do it."

"Yeah, yeah. What's got your goat?"

"Who's got your goat?" He corrects me.

"That's what I meant."

"Not the same thing."

"Stupid semantics."

"You need to be precise in what you say and do, else it leaves room for error," he retorts.

"You need to decide whether you like me or hate me because this seesaw mood of yours is giving me whiplash."

He leans around to prop up the pillows at my back, then touches the side of my neck. "You don't have whiplash, do you?"

I shiver, then cringe away from his touch. "I am fine, as long as you don't touch me," I choke out the words, and he stiffens. He pulls away and I instantly miss his proximity. Damn it, this is crazy. This push, pull between us... It is doing my head in.

He walks over to the table, picks up the tray, then returns to place it across my thighs.

He pulls up a chair, sinks into it, then picks up the spoon and dips it in the soup. He holds it up to my mouth and I purse my lips.

He blows out a breath. "Eat," he growls.

I feel about ten. Hell, I want to throw a tantrum like I am ten and refuse to touch my food. I fold my arms across my chest and stare at him.

He meets my gaze, and his own softens. "Please," he murmurs. "Eat; the food will warm you up."

And there he goes again, revealing his caring side which, to be fair, disarms me more than his dominance.

I open my mouth and he slides the spoon in between my lips. The taste of tomatoes and peppers explodes on my tongue. "It's good," I say.

"Of course, it is," He smirks.

"Modesty, thy name is not Arpad f'ing Beauchamp," I grumble under my breath.

He chuckles and scoops up more of the broth and holds it up for me. I eat my way through the rest of the soup and soon the bowl is empty.

He sets the spoon back on the tray, then uses his sleeve to dab at my mouth.

I blink up at him. "You seem to feed me an awful lot."

"Need you strong so I can feed you something other than food."

Heat flushes my face. I glower at him and he laughs. "Couldn't resist that."

"Right." I yawn so hugely that my jaw cracks.

"You should get some more rest." He picks up the tray and rises to his feet. He turns to leave and, somehow, I can't let him go. Not yet.

"Will you be back?"

He turns to glance at me. "Do you want me to return?"

I nod.

"Then I will."

He heads out of the room. I switch off the lamp next to me, snuggle in. I must have passed out again. When I wake up its dawn and the bed next to me is cold.

I push the covers aside, slide out of bed, and stretch. I walk out into the living room and come to a stand-still. "What are you up to?"

31

Arpad

"What does it look like?"

I look up from the doorway where I've slipped on my jacket.

"Looks to me like you are leaving?"

"So are you."

She rubs one bare foot over the other, and of course, my gaze is instantly drawn to the length of her legs. The T-shirt she wears—*my* T-shirt, reaches the tops of her knees. She folds her fingers together in front of her, then tips up her chin. "We're leaving?" she asks.

I jerk my chin toward the window where sunshine streams in.

"I've been up since dawn making sure the yacht is ready to sail.

"Oh." She swallows, then folds her arms in front of her. "So that's it, then?"

"That's it." I nod.

"You said you'd come back to bed last night." She squeezes her eyes closed. "No, wait. What am I saying? Forget I said it… I mean…" She rakes her fingers through her hair, messing it up some more.

My fingers tingle and I want to move toward her and smooth down the errant strands. Instead, I stay where I am. "I did come to bed. You were asleep by then, and when I woke up this morning, you were still sleeping."

"Right," she swallows, "give me a few minutes to jump into the shower." She turns to leave, then winces, and glances down at her ankle.

I take a step forward. "You okay?"

"Yes, of course." She heads off to the bedroom.

I call after her, "I'm sorry."

She pauses, then turns to face me, "For what?"

"For allowing you to leave the house yesterday. If I hadn't, you wouldn't have run through the rain or fallen over the side and—"

"Hold on… You allowed me to leave the house? *You* allowed *me?*"

I narrow my gaze. "I should have stopped you."

"You didn't make me do anything," she snarls. "I ran out because it was the only way I had a chance of outrunning you."

"That's what I mean, I shouldn't have let you out of the house."

I take a step forward and so does she.

"I should have tied you to the bed when I had the chance and fucked you until you couldn't walk again."

Her chest rises and falls; her pupils dilate. "Think again, buster." She hobbles over to me, then stabs a finger in my chest, "You can't make me do anything I don't want to do. You are not the master of me, asshole."

"Don't tempt me to prove otherwise."

"What are you going to do? Use your stupid ego, and over-the-top possessiveness to put me in my place?"

"That might be a start." I don't stop the sneer that curls my lips. "Better still, I might throw you down on the floor right here and bury my cock inside you all over again."

"So why don't you do it?"

She digs her finger into my chest and I snarl, "Don't tempt me."

"I am challenging you to do it, you asshole."

"Alphahole, remember?" I step back and her hands fall away. "And no, thank you. I do believe I've done my duty toward you. I shagged for nearly 48 hours past your ovulation window. Realistically, I do believe the chances of you conceiving are slim now, so…" I raise a shoulder, "I think I'll pass on the offer, babe."

She lets loose with her hand and I catch her wrist. "Watch it," I growl. "I am going to overlook your error this time because you're still recovering from your fall yesterday."

"Oh, sod off," she snarls. "This contract, or whatever it is that we had, is over now."

"No, it isn't." I click my tongue, "I pumped you up with my cum, the results of which are still unknown. In return, you're going to come with me to see my family, and we have another 29 days within which to try again. Besides, we are getting married, aren't we?"

"You're crazy." She tosses her hair over her shoulder, "You only came once where it would be useful. The rest of the time you were just playing around, using all sorts of other ways to get you and me off, but not in a way that would impregnate me."

"Are you denying that I came inside you and that you could be pregnant as we speak?"

She sets her lips.

"That's what I thought." I look her up and down, "Suddenly, everything is clear to me, Sparks."

"Don't call me that."

"Sparks." I smirk and she makes a sound deep in her throat.

My dick instantly twitches. Why is it that the more I annoy her, the more I seem to like her? That spirit inside of her... My God... It seduces me like nothing else ever has.

"As I was saying, after yesterday's escapade, it's clear to me that you need a keeper."

"What I need is to have my head examined that I was ever attracted to you."

"So, you admit it then?"

"What?"

"That you find me attractive."

"I find gorillas attractive." She tosses her head. "Doesn't mean anything."

"It means something that you proposed to me."

"I'll never live that down, will I?" She flicks her hair over her shoulder. "Put it down to temporary insanity."

"Or clarity? Maybe that's the only time you were thinking straight?"

She lowers her hands to her sides, fixes me with her gaze, "What do you want me to say? That yes, I did think we had a connection? In fact, yesterday when I was alone on that ledge and waiting for you to return, I promised myself that if I made it back in one piece, I'd tell you the truth about what I felt. And then, when you rescued me and carried me back in your arms and took care of me, I was sure that the connection between us was more than sex. But then, you have to go and make a complete wreck of everything with your over-the-top dominance."

"That's me, sweetheart. I can't apologize for what I am."

She throws up her hands, "Jesus, you take my breath away, you know that?"

"I'd always suspected it. Thank you for confirming it." I widen my smile and she curls the fingers of her palms into fists at her sides.

I click my tongue, "Don't even think about it."

"Argh." She throws up her hands. "Let's just agree to disagree, shall we?"

"What-bloody-ever." I yawn. "Get dressed, will you? I don't want to be late for lunch."

32

Karina

Half an hour later, we're on his yacht, which honestly, doesn't look much worse for wear. Apparently, it's sturdier than I had assumed.

On the other hand, I had given the alphahole steering this vessel too much credit, and for all the wrong things. For some reason, I'd thought that behind that callous exterior of his, beats a heart that is much more sensitive. Surely, those little glimpses of affection he'd shown me, that tenderness and caring that he sometimes revealed… There's more of that where it came from, right?

I bite into the sandwich that he'd handed over to me, along with the bottle of orange juice that he'd carried with him. When I'd refused to take it, he'd simply reminded me to think of the possible life I may carry.

I flatten my palm to my stomach. Bloody hell, I couldn't be pregnant, could I? I don't feel any different, but then, how is one supposed to feel in the days following conception?

And if I am? What then? Would the sham marriage we are pursuing turn out to be real? Why the hell does he still want to go through with it, anyway?

I stare at the man who stands on the deck. He's wearing his jacket and boots, with a cap perched on his unruly hair. He steers the boat with a firm hand... Just as he had pulled me up the cliff-side without hesitation. And those terms of endearment he had used after that? No, I hadn't imagined that. He feels something for me, but he is fighting it. What is it that holds him back from sharing the real reason for his bad mood, anyway?

I walk up the steps from the cabin and onto the deck. As I draw abreast of him, I smooth my hands down my jeans... A pair borrowed from him which, despite having been cinched in at the waist with a piece of rope that he'd loaned me, is perched precariously low on my hips. I also had to roll up the legs to almost half the normal length. And the shirt is so big, it swallows me. I'm not fit for company. When I'd told him, he'd said that his family wouldn't care.

Men. Honestly. No way, am I going anywhere without the proper attire.

When I'd insisted, he'd relented. He'd said that we would stop at a shop on the way to his family's place, where I could pick up some new clothes.

That's something, I suppose. A minor victory, but still, he'd ceded to me. One step at a time.

I stop next to him, peer through the windshield at the stretch of water ahead of us. "How much longer?" I ask.

"We should be docking in half an hour," he replies.

"Does your family know that we are coming?"

"They know that *I* am coming."

"Of course." I snort. "Thanks for the heads-up."

"Anytime." His lips twist. "You don't have to worry yourself about the visit."

"Yeah, it's only every day that I go to meet the family of my fake husband, soon to be my real husband—which would make them my fake-real to-be in-laws, so yeah, and by the way, I could already be pregnant with his child...or not..."

I draw in a breath, and he chuckles. "That's some twisted shit, right there, you've got yourself into, Sparks."

"You're telling me." I turn to him, when my phone begins to ping with incoming messages. Guess we are back within reach of the non-satellite networks then?

Not that he'd have refused to let me use the satellite phone if I'd asked. Except, that would have meant that he'd listen in on my conversations, which is not what I wanted.

"Umm, I need to make a call," I venture.

"Not stopping you," he replies, his voice preoccupied.

"I'm going to step out."

"Suit yourself." He turns to fiddle with the dials on his dash.

Jerk, could've pretended that he wanted my company for a little longer, right?

I flounce out and back into the bedroom on the far end of the boat, then close the door and lock it behind me for good measure.

I call up Samuel, my right-hand person, who confirms to me that everything is fine. Clients are all happy, there's nothing pending, no fires to put out, or if there were, they've already been resolved. Huh? So, guess I wasn't missed at all? A heavy feeling invades my stomach. Yeah, this is what I've been dedicating my days and nights to; for building my business and my team. Apparently, I've done a thorough job of it, because my company can run itself without my direct involvement for a few days. I draw in a breath. No one is indispensable; I know that. But this is my enterprise; so, you'd think things could have, at least, collapsed a *little* when I wasn't there to directly steer things along, right?

I bite the inside of my cheek. Now, I am being childish. It's a good thing that my business is on track. When I have kids, if I need to work remotely or go part-time for a while, it means I'll be able to do that without the work suffering. I bid him goodbye and hang up before he can ask me about my holiday—or lack thereof.

Then I dial Isla's number.

"Heyyy youuu!" She comes on the line breathless, "Where have you been? I've been trying to reach you, but I kept getting an out-of-range message."

"That's because I was."

"Oh?" Her voice comes through clearer. "Just took you off the speaker."

I hear voices in the background, which recede.

"Where are you?"

"At a wedding rehearsal, and OMG, this bridezilla is so annoying. She just found out that her friend got engaged as well and is planning to get married this year."

"So, what's the problem?"

"Apparently, it's her special year, and not just a day. The woman's convinced that her friend is getting married to steal her thunder." Isla snorts. "Because no one else can have a life at the same time as her, right?"

I hear the sound of something crashing.

"What was that?"

"She just yanked the table cloth from the table and all the crockery was on it," Isla says, her voice calm.

"At least, there was no food on the table, or as Ari would say, that would be a travesty."

"Ari?"

"I mean Arpad."

"So, it's like that, hmm?"

"That's not why I called you."

"Are you with him now?"

"What if I am?"

"You're definitely with him," she crows. "Give it up, girlfriend. So, you finally did it, didn't you?"

"Did what?"

"Want me to spell it out for you?" She laughs. "Give it up, babe. You know I won't stop asking you about it until you do."

I blow out a breath, "Fine, fine," I grouse, "I'm with the asshole aboard his yacht."

"I knew it," she yells. "Fist bump, fist bump."

"It's nothing to celebrate, though."

"Of course, it is," she sings out. "Ari and Kari making out on a yachty."

"Yachty?" I wince. "Really? What are you? Ten?"

"Just soooo happy that you two finally decided to do it."

"And how," I mutter under my breath, but she catches it.

"That's what I want to know. Details, girlfriend."

"No way," I reply, horrified. "I am not going to share details about my sex life with you."

"Aww, party pooper."

"That's me." I shuffle my feet, then walk over to the large window of the cabin and glance outside.

"At least, tell me if it was everything you expected?"

"It was...." I stare at the shore that I can now see in the distance, "different."

"Different?" she yells. "That's all you're going to give me? Come on, take pity on someone who's been living vicariously through the exploits of all you women who've been hooking up with the Seven."

"Why don't you get one of them for yourself?"

"Nope, no way, nada," she protests. "Those a-holes are way too possessive for me. I like someone who gives me my space, you know?"

"That's why you've been eyeing up the only man who'd possibly beat the Seven at their own game?"

There's silence, then she groans, "Not you as well?"

"So, you know who I am talking about?" I chuckle.

"Erm…" she clears her throat, "who were you talking about?"

"First you," I insist. It's delightful how quickly I've managed to distract her. Whew.

"Yeah, okay, Liam…the fierce-as-fuck, sexy as-a-delicious-grooms-man, mean-as-a-bride-to-be-before-her-wedding, Kincaid."

I laugh. "Those are some interesting comparisons you have there."

"That's what comes of organizing weddings for a living." She continues, "I have the caricatures of those I've encountered on my brain. I'm afraid it's turning me into a cynic."

"Cynical, and you?" I shake my head. "Nah, you're the most optimistic woman I have ever met. I mean, come on, you have to be, to put together as many weddings as you have and still keep your sense of humor, not to mention your energy levels."

"Hmm," she grunts, "why are you buttering me up like I am a three-tiered wedding cake?"

"Aww, come on. Can't I compliment a friend?"

"You don't do compliments, Karina." I sense the smile in her words.

"What do you mean?" I twirl a strand of hair around my fingers. "Haven't I been complimentary of you in the past? Or Julia? Or Summer?"

"Umm, no?"

"Hold on," I stiffen, "are you saying that I am unfeeling?"

"No, no," she protests. "On the contrary, it's clear to us that you feel a lot. You tend to have it all bottled inside, which is fine. It's the way you are you. It's why, when you say something, we all end up listening. We know it's significant."

"You make me sound… " I chew on my lower lip, "like a reserved, stuck-up bitch."

"You don't come across as reserved or stuck up. More like cautious, like you take your time getting to know people before you open up to them."

"Hmm." I hunch my shoulders, not sure what to make of it. I do take my time getting to know people before I trust them. Which is why my reaction to Mr. Grumpy pants is a complete mystery. I thought I hated him... And then, at the first opportunity, I'd pretty much agreed to sleep with him...and...and... "I proposed to him."

"Wait...? What?" There's the sound of something crashing.

"Isla?" I frown. "Isla? You there?"

I hear the sound of footsteps then more thumps. "I... I'm here," she finally says.

"You okay?"

"More to the point, are you okay?"

"I'm not sure." I walk over to the bed... The bed where he fucked me. The covers are still a mess, with dents in the middle of each pillow, indicating that, clearly, it had been a couple who had shared this space not too long ago. I sink down onto the mattress. "It's why I called you."

"And here I thought you were calling to say 'hi' to me and check in how my day was going."

"Of course," I swallow, "that too... I mean... I... Ah." Tears knock at the backs of my eyes. Fuck. The hormones I'd been injecting myself with in advance of the IUI are clearly messing me up.

"And...and...before that, I asked him to father my child."

"You did what?" Her voice rises in pitch.

"Yeah..." I nod, "I was scheduled to get artificially inseminated, only instead of making it to my appointment, I ended up being stuck on the yacht with Arpad."

"So, you asked him to step in?"

"Pretty much."

"And... uh... How did your proxy jizz maker perform?" There's a hint of laughter in her voice.

"Can't complain," I mumble. "And now you're having fun at my expense?"

"No, babe. Of course, not. It's just, you have to admit, as stories go...and trust me, I've heard some pretty crazy shit from each of the other women as they got together with one of the Seven... But your story—" She blows out a low whistle.

I press the heel of my palm into my forehead. "That bad, huh?"

"It's…up there with how Harry met Sally or Ennis and Jack in *Brokeback Mountain* or Blake and Dan in *Gossip Girl* or…"

"I get the picture," I say hastily. "So," I jump up and begin to pace, "what do you think I should do?"

"What do you want to do?"

"I don't know what I want to do; that's why I'm asking you."

"Bullshit," she snaps, "of course, you do."

"No, I don't." I pull the phone away from my ear then speak into the mouthpiece, "Are you going to give me the benefit of your advice or what?"

I hold the phone to my ear again, and she blows out a breath.

"Do you want to walk away from him?"

"I'm not sure."

"Do you want to stay with him?"

"Not sure either."

"Maybe you should give it some time. Perhaps you're not ready to make the decision yet?"

"May…be." I stop again by the window. "There are times I want to punch his face, other times I want to kiss it… But most of the time I want to—"

"—Be close to him?"

"Not quite…" I bite the inside of my cheek. "I admit, I don't want to give up this chance of getting pregnant, you know? It's the one thing I have always wanted, a kid of my own."

"You're brave, wanting to do this by yourself."

"Or a coward?" I raise a shoulder. "It seems less stressful if I don't have a man to deal with. Besides, this way, I get to do what's right for the kid without always having to fight it out with the father."

"Or maybe, you and the father would discuss it and arrive at a decision that would benefit the child the most?"

"Are you trying to push me in his direction?"

"Hey," she protests, "you asked me for my opinion."

"You're not in favor of my bringing up a child on my own?"

"You're strong enough to do anything, including having a family by yourself without a man." Isla hesitates, "I guess, me personally, though… I can't see myself doing it without a partner. Maybe I am old-fashioned that way. I want security, and the man I marry needs to be able to provide that, above everything else."

"And love?" I chew on my lower lip. "What about finding love? Don't you want that?"

She laughs, "I knew you were a closet romantic."

"I'm not."

"Of course, you are." She snickers. "The tougher career-minded ones are always the ones who fall the hardest."

"Hey," I protest, "I thought you were on my side."

"I am, babe. It's why I am telling you to follow your heart."

"Like that's going to help me?" I huff.

"Why don't you bide your time? Go with the flow, see how things turn out, you'll know when you'll know."

"Right." I hang up, then turn toward the door. Guess I've put this off long enough. It's time to go out there and face the sullen beast.

I square my shoulders and head for the door.

33

Arpad

"Would you like something to drink, Sir?"

I glance up from where I've been tracking my investments on my phone. We are in the most exclusive boutique in Lille. One that showcases British designers—something unusual when you're on French soil—and which is why my grandmother loves to come here.

"A hot chocolate, maybe, Sir?" she prompts.

I glare at the saleswoman, "Do I look like the type who drinks hot chocolate?"

"Yes, Sir. I mean, no, Sir." She blinks rapidly. "I mean—"

"Whiskey," I snap, "hold the ice."

"Of course, Sir." She turns and scampers out.

"Still frightening the hired help, I see?" Karina drawls. "Why don't you pick on someone your own size?"

"You mean like…" I take in her outfit and stare and stare, "like you?"

"Like the dress?" She juts out a hip, then props her hand on it.

"Like it?" I drag my gaze down the modest neckline that hints at cleavage, though I know that the fabric covers the most luscious tits I have ever laid eyes on. The belt that's cinched in at the waist, except I know that underneath it is the smoothest belly, with the delicate nip of her belly button. The flare of her hips, that no dress in the world can hide. Stocking clad legs, and on her feet, she wears delicate ankle-length boots.

I frown and she straightens. "What's wrong with it?" She looks down at herself.

"You're showing too much flesh."

"What?" She gapes. "This is a long-sleeved dress."

"It's too short."

"It's goes to my knees."

"Ankle length," I nod, "Get an ankle length one."

She stares, "Are you serious?"

"No, actually," I snap my fingers, "something that comes to your toes." Yes, that's better. That way, no one can catch a glimpse of her gorgeous ankles either

"You've lost it." She turns and walks into the changing room. I jump up and follow her, close the door to the space and lock it.

She freezes, turns around. "What are you doing here?"

"What do you think?" I take a step forward, "I think we should continue with our original plan of getting you pregnant."

She glances around the space, "Here?"

I nod, "Right, here."

She stiffens, "We don't have time."

"Ordinarily, I'd say I need more time, but in this instance, considering how luscious you look in that dress —" I close the distance between us and she puts up her palms.

"This is just a simple, everyday wear outfit, you know?"

"But on you," I stare down at her chest, "it looks fucking incredible."

"Why don't you say that to my face," she grumbles.

I tip my chin up, "Sorry, babe. Your tits are just the most gorgeous things I've seen, since the money from my first £1 million pound deal hit my bottom line."

"Are you comparing me to a transaction?"

"I know right?" I shake my head. "What could be more flattering?"

She scowls up at me. "Maybe just appreciating me for what I am?"

"But I do." I stare. "Come on, babe. You're a business woman. You understand the value of money and how important it is, and especially your first big win… There's nothing sweeter than the taste of it, so the very fact that I compared you to that shows how much respect I have for you."

"Respect?" She purses her lips. "Sounds more like you think money can buy anything."

"Can't it?"

"Not me." She tips up her chin. "I have enough of my own; I don't need your cash."

"Only my sperm." I tilt my head. "That's still something I have which you want, and I am ready to give it to you now."

Her cheeks smear. Interesting. The hardnosed business woman I'd first met in LA wouldn't have flinched or blushed at anything. Somehow, the last few days have softened her... There is a glow about her which, surely, has to have come from all the ways I've fucked her, and yet, I want more of her.

I whisper my knuckles down her cheek. "What do you say, Sparks? One for the road?"

She glances past me at the door. "What if someone knocks?"

"They won't."

"How can you be sure?"

I stare at her and she grimaces. "Right, of course, you know the owners."

"That too." I smirk. "Trust me, they'll know when I am in here, I am busy."

"Have you brought other women here?"

I frown. "Only my grandmother, and I've never been inside this changing room before."

She frowns. "How do I know you're not lying?"

"One thing you can be sure of, I'll never lie to you. I'll always tell you what I want from you upfront." Only I haven't been able to confess the part I'd played in changing the course of her life thus far.

She tips up her chin. "Promise you won't be with another woman for as long as we are together."

"I haven't been with another woman since I saw you in LA."

"But that was...was...a year ago?"

I nod. "Why do you think I couldn't wait to get inside your pants? Speaking of—" I reach forward and tug on the belt of her wraparound dress. It unravels—thank you God for fashion trends. The ends part to reveal the creamy skin of her breasts, the curve of her stomach, the sleek thighs and between them black panties that hint at the flesh within.

"Jesus," I growl, "you're too fucking beautiful."

She raises her hands to my shirt and I shake my head. "Hold them behind your back."

"What?"

"Do it," I snap.

She swallows, then complies. The movement makes her breasts thrust out further. I lower my head to kiss the top of one of her creamy mounds and she shivers. I curl a finger under the waistband of her panties and tug. The fabric snaps and she draws in a breath. I tear off the material, then pocket it, before reaching down to lower the zipper of my jeans.

She glances down, then swallows. "No briefs?"

"I came prepared."

"You mean you planned this when you brought me here—?" She squeaks, for I've hoisted her up so she has no choice but to wrap her legs around my waist. I walk forward until her back is flush with the wall.

Then, cupping her butt, I balance her, before reaching down to position my dick at her entrance.

She tips up her chin, her pupils dilated, her breath coming in short pants.

"Shit, this excites you, doesn't it? The thought of doing it in a place which is only semi-private, where it will be clear to anyone outside that we are here, fucking?"

"Of course, not." She huffs, but her chin trembles. She licks her lower lip and the blood engorges my shaft.

"I need to be inside you, Sparks," I growl. "Now."

She tilts her hips forward and the crown of my cock breaches her. So fucking soft, so hot. A groan tears out of me. Her chest rises and falls, her tits spilling out from her bra.

"Touch your breasts," I urge her.

One arm still about my shoulders, she reaches up with the other to cup her breast, then pinches her nipple. That's when I plunge inside her. She gasps, her hips flattening against the wall as I thrust into her again and again.

"Ari," she moans and my cock lengthens further.

Every time I pound her, her tits jiggle, and fuck me, if it isn't the most erotic sight I've seen.

"Pinch your other nipple," I command.

She obliges instantly. Perhaps because she's caught up in this combined lust that we share? The one time that we don't need to negotiate or jostle for power. When I can give her pleasure and she can take. When the only thing separating us is the skin between us. Nothing else.

She tweaks the other pebbled nub, and a groan tumbles from her lips.

"Harder," I snap. "Pretend it's my hands doing the job."

Her knuckles whiten and she increases the pressure on the hardened nipple just as I tilt my hips and impale her. Her body bucks and she digs her heels into the curve of my butt. I squeeze the backs of her thighs, yank her forward as I tilt my hips and thrust into her again and again.

She shudders, color smears her cheeks, and a bead of sweat trickles down her throat. I lean down and lick it up. "Oh, Arpad," she moans. "Please… please…"

"What is it?" I raise my head, and peer into her eyes, "What do you want?"

"I want to—"

I plunge into her with enough force that the ridge of my pelvis grinds down on her clit.

"Oh…" she gasps, "oh, I'm going to—"

"Come with me," I hold her gaze, "only me."

I thrust into her as her back curves, her eyes roll back in her head and she opens her mouth to scream. I close my mouth over hers, absorb the sound as I come inside her.

I hold up her weight, thrust into her a few more times as aftershocks grip her.

Her body slumps and I widen my stance to support her. My shoulders burn and my thigh muscles tense under our combined weight. It reminds me of how I'd pulled her up from the ledge at the side of the hill. How I'd almost lost her. Never again. I bend down and press my lips to her forehead. "It's time to go, Sparks."

She mumbles under her breath, and I kiss her upturned nose. "Yeah, nothing I'd rather do than curl up with you in bed, but I'm afraid we've got to see this through."

I lower her legs to the ground, then pull out of her and step back. Our joined cum slides down her inner thigh. I glance around, then grab a scarf from a peg on the wall and press it to her pussy. I clean her up and she stirs. She looks down, then gasps, "That…that's a Hermes scarf."

"So?"

"It's expensive."

"I can afford it."

I drop the scarf on the ground then hold out my hand to her, "Come on, let's get you dressed."

34

Karina

I run my fingers down the soft fabric of my dress—my shoulder-to-toe, knit, wool dress, which he'd picked out for me. I'd refused; he'd insisted. I'd begun to protest and he'd asked me to try it on first. I had, and you know what? When I looked at myself in the mirror, I liked it. The long length highlights my figure, brings out the curve of my hips, and that, combined with the long sleeves and high neck, showcases my breasts in a way which is demure yet alluring.

I'd also managed to refresh my make up—making sure to cover all remaining evidence of the headwound—just as he'd appeared behind me in the mirror, a tumbler of whiskey in one hand. The other, he'd placed on my hip possessively.

"Well?" He'd smirked at my reflection in the mirror.

"It's not bad," I'd finally offered, and he'd laughed.

"You look magnificent, Sparks."

"And I'm covered from head to toe," I'd grumbled.

"Good," he'd met my gaze in the mirror, "your body is only for my delectation."

A thrill of lust had swept down my spine, and something else... A sensation of warmth had suffused me.

It feels good to be the object of his possessiveness, this single-minded focus of his, a tractor beam that bathes me in its spotlight and highlights me to myself in a way nothing ever has before. How strange. Did I actually need to be measured by someone else's gaze? Isn't my opinion of myself enough anymore? That I'd once dressed to feel good, had groomed for my comfort, and carved a path through the world for my self-confidence... Why does all of that seem unimportant compared to being at the cynosure of his attention?

I'd pulled away, then brushed past him and headed for the door. "We're getting late." I'd pointed out, and he hadn't protested.

I'd pulled out my wallet and handed over my credit card, but the sales woman had simply said that it had all been taken care of.

Of course, it had.

I'd snorted and his grin had widened as the sales woman had walked away. "You didn't think I was going to let you pay for it, did you?"

"I can afford it," I'd huffed.

"So can I, and I much prefer if I bought it for you."

"Why, so you can make me a kept woman?"

"Can't I buy you something because I want to?"

"A generous thought from you?" I widen my gaze. "Why don't I believe it?"

"Better believe it, babe. Where you're concerned, my thoughts run the entire spectrum from lust to anticipation to dominance to—" he'd leaned in close enough for our eyelashes to touch, "your submission."

"Which you'll never have. That, I promise."

"We'll see." He'd straightened, taken my arm, and I'd allowed him to lead me out and into the waiting car—a Porsche, which he'd had waiting for him at the marina... Apparently, he'd called ahead and had it readied for him.

Oh, and did I mention that he'd bought out half the shop? Or so it seems, given the number of bags they'd loaded into the back of the car. I had protested, but he'd simply countered that since I'm playing the role of his wife, I need the clothes to look the part. I have no argument for that.

Also, yeah, I have a weakness for designer wear. Although I do prefer to buy them for myself... Besides, this is an entire freakin' wardrobe. WTF? The mind boggles. So, this is what unlimited money can get you? Not that I am lacking for anything; but in comparison to Mr. A'hole here, I may as well as be as poor as…a crow; and I am not talking about the yoga pose by the same name, either.

I shoot him a sideways glance, take in that stern profile, the hooked nose, that square jaw that should have warned me of his imperious nature. "Were you always like this?"

"Like what?"

"Always confident that you'd get your own way.

His lips kick up. "Especially when I'm with you, Sparks."

"No, seriously," I huff, "have you always commanded people, confident that they'd do your bidding?"

"After the incident," he stares through the windshield, "the Seven of us fought a lot. Damian and me, in particular. We'd been locked up together by our captors, who liked to pit us against each other. We had to fight until one or both of us lost consciousness. It became a game for the two of us, how to keep hitting each other, without hurting the other too much, but making it believable enough for our kidnappers to buy it. When they caught on, Damian took the blame for it, only they didn't spare me."

My heart begins to race. Finally, finally he's beginning to share more about what happened to him.

"What did they do to you?"

"They whipped me."

I draw in a breath.

"Wh…whipped you?"

"They took turns, went at it day and night. They tied me up, strung me up from the ceiling, and whipped me until I'd lose consciousness. Then, when I had recovered, another man would start the process all over again."

"H…how long did that go on for?"

"Days…" he swallows, "weeks maybe… Or so I thought. I found out later it had been closer to ten days."

"Ten days?" I burst out. "Oh my god, Arpad."

He stares straight ahead, "My injuries were only physical, compared to what was done to some of the others."

"What…did they do?"

"That's for them to share."

"Of course," I swallow, "from where I am, though, I wouldn't say that you got off lightly."

He glares at me, "I don't want your pity."

"Oh, I am not pitying you." I swipe my hair over my shoulder. "All I'm saying is that a physical beating like that when you are a child—"

"I was almost a teenager."

"A child," I say firmly. "Something like that scars you for life, and not just physically." I twist my fingers together. "No wonder you need to tie up a woman to get off."

"See, that's where you are mistaken." He turns off the highway. "I was born this way, Sparks. This cruel streak is a part of me. It's what made me resilient enough to withstand what those bastards put me through."

"So, you're saying the very trait that makes you an asshole is the one that's helped you survive thus far?"

He tilts his head.

"So, you don't think your need to tie women up before you fuck them is…unusual?"

"Oh, it's different, all right. And it doesn't take a psychologist to tell me that, clearly, my losing control because of being tied up, is the reason I like to tie up my partners."

"It helps you feel in control?"

"It's the only way I can let go." He slows down at a crossing, then turns right. "I have no doubt that my experience drew me to Kinbaku. It's very tactile, very sensual, more so than other forms of foreplay."

"And here I thought you'd do anything to avoid intimacy." I mutter.

"Who said anything about intimacy?" He smirks, "It's how I prefer to experience pleasure." His eyelids grow hooded, "when I have a woman tied up and splayed open for my delectation, when I know that I am in charge and all it takes is a look," his lips part, "a flick of my fingers on her nipple," his lowers his gaze to my breasts, "the swipe of my tongue up her cunt, to have her writhing and groaning and falling apart under me and asking for more."

"Right." I squeeze my thighs together. Why am I wet again? Because he's revealed the rationale behind his choice of kink…because he's finally shared some of his secrets with me? Or is it because I want him to tie me up again? Heat suffuses my cheeks and I glance out of the window.

We turn into a driveway and I take in the well-maintained lawn, the profusion of flowers that line the flower-beds. My heart begins to thud again. I wipe my damp palms on my thighs. I can do this. I don't need to be nervous. It's only fulfilling my part of the bargain, meeting up with the family of my currently-fake-but-soon-to-be-real husband. I swallow as he eases the car to a stop.

My pulse rate ratchets up. I clutch at my handbag, then glance straight ahead through the windshield.

He reaches over and takes my left palm in between his large hands. "Hey, it's going to be okay."

"You're so clueless, you know that?" I snarl under my breath. "Of course, it will be okay. After I've been given the third degree, no doubt."

"It's not going to be that bad."

"Right," I draw in a breath, "speaking of, what story are we going to give them about us?"

"How about the truth?" He quirks an eyebrow.

"You're joking, right?"

"Why not?" He raises his shoulders, "We met a year ago, in LA, before you came to London and we reconnected. Why would that not be okay?"

I frown, "You know that's not what I am referring to."

"If it's our agreement you're worried about, then relax, we don't have to bring it up at all."

"Fine, easy for you to say." I mutter, "It's not your in-laws that you are going to visit."

He rubs his thumb across my wrist and goosebumps pop on my skin. "I'm sure you'll do great."

I swallow; my throat dries. *Christ, pull it together. You are about to meet his family.* It won't do to entertain carnal thoughts about the man while you do so, right?

He peers into my face, "I promise, it will be fine."

"Fine." I blink at him.

"Fine?" He tilts his head.

"Fine." I nod.

He pulls back his hand and I reach over to open the door. That's when I notice the band on my ring finger.

35

Arpad

Her gaze widens, "Wh…what's this?"

"What does it look like?"

"A ring?" She holds up her fingers. "You placed a ring on my finger?"

"It's been known to happen."

"But why?" She frowns at me. "Not everyone who's married wears a ring."

"It's more convincing this way."

She glances at my hand, "And what about your ring?"

"I don't need one."

She firms her lips. "So as your wife, I am supposed to wear a ring, but as my husband, you don't need to wear one?"

I scratch my jaw and pretend to think, "Sounds about right."

She stares at me. "Only you could take a gesture that could have meant so much, and turn it into something so…so…"

"Real?"

"So dominating," she snaps.

"That's me, babe, and don't forget it."

"Stop it," she snarls. "Why do you insist on being so offensive?"

I tilt my head. "This is me, being myself."

"You don't say." She fingers the ring on her finger, "Don't you think you're taking this charade too far?"

"Not far enough." I get out of the car, walk around to open her door, but she's already out and standing.

I hold out my hand, "Shall we?"

She brushes past me and I let her lead the way… This once. We head for the door as it swings open.

"Arpad." My father stands in the doorway. His full head of hair, is more flecked with grey than when I last saw it. His frame seems to be leaner than before, like he's lost weight, or is that my imagination? He glances from me to Karina and his forehead furrows. "And you are…?"

"I am his…" she hesitates.

"This is Karina, my wife." I pull abreast with her, and wrap my arm around her shoulders.

"Ah." His gaze widens. "Wife?" He glances to me. "A little bit of advance notice would have been welcome."

I tilt my head.

He nods toward Karina, "I'm Philippe, Arpad's father. I'm happy to welcome you into my family." He turns to me, "And you? Why are you here?"

"It's nice to see you," I snap.

Karina draws in a sharp breath. I ignore her. So perhaps I should have warned her a little about our family dynamics, but if I had, she'd have never agreed to this arrangement. Besides, nothing like full immersion, all at once, right? Get thrown off the deep end and you have no choice but to swim.

Footsteps approach, then my younger brother appears at my father's shoulder, "You made it," he drawls, then he glances at Karina, "and this is…"

"Karina," my father replies, "his wife."

"Wife?" He blinks, then turns to her. "You actually agreed to marry him?" His lips curl. "Will wonders never cease? My brother, the asshole, confirmed bachelor, finally meets his match, then?"

"The obnoxiousness is a family trait, then?" Karina scowls at him.

My brother seems surprised, then he chuckles. His features split into a grin.

"You're Declan Beauchamp, the film actor," she states.

He tilts his head, "Guilty as charged."

He holds out his hand and Karina takes it. He turns her palm over then presses his lips to her knuckles, "Welcome to our dysfunctional family. I promise you'll never find things boring here."

I stiffen at that little gesture, then place my arm around Karina. Declan straightens. He stares between us and his grin grows wider. I glare down at where he still holds Karina's hand in his, then at his face. He laughs, but releases her hand.

"I assume you just got married?" He straightens. "Shouldn't you be on your honeymoon, or," he turns to me, "did you decide it was best to get the family drama out of the way upfront before you head off?"

"Family drama?" She squints at him.

My father shoots him a sideways glance. "That's enough, Declan." He steps aside. "I suppose you had better come in."

I purse my lips. "Never let it be said that you were lacking in manners, Father."

Karina hesitates, and I guide her forward with a hand on the small of the back. She glances over her shoulder, "The luggage —"

"The staff will get it," I reply.

She nods, follows my brother as he leads the way into the spacious living room. The sliding doors at the far end open onto the garden. In front of it, in an armchair, is the woman who's the primary reason for this charade.

Karina's steps slow, and I walk past her to reach the other woman. I sink down to my knee in front of her, take her slim hand in mine, "Grandmama," I say, "how are you?"

Her face splits in a huge smile. "Arpad, my boy." She frames my face with her palms, then leans forward and kisses my forehead. "It's wonderful to see you." She leans back and peers into my features, "You look good." Her forehead wrinkles. "Something's different about you."

"It is?"

She nods, "I can't put my finger on it, but you seem... Happier? More content?"

"Maybe it's because he's gotten married since we last saw him?" Declan's voice sounds from behind me.

"Married?" Grandmama gasps at the same time that I shoot him a dirty look over my shoulder.

"Thanks for nothing," I growl.

Declan chuckles, "I aim to please, bro."

Karina walks up to stand next to me. "I'm Karina," she says, "I'm his—"

"Wife." Grandmama holds out her hand and Karina takes it. "Help me up," Grandmama commands.

I straighten to help her and she waves me away. "Karina will help me," she declares.

Right.

I step back and Karina helps Grandmama to her feet. The older woman hooks her arm in the nook of Karina's. "Come, my girl, walk with me to the dining room."

The two women move forward.

Karina shoots me a sideways glance and I nod at her.

"I won't bite," Grandmama chuckles, "and your husband will be right behind us."

"Not my—"

I stiffen, and Karina flinches. "I mean, of course, I would only be too happy to accompany you."

Grandmama's forehead furrows and she glances between us. "Not used to calling him your husband yet?" She laughs lightly. "It took me a little while after I married Francis to get used to my new status, too." She pats Karina's hand, "Come dear, why don't you tell me about yourself?"

The women walk ahead and I blow out a breath. I am sure Karina can handle herself. She is smart and can think on her feet, one of the qualities that had attracted me to her right away. So why am I so concerned about her right now? I take a step forward and Declan snickers, "Can't let the woman out of your sight, eh?"

"Nothing of the sort," I mutter.

"You could have fooled me." He chuckles. "When did you get married anyway?"

"None of your business."

"Didn't realize you were serious about anyone," he persists.

"Lots of things you don't know about me," I snap back.

"Likewise, bro, likewise." He brushes past me and follows in the wake of the women.

I take a step forward when. "Arpad?" My father calls.

Oh, fuck. I know that tone of his voice. It normally means I am in trouble, only this time, he doesn't know just how deep I am.

I slow my steps and he catches up with me. "Hold on a second, my boy, what's the rush?"

I glance in the direction the women have gone.

"Can't stay away from the wife, huh?"

"Something like that," I mutter.

"I don't recall you being involved with anyone."

"It was sudden."

"Like all of your decisions in life, huh?"

"What's that supposed to mean?" I turn to him. "If you want to tell me something, why don't you come out and say it?"

He stares up at me, and his gaze intensifies. He draws in a breath then grips my shoulder, "All I'm saying, is that some advance notice, a phone call that you'd decided to get married, would not have been amiss."

"I'm here now, aren't I?" I declare, my tone belligerent. Jesus, a few seconds back under the roof of my family; and I am already relapsing to my younger self. "Look," I drag my fingers through my hair, "everything happened quickly. It was one of those things where my instinct seemed to get away from me, and I followed. But I came as soon as I could."

"And I'm glad you did." He grips my shoulder. "I'm glad you've finally decided to settle down. If your mother were here... She'd have been thrilled to welcome your bride." He steps back, slides his hand into his pocket. "Not a day goes by when I don't miss her." He glances some-where beyond my shoulder. "Every day, I regret the opportunities I lost to tell her that I loved her. If I could only turn back the clock, I'd have never spent the time away from her that I did to grow my business."

I hunch my shoulders. It's another reason I'll never forgive those behind the incident. The shock of those few days when I'd been kidnapped and she'd feared I was dead, had brought on a heart attack. By the time I'd been rescued and returned home, it had been too late. I never got to see my mother again. The fucking bastards who were behind my kidnapping also took her from me. When I finally track them down, I am going to make sure they pay.

"You were a good husband," I mutter. "You have your faults, and while I wouldn't say you were the best father, when it came to her, you did your best by her."

My father winces. "Thanks for the backhanded compliment... I guess."

"You're welcome." I raise my shoulders. "Why are you telling me all this now?"

"Because," he widens his stance, "I don't want you to make the same mistakes I did. I want you to understand what's most important in life and when you find out, I want you to hold onto it. I want to make sure you use every moment you have to its utmost."

"You mean her?" I jerk my head in the direct of the dining room

"Your wife." He nods. "If you do love her, and I believe you do," he peers into my eyes, "then you'll try to make her happy the way I tried with your mother. It takes the love of a good woman to ground a man, and not everyone is lucky enough to have that."

I shuffle my feet. "Right."

"If you've found the love of your life, then I hope you'll grab this opportunity with both hands and not let go of it. It's your one chance to become a decent human being."

"You mean, it's a chance to undo all the years of harm your neglect caused us?"

He pales, then raises his hand. "You hate me. I understand where you are coming from."

"Do you?" I peer into his eyes. "Do you understand how it is for a boy of twelve to return from an ordeal that turned his life upside down, only to find that his mother is dead? Then, his father decides to withdraw from the world instead of trying to be there for his children?"

"I was there," he grinds out, "I provided for the both of you, ensured you had the best education, that you didn't want for anything."

"A-n-d that's the problem. You assumed money would compensate for the lack of family."

"Is that what you're doing now? Using your money to buy yourself the family you never had."

Anger pumps through my veins. I raise my hand, take a step forward, when, "Arpad," my brother's voice calls out from the doorway, "Grandmama's asking for you."

36

Karina

Arpad walks in, his features stonier than usual. He takes the chair next to me. His father moves to the other side of the table and sits down in a chair the farthest from Arpad. Tension between the two of them stretches. The hair on the back of my neck prickles. I glance between them. What had they been talking about? Is this kind of fighting between the two of them normal? It certainly feels that way. Declan quirks an eyebrow at me from next to Philippe.

As security consultant to the Seven, I know about their families too. So, I'd been aware of Declan's status as the most promising upcoming star in the world. Since his lead role in a series which had launched over Christmas, he is the epitome of many a girl's dream. The internet is abuzz with speculation about his next movie, his personal life, what he had for lunch, his workout routine, you name it. I'd known all this, yet not been prepared to meet him face to face. Guess fame can do that. It turns ordinary men into superstars, so when you meet them in real life, you're convinced there's something different about them.

I take a sideways glance at my not-yet-but-soon-to-be-husband… To be honest, there's no resemblance between Declan and Arpad. If anything, Arpad seems more handsome to me, with that brooding gaze, thick eyebrows, the pouty lips of his that I'd do anything to feel against mine. Arpad glances up, holds my gaze. I flush, look back to Declan.

"So how is it to be famous overnight?" I ask

Declan chokes on the water he'd been drinking. He swallows, "I am getting used to it. You know…struggling for ten years to be recognized, going to countless auditions, then boom…" He chuckles. "All of a sudden, one of your TV series is a hit, and suddenly everyone wants a slice of you."

"Isn't that good? I mean, isn't that what most actors want—fame?"

He grimaces. "It comes with the territory, but that's not why I got into acting."

"No, it was to get women throwing themselves at you, no doubt." Arpad snorts.

Declan grins. "You are just envious because I am better looking than you."

"And you're so full of shit." He glowers at his brother.

"Why don't we let Karina decide?"

"Me?" I pause, "Oh no, I am not being dragged into this."

"Come on," Declan prompts, "look at him." He jerks his chin at the alphahole. "Now me," he gestures to his face. "Who do you think is better looking, huh?"

I stare between them. "Hmm." I chew on my lower lip. "If I had to pick one person," I glance from Arpad's face to Declan's then back to Arpad's, "it would have to be—"

Arpad's face grows thunderous.

"I think," I bite down on the inside of my cheek, "I think you're better looking." I nod at Declan.

"Aha!" Declan crows.

Every muscle in Arpad's body stiffens. He glares down at me.

"But," I glance up at him and his gaze intensifies, "but my husband has more presence and more charisma. He'd beat you outright when it comes to personality and magnetism."

Arpad's eyes gleam. The skin around his eyes tightens, then he reaches up to touch my cheek. "Thank you," he whispers.

"You're welcome," I half smile back.

"Aww…come on, Karina," Declan protests, "that's not fair."

"Life's not fair." I turn to face him. "Not that you have anything to complain about, Mr. Flavor-of-the-month-hot-shot-film star."

"Flavor of the month?" He chokes. "You sure do know how to come to the point, don't you?"

"It's the trait I like most about her." Arpad wraps his arm about my chair and pulls me closer.

Heat flushes my cheeks. I stay frozen, trying not to lean back further. If I do, I am sure to brush against his arm, and that's only going to turn me on. Something I definitely don't want happening here in front of his family.

"Do you now?" Declan stares at Arpad. "It's certainly a change from your other girlfriends."

I gape. Did he actually say that?

Arpad's muscles tense and he leans forward in his seat. "That was unnecessary and disrespectful. Apologize to Karina," he growls.

"Declan Beauchamp," Grandmama snaps, "I raised you better than to insult a lady."

The brothers stare at each other, then Declan blows out a breath, "I'm sorry." He clears his throat and turns to me, "I didn't mean to come across as so rude." He drums his fingers on the table. "I am afraid your husband rubs me the wrong way."

Arpad scoffs, "At least, find a better excuse."

"Yeah, no." Declan chuckles. "You know we bring out the worst in each other, brother."

"And the best too," Grandmama interrupts from the head of the table. "When you are family, you are bound to fight and then have each other's backs when the going gets tough. Remember that, boys. When things get hairy, it's your family—made or blood—that will be there for you."

"Like the Seven?" I pipe up.

Grandmama's eyes gleam. "The Seven." She takes a sip of water "A kinship that can only grow more solid with age." She turns to Arpad. "They'll also be there for you, when you most need them," she says. "Along with Declan, of course."

"Like I have a choice," Declan quips.

"You always have a choice," Grandmama raises a small bell next to her and rings it, "but your bark is worse than your bite." She turns to Arpad. "When you need him most, he'll be there to help. That's what family does."

The door to the dining room opens and two members of the staff walk in. They're dressed in uniform—of course they are, how had I forgotten just how rich Arpad's family is?—and place plates in front of Philippe and Grandmama. Once we are all served, I dip my spoon into the soup, a bacon and mint combination I've never had before. "This is delicious." I scoop up some more.

"You should tell our chef that; she'd be very happy. She's the one who taught Arpad to cook," Grandmama replies.

I shoot a sideways glance at Arpad, trying to imagine him learning anything from anyone. I mean, of course, he'd gone to school and had teachers, but somehow, it's easier to think of him as having arrived fully formed and growling at everyone he sets eyes on. I snicker to myself, then turn it into a cough.

Arpad meets my gaze, and frowns. He pours a small amount of wine into a glass for me, then fills his own.

Grandmama raises her glass, "To Arpad and Karina."

Philippe raises his without comment.

"To the woman who turned my brother into an adoring lovesick Romeo," Declan jokes.

Arpad makes a snarling sound low in his throat. I touch his arm, "He's only trying to wind you up."

Arpad turns to me, "You sounded so British when you said that." He smirks.

"Maybe your influence is rubbing off on me."

"Is it?" He holds my gaze and the air between us thickens. My core clenches. I shift about in the seat to make myself more comfortable.

"So, Karina," Grandmama asks, "your name... Is it... Slavic, in origin?"

"Russian." I turn back to my soup. "Both sets of my grandparents immigrated to the US. My parents were born in the US, so I am American." I raise a shoulder.

"But you're in touch with your roots?"

She raises her soup spoon and drinks from it.

"I guess." I stare down into the depths of the liquid in my bowl. "My father holds onto his culture. He instilled a...respect for his homeland in us."

"Sounds like he was a good father."

"The best." I reach for my wine glass. "He was strict, but a fair parent." I glance sideways in time to see Arpad scowl. What's his problem? He seems like he wants to say something, then changes his mind and goes back to eating.

I bring the wine glass to my nose and sniff it — I'm still not drinking, but I don't want to turn down the wine and raise his family's suspicions that I may be pregnant or trying to get pregnant. I'd even taken a sip when Grandmama had made the toast. Now I indulge in another cautious sip.

The rich flavor coats my tongue. "This is excellent." I stare at the glass, then at the bottle. "Where is it from?"

"My vineyard," Arpad replies.

"You own a vineyard?" I stare at Arpad.

"A few," his lips kick up, "in Napa, in the UK, in Australia, in Argentina —"

"Stop," I frown down at the wine, "I could have sworn this tasted French."

"It is; it's from Burgundy."

"Of course, it is." I set down my glass. "So, do you all meet often for a family lunch?"

Philippe and Arpad stiffen. Declan chuckles. Only Grandmama's features don't change expression. She rings the bell again, then turns to me. "We don't get to dine as a family as often as I would like." She glances around the place, "Hopefully, in the time I have left to live, we'll have a few more such occasions."

"Now, Grandmama," Arpad admonishes, "you're not going anywhere soon."

"You'll outlive all of us," Philippe declares.

"You're healthier than most people in their twenties," Declan bumps his fist into his chest, "me included."

She stares around the table. "You know, my doctor doesn't agree with that prognosis."

There's silence for a beat, then another.

"Now, come on boys, I am not dying that soon either." She chuckles. "Not before I've seen my grandchild." She looks at me.

I swallow. "Right. Of course." I stare down at my plate of food. Is this why he'd agreed to my proposal of his impregnating me so quickly? Had he wanted to use this entire set-up to his own benefit? Of course, he had, and who am I to blame him, when I had done the same? Only, he could have told me up front that there is a bigger reason for his ready acquiescence. After all, if he is doing so because he wants his grand-mother to be happy… Well, I could hardly fault him for that, right? But, typical Arpad, he couldn't come out and tell me his motives clearly. Or he'd simply assumed that it didn't matter if I knew or not. Likely, that was the reason.

The door to the dining room opens again. The same staff comes in, remove our soup bowls, then bring in plates of food covered with stainless steel domes, the kind I've only ever seen in fancy restaurants. Not that this is any less. The food here is better than at many of the Michelin-starred restaurants where I've dined.

They remove the covers with a flourish.

"Roasted Cod in a cream sauce with parsnip puree, shrimp, brown butter, and capers," one of the servers declares.

"Thank you, Hugo." Grandmama beams at him.

"My pleasure." Hugo half bows and departs.

I tuck into my food with gusto, not stopping until my plate is empty. I glance up to find the rest looking at me. "What?"

Arpad grins, glances down at his own plate, which is still almost full.

"Guess I was hungry... And the food is incredible," I say sincerely. "Besides, it's nice to be eating with family, isn't it?"

"It is," Grandmama nods, "and it's refreshing to see a woman eat well."

I laugh. "My father would never let me leave anything on my plate. His military training wouldn't allow him, and besides, he was very careful of any waste."

"And your mother?" Philippe asks.

"She died when I was eighteen." I fold my arms in my lap.

"I am so sorry for your loss, my dear." Grandmama places her fork on her plate.

"Thank you." I murmur.

"Let's have dessert." Grandmama leans toward me, "Then, why don't you and I take a short walk?"

❄ ❄ ❄

Ten minutes later, I trail behind the older woman as we walk through the fading sunshine. She waits for me to catch up, then hooks her arm through mine. We proceed in silence along the garden path. The grass is mowed while evergreen shrubs line either side of the path. We reach a circular conservatory; she pushes open the door and I step in after her. The heat instantly warms my ankles. I follow her until she reaches a wooden swing in the center. She sinks down, then pats the space next to her. I reach her, unbutton my coat, then sit down next to her. The swing moves back and forth as we push back with our legs.

"So, you and Arpad," she finally says, and I brace for the inevitable questioning. This is the lady of the house and someone who Arpad regards very highly. She is the matriarch of the family, and surely, she wants to protect her family.

She turns to me, fixes that blue-grey gaze, so like his — on me.

"How long has this charade been in progress?"

37

———————

Karina

"Excuse me?" I blink.

She tilts her head and stares down her patrician nose. "Arpad is smart and he thinks he can humor me. And bless him, his intentions are all in the right place, I am sure, but I am not that easy to fool."

I blink rapidly, not sure what to say.

"Not that the two of you are not in love —"

"We're —" I bite down on my lip. Shit, what's wrong with me? I am almost blowing our cover here. Why the hell can't I get my story right? It's Arpad, that asshole's, fault. We could have rehearsed before coming here. He could have apprised me about the situation, that his grand-mother was unwell. A detail which hadn't come to light in all the infor-mation I'd had access to so far.

"You were saying?" Grandmama holds my gaze, and those blue-grey eyes of her seem to read all of my secrets.

I glance away, "N...nothing." I swallow. "You were talking about me and Arpad..." my voice trails off.

"And the elaborate front the two of you have constructed for me."

I bite the inside of my cheek. What the hell am I supposed to do? Why had we never discussed this possibility—that our story could have been found out? I glance about the space, taking in the foliage, the flowers—amaryllis, pansies, snapdragons… And orchids, so many orchids. I drag in the sweet scent of the flowers and it's as if I've been transported into an English garden in the middle of summer.

"You're English?"

"British," she replies. "I married a French man, and brought up my children in this house. I've lived here since I got married fifty years ago."

Fifty years. Wow. I glance toward the house we'd just left, then back at her.

"I know what you're thinking." She curves her fingers around the thick rope that connects the swing to the ceiling. "It's such a long time, a lifetime of living, of memories, decades of the world changing and you changing with it, and yet, some things inside stay the same. All gone by in the blink of an eye, a snap of a finger, a flutter of butterflies' wings somewhere in the Amazon, and everything changes. You're no longer a bride of twenty, stepping across the threshold, but a woman at death's door."

"Grandmama—"

She raises her hand. "You don't need to coddle me like the men in there." She jerks her chin toward the house again. "They know the truth, but they avoid it, thinking if they don't acknowledge it, it ceases to be real. But you and I... We know better, don't we? We know that life is short, and we need to make the most of what we have right now in the moment." She peers into my features. "We do, right?"

I hold her gaze and my throat goes dry. This woman... She's way too sharp, more than anyone I've ever met. There's no pulling the wool over her eyes.

Damn Arpad, he should have known there was no way that we could fool her into buying our story. But of course, he wouldn't give anyone credit for being as smart as him. He'd seen an opportunity and taken it, and so had I. And here I am, faced with a dying woman whom I had deceived, straight to her face. Damn. I fill my lungs with the scent of the flowers, then turn to her. "You're right. Arpad and I… We…have … This is an arrangement."

"What kind of an arrangement?"

A hot sensation stabs at my chest. Why the hell is it so difficult to tell her the truth? She's guessed most of it already, so why does it feel like I am, somehow, betraying her and Arpad and myself? Gah! I jump up to my feet and begin to pace. "We, uh, decided that I'd pose as his wife for thirty days, including the duration of this trip, after which, we are getting married for real."

"But you're not sure about it?"

I stare at her features. How did she guess? Am I that bad an actress or is she simply that perceptive?

I play with the ring on my finger. "We've gotten to know each other better over the last few days," I hesitate, "but—"

"You're still not sure about your feelings for him?"

"No...it's not that."

"So, you're not sure if he loves you?"

I open and shut my mouth. How do I explain? That he does feel something for me, somewhere deep down, under the alphahole exterior of his, but... That he's not going to say it.

"Or you know he does, but he hasn't told you so yet?"

I stare at her. Jesus, this woman is frightening. The way she reads my mind, it's as if she knows what I am thinking.

She kicks off again, the swing creaks on its hinges, and her silver hair flies back from her face. For a second, I can imagine her as a young woman, her eyes huge in her unlined face with, her dark hair falling in a cloud about her shoulders. I blink and the mirage disappears. She smiles at me. "I need to share a secret with you."

"You do?"

She nods. "Come," she pats the seat next to her, "sit down with me for a few more minutes."

I retrace my steps, sink down onto the swing.

"You see, men... They are simple creatures."

"They are?" I swallow.

She nods, "They like to eat, to get pissed, then indulge in pissing contests, and to fuck."

My jaw drops.

"What?" She chuckles. "I am old, so I can't use the F word, is that it?"

"No," I twist my fingers together, "of course, not."

"You have to lure them in, you know?"

"O-kay." Where the hell is she going with this?

"You have to show them what they are missing out on, appeal to the caveman in them. Know what I mean?"

I bite down on the inside of the cheek, "Is that what you did? With uh, Mr. Grandmama?"

She laughs. "Absolutely. Given a choice, my Francis would have happily continued his single existence without ever committing. It's just, I knew better."

"You did?"

"Of course. It's why I left him."

Huh? "Then what happened?"

"He came after me, of course, wanted me back. I told him only if he committed to me.

"And he did?"

She swipes her hair over her shoulder. "We were married within the week."

"Wow."

She holds up the ring with the single diamond that graces her ring finger, "I've never taken this off, since that day."

I draw in a breath. "So, you're saying I need to, somehow, play hard to get, show him what he could be missing out on?"

"Now, now, don't go putting words in my mouth. You're a smart woman, aren't you? Surely, you'll figure something out?"

Arpad

I slide my razor down my cheek, then shake it off under the tap. It's an odd time to shave but my whiskers had begun to bother me, and I wanted to shave before we headed out again.

The bathroom door opens and she walks in. She meets my gaze in the mirror, then heads over to the commode at the far end. She pushes down her panties, perches on the ceramic bowl and her piss tinkles down the sides.

What the—? I blink. Did she just do that? The audacity of the woman… The complete comfort she has in her own skin, the way she tilts up her chin and watches me watch her as I stand there with the razor poised half-way to my face. Why the hell do I find this everyday

act of hers so erotic… Not to mention, the domesticity of this scene…
It's mind-blowing, and real, and so natural, so easy. Is this how it would
be if I had her in my life always?

I watch as she tears off a piece of tissue paper, slides her hand under
the skirt of her dress to wipe herself. Then rises to her feet, pulls up her
panties and straightens her dress about her hips. She flushes, then heads
to the sink and washes her hands, before drying them. She turns to
leave and I call out, "Hold on."

She ignores me, and I scowl. As she brushes past me, I grab her arm
and stop her.

"What?" she snaps.

"Don't ignore me."

"And what if I do?"

"Try it and find out."

She peers into my face, then huffs, "Fine, I'm here, aren't I? What
do you want from me?"

"What did you and Grandmama talk about?"

"Let go of my arm first."

"Tell me first."

"No."

"Yes."

"You're such a bully."

"And your husband, for as long as we are under this roof."

She throws up her free hand. "Why do you always have all the
answers? It's so annoying."

"It is." I nod, "Being perfect can sometimes get to be too much for me
as well."

She gapes, "Whoa, have you ever heard yourself?"

"All the time, babe." I place my razor on the counter, then turn and
haul her to me. Her gaze widens, her breasts brush up against my chest,
and color smears her cheeks. Good. I like her off balance, a little
surprised, a little breathless. "Now, tell me what you two spoke about."

"It's a secret."

"A secret?"

She nods. "It's a woman thing, you know?"

"Is that right?" I scowl.

"Yep." Her eyes gleam, "Not something I can share with you."

I take in her flushed features, the satisfied look in her eyes, then
release her. "Fine." I turn back, pick up my razor and begin to shave.

"Fine?" She blinks at me rapidly in the mirror. "What do you mean fine?"

"If she told you something in confidence, then I guess you'd better keep it that way, right?"

"So, you don't mind that your grandmother told me something that she may have not mentioned to you?"

Her tone is shocked. I set down my razor, then turn to her. "You're my wife."

"Fake wife."

"Wife," I insist, "for as long as we are under this roof, remember? And if my grandmother took to you so quickly—which I had no doubt she would—if she trusts you enough to share with you, then I am more than pleased about it."

"You…you are?" She frowns.

"Why wouldn't I be?" I cup her cheek. "It's the reason for this entire arrangement, after all. She wanted to see me married and settled, and now she knows I am."

"It's wrong," she says. "You shouldn't try to tell her an outright lie."

I grasp her left hand and hold it up, "It's not an outright lie. You wear my ring and we will be married at the end of the thirty-day period."

"Something I still don't understand." She bites down on her plump lower lip, and damn, if the blood doesn't rush to my cock instantly.

"What don't you understand?"

"Why do you still want to marry me?"

"Maybe you're growing on me... Maybe it's easier to pretend than to want the real thing... Maybe this is the real thing..."

"No, it's not." She tugs her hand and I release it. "This is one big ego trip for you; that's all it is."

"Is that what you think?"

"Isn't it?" She drags her fingers through her hair. "Honestly, right now, I don't know what to think."

I grab the towel and wipe my face, "Why don't you give me a minute to get dressed? I have something to show you."

Half an hour later, we are on the highway.

"Where are we going?"

I don't reply, stare ahead through the windshield.

"You can, at least, tell me," she complains. "Is this another surprise?"

"Something like that."

I hadn't wanted to do this. I'd wanted to make sure I spent the thirty days with her before arriving at a decision, but something about that scene earlier, the comfortable routine we had fallen into, had shaken me. If I stay on in this fake relationship… Well, it won't stay fake for much longer. I'd always wanted her body…but somewhere along the way, I had started hankering for more. A real relationship, a real wife… A real mother to my child. The child she may already be carrying. Shit. I tighten my fingers on the steering wheel. I shouldn't have embarked on this relationship. I should have turned her down upfront. But I hadn't and now here I am.

We drive for another half an hour in silence. Then I turn off onto a sideroad. Another ten minutes, another turn off, this time onto a narrow unpaved road. Five minutes later, she gets restless. Ten minutes later, she's peering out through the window at the foliage that grows wilder, thicker. Another few minutes and she turns to me, "Do you know where you are headed?"

"Do you?" I ask her.

"Obviously, not," she snipes. She turns away from me to look out the window.

I guide the car to the very end of the road as it opens out onto a driveway. One overgrown with weeds and trees whose limbs reach out to each other to form a canopy overhead.

The sunlight seems to dim as I pull up next to a two-story bungalow.

I come to a stop in front of the steps that lead up to the house, then shut off the car engine.

Silence descends.

I push open the door, come around to find she's already stepped out. Good. No use delaying this further.

I begin to climb the steps, then turn to find she hasn't moved.

"Are you coming?"

"Are you going to tell me where we are headed?"

"You're about to find out."

"I don't like being surprised." She folds her arms around her waist.

"Too bad; you don't have a choice in this."

She stands there for a second, then pulls up to her full height. "Fine, have it your way."

You bet I will.

She walks up the steps, brushes past me and bangs on the door.

It swings open and a man's shoulders fill the doorway. He's dressed in a dark suit, dark hair cut close to this scalp. He jerks his chin at me, then his gaze lowers to the woman at my side.

Karina's muscles freeze.

"Victor?" She stutters, "Wh...what are you doing here?"

38

Karina

"Kaykay," My middle brother addresses me by the name that only my siblings call me.

"Why are you here, V?" I frown.

He exchanges glances with Arpad, "You haven't told her yet?" Victor scowls.

"I didn't have time." Arpad grimaces.

"What is it?" I stare between them, "Tell me what?" I turn to Arpad. "What's happening here?"

"Why don't you go inside, and I'll explain?" Arpad tilts his head.

"I have a better idea," I snap. "Why don't I leave instead?"

I turn to go, but Arpad plants his body in my path. "Not so fast, Sparks. We have unfinished business."

No. I shake my head. I tip my head up to meet his gaze. His eyes narrow and there's a harsh set to his features. He glares at me and I swallow.

"Don't do this," I whisper.

"Too late." His emotionless expression seems carved in stone. "It's happening; you don't have a choice now but to comply."

"You'll regret this." I search his features, trying to catch a glimpse of the man who had kissed me, fucked me, who'd put his ring on my finger. I hold up my hand, turn it around so he can see the ring on my finger.

"I already am," he growls.

I swallow, then pull myself up to my full height.

I pivot and Victor steps aside. I walk into the house. The remnants of sunshine disappear and the cold instantly seems to wrap itself around me.

I shiver, hunch my shoulders, then warmth sears my back. It's Arpad, and for a second, I want to lean back, wallow in his comfort. Instead, I take a step forward.

I glance around.

Victor beckons me, "This way."

I follow, Arpad on my heels.

I cross the hallway, walk inside a room. There's a rectangular table in the center, chairs around it; on the wall behind is an insignia with which I am well familiar. A single white rose, with a drop of blood marring the perfection of its petals… Or adding to it, as I'd often thought.

I walk over to a chair in the middle of the table and drop into it. "Let's just get this over with."

Footsteps sound, then my chair is spun around with such force that a cry bursts out from me, "What the hell?"

"Shouldn't that be my dialogue, Sparks?" Arpad snaps.

"You're the one who brought me here. Why don't you tell me?"

"That's all you have to say for yourself?" He scowls.

"Hey," I protest, " you're the one who brought me here, and now for some reason you seem to be pissed with me? What's your bloody problem, Arpad?"

His scowl deepens. He seems on the verge of saying something, when a familiar voice rings out from behind me, "Karina."

I stiffen, then turn to face the new arrival. He's tall, broad-shouldered, dressed in a slate grey suit that I know costs more than the economy of a third-world country. Nothing but the best for Gregory Solonik, as befits his status as the head of the Bratva.

"Hello, Papa." I blow out a breath.

My father narrows his gaze on me, "I told you to keep out of trouble."

"And I told you I could manage on my own."

"This—" he jerks his chin toward the glowering Arpad, "this is what you mean by managing?"

"This..." I fold my arms about my waist, "this is not what it seems."

"Why don't we all sit down?" Victor glances between us.

Arpad's jaw tics. A nerve throbs at his temple. He releases me so suddenly that I crash back into the chair. He backs away, and instantly, the cold closes in on me. I turn my chair around just as my father walks over to take his seat at the head of the table.

"So?" My father digs his elbows into the table, then places the tips of his fingers together. "You leave the country and sever all family relationships because you want to build your career on your own steam, then you turn up married? When were you going to tell your family about it?" He scowls at me and I shuffle my feet.

Shit, why does it feel like I am five again and sneaking off behind his back to do something I shouldn't?

"There's nothing to tell, because we are not married...yet."

"And the ring?" My father scowls at my hand, "What's that about?"

"That...uh..." I toy with the band but don't take it off, "that was for the benefit of Arpad's family. We were trying to convince his grandmother that we were married, because she's unwell and may not have much longer to live and—"

My father's gaze narrows. "So, you lied to her?"

I flush. "Uh, yeah, that was the general idea," I mumble.

"And the marriage? Whose idea was that?"

"It...uh, it was his idea."

I jerk my chin toward Arpad, at the same time that he says, "It was her idea."

My father glances between us.

"So, both of yours?"

"No," I say.

"Yes," Arpad snaps.

My father's gaze widens.

"So, did both of you come up with the idea?"

"He suggested a pretend marriage first," I nod toward Arpad. Not that I am going to tell my father why. If he finds out that I'd been trying to get pregnant through artificial insemination he'll have a cardiac, and I definitely don't want that to happen. "Then," I swallow, "I proposed to him."

My father turns to Arpad, "And you accepted."

"Yes." Arpad glowers at me.

"Hmm." My father scowls, "Unconventional." He rises to his feet, walks over to where Arpad stands over me. My dad looks him up and down. "So, you want to marry her?"

Arpad holds his gaze, "Yes, Sir."

"And you promise to take care of her, for the rest of her life?"

Arpad opens his mouth to reply and I throw up my hands.

"Hold on, him taking care of me? I can take care of myself."

"I'm not talking to you," my father informs me.

"But both of you are talking about me."

"Don't talk back to me," my father snaps, and I wince.

"Why is it that all of the men in my life think it's their right to tell me what to do?"

"Because I'm your father."

"And I'm your husband," Arpad growls.

I gape. What the hell? Now they are uniting against me? At least, on this issue. Speaking of, I scowl up at my father. "Why is it that you are not more upset about him marrying me?"

My father glances down at me, then back at Arpad. "Of course, I'm upset." He shuffles his feet. "But, you could do much worse than him..." He tugs on his shirt sleeve.

"Bullshit." I stare at him. "You used to lose your temper if I so much as mentioned dating a boy. You'd put them through the wringer with your questions. You'd show them your collection of guns to throw a fright into them. You made sure you scared away any boy who dared look at me, something you didn't stop doing even after I grew older and began dating men. No one was good for me and now... You...you...just accept this guy... This complete stranger... As my possible future husband. You..."

I blink, glance between them again.

Arpad's staring at my father, who's looking back at him. Something passes between them.

"Oh." I gulp. "Oh." I grip the arms of my chair. "Unless," I blink rapidly. "unless you are not strangers?"

Neither of them replies.

"I mean, Arpad interrupts his trip to visit his family... To bring me here and meet mine. The family I've tried to keep my distance from..."

My voice trails off. I swallow. My heart begins to beat faster. "No." I turn to Arpad. "It can't be."

"Stop." Arpad frowns. "Don't let your imagination run away with you."

"Oh, you have no idea what I'm thinking right now." I try to rise to my feet and Arpad presses down on my shoulder.

"Sparks, stay for a while longer."

"Are you threatening me now?" I scowl at him, then turn to my father, "And you... Why aren't you telling him off for manhandling me?"

My father's jaw hardens, he opens his mouth, then closes it again. What the hell? Since when has my father stayed quiet before anyone? I glance between them, then shake my head again. *Shit, shit, shit. This can't be happening.* Whatever I'm thinking, it can't be true, can it?

"Sparks," Arpad's voice grows urgent, "don't work yourself into a panic. I'll explain everything, in just a few more minutes."

"Why?" I glower at him, "What are we waiting for?"

That's when the door opens and two guys stride in — tall, broad-shouldered, wearing suits in a different shade of, you guessed it — black. Of course, it had to be them. Somebody really needs to tell my family to tone down this entire over-the-top villain-in-a-Bond-flick thing they have going.

The slimmer of them, my second brother Roman, pulls up a chair at the far end.

My oldest brother, Nikolai, prowls over to Arpad. The two men size each other up. Arpad's shoulders seem to bulge and grow bigger, his entire demeanor taking on that of a man who's had his favorite plaything threatened. Or rather, a dog who's about to have his bone snatched from between his jaws.

Soon, they'll indulge in a pissing contest, which is par for the course amongst my family and others with whom my brothers associate. But Arpad? He's a billionaire investor, for hells' sake. Sure, he's alpha, but he hasn't seen the kind of violence these guys have... Or the bloodshed. Arpad widens his stance. "You have something to say to me?" he growls.

Niko cracks his knuckles and Arpad laughs. Outright. In his face. I wince. Shit, that was a bad move.

Arpad raises his fist, draws it back. So does Niko. I squeeze my eyes shut, waiting... Waiting...for the inevitable clash between them.

"Niko fucking Solonik."

"Arpad motherfucking Beauchamp."

What the —? I snap open my eyes to find my brother and my husband bumping their fists, then doing that half-hug thing that men do, when they like each other, but don't really want to show how much, but still want to acknowledge the bond between them.

I blink, once, twice. My pulse rate ratchets up. Sweat beads my palms. "What the hell is happening here?"

39

———————

Karina

"Seems you're not the only one with secrets, my darling *wife*." Arpad releases my brother and turns to me. His features wear that smirk that is hot and sexy and so bloody annoying.

I grip the edge of the table and lean forward. "How do you two know each other?" I snap.

"We went to school together," Niko replies.

"No. You didn't."

Arpad's grin widens, "Oh, it's not the kind of school that you're thinking."

"Oh, yeah?" I firm my lips. What the hell is this man up to now? Just when I think I have things under control, he pulls the rug out from under my feet.

Niko nods. "We met, shall we say, in the kind of academy to which only a certain few have access."

"The Seven included," Arpad drawls.

"And what kinds of things were you taught there?"

"Do you want to know?" Arpad's eyes gleam. He leans forward on the balls of his feet, and his gaze bores into mine. Damn him, he knows how curious I am, that I'll do anything to find out how he knows my family.

"No," I snap my lips closed.

"No?" He blinks.

"What do I care?" I lean back in my chair and pretend to yawn. "Clearly, you're in cahoots with them. Perhaps you've been planning this all along. If you think you've surprised me, forget it, buster. I've known worse."

"Oh?"

"Yeah," I draw in a breath, then turn toward my father, "I am not sure what game is being played here, but you know how I feel about my involvement in matters of the Bratva. Suffice to say, I want no part of it." I rise to my feet.

My father's gaze grows stormy. The tips of his ears grow red. Shit, never a good sign. Now you know where I get my temper. My stomach twists. I think I am going to throw up now. That's all I need to embarrass myself. I swallow down the bile that rises to my throat.

"You okay, Sparks?" Arpad asks.

"Water," I croak.

He reaches over, grabs a bottle of water from the table, twists off the cap, and offers it to me.

I snatch it from him, tilt it to my lips and chug down a few mouthfuls. My stomach seems to settle. Thank god. I place the bottle down on the table, sit back in my seat.

"I'm sorry I surprised you like this." He squats down, takes my hand in his. His palms, wide and warm, make me aware of just how cold and clammy I've gone. Shit, it's okay. No big deal. Just my family pulling a fast one on me… As they've been prone to do in the past. Which is why I'd decided to go my own way. Then, of course, I had to meet Arpad and fall for him and screw it all up. I yank my fingers from him.

"I'm not sorry for anything," I snap.

His jaw tightens. He rises to his feet, then turns to my father, "Gregory, let's get to the business at hand, shall we?"

My father glances between us, then nods. "Why don't you sit down?" he asks Arpad, who slips into the chair next to me. The warmth of his body calls to me, and damn it, but I want to lean toward him. I grip the side of my chair, and turn toward my father.

"I have nothing to do with what's happening in this room."

"On the contrary, Karishcka, you are at the center of the discussion that's about to take place."

"I am?" The blood drains from my face. I lean back in my chair, twist my fingers together. "Don't tell me. Let me guess," my voice breaks and I clear my throat, "you're going to tell me that I need to marry this man for real because it's the only way for you to get power on this side of the pond, something you've been wanting for a long time."

My father gazes at me steadily, "You always were a clever girl. If only you had agreed to join us."

"And you know my answer to that. I don't want anything to do with the family business."

"And yet, you had no qualms taking on the security agency and growing it." Nikolai leans forward in his seat.

"That was…legal."

"That was…" Niko puts his fingertips together, "naïve of you."

"Naïve?" I snap, "*I* was naïve?"

He regards me with a steady gaze. "If you thought you could just run part of the family business and not be involved…" He raises his shoulders.

"What do you mean?" I scowl. "I made sure to keep my distance from any of your illegal activities. Besides the security agency had always been run independent of the other companies."

"On the contrary, it was the best cover you could provide for our activities," Niko replies.

"What?" I stare. "How is that possible?"

"Technology, and the best hackers money can buy." He tilts his head, "It's amazing how it helps get through the most secure of firewalls."

I pale, "Do you…do you mean to say you have been using my company as a front all along for whatever activities it is you guys get up to?"

He flattens his lips and that's reply enough. Anger thrums at my nerve endings. "So all this time, I thought I was building my career and my company in as honest a way as possible and you were using it as a front? Do you even realize what a breach of confidence that is to my clients?"

"We made sure never to compromise them in any way." Niko raises his hands. "We simply used the information you turned up, on a strictly need-to basis."

"Need-to basis?" I curl my fingers into fists.

"We made sure we didn't undermine your company in any form," Niko adds.

"Is that what you think?" I swallow. Everything I'd built thus far was a lie. Anger thuds at my temples. My fingers tremble and I press them together to stop myself from doing something I'll regret later.

"Besides, Karina," Roman, who's been silent so far, speaks up, "you know the work we do benefits the thousands we employ around the world."

"And they have no idea of the kind of people they are working for. Sure, it's one big deception, but hey, if you don't want to see the truth, what can I do about it?"

"I had no idea you were so against us." Niko frowns. "I knew you didn't particularly care for what we did, but you never told us how much you were vehemently against our family business."

"That's the problem." I square my shoulders. "None of you ever bothered to listen to what I was trying to say."

Silence, then I glance around the table, "I demand that you stop using my business for your interests unless you want me to quit."

The silence stretches, then Nikolai finally replies, "I'm afraid that won't be possible."

"Of course not. Why does it matter that it's my business? One I've poured my life into. One I've nurtured and built up from the ground up." I stare at Niko, then turn to my father, "If mama was alive, she'd understand. She's the only one who was ever there for me." Tears trickle from my eyes and I swipe them away from my cheeks. "And she'd still be if it weren't for the 'family business.'" I make air-quotes with my fingers. "It's the reason she was killed, and yet, all of you refused to walk away." My chest hurts and my head begins to pound. "It's your fault she's not here with us. You are responsible for her death. You murdered her."

"Enough." My father's palm strikes the table again and I flinch. Jesus, why the hell can't I shut my mouth? What's wrong with me?

I clearly have a death wish. Nothing else can explain why I've decided to dump all the dirty family laundry on the table, and in front of the man who…is likely the one person who can actually understand what I am going through now. Shit, why do I have to think that? Because it's true. Because he'd get why I hate this entire business so much. After all, he too, had been a victim of the Mafia. And sure, his methods of hunting them aren't all that orthodox, but he hates the organized crime syndicates with almost as much of a passion as I do.

"Is that what you believe?" my father asks. "All these years, is that what you thought of me?"

I draw in a breath, then shake my head. "I'm sorry," I mumble. "That was uncalled for."

"But you hold me responsible for her death?"

I wring my hands together. "No," I bite the inside of my cheek, "Yes. I don't know." I hunch my shoulders. "Nothing changes the fact that she was shot because of the enemies you made, and yet, you refused to leave this life."

"Because... I can't," my father thunders. "You can't leave the Bratva once you're in. And your brothers... They made their choices when they came of age."

"And I made mine." I set my jaw.

"And I don't want what happened to her to happen to you."

My father glares at me with the kind of look that has quelled many in his organization. The kind he's only used a few times with me—notably, when I had broken into his study and stolen his cigars and his favorite whiskey and managed to get really drunk and sick. My stomach churns again. I grab the bottle of water and swig some more of it.

"I know how much you miss her." My father's voice lowers, "We all do."

"I know." I hang my head. I had lost a mother, but he had lost his wife, his other half. He'd sworn he'd never marry again. He'd devoted his life to being a good father to all of us. He'd tried his best... In the only way he knew how, and here I am, throwing it back in his face.

"I am sorry, Papa." I hang my head. "I shouldn't have said that. I am really upset that, despite trying to leave my past behind, here I am, slap bang in the middle of it again."

"The more you try to run, the more your issues are going to follow you. The only way out is to turn around and face them."

"And here I am." I blow out a breath, "So, are you going to finally tell me what this is all about?"

"May I?" Arpad asks from next to me.

My father frowns at him. The two lock gazes, something passes between them, then my father leans back. Huh? The *Pakhan* of the Bratva never allows anyone else to take over his meeting. Certainly, not an outsider.

But then, Arpad is no longer an outsider, is he? How long has he been in touch with my family?

Arpad leans forward. "Karina, there's something you should know."

Now what? My heart begins to thud, my throat closes, sweat beads my palms and I squeeze them together. I sit upright, tilt my head in his direction. "What is it?" I ask.

"You see, this is not the first time I've been in touch with your family."

"No shit," I snort.

"No," he shakes his head, "you don't understand."

"You're the hotshot financial wiz, so why don't you explain it to me?"

"That's the thing." He reaches for my hand and I pull it away.

"Say it." I scowl. "Just do it already."

He draws in a breath, glances up at my father, then back at me. "I am not who you think I am."

"I could have told you that for free." I chuckle, then wriggle around in my seat. "Well, go on then, what is it?"

He reaches down, and closes his hand around mine. I try to pull away and his grasp tightens.

"I am one of you."

"What?"

"I am one of the Bratva."

40

Karina

I throw back my head and peals of laughter spill from my lips. If I sound hysterical, it's because that's not far from the truth.

"Sparks, you okay?" Arpad scowls.

I wipe the tears from my cheeks, then sit back in my chair. "Why shouldn't I be? I mean, just because you can say any damn thing that comes into your mind, doesn't mean I am going to believe it, right?"

Arpad glances between my father and brothers, then turns to me. "Sparks, I—"

I hold up my hand, "You...you can't be part of the Bratva. You don't have the tattoos—"

"If I may?" Niko asks Arpad, who nods.

Niko taps his fingers on the table, "If you'd bothered to keep in touch with us, you'd have known that, along with the times, we too, have changed. From a business standpoint, we understand how important it is for the brotherhood to blend in with the mainstream. So, the tattoos are not compulsory anymore."

I frown.

"Besides, tattoos don't buy loyalty," he adds. "It's actions that do."

"And clearly his actions," I nod toward Arpad, "have confirmed his loyalty to you?"

Niko tilts his head.

"Even if I buy that, which somehow, I am finding it difficult to believe," I turn to Arpad. "I am a security consultant, remember? I checked out all seven of you before I took you on as clients."

"You looked into our background?" He draws himself up to his full height. "You had us investigated?"

"Of course, I did. I wouldn't have accepted the lot of you as clients without doing it."

His jaw tics; a nerve throbs at his temple. Then, he nods. "Smart." He rubs his jaw. "I'm glad you did."

"I am not looking for your approval." I grimace. "All I'm trying to do is make a point that what you told me can't be possibly true."

He firms his lips. "I'm afraid it is."

"So, your job... All the investments in startups that you make—"

"I have staff to oversee them." Arpad scowls.

"And your past... You lived in LA. You used to be a full-time angel investor, you were known for finding and launching new ventures."

Niko turns to me, "You need to get over the outdated concept you have of the Bratva. Someone like Arpad is part of the new generation of the Brotherhood. We look, sound, walk like anyone else in the real world. But when tested, our loyalties and interests lie with 'the family.' It doesn't mean he's out killing—"

I wince.

"—or committing illegal acts. His financial and tech expertise are what makes him an invaluable asset to us," Niko adds.

"So, financial and cyber frauds?" I venture. "That's what you are talking about?"

Niko's features stay impassive. I know that look. It means he won't say anything more. He won't confirm or deny the statement, which means it's more true than not. Normally. Which doesn't mean it is fact. It's what I am used to from my family. As the youngest and the only girl, they'd done their best to protect me from the details of what the Bratva were associated with. And then, they wonder why I am so against the family business.

I turn to Arpad, "Tell me it's not true," I plead. "Tell me you are saying all this just to get a rise out of me."

"Sparks," he squats down so he's eyelevel with me, "all I can say is that I am not involved in anything illegal."

"How can you say that?" I laugh. "You are part of the Bratva."

"Haven't you listened to anything I have been saying?" Niko explodes.

Arpad holds up a hand. "Let me handle this from here," he snaps at Niko, whose face grows thunderous. But he tightens his lips, then nods at Arpad.

Whoa. My oldest brother, who in some ways, I've feared more than my father, who is known for his ruthlessness, just backed down?

I turn back to Arpad, who scrutinizes my features. "Niko and I have a bond that is almost as strong as what I share with the Seven. When he asked me to help him out, I couldn't say no."

"So, you became one of them?"

"I only deal with Niko, and only when it's absolutely essential. I help him by steering things along in the business world. A carefully placed word here, a play on the stock market there, snapping up a startup that could send more business his way."

"You're his Ace," I conclude. "He plays you when he needs that extra edge."

Arpad nods.

I stare into his features, take in his clear gaze, the set of his shoulders. That half-pleading, half-defiant look on his face. It's true. Everything he's said so far is true. My throat closes. The band around my chest tightens.

"Karina," He moves closer.

I lean back, trying to put as much distance as possible between us as my seated position will allow.

"Stay away from me."

The skin around his eyes tightens. "Let me explain."

"Too late." I swallow. "All this time we spent together, and you couldn't have mentioned this to me?"

"You didn't mention your connection with the Bratva either," he points out.

"Oh, don't put this on me. I'm not the one who has an entire other life that I just failed to bring up."

"But you do, babe." He firms his lips. "You, too, have another, undisclosed life, even if it's in your past."

"It's different for me."

"Oh?" He growls, "How's that?"

"I was born into the Bratva and decided to cut ties with them. You weren't part of them, but decided to join them."

His jaw tics.

"So your deception is greater because you made the choice."

A nerve pops at his temple.

"My silence was a necessary part of changing who I was." I insist.

"Was it?" His lips twist.

"How can you even ask me that?" I snap back. "You know what? Sod this." I push back my chair, and rise to my feet, or try to, because he's still holding my hand and I find I can't shake him off. So, I half hunch and try to free my hand, but of course, the asshole doesn't let me go.

"Please, Sparks, listen to me."

"No."

"This once."

"No fucking way."

"Karina," my father admonishes me.

Arpad peers into my features. His gaze intensifies; he seems to be pleading with me, and at the same time, trying to coerce me and dominate me. The skin around his eyes tightens. "Please," he reiterates, "give me just a few more minutes of your time to explain."

"A few more minutes?"

"Five minutes." He holds up his hand. "That's all I need, I promise."

"Five minutes."

"Just five."

I gaze into his features—those gorgeous blue-grey eyes, those lips I want to kiss and suck on. *Ugh, stop thinking about his sex appeal in front of your father.* "Fine," I mumble.

"Fine." He lessens the pressure on my hand, but doesn't let go.

"After the incident, you know how the Seven of us took to the streets? A bunch of posh prats like us, and we felt unhinged. We didn't belong in school, couldn't fit in at home, since our families, when they tried to help, didn't have a clue as to the kind of emotional toll it had taken on us. I was spiraling out of control when, I met… Niko." He jerks his chin at my brother. "I was itching to fight and your brother was already running an underground fighting ring in London."

"So that's what your frequent trips to the UK were for?" I scowl at my brother. "And here I thought, you had a woman."

"That too." Niko's features harden. Of course, my oldest brother is every bit as much of an a-hole as my previously soon-to–be but no longer to-be real husband here… No, probably worse, in some ways, given he's been groomed to take over as the scion of the most powerful organized crime syndicate on the West coast… And likely soon, this side of the pond as well.

"So, you two met, found kindred spirits in each other, likely fought each other, I am guessing, and that was the beginning of a beautiful relationship?"

"Relationship?" Arpad and Niko glare at each other with something like distaste.

"I can assure you there's no relationship between us…" Arpad retorts.

"Unless you count the fact that both of you are part of the Bratva?" I snarl

Arpad winces, "There is… That…"

"You're right," Niko adds, "but we wanted something more binding."

"So, you asked him to seduce me?"

Niko draws in a breath.

Roman's face hardens.

Victor shifts in his seat and my father explodes. "Your brother asked his friend to take care of you."

"How?" I jut out my chin. "By marrying me?"

"Yes," my father snaps.

"Do you see how insane this is?" I throw up my hands. "My family goes behind my back, and asks someone who is a complete stranger to wed me?"

"He wasn't a stranger to us," my father points out. "Also, the war between the Bratva and our enemies was escalating in LA. We needed you out of there."

"You could have asked me to leave."

"Would you have left the country if we'd asked you to?"

I bite my lips.

"I thought not." My father nods, "We knew him and trusted him to keep you safe."

"He was one of us, yet part of the mainstream," Niko interjects. "The kind of man who could protect you. The kind we hoped you'd fall for."

"So, you asked him to contrive an excuse to make me move to London and then get me to marry him?"

"It would've worked out for everyone."

"Everyone but me." I twist my lips. "This..." I point my finger at him, "these meddling ways of you guys is exactly why I chose to leave."

"You can't blame your family for trying to protect you," Arpad interjects.

"Was that the only reason you agreed to this...this deal?" I turn on him. "What else did they promise you in return for marrying me? Did they promise to help you track down whoever was responsible for you and the Seven being kidnapped?"

Silence around the table.

Arpad stares at me with something like pride in his gaze.

"Oh, no," I shake my head, "no, no, no." I groan. "This isn't happening." I left my country, tried to forge a path of my own. I'd been so sure I'd be able to shake off the grasp that the Bratva had on me. I'd been so clear that I'd avoid the kind of arranged marriages that are common among the children of the Bratva, and all along, I had been manipulated by my family. I am being coerced into the exact kind of arrangement that I had sworn I'd never fall into, and... By the man for whom I have developed feelings. He's been hiding things from me all along. If that isn't the start of the makings of a disaster, I don't know what is.

My stomach protests again and bile rushes up my throat. "Excuse me," I gasp, "I think I am going to be sick."

"What?"

"I need to puke." I yank my hand from his hold, jump up to my feet and race to the doorway

I wrench open the door, race out and stare about me. Oh, shit, where do I need to go? Where's the bathroom? Arpad reaches me. He scoops me up in his arms, races down the corridor, shoulders open a door and darts in, then deposits me near the commode. I drop to my knees, and hurl. Ugh.

I retch and retch, emptying the contents of my stomach. My hair is pulled back and held. Bloody hell. How romantic. The man I'd fucked... Who I'd fallen for, who had tricked me into the kind of arrangement I'd wanted to avoid my entire life... When I finally stop, he reaches over and tears off a sheet of tissue paper for me. I wipe my face with it, while he reaches over and flushes.

I slump back against the wall, too exhausted to move. He scoops me up in his arms again.

"Don't touch me." I whisper, but he doesn't acknowledge me. He walks over to the counter, lowers me to the ground, then turns on the tap. I reach over, rinse out my mouth, then splash water over my face. He hands me a paper towel. I turn away, snatch up a different tissue and pat my face dry.

"Better?" he asks. "Is it something you ate? Do you want to lie down?"

"It's the bloody company I am keeping right now that's making me want to throw up," I snap.

He stiffens, reaches for me. I evade him, drop the tissue in the waste-paper basket and walk out.

"Sparks?" He draws abreast. I speed up my pace. The last thing I want to do is talk to him.

"Karina." He grips my shoulder.

I angle my body and pull away from him.

"Karina, please listen to me."

"No," I yell, "you lost the right to ask anything of me."

His features tighten and a nerve throbs at his temple. "Don't talk to me like that."

"Oh yeah?" I stab a finger into his chest. "How about, I don't talk to you at all? You dare dictate to me about how to converse with you? When you are the one who's pulled a fast one on me all this time?"

"It's not what it seems."

"Ha!" I blow out a breath and the hair on my forehead rises. "That's what they all say. Pray, tell me, what it is then? You are in cahoots with my family, you know how much I hate their profession, how I've tried to keep away from anything related to them, personally—"

"Even as you helped us investigate the Mafia who are behind our kidnapping?"

"The Mafia are Sicilians; they are different from the Bratva, who are Russian in origin." Why the hell do I feel the need to point that out. Apparently, even though I'd tried to keep myself aloof from my family, their biases and opinions had rubbed off on me.

"Besides, that was professional," I mutter.

"So is this."

I gape at him.

"Bloody hell." He sets his jaw. "I didn't mean it that way."

"You're the one who's always said that he never says anything he doesn't mean."

"No, I said I wouldn't lie to you."

"And isn't this a lie of omission?"

He drags his fingers through his hair and I stare. Jesus, this man... I've only seen him as authoritative and confident, but this... The way he stares at me with an unreadable expression in his gaze... It's not something I would have expected.

"I admit my interest in you started off as a way to get in your pants." He shifts his weight from foot to foot. "Then when your father and brothers approached me with the proposal of marrying you—"

I snort, his gaze narrows, and he shoves his hands into his pocket, "—that's when I decided to offer you the contract to run security for the Seven," he says.

"You offered me the contract?" I explode, "I got it because I am the best in the business."

"You are, and that's why you did," I agree, "but I also had a vested interest in making sure that the contract went to you."

"Wait. Hold on." I raise my hand, "So, you're saying that you influenced the Seven into ensuring that I was the preferred contractor for the job?"

"Because you're the best." he reminds me.

"But you influenced the outcome?"

He raises his shoulders, "I may have hinted that you had my vote and that I trusted you."

"Too bad I can't say the same about you anymore."

He sets his jaw.

"You made sure that I won such a lucrative contract that I had no choice but to move countries." I stab my finger at him. "You made me upturn my entire life, and why? So you could benefit from the deal that you struck with my family?"

"I did it to keep you safe."

"I can take care of myself," I yell.

He sets his jaw. "Do you have any idea of how many people bear a grudge against your family? The kind of enemies one makes in the line of business they are in?"

"You mean the line of business you are in?"

"No. No one knows of my affiliation with your family. That means that I can protect you."

"Oh yeah?" I snort, "And how do you plan on doing that? By manipulating my life? By arranging for me to stowaway on the yacht?"

"I didn't arrange for you to stowaway on the yacht. That was all you, and you know it."

I toss my hair over my head, "But you do admit to controlling my life?"

"If you mean, did I seduce you into falling for me?" He smirks. "Then it's natural that you feel cut up about it. After all, you didn't have a chance."

I fold my hands over my chest. "Excuse me?"

"I mean, it's only natural that you'd want to be with me after I shagged you."

I gape at him. "Is that an apology? Because it's certainly not sounding like one to me."

He cracks his neck. "You're right, I totally suck at this."

"Finally," I raise my eyes skywards, "something you're not good at."

"I'm also not good at this." He gets down on one knee, takes my left hand in this.

"Oh, no, no, no." I try to pull my hand but he holds on.

"Karina Solonik, will you marry me?"

41

Arpad

"No." She stares down into my face.

"What?" I blink. "What did you say?"

"You heard me." She tugs on her hand and I release it. "I said no. No, I will not marry you. No, I don't want to be with you. In fact, I hate you as much as I hate myself for ever allowing myself to feel anything for you."

She turns to leave.

I spring to my feet and grab her wrist. "You don't mean it."

She turns on me and stares down at where my fingers encircle her wrist.

I release her and she folds her arms in front of her. "I've never been more serious about anything in my life."

She heads toward the doorway, then stops. "I'll leave it to you to make excuses to my family."

"Stop, Karina, don't leave like this." I walk toward her.

"I don't want to stay a minute longer with you." Her back is stiff, her shoulders straight. Her dark hair swishes about her shoulders as she yanks open the front door.

"At least, wait a minute. I'll drive you back to my place."

"If you think I am coming back with you to see your family again, you have another think coming."

"Fine, so don't come back to my place. At least, let me take you to… to wherever you are going." I reach the front door as she heads outside.

"No, thanks." She walks down the steps.

"Karina, come on. Let me make sure you reach your destination safely."

"Ha," she snorts, "I'll be safe as long as I am away from you. Besides, you lost the right to care about my wellbeing. No," she holds up a finger, "let me rephrase that. You never earned the right to worry about my happiness, and now," she peruses my features, "now you never will."

She reaches the bottom of the steps. Hell, I need to stop her. I need to figure out how the hell I am going to get her back. "What if you're pregnant?"

She pauses.

I take the steps two at a time and reach her. "You were sick all of a sudden, weren't you?"

Her shoulders shake.

What the—? "Karina, you okay?" I touch her shoulder. She shakes it off and turns to me.

Her mouth is open, tears run down her cheeks.

"Why are you laughing?" I growl.

"OMG." She wipes the moisture from her face. "I puke and you think I am pregnant? It's less than a week since we had sex, and you think I am already carrying your child?"

"It's possible, isn't it?"

"It is," she admits, "but no way, would I be feeling the effects of pregnancy so quickly that I'd be vomiting as a result."

My neck heats. Of course, she is right. And I knew that, I swear, I did; I just wasn't thinking straight. When I am near her, my thoughts seem to get all twisted up inside until I am a mess. Why the hell does she screw me up so?

"So, what is it then? Was it something you ate? Should you be traveling in this condition?"

She snorts. "It was your proximity that resulted in my being physically sick. Now that I am leaving you—" She takes a step away from me, "See, I already feel better."

She holds out her hand.

I stare at it, then back at her face.

"The keys," she says impatiently, "the car keys."

"If you think I'm going to give you —"

She stares at me.

I glare back.

She purses her lips, and fuck me, but she has me where it hurts the most. If I stop her, then clearly, I don't have a chance of winning her over. If I let her go —? *Not happening*, but I have to, at least, comply with her wishes — or be seen to. It's the only way I stand a chance of showing that I am serious about winning her back. Winning her back? This woman has me by the balls. Does she even realize it?

She tilts her head.

I dig the keys out of my pocket and place them in her palm. Before she can pull her hand away, I've gripped her wrist and hauled her to me. I lower my head and press my lips to hers.

She stays unmoving in my embrace and I deepen the pressure of my mouth on hers. I tilt my head, nibble on her lower lip. She sighs, then melts against me. She opens her mouth and I sweep my tongue in between her lips. I bend her over, kiss her, suck on her tongue and —

Pain explodes between my legs.

"What the —" I release her, stagger back. "Did you knee me?" I growl.

She squares her shoulders. "Bye, Mr. Beauchamp. Don't bother coming to grovel; I am not going to give in to you anytime soon."

I straighten, track her as she marches over to my car. The lights flash as she unlocks the car. She pulls open the car door, then turns to face me, "By the way, I'll be billing you for the time we spent together."

She slams the door shut.

Wait, what? I stalk toward the vehicle, when she turns the car around and drives off.

I stare after her. I can't believe she just did that. Left me, literally, eating her dust and driven off. More to the point, I can't believe I allowed her to do that.

"Arpad," Niko calls out, "you'd better come inside. Gregory needs a word with you."

Of course, he does. I pivot and march up the steps. I brush past my one-time friend and now collaborator, then march inside the house.

I stalk into the room, drop into the chair vacated by her. The warmth of her body clings to the chair; the soft feminine scent of her clings to my nostrils. Jesus, fuck, why the hell can't I get her out of my mind?

"Karina."

I raise my head, stare at her father, "What about her?"

"You're going to marry her."

"I am."

Niko bursts out laughing and I stare at him. "What's so funny?"

"You are."

"Explain your motherfucking self."

"My sister just walked out on you, left you in a cloud of dust, and you think you're going to convince her to marry you?"

"Consider it done," I snap with more confidence than I feel.

Ivan snorts from his position near the door. Niko and Roman chuckle at me.

"Still don't see what's funny."

"You are." Gregory's eyes twinkle for a second. "My daughter is stubborn."

"Tell me something I don't know."

"She is very stubborn," he reiterates. "When she makes up her mind about something, it's very hard to sway her."

"And you're telling me this…because?"

"Clearly, she's angry with you."

I raise one eyebrow, challenging him to continue.

"You're going to have to woo her."

"Woo her?" I stare at Gregory.

"You know, the thing that men who've lost their balls do, when they've set their sights on a woman?" Niko interjects.

I firm my lips, "I didn't lose my heart—"

Now it's Gregory's turn to stare at me.

"—my balls," I say. "I'll keep them, thank you very much."

"You do love her, don't you?" He frowns.

I hesitate.

"You finally agreed to marry her," Niko points out.

Shit, what do you tell your future father-in-law and brother-in-law, both of whom are staring at you, like they would have the aforementioned balls for breakfast if you say something to displease them? Not that I'd hesitate to take them on. Those years of fighting, first on the streets, then in Niko's cage fights, have left me with a trick or two up my sleeve. But they are going to be family… And picking a fight with them is not the way to get back in Sparks' good graces.

"I will marry her." I look between them. "This, I promise you."

"I am counting on you to take care of her." Gregory fixes me with those piercing brown eyes, so like hers.

"I give you my word." I knock my knuckles on the wood. "I'll marry her, give you access to all of my contacts, and introduce you to the Seven so you can expand your reach in the UK. In return, you'll help us track down the perpetrators of our kidnapping."

"It's a deal," Gregory leans forward, "assuming you are able to woo her back."

42

Karina

"You did what?" Isla stares back at me from the phone screen.

"I left him." I hunch my shoulders.

More precisely, I had driven away from him and all the way back to London. Then I had headed back home and crept under the covers. I had since taken to ordering my groceries online, binge watching my favorite series, and except for one call to my team to make sure that things were on track — they were — I had holed up in my apartment for the last week.

"And you didn't pick up my calls all these days?" She frowns at me.

"Uh, yeah." I see myself on screen and wince. My hair is unbrushed, my complexion pale, and the black circles under my eyes are so pronounced, I swear, I look like a sleepwalking raccoon. "Sorry, I didn't feel up for company."

"Company?" She stares at me. "You're calling me company? Me, the woman who held your hand while you dithered over Arpad."

"You mean Arpad the douchehole, don't you?" I retort. "Arpad A-hole Dickasaurus."

"Very creative."

"I've had time to think up a few names," I admit.

"So, you've been hiding away in your apartment all this time?"

"Call it a vacation." Yeah, so I am using his words. Big deal, doesn't mean that his voice is stuck in my head or anything.

"You mean staycation."

"Yeah, yeah." I purse my lips. I love Isla, honestly, but right now, I just want to be left alone with my thoughts, preferably with a big carton of Cherry Garcia, my fave ice-cream, and a romantic comedy to watch and cry over. Yeah, I cry over rom-coms, because they remind me of what I can't have. What I set out to find and got hoodwinked by that scoundrel. That rake. Gah! I wind a strand of hair around my finger, and tug on it. "Same thing."

"No, it isn't. If you were on vacation, you'd be on a yacht, sunbathing, sipping margaritas and making out with a hot stud."

"Remember, I did the first and the last?" I point out.

"And how was it?"

"Underwhelming," I lie.

"At least, did he fuck well?"

I make a motion of zipping my lips.

"Aww, come on, give me something," she whines.

"Nope, not going to kiss and tell, babe."

"So, it was good then?" She waggles her eyebrows.

"It wasn't not good."

"Whoa." Her eyes widen. "That good?"

"You're not listening to me."

"Oh, I totally am." She nods. "Bet it was scorching hot."

"No, it wasn't."

"And lascivious."

"Of course, not."

"Blistering, intimate, brazen, amorous?" She snickers.

"Are you consulting a thesaurus?"

"Close," she chuckles, " I made a list of excitable words from the last few romance novels I read."

"Why in the world would you do that?"

"It helps me when I'm pitching for my next wedding, to drop in the right word at the right time."

"Really?" I frown. "Do your customers actually fall for that?"

"You'd be surprised." She changes position on the sofa where she's stretched out, "So what happened, that you came rushing back home and decided to shut him out."

"It's not going to work out."

"What are you not telling me?"

"Nothing."

"And the baby?"

"What about it?"

"What if you are pregnant?"

"I'm not," I snap.

"Are you sure?"

I shake my head. "Even if I am, I plan to bring him or her up alone."

"Do you want to do that?" She scowls.

"Yeah."

"Are you really sure?"

"No, but it has to be enough." The small of my back hurts. Shit, this is what comes from being cooped up in one position for too long. I spring up to my feet, begin to pace the living room of my cozy two-bedroom apartment off Regent's Park. It's not a small space, by London standards. Also, not as luxurious as the kind of real estate that the Seven tend to frequent. "To be honest, I don't know what I want," I muse.

"You want him," she retorts.

"Well, too bad. I am not going to have him. That lying, conniving, bastard," I burst out.

"Whoa, whoa, whoa," she holds up a hand, "what's going on there? What are you not telling me?"

I lower my phone and hang my head. Nothing; everything. Shit, where do I even begin without giving away the truth about who I am? Something I've been hiding from everyone, including the Seven. If they found out about it… Clearly, I'd lose their account and much more. I think. I'd probably lose my friends too… Or not. Arpad knows about it, of course, but considering he is in on this with me, I don't think he would tell the rest of the Seven.

Strange, somehow, he's the only one who knows everything about me… Apparently, he and I have more in common than I thought. Is that what had attracted me to him? The fact that, under that sophisticated, billionaire exterior, he is so similar to my father and brothers... Cut from the same cloth.

Hell, even his experiences are similar to theirs. And he knows them. What are the chances? So, not only had he manipulated my life over the last year, but he'd also been luring me toward this possible marriage. Wow. I shake my head. The one man I'd been attracted to... Turns out, he is exactly the person I should have avoided at all costs. And, of course, he has to be the person with whom I'd chosen to have a child.

"Karina? Kaaareeeena? You there?" Isla's voice reaches me. Shit, I'd forgotten I was still on a call with her.

I raise the phone and peer into her angry features on the screen. "I'm here."

I rub the small of my back again.

"You okay?"

"Of course, I am." A twang tugs on my lower belly. I pale.

"Karina?" She frowns. "What's wrong?"

"N...nothing."

Another jolt of pain hits me. I press my palm to my stomach.

"Karina, you're worrying me. Do you want me to come over?"

"No…no, I'll be okay."

"Karina, don't—"

I disconnect, toss the phone on the bed, then head to the bathroom. Tears prick the backs of my eyes. Shit, don't cry. It's okay. Why the hell am I so upset?

Something hot stabs at my chest and waves of pain coil low in my belly. "Ah!" I stagger over to the bathroom cabinet and open it. Of course, I can't find what I need. Damn it, I should have been better prepared. I'd known it was possible that I might not conceive the first time I tried, but somehow, I had refused to consider that option. I had been so sure that it would work, that I would get pregnant. Is that why I had neglected all the signs of my impending period over the last few days? Tender breasts, the discomfort at the small of my back, my feet, which ache more than usual? No choice. I have to head over to the shop and get what I need now.

As I turn, another wave of pain slices through my middle. Damn it, it bloody hurts; it hurts. I double over, draw in a breath, then another.

Shit, this can't be happening; it can't be.

The doorbell rings just then and I jump. I should go get it, but fuck that. I am not in any mood for company.

The doorbell sounds again, and again. "Go away," I yell. Then head inside the bedroom to reach for my bag, when the sound of the door opening reaches me. What the ever lovin' hell?

I turn to the door as footsteps near. Arpad bursts into the room.

43

Arpad

"Sparks, what's wrong." I spring forward, covering the distance between us.

She straightens, then moves to the side. "Don't touch me," she warns.

"Fuck that," I growl. "Are you okay? Are you in pain?"

"No, I'm dancing around, getting ready to go on a date."

I frown. "Are you?" I look her up and down. "Is that what you're doing?"

"No, of course, not." She clutches her middle, then hobbles toward the door.

"Where are you going?"

"To the shops, you ass."

"Wait, what? You're going like this?"

She turns, "Of course, like this. What's wrong with you?"

"What do you need? I can get it for you."

"Oh, no. No way. I don't want to be beholden to you." She stiffens, then groans again and grabs at her stomach.

My heart begins to race. Sweat beads my palms. Shit, it can't be... Is it? She can't be pregnant this soon, let alone having a miscarriage. "Sparks." I reach for her and she slaps away my hand.

"I said… Don't touch me," she snarls.

"Fine," I hold up my hands, "at least, let me help you."

"You've done enough so far, haven't you?"

I wince. "Look, I'm sorry about what I did, but honestly, now is not the time to talk about it."

"Oh yeah?" She staggers back, until she reaches the wall, then leans against it. "Now is exactly the time to talk about it."

"Not when you are in pain, and bleeding out."

"Exactly now, because I am in pain and bleeding out." She wraps her arms around her middle, bites down on her lower lip. "Shit, this is all a mess." Tears stream down her cheeks. "Why did it have to happen like this?" Her face crumbles and she sinks down to the floor. "Why the hell couldn't it work out? I'd thought it wouldn't matter either way, but clearly, I had allowed myself to believe it was possible. I mean, damn it. I'd really thought I was pregnant, and now I'm not."

"You're not?" I frown.

"Of course, not. I just got my period, you ass."

"Ah," my shoulders sag, "it's only your period."

She shoots me a look from under her eyelashes. "Spoken like a man," she snaps. "Like you'd know how it is to be struck with tender breasts, mood swings, upset stomach, headaches, cramps, aching hamstrings, swollen feet—"

I pale.

"—not to mention that you have to walk around with a wad of cotton stuck up your cunt."

I grimace.

"And take painkillers that make you woozy, so all you want to do is curl up under the covers and sleep. But instead, you are curled up on the floor of the bloody bedroom, watching as the man you thought you loved, the bastard who did a number on you by going behind your back to gang up on you with your family, is watching as you slowly bleed from between your legs like a pig stuck in a hole."

The blood drains from my face. Shit I really hurt her. I'd told myself to stay away after she'd left, to give her time, but hell, if I haven't reached the end of my patience as well. I have to find a way to make her believe in me again. But how? Gregory had said woo her, but hell, if I am going down the tried and tested flowers and candles and dates route… Not that there is anything wrong in that, but seriously, this is Karina, a princess for whom nothing less than the very best will suffice.

I swallow, force myself to meet her gaze. "You're not a pig." I scan her face. "Nope, definitely no resemblance."

She half snorts, then clears her throat. "Is that all you caught from everything I just said?" She sighs.

"The list of symptoms was impressive." I swallow, "Clearly, I'll never know what it is to be on my period, but I can empathize."

"Oh yeah?"

"Sure, I mean, it's like breaking your arm?"

"Arm *and* a leg," she mutters.

"Arm and a leg," I agree, then take a step forward.

"And stubbing the big toe of the foot of your uninjured leg."

"That too," I nod, and move closer to her.

"And…then banging your elbow into the edge of a doorjamb."

"Totally." I reach her.

"And.. And…" her features scrunch up, "and like…losing the chance at having a child." She bursts into tears.

I swoop down and pull her onto my lap. "Shh! Baby, shh!"

She buries her face in my throat and weeps. Her shoulders shudder, her entire body shakes with the outpouring of her disappointment. A lump sticks in my throat. "Oh, sweetheart, I am so sorry."

She only cries harder.

I drag my fingers down her thick soft hair.

"Why did it have to turn out like this? Why?" She curls her fingers into fists and beats against my chest. "I wanted one thing…one thing. To have a child, someone of my own, to bring up without the shadow of my family and my past sullying it. I wanted this child, I really…really wanted it. I… I.."

Her breath hitches and more tears flow down her cheeks.

"I am so sorry, Sparks. I understand how you feel right now."

"You don't." She hiccups. "You have no idea how it feels to be convinced that you're pregnant and then have your bloody period arrive."

"Periods are meant to be bloody aren't they?"

She pauses, stares up at me, then bursts out crying again.

"Shh, baby, please don't cry." I hold her close and rock her. "I'm so sorry, Sparks, truly I am."

"Are you?" she blubbers. "Are you really sorry? Surely, you must be happy that you don't' have to contend with a child, considering we broke up."

My heart stutters. My blood pounds at my temples. We may not be together now, but hell if I am not going to do my best to rectify it. "I didn't realize how much I wanted you to have a child until I walked in and found you doubled over in pain and thought you were having a miscarriage."

"Miscarriage?" She stills. "It's too soon for that."

I wipe the moisture from her cheek, "I know… Stupid of me, but I was concerned and besides, it's all your fault."

"What?" She scowls. "Why?"

"Because of you, I have babies on my brain, and when I saw you in pain, and clutching your middle... Well, come on. It was a logical conclusion. And then, when I thought you'd lost the child… I…" I set my jaw, "I only, then, realized how much I wanted to give you the baby you long for."

"Something which is never going to happen now. She pushes away from me, and jumps to her feet. "What are you doing here anyway?" She flicks her hair over her shoulder, "How dare you barge in here and put your hands on me as if you are…?"

"Mine," I say simply. "You are, Sparks, and I am not letting you forget it that quickly."

"You did a damn good job of it this past week."

"I was trying to give you space. I didn't want to crowd you."

"Well, you're crowding me now."

I rise to my feet, drag my fingers through my hair. "Look why don't I go get whatever you need from the shops, and then we can talk?"

"You can get me what I need, and hand it to the porter downstairs to bring it up. Speaking of," she glances at me with suspicion, "how did you get past him and get inside?"

"Uh…" I shove my hands in the pockets of my jeans. "I have my ways."

"Oh." She stares at me, then the wrinkles on her forehead clear. "Ohhh! I see."

"What?" I take a step forward and she throws up a hand, "Don't come any closer, you…you… Conniving ass."

I stiffen. "Now look here a minute—"

"No, you look here." She draws herself up to her full height. "I thoroughly investigated the ownership of this building, and it hadn't revealed any connection to you," she says slowly, "but you do have a connection, don't you? You own this building."

"Through a company that acts as an interface," I admit.

"Which means the porter is your employee, of course," she snarls, then stiffens. "But I checked out the apartment. There were no cameras in the apartment, so how did you know when to rush in?"

"I waited until you'd completed all of your checks and were all moved in."

"So, every time I was in any of the rooms, you spied on me?" She glances around the space wildly. "And the bathroom? Did you also bug the bathroom?"

"No." I scowl. "Of course, not. I don't have cameras in the bathroom. I am not some creepy-ass stalker."

She bursts out laughing. "You're not, huh? I can't think of another way to define your stalkerish behavior."

"Hey," I hold up a hand, "Cut me a break, will you? I wanted to give you your space, but I wanted to be sure you were safe."

"So what? You jerked off to watching me crying into my ice-cream?"

"Uh… Not exactly." I shuffle my feet.

"So, you did jerk off?" she asks carefully.

"I…uh, I may have." It's one thing to do it, another to admit to it, and to the woman I'm trying to make a good impression on. Shit. "I mean, you're so fucking beautiful when you sleep."

"You watched me as I slept?" She opens and shuts her mouth. Then her cheeks redden, "So, you saw me when I… I…"

I nod, "I saw you shove your toys inside yourself and bring yourself to orgasm. That's when I almost came over and—"

"Hold on," she tilts her head, "you almost came over then?" She stiffens, "And this time when you saw me in pain... How did you get to me so quickly?"

I am not going to lie to her, not after everything we've been through. If I have a chance in hell of winning back her trust, I need to be up front with her. She needs to accept me, faults and all, as I want her in my life. Completely unvarnished, without any masks. That's how I want us to be able to see each other. I square my shoulders, "I am in the apartment down the hallway, actually—"

"What the hell?" Her cheeks redden, but it's anger, not embarrassment. "All this time, I have been crying over you and you've been watching me and enjoying yourself at my expense."

"No, no, no. It's not like that." My throat closes. Shit. This isn't going how I'd imagined it would. "I had to make sure you were okay."

"I was fine, until I met you."

"I promised your family that I'd look out for you."

"Oh, yeah?" She tips up her chin. Her gaze narrows, "If this is what you mean by 'looking out'" she makes air quotes with her finger, "then I am sorry, but clearly, you and I have a different definition of what that means."

She clutches her stomach again, and something hot stabs at my chest.

"You're in pain. You shouldn't be exerting yourself emotionally, physically—"

"It's only my period, you blundering neanderthal," she yells. "It's not like I am pregnant." Her face crumples again, but she takes a few deep breaths and composes herself. "Shit, I am not pregnant. Not pregnant." She holds herself and begins to rock.

A ball of emotion lodges in my chest.

I take a step forward, and she snarls, "Don't you dare come near me."

"But—"

"Are you happy now? Clearly, you didn't want me to be pregnant. Your plan worked."

"What do you mean?" I frown. "You know I wanted you to have my child."

"Did you?" Her gaze narrows. "The number of times you could have come inside me and you didn't. You pulled out, you came on me, you fucked me in the ass, but you held off coming inside me until—"

"Until I was sure you were ready to submit to me."

She stares at me, "So you admit it? You admit that you were playing with me, even though we had an agreement?"

"I kept up my part of the deal," I insist.

"You were supposed to get me pregnant. Instead, you were too busy playing your mind games. You were more concerned with holding onto your power. You wanted me to give in to you, you wanted me to beg, before you delivered on your part of the bargain."

Her jaw firms.

"If you hadn't been so hung up on the powerplay, if you hadn't been so obsessed with dominating... If you had been less selfish, you'd have focused on our deal. You wouldn't have held back on me. You'd have tried to get me pregnant every opportunity you had. In fact," her chin wobbles, "if you had, for one second, thought about anyone else but yourself, I'd probably have conceived by now."

My heart begins to race and the band around my chest tightens. I move toward her and she holds up her hand. "Please," her voice wavers then she draws in a sharp breath, "please don't come near me. In fact, it's best you stay away from me from now on."

"Let me help." I close my fingers into fists. What can I do? How can I help her? Is everything she said true? Had I been so engrossed with staying in control, had I been so wrapped up in my own emotions, so preoccupied with what I wanted from her, that I had forgotten about why I had entered into the agreement with her in the first place?

My throat closes; a bead of sweat runs down my spine.

Damnit! I have faced down the Bratva, sat across from the sharpest of investors in Silicon Valley, but none of it has prepared me for the absolute helplessness I feel as I watch her grapple with her pain, her anguish.

"Let me at least hold you," I plead.

"No." She wipes the tears off her face. "You lost that right with how you've treated me."

"I treated you like you are my—"

"Like your possession," she spits out. "Like you…you could manipulate my life to suit your needs. Like you could arrange the trajectory of events to your convenience. Well, I have news for you Arpad f'ing Beauchamp. I am Karina motherfucking Solenik, and I am going to make you sorry for the moment you set eyes on me."

44

———

Karina

"He spied on you?" Isla scowls at me from across the table.

We're at the bar above the National Portrait Gallery, my favorite drinking spot. Also, the second favorite place I like to go to when I want to think. Normally, I'd have gone for an Ashtanga yoga class, but my bloody period means that's out. Not that I haven't tried to fit in yoga sessions when I have my period, but given the kind of cramps I have during this time, I find it uncomfortable to take part in any overt physical activity. For all of my best intentions, my body has a will of its own, apparently. Just like my wanting to get pregnant and my body declaring otherwise.

It's been forty-eight hours since I told off that asshole. Forty-eight hours since I found out I hadn't conceived. Which means I can drink all I want, right? Bonus: it will help with the cramps. I raise the shot of vodka, and toss back the remnants.

Isla's eyebrows rise. "You okay?"

"What do you think?"

"Considering how you're tossing back the alcohol, I'd say you're upset."

"Understatement of the year." I gesture to the bartender for a refill. "And just so we are clear—he didn't spy on me; he stalked me."

"Stalked you?" She frowns.

"Asshole had cameras in my house. " My fingers tighten around my glass of wine. "The bastard rented the apartment down the hall from me so he could keep an eye on me."

"Whoa." She leans back on the barstool. "That's some crazy shit."

"Exactly."

The bartender tops up my vodka and I nod my thanks.

"How do you think Sinclair, Saint, Weston and Damian found out everything they wanted about their women?"

She frowns, "Are you saying they stalked their now-wives and girl-friends?"

I stare at her. "I can't reveal client confidences."

"So, they did stalk the girls?"

I raise my shoulders. And now I know how it feels to be on the other side. I lower my face, stare down into the depths of my shot glass.

She sighs. "The Seven are complicated men. Alphaholes to the extreme, and yet, when they set their hearts on something—or someone, they don't stop until they possess the object of their obsession."

"Tell me about it." I snort. "I've seen it all unfold in front of me."

"You have to admit, there's something hot about being the focus of all that intensity."

I stare at her in disbelief. "It's more like an invasion of my privacy."

She nods. "Shows how much he wants you—that he'll go to any lengths to get you."

"Well, he can fuck right off if he thinks that's the way to woo me," I snarl. "And I can't believe you're saying this. This is real life, Isla. It's not one of those romance novels you like to read so much."

"Hey," she protests, "don't mock my kink, and I won't mock yours."

"Kink, what kink are you two talking about?" A new voice asks from behind me. I turn to find a young girl…dressed in skinny jeans, chucks, a purple blouse that matches the highlights in her hair.

"Ava," Isla exclaims, "what are you doing here?"

"I came to the gallery to complete a project, then my friends and I decided to come up here for a drink." She laughs.

"Are you of legal age?" I huff.

"You can order your own drinks if you are over eighteen, which I am." She tilts her head and furrows her brow. "After all, this is England."

Of course, it is. And I am here, why? Because the asshole manipulated my life so he could ensure that I was close enough for him to keep tabs on me.

I raise my glass and throw back more of the vodka.

"Have you two met?" Isla looks between us. "This is my friend Ava, and this," she turns to me, "is Karina—"

Ava's face brightens. "You are Arpad's—?"

"Not Arpad's," I growl.

She blinks, then her cheeks redden. "Sorry, didn't mean to imply something where there isn't anything."

"There was, but now there isn't." I toss back the vodka so quickly that my stomach protests. A numb feeling grips my hands and legs. Good. Not that I like getting drunk... In fact, I can't remember the last time I did. But nothing like starting in the present moment, right?

"Oh," her lips tilt down, "I'm sorry."

She turns her body away from me, and I know I'm being mean. Isla glowers at me. I frown back. I am not really ready for company. But I couldn't bear to be inside the apartment, even though he'd promised me that he was disconnecting the cameras. Not that I trust him.

I had dumped my phone, gone through the space to ensure I had found and destroyed each of the cameras—all of it expensive, top notch equipment, that I had taken great pleasure in wrecking under the heels of my favorite pair of designer shoes.

I nod at the bartender and he refills my shot glass again.

Isla grabs my hand. "You're going too fast," she protests.

"Not fast enough," I grumble.

Ava pulls out her phone and taps out a message, then she slides onto the barstool on my other side.

"I'll have what she's having," she beckons to the bartender.

"You will?"

She nods.

"What about your friends?" I scowl.

"I just messaged them to say I'll catch them later. It's more important that I am here to keep you company while you get over your heartbreak."

Heartbreak? Is my heart broken? I thought it was more the disappointment that I hadn't conceived. Hell, this was only my first time trying. The band around my chest tightens and I feel a hot, stabbing sensation. How do the women who try for children for months, years, decades sometimes, manage to keep going? Do they have more self-confidence than me? Are they simply luckier than me? Maybe it isn't meant to be for me? *Oh, stop that.*

Ava raises her shot glass of vodka to me. *"Salut."*

"Nostrovia." I clink my shot glass with hers. We down it at the same time.

The alcohol slides down my throat, leaving a trail of heat in its wake. The lack of sensation that follows is totally awesome. My head spins, then everything in my vision seems to pop and sparkle. Jeez, it's like I finally took off the blinkers I've been wearing so far.

"I am sorry for my mean girl attitude earlier," I mutter. "It's just... Well... You know..." I stare at her face, the trusting features, as she watches me, unblinking. Bloody hell, this girl really is so young. "Forget it." I wave a hand. "It's not worth discussing. Just please know, I am not normally this horrible."

"Yeah, normally she wouldn't have spoken to you at all," Isla chimes in.

"What?" I gape at her, "Are you telling me I'm normally a nose-stuck-in-the-air—"

"Haughty, condescending, bitch?" She nods.

I open and shut my mouth, and she chuckles. "I was only joking, silly."

"No, you weren't." I swallow. Shit, is this what the few friends I have think of me? Why the hell do I have so much trouble hanging onto the people who mean something to me? Like him? Why did everything have to go so pear-shaped with him? It could have been different, couldn't it? He could have meant everything he'd said to me. He could have actually wanted me. He could have married me for real and I could have gotten pregnant in my first try and we could've lived happily after, raising little Solonik-Beauchamp babies... In a suburban neighborhood with white picket fences... Not. I can't stop myself from snorting. As if we'd ever be something so...bourgeois? Shit, now I was even thinking like him.

I turn to Ava, then reach for her hand and squeeze it. "I am sorry for being such a bitch," I swallow, "I really didn't mean to come across so... so..."

"Preoccupied?" she helpfully offers.

"You really are too kind to be real." I half laugh.

"Yeah," her forehead creases, "I get told that a lot. My friends think I am too trusting. I prefer to think I am an optimist."

"I'd settle for being a realist," I mutter.

"You do realize realists are secretly much more romantic than the rest of us?"

I scowl and she bursts out laughing. "That was a joke, but honestly, I believe there's a grain of truth in it."

Hmph. "God, I hope not. I am as far from a romantic as you can get."

"That's what they all say." She flashes me a huge smile. "It's only until you meet the one, you know, and when you do, all these preconceived notions will fall by the wayside."

"So, have you met the one?"

"Not yet, but I am confident he's not far off now either." Her grin widens, if that is at all possible. Her eyes sparkle.

Wow, she actually does believe that. If only I had half the hopefulness she has. When had I turned into such a cynical woman that I can't believe in a happily-ever-after for myself?

On impulse, I rise to my feet and hug her. "I hope we'll get to know each other better."

She hugs me back. "I am sure we will."

I step back and she slides off her stool, then turns to Isla. "Sienna mentioned that you have a big wedding coming up, that you might need some help with the planning?"

Isla's jaw hardens. "I do." She doesn't elaborate, which is strange. Isla's the kind who loves her job so much, she only needs an excuse to run her mouth off about it.

"Whose wedding is it?" I peer into her features. "Anyone I know."

"Yeah," she blows out a breath, "Liam's."

"Liam?" I frown, "Weston's older brother? But I thought…"

She glowers at me. "What? What did you think?"

"That you and he…"

Her glare deepens. "That he and I…?" she prompts, and I cough.

"Nope. Nothing. Forget I said anything."

"Honestly, all of you'll going on about Liam and me... How many times do I have to say, there's nothing there?"

Right. "So why do you look so pissed off?"

"Probably because I'm not pissed enough."

She turns around to the bartender. "I'll have what they're having," she snaps, "and make sure you top up their glasses too."

I exchange glances with Ava, who's watching Isla with a look of concern. "You okay, Iz?"

"Of course, I am." She flashes us a too-bright smile that's patently false.

"Have you spoken to Liam?" I prod. "Maybe if you told him how you felt about him — ?"

"Feel?" She scoffs, "I have no feelings for him. Hell, I barely know the man."

I frown. "But I thought — "

"That I had a crush on him or something?" She tosses her hair over her shoulder. " I have spoken to the man… Twice… Maybe."

"One look is all it takes," Ava interjects. "When you know, you know."

Isla shoots her a sideways glance. "What I know is that he's all wrong for me. I've sworn off the Seven…"

"He's not one of the Seven," I remind her.

"And their friends," she snaps.

"But not us, I hope?"

"The girls don't count. If it weren't for their women, the Seven would have burned in hell by now."

"True that." I push the shot glass of vodka over to her. "It's the women who've saved the Seven from themselves."

"Maybe that's why Arpad wants to pursue you," Isla runs her fingers around the rim of the shot glass, "because he knows you are his last hope at redemption."

"Or maybe he simply wants to show how easy it is to control me?" I snarl.

"I don't mind being controlled."

Both Isla and I turn to Ava.

"Woman, do you even know what you are saying?" Isla huffs.

"I may be younger than you all, but trust me when I say that the control goes both ways. The person who thinks he or she is in control isn't really, and the one being controlled? Let's just say, that's the person who has the power."

I blink. "Wow, so not only are you perfect, you're also wise?"

She laughs. "I know, I was born with an old soul. That's what my sister says too."

"I guess I wouldn't mind ceding control to a man," Isla retorts.

"What the—?" I stare at her. "Really? You had to say that now?"

"On one condition..." She raises her finger. "If he wanted to wield power over me, he'd better damn well make it worth my time."

Ava reaches for her shot glass. "Money isn't everything. You realize that, right?"

Both Isla and I stare at her again.

"What?" She scowls. "Did I say something wrong?"

"How many eighteen—?"

"Nineteen-year-olds," she corrects me.

"Nineteen-year-olds today, would say that, you think?"

"Why, don't you feel the same?" She takes in my features. "Go on, you can tell me."

I rub my temple, feeling a headache coming on. Or maybe I just haven't had enough alcohol. I reach for my shot glass, when she says, "Surely, you don't believe money is the be-all and end-all of everything?"

If she only knew my background and my family's view on that.

"Of course, not," I mutter. "Money isn't everything, but it's definitely important."

"Not as important as love," Ava insists.

"Love," I snort, "that stupid thing that doesn't really exist, and even if it did, I don't believe in it."

"Of course, you do." She nods her head. "You only need to adjust your expectations."

"Expectations?" I blink rapidly. "Whatever do you mean by that?"

"That maybe, falling in love means you need to give first, before you get back."

The headache behind my eyes intensifies. "But what if the other person did something that hurt you so much, you can't forgive him?"

"Can't forgive him, or don't want to forgive him?"

I hunch my shoulders. "I'm still trying to figure that out."

Ava's gaze softens. "Maybe you need to give this time before arriving at any conclusions?"

"I'm with young Ava here." Isla nods. "It seems whatever Arpad did was because it was the only way he knew how to express what he was feeling."

I snort, "You mean being a neanderthal is all that any of the Seven know?"

"You've worked with them; you should know," Isla replies. "Either way, just take SOME time to reflect on how you actually feel about him."

"Right." I do know what I feel about him. Problem is, I don't like it very much. But there's no need to reveal that here, is there?

"Meanwhile," Isla adds, "focus on moving forward, you know? Concentrate on your job, your life —"

"Shit, my job." I blow out a breath. "The Seven are my biggest clients at the moment. If they decide to take their business elsewhere —"

"They won't." Isla frowns. "Will they?"

"I hope not." I square my shoulders. "Either way, I'm going to use this opportunity to expand, look for new clients. Something I should have done a long time ago." I've become complacent, happy with the easy business the Seven send my way. No more. I am going to take things into my own hands, forge my own way out of this mess.

I raise my shot glass. Ava and Isla clink their glasses with mine. I toss the drink back and it explodes in my stomach. A fire sizzles down my spine, and I slap my glass upside down on the bar counter.

"Right then," I laugh, "who's ready to party?"

45

Arpad

I watch from the edge of the dancefloor as she sways her hips to the music. I'd tracked her to the bar earlier. Yeah, yeah, I'd said I'd leave her alone. Doesn't mean I can't look out for her, right? From a safe distance. That is, until the evening had worn on, and she still hadn't come out. So I had taken things into my own hands and walked in to find her dancing.

The vibrations pulse out across the bar, the beat picks up, and she raises her arms in the air. She closes her eyes, throws her head back as she grinds her hips, once, twice, thrice.

She sinks down until she's almost squatting, then bumps her way up to standing again.

Eyes still closed, she places her palms flat across her stomach, rotates her hips again, moves her shoulders in a sinuous shimmy. The blood rushes to my groin. My pulse begins to thud.

A man steps in front of her — tall, broad shouldered, asshole has a mohawk which, no doubt, he thinks is cool. He mirrors her moves, moving to the right, then the left. Drops down with her, then rises to his feet. He leans in, touches her shoulder and I see her jerk visibly.

What the hell?

He moves with her and she smiles up at him. Eyes gleaming, she increases the pace of her rhythm, swivels her hips, thrusts out her breasts, and his gaze lowers to her chest. He plants his hands on her waist and my anger pumps through my veins. How dare he touch her? How dare he dance with her? She's mine. Only mine.

I shoulder my way through the crowd on the floor. A couple gets in the way and I growl at them. The man and woman glance at me. Their gazes widen and they skitter away. Good. I plough forward and a man steps in my path, jumping up and down in tempo with the rhythm of whatever godawful song they are playing over the sound system. I glare at him. He pales and leaps aside. Wanker of the first order. I stomp across the remaining distance, reach the bastard who's dancing with my woman.

I plant myself in front of them, fold my arms across my chest. They keep moving, don't even glance at me. What the bloody hell? I tap his shoulder, and he swivels his head to stare at me. "Move," I jerk my chin.

He frowns, then mouths, "Fuck off."

I bare my teeth, raise my fist and plant it in his grinning countenance. He staggers back, then rights himself and comes at me. I move aside and he charges past me. I kick his legs out from under him and he hits the floor face down. The entire floor seems to shake with the impact. The music pumps up another notch, the laser lights swiveling across our faces. The asshole on the ground stirs, and I move toward him, when a hand grabs at me and tugs. I turn and her green gaze collides with mine. "Don't," she mouths, shaking her head frantically, "he's not worth it."

"He touched you," I yell back at her. The music drowns out my voice but she must lip read me, for her grasp on me tightens.

"Don't." Her chest rises and falls; her eyes widen with apprehension. "Please don't, Ari."

"How dare he get close to you?" I growl. "I am going to kill him." I turn my attention back to the tosser on the floor.

She steps in between us, throws her arms around my waist. She tips up her chin, holds my gaze, "Dance with me."

I stare past her at the bastard on the floor. He stirs, then lurches up to his feet. I strain forward and she begins to move against me, thrusts her pelvis into mine, then rubs her gorgeous tits into my chest. The little tease. I watch her as she rotates her hips, grinding her core against the growing bulge in my jeans. She licks her lips, and fuck, if I don't come right then.

A movement catches my attention. I look up to find the asshole staggering away.

She cups my cheek, forcing me to look away and at her. She goes up to tip-toes, lifts her head, and my gaze drops to the gleaming flesh of her lips. My throat closes.

She continues her exaggerated hip movements, and I take in the swell of her breasts, the slim waist that flares out to the curve of her arse that she wiggles as she undulates her body against mine.

My cock thickens, my balls harden, and damn, if I don't want her right now.

I lower my head, try to kiss her, but she evades me. She steps away, pivots so her back is to me, then continues her bump and grind routine. She juts out her butt, wiggles it, all the while moving, shaking that gorgeous body of hers in a way that's sure to have every man and woman here salivating after her. I glance around to find that, sure enough, we have an audience. People closest to us have stopped dancing, formed a circle as she gyrates, trails her fingers about her neck, sweeps it over her breasts, down to the flat of her stomach as she circles her hips again. She turns to throw me a coquettish glance, her eyes gleaming.

I quirk my finger at her; she shakes her head.

I frown and she chuckles. She turns to face me again, digs her fingers into her hair and piles it above her head in a move that's meant to seduce. She moves in again, presses herself to my front, from breast to pelvis to thigh, and that's when something inside of me snaps. I am going to have her all to myself. End of story. I bend my knees, grab her around the back of her thighs and throw her over my shoulder.

Instantly, she twists in my grasp, almost pulling free. Sneaky. But nothing less than I expected. After all, she is a security consultant. Surely, she's trained in martial arts. But hell, if I am not a match for her. I tighten my hold around her and she only wriggles harder.

She pushes her breasts into my back, and I am sure she must be hurling insults at me. Good thing I can't hear her above the music, eh? She buries her fists in the small of my back, and I feel it all the way to the tip of my cock. Yep, definitely needs to be taught a lesson. I bring my palm down on her butt and she stills. Then begins to squirm and writhe against me, and that only makes me harder. Damn it. I walk off the dance floor, out of the room, and down the corridor.

Reaching the door at the far end, I twist it open. A snogging couple breaks apart. "Out," I growl. They break apart, careen out. I step in, slam the door shut and the noise cuts out.

"Let me the fuck go, you swine," her scream almost takes my ear off.

"Your wish is my command."

I pull my arms away and she topples to the floor.

46

Karina

"What in the ever lovin' hell?" My back connects with the floor of the restroom. The godawful bathroom of the bloody bar, where god knows how many people have been today? "Argh!" I shake the hair out of my eyes, then spring up to my feet, rubbing my ass. "Why did you drop me like that?" I yell.

"How dare you dance with another man?" he growls back.

"It's a free country, you ass. Besides, I thought I told you to stay away from me."

His jaw firms. "I tried," he rotates his shoulders, "but it's your fault that I can't keep away."

"My fault?" I gape. "What the hell do you mean?"

"You were all over that man—"

"I wasn't."

"You were shoving your tits at him—"

"It's called dancing, you bastard."

"You gyrated your hips and all but plastered yourself to him—"

"There was space between us the whole time we danced, you prick."

"Language," he growls, "And what the hell are you wearing?" He looks me up and down.

"What does it look like?" I tug on the hem of my dress, which I confess, is shorter than what I would normally wear, but hell, if it doesn't look good. "It's a designer dress, I'll have you know. The latest of the season, and yet, a classic." I pull back my shoulders, thrust out my hip and prop my hand on it. "What the hell are you doing here, anyway?" I scowl.

"What are *you* doing here?" he demands.

My jaw drops, "I am a single woman, living my life, out on the town —"

His gaze narrows.

"—ready to take the first eligible man I meet home for a shag."

Color smears his cheeks and his nostrils flare. Ooh, this is more fun than I would have anticipated.

"I was doing so well too, until some tosser —" I tip my chin up, "showed up."

His jaw tics. "Don't talk to me like that."

I blink, then burst out laughing. "You're asking me to be polite? After everything you did?"

"What did I do? Except try to give you what you wanted?"

"And yet, you failed."

The color leaches from his face, and for a second, a tiny second, I am almost sorry that I've hurt him. Sure, I'd found I wasn't pregnant but had he…also been disappointed by the outcome?

Nah, not possible. This man? He's too selfish. He only thinks of himself, after all.

He balls his fists at his side, "I can't tell you how sorry I am that you aren't pregnant."

"Not as much as me." I drag the back of my hand across my face. The light from the overhead bulb seems to burn into my brain. Shit, how much have I had to drink? What am I even doing here, with him? "Let me go, Arpad." I wrap my arms about myself. "Just let me out of here."

"No." He widens his stance, seems to draw himself to his full height. "You're not leaving until you listen to me."

"I don't care about what you have to say."

"Just a minute of your time, Sparks."

"What? No commanding me to stay?" I snarl. "No tying me up so I can't leave?"

He drags his fingers through his hair. "Will you just listen to what I have to say?" He lowers his voice to a hush, "Please." And there's that word again. Damn it, alphahole Arpad f'ing Beauchamp, trying to be polite and failing spectacularly. *But he's trying, isn't he? Gah. Tell him to go to hell. Do it.* I draw in a breath. Instead, I find myself complying. "Fine," I mutter, "you have sixty seconds."

He nods, then pinches the bridge of his nose, "I'm sorry that you didn't get pregnant, but I won't apologize for manipulating your life."

I open and shut my mouth, "You won't?"

He lowers his hands to his sides then thrusts his chest out. "I saw you and I wanted you. I've learned that life is short, and when you see something that resonates with you, you have to go after it, so that's why I did."

I shake my head, try to speak, fail. I simply stare at him.

"Look, Sparks," he steps forward and takes my hand in his, "I know how much you hate me now, and I can only imagine how disappointed you are that you didn't get pregnant. I can't tell you how much I wanted to give you a child."

I glance down at where his large palm engulfs mine.

"If only things had worked out otherwise, but they didn't, and I am sorry. But that was just one time, right?" He rubs his thumb across my wrist and my pulse skitters.

"We can try again." His voice takes on a cajoling tone.

I tip up my chin. "We can, huh?"

He nods, his features taking on an earnest expression. "Let me give you what you want. Let me take you away from the city to a place where there is no stress, where you don't need to worry about anything, but can focus on yourself. After all, if you are less tense, it helps to conceive right?"

"You've been reading up?"

He smiles and his features light up. "I confess that I may have researched it." He lowers his head and kisses the back of my palm. "Let's do it right this time. Let me marry you, make you my wife, and then we can try for a child."

"Is that your command?" I stare at him.

He rakes his gaze across my face. "And if it is?"

"Well then…" I flutter my eyelashes at him, "it's a 'no' from me."

"What?" His gaze widens. "You don't mean it."

"Better believe it." I flick my hair across my shoulders. "I thought you were going to apologize—"

"I already did, didn't I?" He scowls.

"Did you?" I look him up and down. "Clearly, you and I are not talking about the same thing if I have to remind you about what you have to apologize to me for."

I turn to leave and he grabs my wrist, "Don't leave." He growls, "Don't you dare turn away from me, Sparks."

"Oh, I am going to do more than that." I smile grimly. "Let go of me, Arpad."

"No."

"See, this is your problem." I shake my head. "On the one hand, you want to convince me to marry you. On the other, you're still trying to control me into doing what you think is right for me, and that's only going to push me away. You know that, right?"

He glares at me and his grip tightens. His jaw tics and his muscles coil. Then he squares his shoulders, and releases me. "See," he growls, "I am doing what you want, aren't I?"

"It's a start." I tuck my elbows into my sides. "Now, you can stay the hell away from me."

"Don't ask me to do that." He bunches his fingers into fists. "Anything but that."

"That," I tilt my head, "is the price."

"For what?"

"For a chance at convincing me that you're the man for me."

"I am the only one for you. You know that already."

"Do I though?" I scan his features. "All I see is a man who wants to control me into doing what he wants."

"Because it's right for you."

"Let me be the judge of that." I draw myself up to my full height. "Promise me, you won't interfere in my life."

His chest rises and falls. Anger rolls off of him in a dense cloud and his shoulders seem to grow even bigger. He takes a step forward and the strength of his dominance crashes into my chest. I throw up my hand. "Promise me," I force out the words through a throat gone dry. "Do it Arpad, if you want a chance at us being together."

"Will you come back to me if I do?"

"I don't know."

"What?" He blinks. "You expect me to let you go, not knowing if you will return to me?"

"That's the whole point. It's called taking a risk." I twist my lips. "Do you have the guts to take this chance on us? Do you, Arpad?"

"And if I refuse?"

"Then you've lost me anyway."

He squeezes the bridge of his nose, then mutters, "Fine."

"What?" I stare. "What did you say?"

He lowers his hand to his side, stares at me, "I give you your freedom," he snaps, "for now."

"And you promise that you won't come after me."

"I," his jaw tics, the skin around his mouth tightens, then he nods, "I promise."

"No matter what you see, you won't interfere in my life?"

His lips firm and he looks like he's about to refuse, then he nods again. "I won't interfere, no matter what."

"Promise." I hold out my hand, palm face up.

"I promise." He stares down at my palm. "If I touch you, I'll never let you go."

His shoulder muscles bunch, his chest planes ripple, and anger rolls off of him in waves. A drop of sweat slides down his throat, drawing attention to his sculpted torso. Jesus, why does he have to be so hot?

I hesitate, and he jerks his chin to the door. "Leave," he growls.

I blink at him.

"Now," he snaps. "Get out while you can, Sparks."

47

Arpad

"You agreed to let her go?" Edward frowns at me from across my cabin on the *Heartbeat.*

"I told her to leave while she still could." I raise the bottle of vodka to my lips and chug it down. The alcohol slides down cold, only to hit my stomach, and heat explodes up my spine. Even the bloomin' alcohol from her country of origin is full of contradictions. Just like her. Hot and cold. Giggling one second, all flashing eyes and heaving breasts the next. And why the hell am I still thinking about her?

Perhaps it's because I'm still on the yacht? I couldn't bring myself to leave here though. After all, I'd first made love to her here. When I am here, I feel closer to her; yet the ghosts of our coupling make me miss her more intensely. The pain is a dull throbbing ache somewhere behind my rib cage. Good, I deserve it. A reminder of how I'd screwed up. Edward had tried calling me, and when I hadn't answered he'd tracked me down here.

"Vodka?" He eyes the drink in my hand, "Since when did you start drinking vodka?"

I glare at him and he chuckles. "Is it because it's her favorite drink?" he asks.

"Who's favorite drink?" I grumble, then drink more of the liquor.

"Are we going to pretend that you're not heartbroken because of how you acted toward her?"

"No," I polish off the remaining alcohol, then slam the bottle down on the bar counter, "we are going to pretend that you never said that." I point a finger at him, then blink when his image splits into two.

Shit, maybe I drank too much. On the other hand, I'm still standing, so perhaps it's not nearly enough.

I pull out the pack of cigarettes from my pocket, toss one between my lips. I light the cigarette. The flames lick my fingertips and I hiss, before dropping the lighter on the counter.

I take a healthy drag, then cough. What the hell? Have I become so pussy-whipped that I've forgotten how to smoke?

My head spins. I pull the cigarette out from between my lips, stare at it.

"Thought you were trying to quit?"

"Trying." I growl. "The operative word is trying."

Like I'm trying to quit her. And succeeding at neither. No, strike that. The withdrawal pangs for nicotine cannot compare to the withdrawal symptoms I am facing at the thought of moving on from her. Shit, and I clearly have lost all my balls. I stub out the cigarette in the ash tray, then reach across the counter, and grab a fresh bottle from the inside shelf.

I straighten and the blood rushes from my head. The world tilts, I grab at the counter, and steady myself. Shit, guess I am more drunk than I thought?

I place the bottle on the bar, slowly, slowly, then try to unscrew the cap. My fingers slip and the bottle tips over. It hits the ground, then rolls toward Edward, who stops it with his foot.

He picks it up, then holds it behind his back.

"Aww, come on," I huff, "don't be such a spoilsport."

He walks over to the couch, then points to the one on the other side of the coffee table, "Take a seat."

I scowl, "Not particularly in the mood to confess anything, Father."

He sighs, "Sit down, will ya?" He stares at me with his patient all-knowing eyes.

"Don't you ever lose your shit?"

He arches an eyebrow. "Typical defensive mechanism," he drawls. "When you don't like what you see, you point the mirror at the other person."

"Is that an euphemism?"

"A metaphor. It's my way of saying you need to face the problem at hand, instead of running from it."

"And haven't you ever run from your issues? Have you always been so perfect that you've faced your fears head on?"

"If you only knew what goes on in the recesses of my mind." He purses his lips.

"Ooh, do tell." I reach over, grab another bottle of vodka, then amble over to drop into the seat he'd pointed to earlier.

I tilt the bottle to my lips, take a healthy swig. The liquid goes down smoothly. It hits my stomach and a low heat creeps up my spine. At least, this shit is good. Worth the odd million I'd paid for it.

Edward raises his own bottle and unscrews the cap.

I stare. "You're joining me, Father?"

He chuckles. "I do drink, you know. I simply try to do so in moderation."

"Booorinnng," I mutter, then drink some more. "So, are you going to tell me why you've made me sit here? For that matter," I lean forward, "why the hell did you come here anyway?"

"I'm not here alone, actually." He tilts his head, as if listening intently.

"No shit, I am here with you," I guffaw.

He holds his palm behind his ear.

"The hell you up to, Father?" I scowl.

"Wait for it; wait for it." His lips turn up in a smirk. And Edward never smirks. Which means this must be bad. Like really b-a-d.

I hear the sound of footsteps hitting the deck of the yacht, which rocks under the combined weight of whatever... Or whoever is headed for us.

"Oh, bollocks," I purse my lips, "don't tell me the rest of the Seven are —"

The door to the cabin is flung open and Saint marches in.

"Oh, for fuck's sake." I raise the bottle, chug down more of the drink.

It doesn't help dispel the nightmarish scenario that's forming in front of my eyes.

Sinner saunters in, followed by Damian, and Weston. "Bugger." I slouch down deeper into the sofa. The guys walk to the bar. Damian circles the counter, then pulls out a bottle of whiskey. "So, this is where you've been hiding the good stuff?" He holds up the MacAllan's 72-year-old whiskey… Which I admit, is something I'd bought on a whim.

Weston turns to me, "You mean you've been storm chasing with this expensive shit on board?"

"It's bolted in when I'm at sea, you twat." I swig back more of the vodka, then wipe the back of my palm across my mouth.

"He means he's not drinking whiskey anymore," Edward pipes up.

"What do you mean?" Saint looks between us. "The bastard's whiskey collection rival's only Sinner's." He glances around at the others, "No offense to the rest of you tossers."

"None taken." Damian chuckles, Weston laughs, and Edward watches the proceedings with his steady gaze. Damn it, doesn't the man ever take a day off from being a serious priest to simply, being…?

"I should be the one offended," Sinner drawls, "considering Beauchamp, here, wouldn't know taste if it bit him in the arse. Except when it comes to his choice of woman, of course."

"Don't talk about her, you bastard," I mutter.

Sinner arches an eyebrow. "This is not looking good."

"Nope, it isn't," Damian agrees.

Weston holds out his hand and Saint slaps a note on his outstretched palm.

"You guys bet on me?" I scowl at them, wondering why I don't feel angrier toward them. I should be livid, should toss them out of the only space where I feel at home, but hell, when you hang out with boys who've turned to men in front of your eyes, and who sometimes you hate almost as much as you love them like brothers… Then it's a little difficult to take offense at their shenanigans.

Edward jerks his chin toward me, "The man's taken to vodka like a mermaid to dry land."

"Uh?" Weston frowns at Edward, "Aren't mermaids supposed to find dry land difficult to navigate?"

He lowers his chin, "Keep up, Doc."

Weston rubs his chin. "So you mean he hasn't really taken to vodka?"

Edward winds his finger in the air.

"So, you mean he actually hates vodka but he's drinking it because..." Saint's voice trails off. "I see." He looks me up and down, then glowers, "Jesus, Arpad, couldn't you have held out just a little longer?" He pulls out his credit card and hands it over to Weston, who pockets it.

"The way Mr. No-strings-attached is going, it's best I keep it, don't you think?" He smirks.

"Whatever." Saint rocks back on his heels. "If the fucker's spirits sink any lower, he'll be drowning without water."

"Har, har." I lift the bottle of vodka and toast them, "Aren't all of you the soul of wit today?"

"Someone has to be, considering you've lost your mojo." Weston grabs his glass, then prowls over and drops into the seat on my right. Damian follows, drink in hand, and sits down on my left.

Saint and Sinner position themselves on either side of the sofa and Edward completes the hexagon from where he's seated opposite me.

I recognize it for what it is—an intervention. Hell, I was there for the ones we'd staged when each of the other men had met their match in their woman. Except Edward, that is, and soon he is going to be left alone... Hold on, what am I thinking? I don't have my woman yet. Far from it. In fact, the way things are headed, I am likely to remain a bachelor for a long time. Which is good. Which is what I had wanted not that long ago. So, what changed in the little time I've known her? How has she managed to turn my world upside down in such a short time?

"I proposed to her," I reply. "She agreed, at first, until she found out about my arrangement with the Bratva."

Silence descends on the room, then Saint explodes.

"The Bratva?"

Damian scowls. "Let me get this right. You decided to align with the Russian mafia. Why the hell would you do that?"

"The Bratva? You're taking the piss, right brother?" Weston drawls.

When I don't reply, the rest stare at me.

"Now, why would you do that?" Saint rubs the back of his neck, "It's not for the money, so I can only assume this has something to do with the bastards who kidnapped us?"

"When were you going to tell us?" Sinner's voice is hard.

I set the bottle on the floor, then rise to my feet. Lose my balance, right myself, then fold my arms across my chest. "It's not how it seems."

Shit, why does this have to be so hard? These guys have had my back for so long. Surely, they'll understand why I had to do it, right?

"Hold on, chaps, let's give him a chance to explain." Edward turns to me. "I assume you have an explanation?" Edward's gaze narrows, "You do, don't you?"

I turn to face them, "You know how when we were kidnapped, our captors made me and Damian fight?"

The men nod.

"Well, it didn't stop there."

"It didn't? Edward's face pales. "What..." he swallows, "what else did they have you do?"

I take in his pinched features, his tense body. Shit, what else had they done to *him*? I frown at him, open my mouth to ask, when he shakes his head. Fine, so he doesn't want to talk about it, then? That's okay. There's a time and place for each of us to confess the extent to which the incident had ripped through our minds and ravaged our emotions. Perhaps if I come out with mine, it will help Edward open up about his experiences too? It's another reason to finally come clean to them.

"They," I square my shoulders, "they... made me fight in underground fighting clubs."

"Wait," Damian scowls, "the kidnappers pitted us against each other. They made us fight until one or both of us lost consciousness. It became a game for the two of us, how to keep hitting each other, without hurting the other too much? Remember? And when the kidnappers caught on, I took the blame for it." Damian curls his fingers into fists. "They blindfolded me, took me to an underground fighting ring, where they pitted me against men stronger than me. I fought them, and survived." He rubs the back of his neck. "Hell, it put me off fighting in any form after that... It's also why I turned to music." He shakes his head. "But I put myself forward so you wouldn't have to do it."

"Only," I draw in a breath, "they didn't spare me either."

"Motherfuckers." Damian's jaw tics.

"I don't understand." Saint scowls. "You were the smallest among us."

"Until I outgrew you lot," I snap.

"But at that time, you were smaller than most boys your age," Sinner reminds me. "Why the hell did they make you fight?"

"Because it made for bloodthirsty sport? Because they were

perverted mofos?" I roll my shoulders. "Because they were sure that, unlike Damian, I would fail?"

"Only, you didn't," Edward says slowly.

I curl my fingers into fists.

"I still don't understand." Damian purses his lips. "You were a preteen. Hell, you couldn't hold your own against me, in our mock fights—"

"Until I had to fight for my life."

"So..." Edward clears his throat, "even after Damian offered to fight in your place, they made you face opponents in the underground fighting cages and you never told us?"

I hunch my shoulders. "Have you told us everything they did to you?"

Edward pales.

"That's what I thought." I curl my lips.

"But this isn't about me." He squares his shoulders. "It doesn't change that you took on grown men when you were not even thirteen and managed to defeat them with your bare hands." He leans back in his seat and some of the color filters back into his cheeks.

I straighten my back. "Who said I fought with bare hands?"

"You didn't?" Weston frowns.

"I was given a piece of rope to defend myself, considering I was much younger than my opponents." I glance around the room, "It was their way of giving me a slight advantage... Or so they said."

"The bastards," Sinner growls.

There's silence, then Edward exhales, "So you used the rope to defeat them?" All emotion is schooled from his face. That's the thing with him... Except for the few moments when he lets the mask slip, you can never tell what is going on in that razor sharp mind of his. And the Father has an astute mind... I remember enough of him as a boy to recollect how highly perceptive he'd been. He has a head for numbers and had displayed an early sense of business acumen, which is why all of us had been shocked by his decision to join the seminary. Guess the Lord really does work in mysterious ways... Or he'd simply ordained that the incident turn our lives upside down so we'd each have to reinvent ourselves. Me turning to the Bratva and him becoming a man of God.

"Yes." I take in Edward's stoic features then turn my attention to each of the others in the room. "Turns out, I'm good with my hands." I raise my palms and stare at them. "I didn't have a choice; I had to figure out how to use the single piece of rope to defend myself."

"And you did?"

"Yeah," I crack my neck. "I quickly learned how to tie it around the neck of my opponent and threaten to choke him, until he let me go."

"So, your reputation preceded you?" Damian exhales. "Didn't realize when we nicknamed you Killer, we were only confirming the role you'd already played in the ring."

"Except I didn't kill anyone."

"You didn't?" Edward frowns.

"Nope." I shake my head. "If I spared their lives, they owed me."

"And that's how you built your circle of influence in the underground?" Saint interjects.

I nod, "It's also how I struck up a friendship with Nikolai, the scion of the Bratva."

"Nikolai?" Sinner scowls. "The asshole who first told us that the Mafia were behind our kidnapping?"

"You kept in touch with him?" Edward's jaw hardens.

I draw in a breath, "If you recall, in exchange for the lead, Niko had wanted Damian to face his guy in an underground fight club." I refer back to how the Seven of us had met Nikolai.

"Only, Baron took Damian's place, and lost the fight," Saint says slowly.

"Then you stepped in and defeated the man the Bratva fielded that day," Sinclair recalls.

Saint tilts his head, "That was what, ten years ago?"

"Almost thirteen." I rub the back of my neck. "That day, Niko and I struck up a friendship. We've kept in touch since."

"And you didn't think to tell any of us?" Sinner growls.

I widen my stance. "It didn't seem like a big deal. We simply hung out, kept in touch. Over a period of time, I grew to trust the man. Enough that when he called me with a proposition, I agreed."

"A proposition?"

"What the hell did you agree to?"

"Niko's sister —" I blow out a breath, "She had taken over the family business, the legitimate arm of it. Tensions were escalating between the Bratva and their rival gang. They wanted me to marry her and get her out of LA to keep her safe."

"Hold on." Sinner straightens, "LA? Niko's sister? You aren't talking about Karina, are you?"

I nod, "I agreed to lure her to London, but I stopped short of committing to marrying her. I told them I'd give it some thought. Getting her out of LA was the priority."

"So you made sure that we offered her the gig to take on the security for us Seven?" Edward interjects.

Of course, the Father is the first to put it all together. The man is so intuitive sometimes it's scary.

"Hang on. Something doesn't make sense. You were keeping an eye on her," Saint drums his fingers on his chest, "while she was the one we charged with gathering intelligence on the men who kidnapped us?"

"With her background with the Bratva, she was the right person to suss out any possible gangsters wherever they were."

"This entire picture is one hell of a mess." Edward places the tips of his fingers together.

"You're telling me?" I glance around at their faces. "So, what do I do now?"

They stare back at me. My five best friends, the most feared businessmen in the country, meet my gaze with varying expressions of disbelief.

"If I didn't see it myself, I'd have thought you guys were in shock." I snicker.

"I'm not shocked," Edward finally says. "You guys shocked?"

"Nope."

"Nah."

"No way."

"It's what we expected of you," Damian drawls.

"You did?"

"Sure," Saint scratches his jaw, "fuck up your life royally, more than any of us have done in the past? Of course, it had to be you, Arpad."

I scowl, "Come on, guys, that's not fair."

"You should've thought about that before you manipulated her into your life," Sinner drawls.

I stare at him, "Hello, pot; meet kettle?" I glower at him.

"Hey, sure. I may have steered things so they went my way—"

"Steered, my arse." I snort. "You were gunning for revenge, and decided to marry Summer so you could keep an eye on her."

"The ends justify the means." Sinner shrugs, "I may have gone about it unconventionally, but I was already in love with her."

"And I'm not? " I glare at him, "Now, I want to marry that obstinate woman but she won't hear of it. She told me to stay away from her."

"So, of course, you're keeping an eye on her?" Edward narrows that all-seeing gaze on me.

"Umm. Yes?" I offer.

"You're going to continue to stalk her and get all up in her business, aren't you?" he asks.

I frown. "Is that a trick question, because you know I can't keep away."

He leans forward in his chair. "She asked you to give her space, I assume?"

I nod.

"Yet, you are flagrantly contradicting her request?"

I drag my fingers through my hair. "She's upset, not thinking clearly. I understand—"

"Do you?" Edward glares at me. I blink. Shit, today is a first. The usually placid Father has unbent enough to reveal how displeased he is with me? Well, let's just say, that has never happened before. Hell, the last time we'd seen Edward this worked up was when… We'd intervened on Damian's behalf. I frown. Is the fact that the rest of the Seven are finding their partners getting to him? Nah, not possible. Edward had chosen his path, and he's the kind of guy who'll stay committed to the promises he's made, no matter the price he has to pay.

"Look," I hold up my hands, "given the fact that we're no closer to finding who instigated our kidnapping, and considering her ties with the Bratva, no way, can I go without checking in on her."

Edward rises to his feet. "Given you are in love with her and you want her to come around to marrying you, no way, can you afford to piss her off further."

"Fuck," I swear aloud.

He nods. "My sentiments exactly."

"So, you expect me to simply… What? Stay away from her?'

He nods again.

"And what if she gets into some trouble, and needs saving?"

"Has she needed saving so far?"

"We—ll." I scratch my chin. She needed my sperm. No, not really. She'd had a sperm donor all lined up, until I'd messed up her plans, and then when I told her to pretend to be married to me, so I could take her to see Grandmama, she'd traded that for my impregnating her. And then, every step of the way, she'd matched me. Even when I'd pulled the Bratva surprise on her—asshole that I am—she hadn't flinched. She'd simply broken our arrangement and stormed out of there... Something no one else had done before.

"She's bloody capable of taking care of herself," I finally admit.

Edward nods.

"And feisty." I can't stop the smile that curves my lips.

Saint smirks. "Keep going."

"And gorgeous and full of sass, and boy, when we do yoga together—"

"Hold on," Sinclair chokes, "she's got you to do fuckin' yoga with her?"

I redden. "Uh, it was kind of foreplay," I rush to explain, "but I gotta tell you, those positions, they look easy, but they are not."

"No?" Weston chuckles.

"Nope." I shake my head. Shit, if I am not digging myself in deeper. "I have a whole lotta respect for all those yoga bunnies now."

Damian spits out his whiskey, "Did he just say yoga bunny?"

"He said yoga bunnies." Weston holds out his hand and Saint pulls out another credit card from his wallet and hands it over. "That will pay for our second honeymoon, thank you very much."

"Just try not to come back too soon." Saint grimaces.

"What? Did you guys just have another bet going?" I growl.

"The same one." Weston grins. "Anything else you want to tell us?"

"Nothing that you can profit from." I firm my lips.

"Aww don't be like that," Weston laughs, "you'll get used to it soon."

"What?" I frown.

"This sensation of being unmoored and helpless, and basically, feeling like she has you by the balls."

"You forget one thing," I dig my finger into my hair and tug, "she does have me by the balls."

"Good." Edward looks me up and down, "So whatever happens, you won't intrude?"

"Within limits."

"What does that mean?"

"I won't stalk her, or spy on her. Whatever I do, it will be in the open."

"Don't do anything that'll get you into trouble." Edward walks over and slaps me on my shoulder, "You get me, Arpad? Don't fucking screw this up?"

"Why the hell does it feel like you're warning me, Father?"

"We were put on this earth to learn our lessons, and this, I fear, is the biggest test for you yet."

"And you, Father?" I tilt my head, "What's the lesson you are supposed to be learning this life time?"

He flattens his lips, "Wouldn't you like to find out?"

48

———————

Karina

I walk out of the apartment which I had shifted into a few days ago.

I'd moved out of my earlier place, which maybe had been stupid, considering how much I had liked the place. After all, I'd have been able to clean up the place and spot any cameras or bugs he'd left behind… But somehow, when it comes to that asshole, I don't trust myself. Or rather, I don't put it past him to pull a fast one on me.

So, I had called around to the girls and they'd come to my rescue.

Julia had moved in with Damian, so her place, which was previously Amelie's until she'd married Weston, was free. But considering that apartment block is also owned by one of the Seven, I wouldn't put it past them to find a way to bug that place, as well. So, I had moved into a hotel for a few days, then found this new apartment, which had been a stroke of luck, considering the best apartments seem to be snapped up so quickly.

The place is a two-bedroom apartment on a quiet side street, in a residential area. All of which suits me fine. I had also taken ample precautions, to ensure the space wasn't bugged. Not that I expected it to be, but after what Arpad had done, I couldn't leave anything up to chance.

As is habit, I glance up and down the road as I approach my car. Nothing seems amiss. I scowl. Is that good? That everything looks fine? Has Arpad asshole actually decided to stick to his promise and leave me alone? Would he not even watch me from afar? Or have people follow me and report back to him? I glance about again. A couple walks up the street; a mother, with a stroller and another child, a girl trailing behind her, passes me. I glance down at the baby in the stroller and my stomach flip-flops.

I could have been pregnant with his child. Good thing the alphahole didn't manage to impregnate me then. Who'd have thought he'd turn out to be a lying, manipulative, bastard? Hell, he's a billionaire and a venture capitalist, so I hadn't expected him to be completely sinless… But honestly? Colluding with the Bratva... With my own family. The one thing I had tried to steer clear of, and he'd pulled me right back into the heart of everything I had tried to avoid. *Stop it, stop thinking of him.* He's gone from my life, and that has to be good, right?

I smile at the baby, who gurgles back and points at me. The kid warbles something and the mother laughs. "It's your beanie." She smiles at me. "She likes the color."

"Me too, mommy," exclaims the older child. "I like red too."

"Oh." I laugh as I touch my hat. It's not a color I'd normally wear, but after alphahole had pointed out how much he liked me in it—No, that is not the reason I am wearing it. Is it?

I turn away, whip off the beanie and stuff it in my pocket, then head for my car. My foot connects with an upside-down hat that skitters to the side. Change falls out of it. "Shit." I reach down, and gather up the coins and dump them back in the upturned hat.

"Got a cigarette?" A gruff voice asks.

I glance up into the bright, shining eyes of a homeless man. His hair flows down to his shoulders while an overgrown beard covers the lower half of his face. He's wearing a shirt that's ragged but clean; his pants are a color that must once have been black, but now edges toward grey.

"I don't smoke." I reply.

"Cigars then?" He asks.

I huff out a laugh, "Do I look like I carry cigars with me?"

"You look like a woman who knows what she wants."

"If only." I let out a sigh. "I thought I did, but I don't anymore, know what I mean?"

"Confusion." He nods. "It's a good sign."

"It is?" I scowl.

"It's the first step to getting clarity."

Hmm. "And you know that how?"

"It's the natural progression of things. First, the experimentation. Then the deconstruction. Followed by rationalization. Finally, the reconstruction."

I laugh. "I have no idea what you're talking about."

"Sure, you do." He chuckles. "You just don't want to admit it to yourself."

"Gee, thanks for the words of wisdom," I mutter, "but no, thanks."

I rummage around in my purse, pull out a few notes, then drop them into his hat. He doesn't even look at it. Weird.

"Now, a cigarette, pretty lady? I wouldn't say 'no' to that."

I glance up and down the street. There's no shop in sight. "Why don't you take the money and buy the cigarettes?"

He stares at me and I resist the urge to roll my eyes. "Fine, fine. I'll get some for you on my way back."

"I may not be here then."

"Oh?" I frown. "Where will you be?"

"Here today, gone tomorrow, unlike the love in your eyes, for him."

"Love?" I gape at him. "I'm sorry, but I don't know what you're talking about."

"That's what he said too." He gestures to the signboard he's holding up.

When we two parted
 In silence and tears,
 Truly that hour foretold
 Sorrow to this.

"Cheerful," I grimace. "Personally, I prefer Pushkin."

"I loved you, and I probably still do…" he recites.

"And for a while the feeling may remain." I smile.

"But let my love no longer trouble you," he tilts his head.

"I do not wish to cause you any pain." I toss my hair over my shoulder. Shit, why does that feel…so evocative…so telling, about my current circumstances? Why the hell does the romance in the words remind me of the douchebag I'd decided to break up with? Now wait, I'd never been with him, so we hadn't broken up. Besides, we're just taking a break from each other. That's all, right? I mean, I'd told him to back off… Okay, I'd made him promise to stay away, and apparently, he is doing so.

Bastard. When has he ever listened to what I've asked of him? Never. That's the correct answer. And this time he had turned and left… Okay, technically, he'd told me to leave… Still, I hadn't thought he'd adhere to his promise, considering he hadn't told me outright that he would. And if he hadn't, I'd be mad at him for not leaving me alone. Classic case of, damned if you do, damned if you don't. And now, I am making excuses on his behalf. I really needed to have my head examined.

"Aren't you getting late?" homeless guy asks.

I glance down at him, then back to my car. "Yeah," I huff out a breath, "I am."

"Best be getting along then."

I glance at my watch and wince. I am running late. I head for the car, then turn to him, "Will you be here when I return?"

"Take your chances; live dangerously."

I blink. Why do his words remind me of how the rest of the Seven converse with each other? All the talk about pregnancy and babies, must be getting to me. It's the only reason I'd stopped long enough to have a stream of consciousness conversation with a complete stranger.

I close the distance to my car, get into it and pull away from the curb. I make it to Soho and manage to find a parking spot. Hallelujah. I can see why Londoners prefer the Tube, but hell, if I am going to commute packed into the underground. And no, I don't like being driven around either. Why should I, when I love driving my car? I park and head for the restaurant for my lunch date.

I walk through the buzzing tables toward the back. Niko glances at me from his seat at the corner table. Of course, he has the best seat in the house. Nothing but the best for my family, and I admit, I get my good taste in food, in clothes… In men…? Not that…but everything else, going for the top-of-the-line expensive shit. Yeah, that's my father and brothers for you.

I stomp over and sink into the chair opposite him.

A waitress immediately materializes. Of course, she does. Niko has that way with the women. Somehow, they sense the mean, grade-A asshole that he is; combined with the scent of money that wraps around him like a lover, not to mention, the dark edge of danger that clings to him like a second skin... Yeah, they pretty much come in their panties when they see him.

Niko nods at her, "Two lunch specials."

I frown. "Niko, what the hell? You know how much I hate it when you order for me."

He frowns, then nods toward the menu in front of me, "See anything you want, *Malyshka*?"

"Don't call me that." I frown.

He blows out an exaggerated breath. "What will you have your highness?"

"That's better." I turn up my chin to glance at the waitress who, of course, is staring at Niko like he'll disappear from in front of her any moment.

"The lunch special, please."

She doesn't reply.

"Miss?" I touch her arm and she jerks.

"Oh," she turns to me, "of course, and to drink?"

"Vodka. The best you have," Niko replies, and the woman's gaze widens. Her lips part, and I swear, I can see little hearts in her eyes and more circling around her head.

"Still water for me," I reply.

Niko arches his eyebrows. "Since when do you not want to drink alcohol?"

Since I decided I want to have a child, which clearly, isn't happening anytime soon. So why the hell don't I feel like having alcohol? Especially since I had fallen off the wagon so spectacularly that evening at the bar... That evening when he'd stalked over to me and confessed how much he'd wanted to give me a child... When he'd asked me to marry him so we could start afresh... And I had said no... Shit, why the hell am I thinking about that obnoxious prat again?

"Karina?" Niko frowns. "You okay?"

I cough. "Yes," I nod, "of course, I am. Just parched, that's all."

"Hmm." Niko rakes his gaze across my features.

"So," I fold my arms in my lap, "Why did you want to see me?"

"To apologize."

"Oh?" I glance at him with suspicion. My oldest brother does not apologize to anyone... ever.

"Indeed." He nods. "I am sorry that we used your company as a front for the Bratva's activities. It's not fair given the effort you've put into building it up. We'll withdraw our interests from it."

I blink, "You will?"

He nods.

"Why are you doing this?" I scowl at him.

"Because you're my sister." He half smiles, and his features soften, "my only sister."

I purse my lips. "Why is it that I don't trust where this is coming from?"

He chuckles, "I only have your best interests at heart."

"Not that I don't believe it. Only," I stab a finger at him, "You use that as an excuse... for interfering in my life. You and... and... Papa, both of you."

"You still pissed at us for asking Arpad to watch out for you?"

A-n-d, of course, he'd have to bring up the one person I am trying not to think about.

"What do you think?" I grouse.

"I think you need to look at it from our point of view."

"Which is?"

"You are a weak link for us."

I gape at him. "Weak link? Honestly, Niko, if that's why you called me here... To insult me —" I rise to my feet and he reaches forward and grabs my hand, "Come on, Kaykay, you know it's not like that."

Jeez, why does he have to use the name he called me when we were kids. It takes me right back to our childhood, when I had five brothers doting on me and could pretty much get my way on anything. After all, I was the youngest, and the only girl in the family.

I sink back into the chair and blow out a breath, "Then, what is it like? Explain it to me, Niko, because honestly, all I can see is my family ganging up with that...that bastard, to tie me down in a marriage, and —"

He releases my hand but continues to hold my gaze. "Did he hurt you?"

"Who?"

"Beauchamp, did he fucking do anything to you?"

Nothing I didn't want.

"Answer me," Niko snaps, and I blink.

"N…no, of course, not. He didn't. Arpad's not that kind of man." And now I am defending him? To my own brother? What the hell is wrong with me?

"But he did manipulate me. He tried to control my life, without my realizing it. He tricked me onto his boat and—"

"And—?" Niko leans forward, "What did he do?"

"He proposed to me, you ass. Just like you guys wanted. Honestly, I can't believe you and Papa came up with this crazy scheme. It's not like I can't look after myself."

"Oh course, you can. You grew up with us. You know how to take care of yourself, but our enemies are out to get us, and trust me when I say that you don't want to be caught in the cross fire. And if you are, at all, you want someone to have your back."

I stare at him. "Are things that bad between the Bratva and the Sicilians?"

His jaw hardens, he sits up straight and his gaze grows cold. "It's not good," he replies.

Oh, hell. That means shit is about to go down, and I've eavesdropped on enough meetings that my father and brothers have had without me to know that things will get worse before they get better.

"It's why we wanted to make sure you were safe."

"By ensuring that I left LA?"

"For one."

"And by getting me married?" I burst out.

He stares at me, "If you're married to someone in the brotherhood, you will be safe *and* taken care of. It would put Dad at peace—"

I open my mouth, and he holds up his hand.

"Let me finish, Karina." My brother's tone brooks no argument. In that moment, he sounds so like my father—no, even more scary than my father—that I blink. Good grief. He is already turning into the *Pakhan,* without officially inheriting the title.

"We know you are an independent, modern woman, and you have your views and opinions, and we respect them."

I snort, "If that were true, you wouldn't be here telling me why you thought it was a good idea to arrange for me to marry a man you guys thought was the right choice for me."

"He is, though—the right choice." Niko's gaze moves past me. "Too bad, he seems to have moved on."

"What?"

I angle my head to glance over my shoulder and see him. What the
—? It's him, the jackass who's occupied my every waking moment, and
he's with another woman?

Arpad f'ing Beauchamp looks tanned and relaxed. His dark hair is in
that unruly mess I want to run my fingers through. He's wearing a white
button down, open at the chest. His shoulders seem even bigger than
when I last saw them. Has he been working out? Probably been lifting
that blonde bimbo who's sitting next to him… Not opposite him, but in
the chair next to him. Bet their knees are brushing right now as he
raises his shot glass and holds it up to his date. She lowers her head,
puts her mouth to the glass—to his glass, the one he'd touched with his
lips—and takes a sip.

She coughs, reaches for her water and the bastard grins. He toasts
her with the shot glass then downs it. Bet there's vodka in there too.
Asshole is sharing the drink I introduced him to? With her?

"Karina?" Niko's voice reaches me, but I can't glance away from the
tableau unfolding in front of my eyes. How dare he do this to me? How
dare he flaunt that…that floozy in front of me? No wonder I haven't
seen him in a while. He's been too busy getting his share of vagina from
her, no doubt. Gah! Anger sizzles up my spine. I jump up, turn to go,
when Niko grabs my arm again. "Sit down," he growls.

"B...but..." I sputter, "he's with someone else."

"You walked away from him."

"Of course, I did," I spit out. "That *mudak* had the gall to try to
manipulate my life; he tried to get me to comply with his wishes without
giving me the full picture."

"And if he had, would you have listened to him?"

I guess not.

A peal of laughter rings out behind me, a feminine one. *Don't look
back, don't.* I glance behind, just as he feeds her some food from his
spoon, before scooping up some food and bringing it to his mouth. He
wraps his lips around the spoon, licks it clean, and my belly trembles.
Moisture laces my core. Bloody hell, how can I be so turned on by him?

He lowers his spoon to his plate, then reaches over and whispers a
strand of hair back from her cheek.

That's when something inside of me snaps. I jump to my feet and
stalk over to him.

49

Arpad

"What the hell are you doing?" She slaps her hand on the table with such force that the cutlery jumps, the vodka bottle tilts, and I reach out and grab it.

"Would you like some?" I pour some into a shot glass and offer it to her.

"I'm not drinking."

"Funny," I twist my lips, "that's not how it seemed to me the other day."

"That was a…mistake," she mutters, "I, uh, am not drinking again."

I stiffen, then peer into her features. "Are you uh," I clear my throat. Why the hell is this so hard to say? "I mean, are you… You know, trying to—"

She glares at me, then shakes her head.

I firm my lips. Okay so I can be a class-A dickass… You know what I mean, but even I know not to blurt out the question I have uppermost on my mind… Not in front of a third party.

"Have you met Diana?" I jerk my hand toward the other woman, without taking my gaze off Sparks' sweet face. Shit, the way she narrows her gaze, the sparks in those eyes. Jesus, she's gonna kill me and she's not even aware of it. I part my legs wider to accommodate the arousal that already tents my pants. One glance at her, a whiff of her sweet feminine scent, and damn, if I don't want to simply swing her over my shoulder and carry her out of here. Down, boy. Not yet.

I tear my gaze from her gorgeous features to turn to the other woman. "Diana this is Karina, my…uh…"

"His security consultant," she snaps.

"Ah," Diana glances between us, a frown on her face. "Would you like to join us?"

"Nope." She makes a popping sound at the end of the word. "I wouldn't dream of disturbing your date."

She stares at Diana then back at me.

"However, since I am already here," she juts out her hip and plants her hand on it, "maybe we can talk about the emergency that you called me about earlier?"

"Emergency?" I frown. "I don't think there's an emergency."

She snaps back her shoulders, then schools her features into a pleasant expression. All along, she glares at me. A chuckle rumbles up and I, wisely, swallow it. Not even I am foolish enough to toy with a woman who's working herself up into a temper, the way Sparks is right now.

"You were saying?" I prompt her.

"No, you were." She scowls at me. "I distinctly remember you calling me earlier and telling me you had an emergency." She draws herself up to her full height. "On the other hand, if you don't recall…" She turns away, and damn her, but I can't stop myself from jumping to my feet.

"Oh, *that* emergency," I drawl.

She pauses.

"I remember now."

She stares at me over her shoulder, "Perhaps you'd care to step this way to discuss it then?"

"Of course." I drop my napkin on my chair, then turn to my employee, whom I had enlisted to go along with me on this charade, "You don't mind, do you, Diana?"

She glances at me, then at the retreating back of my woman.

"Good luck," she half smiles, before rising to her feet, "you are going to need it with that one."

Isn't that the truth?

I follow Sparks as she skirts the tables and walks to the door that leads to a hallway at the back.

I step inside and she turns to me.

"How dare you?" she snarls. "How dare you…you flaunt her in my face like that?"

"I was sitting there, minding my own business, and you come along."

"And you happen to show up in the same restaurant where I am eating lunch?" She fumes.

"Heard about coincidences?"

She scoffs, "It's as much of a coincidence as…being able to touch your feet the very first time you attempt a sun salutation."

I blink. "Uh, is that a yoga reference?

"Of course, it is, you moron." She tips up her chin, then purses her lips. "I thought I told you to stay away from me?"

"I was at the restaurant before you arrived," I point out.

"So, you did notice when I walked in?"

Clever woman. She's got me there. I draw myself up to my full height. "I'm always aware of my surroundings and everyone in my vicinity," I mutter. "It comes with the territory."

"You mean of being part of the Bratva?"

"I'm not with them, Sparks." I scowl. "I told you. I merely did Niko a favor—"

"Favor?" she bursts out. "So…so you asked me to marry you as a favor to him?"

"You know that's not true!"

"So, it started out that way, though?"

I fold my arms across my chest. I am not going to lie to her. Not now; not ever again. From now on, I need to be upfront with her if… there is any hope of my winning her over.

"Yes." I hold her gaze. "Yes, it did play a factor in my asking you to accompany me to see my family, but not only. From the first time I saw you, I was attracted to you, you know that."

"What I know," she twirls a lock of her hair around her finger, "is that, since you first saw me, you've been manipulating my life."

"And I told you, that's who I am. I need to be in control, Sparks. You understand that, don't you?"

"No," she shakes her head, "no, I don't. And what you did was not just about control… It was—"

"Over the top?"

"Underhanded," she snarls.

"Passionate?"

"Calculating." She firms her lips.

"Intense?"

"Conniving." Her chest rises and falls.

"See? That is where we disagree." I lower my knees, so I am at eye-level with her. "What you think of as being deceitful is what I term as my killer instinct. It's going that extra inch to ensure that I get what I want. And what I want is you, Sparks."

"Well, you don't have me."

"I will have you, make no mistake about that."

"See, *that's* where we disagree." She narrows her gaze. "Holding too tightly brings nothing but pain. Surrender is freedom."

"That's what I've been telling you, babe." I straighten, "Surrender to me, and enjoy what only I can give you."

"And what is that?" she says in a low voice. "Allowing you to pleasure my body while you don't have any idea what's going on in my head?"

"Ah, now *that's* where we disagree." I allow my lips to kick up at the sides. "There is no pleasure without pain, no gain without torment, no giving in until your mind and body are in sync. And that's what I specialize in."

"I am not a toy, you…you… Wanker."

"Don't talk to me like that," I snap.

"Oh, but I can, and I will. In fact, I am going to make sure you're going to listen to every word I say."

"Is that right?"

She nods, "Read my lips, Arpad Beauchamp. You've fired the opening round; the next move is mine. I am going to do what I think is right for me, and you will have no choice but to watch."

50

Karina

"How dare he follow me, and after he promised he'd step back and let me live my life?" I pace back and forth in the living room of my new apartment. What is happening to me? A month ago, my life was where I wanted it to be, business had been going well and I had been all set and ready to have a baby, and now… Now it's falling apart, and all because of that jackass.

"Are you sure he was following you?" Isla chews on her lower lip. "Maybe it really was a coincidence?"

"Right," I toss my hair over my shoulder, "and everyone who tries to meditate is able to calm their mind."

"Whoa, lady." Isla stares at me. "That's some deep shit you're coming up with."

"It is, right?" I twist my fingers together. "I think my brain cells have melted together. I mean, look at me." I gesture to myself. "I used to love wearing designer clothes. I'd walk into a meeting full of men and enjoy the power I held over them, but now—"

"Now you find all that hot girl shit exhausting?" She nods. "Instead, you want to do the old lady shit, like a puzzle, knit a sweater, sit in a chair while you shower…?"

I glower at her and she chuckles.

"Did you get your knickers in a twist because you saw him?"

I blink. "Not exactly. I'm just going crazy trying to come up with a way to get back at him."

"And that's important?" Isla tilts her head. "That you have your revenge for something he supposedly did?"

"Supposedly?" I huff. "He totally maneuvered me to where he wanted me to be."

"Maybe that's what you wanted, too?"

I turn on her, "What do you mean?"

"Look, Karina," she leans back in the sofa, "you're so strong willed… It's one of the things I love about you. If I had half the backbone you have —"

"Oh, but you do, Isla. You run a successful wedding planning business, which is no mean feat."

She smiles, then shakes a finger at me, "Oh, no, we're not talking about me here."

"But —"

She shakes her head. "Let me finish, babe."

I sigh, "Sorry, that was impolite of me, please continue."

She folds her legs under her, makes herself comfortable. "That's what I mean. You are so clear-headed, doll. There really isn't much anyone can force you into doing."

"Except, he did…" I say slowly.

She nods, "So maybe somewhere inside, you wanted it, too?"

"What?" I frown. "You think I subconsciously knew what was happening, but I went along with it anyway?"

She purses her lips. "All I'm saying is, he's not the only guilty party here."

"Hey," I protest, "who's side are you on?"

"Yours, honey, always yours." She smiles. "I've seen each of the other women go through their own journey before they got one of the Seven."

"Which is why you've sworn never to be entangled with one of them?"

She scowls.

"Yeah, yeah, okay, we're not talking about you." I make the motion of zipping my lips with my fingers.

"Good." She props her elbow on the armrest and supports her chin on her palm. "Each of the other women found a way to strip away the masks the Seven wear to the world, so their true natures were exposed."

"You mean, they found a way to see them at their most vulnerable?"

She nods. "What bothers you the most about what happened with Arpad?"

"That he used false pretenses to first lure me to London, then to make me accompany him to see his family."

"So do the same to him."

"What?" I stare. "What do you mean?"

"You pull a fast one on him… Even the playing field."

"Right," I say slowly. "What do you suggest I should do?"

"What would hurt him as much as he hurt you?"

"I don't want to hurt him."

She frowns.

"I mean, I do…but only in a way that ensures that he apologizes to me." I drag my fingers through my hair. "I just want him to say he's sorry for what he did, you know? Is that too much to ask?"

"No, of course not." Isla presses a finger to her cheek. "He colluded with your family; you should do the same."

"What do you mean?"

"Collude with the rest of the women to put a plan in place. Then spring a surprise on him which he doesn't see coming."

"But," I stare, "why would the others help me? I mean, they are married to men who are part of the Seven, and the Seven are friends with Arpad, so wouldn't they technically want to side with him?"

"Unless they see it as helping him. Why don't you ask them?"

I open my mouth, when the doorbell rings.

"Yay, the troops are here." Isla jumps up and races to open the door. A second later, Summer flounces in, followed by Victoria, now sporting a baby bump, Julia, and Amelie.

"Heyyy!" Summer throws her arms around me. "How are you, Karina? I am so excited to help you in operation Alphaprank."

"Alphaprank?" I blink rapidly. "What's that?"

"It's the plan you're going to come up with to bring Arpad to his knees." Victoria beams at me, then rubs her belly, in the way many pregnant women do when they're adjusting to the new life they are carrying in their body.

I walk up to her. "May I?" I ask.

"Of course." She takes my hand and places it on her belly.

"Oh," I gulp, "it's harder than I thought it would be."

"I know, right?" Her smile widens further. "I'm still getting used to it myself."

I keep my palm pressed to her stomach. "Has he or she started moving yet?"

She shakes her head. "Because it's my first, the doctor says it may be twenty weeks before I feel the little thing move, but I am hoping it will be much sooner."

A soft sensation invades my chest. My throat closes and a pressure builds behind my eyes. Shit, what's wrong with me? I haven't even gone back to taking the hormone shots for anything since I found out I wasn't pregnant. So why is this…affecting me so much?

"You okay?" Victoria peers into my face.

I nod. "Yes," I clear my throat, "I'm so happy for you." I blink back the moisture that threatens to leak from my eyes. I will not let myself cry. Really, in the bigger scheme of things, it doesn't mean anything that I couldn't get pregnant on the first try, right?

So many women have been through so much more when they tried to conceive. I have barely started my journey, so why the hell does my chest feel so heavy?

Victoria releases my hand and I lower my arm to my side. "Come on, you should sit down."

She laughs, but allows me to guide her to the sofa. I place a cushion at her back and she smiles her thanks. "It's a nice place." She beams, "You're going to miss it when you move in with Arpad."

"Or maybe he could move in with me?"

She stares at me, then bursts out laughing. "Why not? It's time the alphaholes realize they can't have their way in everything."

"Damn right," I mutter.

Behind me, Isla claps her hands. "Ladies, who wants a glass of wine? Other than Victoria and Karina, that is."

The women stare at me.

"You're not drinking?" Julia asks.

"Umm." I twist my fingers together. "Just doing a detox thing," I mutter.

"Ah," Amelie nods, "that's wise. Just as long as you are not on a food diet of any kind, because," she places the bag she's carrying on the coffee table, then rummages around in it before producing a container and pulling off the lid. "Tada," she crows, "homemade chocolate chip cookies."

"OMG." Julia jumps toward it and grabs one from the tin. "I am starving." She chomps her way through half of it, then rolls her eyes, "Ohh…. It's almost as good as an orgasm."

"Nothing's as good as an orgasm." Summer smirks, reaching for a cookie as well.

"Especially not when you have an alphahole on hand, ready to use his…uh…hand, and other parts of his anatomy, to provide one on demand." Amelie cackles.

"Pleaaaase, you girls." Isla claps her hands on her ears. "Can you spare me the details? Especially since I know your husbands. Speaking of, can we get back to the topic at hand," she smirks, "i.e. Project Alphaprank?"

All of their faces swivel toward me. I reach for a cookie, then walk back to my seat. "Yeah, tell me more." I bite into the pastry and the chewy chocolate chunks coat my tongue. "Oh." My eyes roll back in my head, "This is incredible." I turn to Amelie, "That's some baking skills you have there."

She giggles, "That's what Weston also says. Although," her forehead creases, "he may have been referring to something more than baking."

The girls laugh and Isla groans. I glance between them and polish off the rest of the cookie.

"So…whatever you have in mind," I address my question to the group in general, "wouldn't the men object to it?"

"Why would they?" Summer raises her shoulders. "Besides, we're not involving the men in this, are we?"

"Nope." Julia touches her earlobe.

"Nah." Amelie shakes her head.

"What we come up with in this room, stays in this room," Victoria says, her tone serious.

"Oh." A warm sensation fills my chest. "You ladies sure about this?" I chuckle. "I don't want your husbands finding out and then being upset with you all."

"Oh, pfft," Summer waves her hand in the air, "our alphaholes are actually tabby cats in disguise."

"Fierce, but all they need is a rub on the tummy, or uh, on other parts of their anatomy, for them to behave." Julia chuckles.

"Ugh!" Isla makes a face. "Stop already."

"I don't want you guys getting into trouble," I mumble, "I mean, isn't it a rule or something that you have to share everything with your husbands?"

Silence for a beat, then another. Then Amelie turns to me, "Umm… excuse me, but where's the mystery in the marriage if you tell them everything? I mean, there are certain things that you're absolutely never going to share with your other half, come what may. Feminine mystique is still a thing, and even more important, once you're married."

"True that," Julia pipes up, as the others nod in assent. "Of course, there's always the chance they'd want to help if we told them."

"Okay, but let's wait on that," I blow out a breath, "if you all are sure about this."

"We are," Summer replies.

"Question is, are you?" Isla fixes her gaze on me.

I twirl a strand of hair around my finger. "I... I don't want to hurt him." I jump up and begin to pace again. " I mean, I want to show him that he can't take me for granted, but really, that's all." I turn to them, "Know what I mean?"

The girls stare at me and my stomach ties itself up in knots. Why the hell do I feel so protective of that ass? After everything he's done to me, I still don't want to do something that would cause him pain… At least, not in a vindictive way... Apparently, I still feel something for him. Okay, face it, I want him, especially the things he can do to my body — the way he seems to make me come alive with just a glare, how he'd said he wanted to give me a child. A child... Hell, I still want to get pregnant, but not by any man. I want his baby. A child who will be the best of both him and me. I squeeze my eyes shut. This is hopeless. Why can't I go even a few minutes without thinking about the a-hole?

She raises her eyebrows, "You worried about him?"

"Of course, not." I snort. "That obnoxious grumpy pants can take care of himself."

"So, you're in?" Isla tilts her head.

I heave out a breath, "I'm in. What do you have in mind?"

51

Arpad

I drive slowly up High Street Kensington, keeping her sporty Mercedes in sight. Where the hell is that woman headed? It's as if she knows I'm on her trail…

Okay, okay, I know I said I'd leave her alone, and I had. For two full weeks, I'd only had my man—someone whom I pay a lot of money, by the way—follow her, because all the other agencies I'd approached had turned me down. Something about professional etiquette… What jerks. More like, they are afraid my little spitfire would give them hell if she found out that they'd helped me keep tabs on her. Unfortunately, as it turned out, the geezer I'd managed to engage to track her had been completely inept. He'd lost her repeatedly. He'd insisted that it hadn't been his fault because the woman is simply really good at covering her tracks. The wanker—the detective I'd employed, I mean—had insisted she was way too good and taking measures to ensure that she wasn't being followed.

Which, I have to admit, sounds like my woman. And she'd called me canny? Sparks is a woman on a mission, and damn, if I am not going to unearth what she is up to. It is my pride on the line. Know what I mean?

She threw down the challenge, and there is nothing I enjoy as much as sparring with someone who is gunning for me. And she is. And I am going to do my best to stop her. Hell, thanks to her, I haven't thought of taking my yacht out to sea, or chasing another storm... Because chasing Sparks around London gives me all the adrenaline rush I need.

What would it be like to live in this perpetual state of high for the rest of my life? To have her go toe-to-toe with me, constantly coming at me with her sass, defying me and questioning me... Until I'd have no choice, but to tie her down and make her submit to me. And submit she will... It is only a matter of time.

I watch as she pulls off onto a side road, then parks and hops out. She's wearing a pant suit that shows off her curvy figure; and those legs, bloody fuck. I can't wait to have them wrapped around me again. I park at enough of a distance so there's no chance of her spotting me. Then jump out and walk toward the boutique she's gone into. I stare at the window display of the understated, elegant shop—What the fuck? It shows wedding dresses. Why the hell is she here? I stare through the display window at the rows of dresses lining the wall on one side. At the far end, Karina speaks to another woman. They laugh, then the woman guides Karina further inside. Why the hell is she here? Is she trying on dresses? Why would she do that? She can't be getting married, can she?

To whom?

Why would she do that?

Maybe because I've been bloody stupid with her...? But I'd asked her to marry me, and she'd refused. Fuck. Bloody. Fuck. I dig my fingers in my hair and tug, then begin to pace the sidewalk. Twenty minutes pass... I know, I counted, as I stared at my watch, then back at the shop window, all the while walking back-forth-back like a douchebag—which admittedly, I am. But seriously, can you believe this? She's thinking of getting married. But to whom? What loser dares move in on my woman, while I... I...pace the pavement outside the shop like a—yeah, a blooming' moron. I fist my fingers at my sides, turn and peer inside the shop. She comes out of the fitting room holding a long white dress in her hand. She beams at the woman behind the counter, then hands over the dress. They speak, then the saleswoman hands over a bag which I assume has the same dress.

Motherfucker! Is that a wedding dress? Did she buy a wedding dress? Who is she marrying?

Karina turns to leave. I glance around, then pivot and race into the adjoining street. I peer around to find her walking to her car. She gets in, then drives off.

I wait a few more minutes to make sure she's turned the corner, then straighten and head for the main road. I am about to turn the corner when a voice asks me, "Have a cigarette, ol' chap?"

I glance sideways to find a homeless man leaning against the wall.

"Sorry," I raise my shoulders, "I quit."

"That's a shame." He looks me up and down, "You look like you need it."

"You're telling me." I blow out a breath.

"Woman trouble, huh?"

"Something like that." I frown. What the hell am I doing talking to him anyway? I shake my head. "Have a good day."

I turn to leave, when he says,

"I loved you so sincerely, so fondly
Likewise may someone love you next."

I pause, then pivot and stalk up to him, "The hell did you say?"

"I loved you so—"

"I heard you," I growl. "Why the hell are you quoting Pushkin?"

"You recognized the poet?" His chuckles. "Funny, could have sworn you were more of a Byron fan."

"I was…" I frown, "I mean, I am." I stare down at his upturned features, the hair matted about his shoulders, the hat pulled down low over his forehead so I can't make out the color of his eyes. The hair on the nape of my neck prickles.

"Do I know you?" I snap.

"Don't think we run in the same circles, ol' sport." He cackles.

Hmm. I frown down at his features. He doesn't seem familiar. So why are all of my senses on high alert?

"Why the hell did you choose that particular line?" I growl.

"Quite evocative, isn't it?" His lips curve. "Do you think he was talking about letting a woman go so she can find a love more suited to her needs?"

My guts twist. I swoop down, grab him by his collar and haul him up. The scent of alcohol and unwashed skin envelops me. I wince. "What the hell do you mean by that? Have you been spying on me? Who are you working for?" I demand.

"No one," he sputters, "just having a conversation, man. If you don't have a cigarette, you only have to tell me. No need to get so worked up."

My grip tightens, and he coughs. He paws at my hand. "Let go, asshole," he chokes out. "The fuck's wrong with you, man?"

I release him and he drops to the ground, then turns and scrambles off.

"Hey," I call out, but he breaks into a run. "What the hell?" I chase after him, but he speeds up. I increase my pace, try to keep up. But the tosser's, clearly, in better shape than he smelled. He turns a corner, and by the time I reach it, he's vanished. Bloody hell. I glance up and down the street, then walk to my car. Once inside, I pour sanitizer onto my palms, disinfect thoroughly, then message the rest of the Seven.

"Meeting. My place. Half hour."

Forty-five minutes later, I glance around at the faces of the rest of the guys. They're sprawled around the living room of the suite I've rented at the Dorchester. It's one of Saint's hotels, so I'd gotten a booking, no problem. Except, the asshole is charging me a premium. Of course, he is. Not that I begrudge him. I'd have done the same in his place. When it comes to money, it's an unspoken rule amongst us to keep the transactions fair for all concerned. Helps preserve the spirit of our friendship. The fact that all of them had dropped what they were doing and rushed here when I'd messaged them is testament to that.

"Whassup?" Sinner drawls from the chair he's sprawled in. "Something got your panties in a twist, Beauchamp?"

"Maybe." I lean forward on the balls of my feet. No way, can I sit down at the moment. First, seeing Karina trying on a wedding gown. Then, the encounter with the bum who quoted poetry? Fuck, what the hell is wrong with this city? Could someone who is clearly educated and well-spoken actually end up on the streets? Or does he simply prefer that lifestyle? If he does, well sure, I'm not going to judge. Still, it's peculiar, to say the least.

"Arpad?" Edward prompts, from where he's seated in the chair across from me. The only straight-backed chair in the room and he'd chosen it. Given a choice, the Father prefers to avoid material comfort of any kind. Sometimes, I think he does it simply to punish himself.

"What's on your mind, Beauchamp?" Damian frowns from where

he's perched on the writing desk in the corner. "Your text sounded like you needed to talk things out?"

"Yeah," I roll my shoulders, "I, uh, saw Karina today."

"What the hell—?" Edward frowns. "Thought we'd agreed that you'd give her space."

I glower back at him. "My exact words, as I recall, were that I wouldn't stalk her, or spy on her; whatever I did, it would be in the open."

"So, you didn't stalk her?" he growls.

"I may have followed her from a distance."

"You didn't spy on her?" He purses his lips.

"I, uh, may have peered into a shop that she went into."

"What the hell?" Edward's jaw firms. "You complete moron. You realize you're acting like a complete twat, don't you?"

"Wait, hold on," I raise my hands, "I had a good reason."

"Can't wait to hear it." Saint blows out a breath. He exchanges glances with Weston, who shakes his head.

"And if you two exchange more money and go on about that bet, I swear, I am going to cut you out of the next round of very lucrative investments I have lined up."

"Easy, ol' chap," Saint mutters, "we're simply concerned about you. All that stress? It's not good for the ticker." He taps his chest. "On the other hand, it's a sign that you're invested in this relationship, which I believe is a positive."

"Positive?" I snort, "Fuck that. There's no positive outcome here, considering she's getting married."

"She is. Of course, she is," Weston murmurs in a soothing voice, "to you."

"You're not listening." I dig my fingers in my hair and tug. "She's marrying someone else."

"You sure?" Edward scowls.

"I saw her trying on a wedding dress, so yeah."

"You spoke to her?" he asks.

I glare at him. "I'm not dumb, Father. I sneaked a peek in the window, paced back and forth like a jackass while she was trying it on…" I flash back to the last time she went clothes shopping. With me. *Don't go there, asshole. Don't conjure up scenarios in your head. Focus, focus on finding a solution to the problem at hand.* I ball my fingers into fists. If only I had some rope right now. I could use it to alleviate this pressure that is building in my head, in my chest, my balls. Except, the only person I want to tie up is her. And she is getting ready to tie the knot with someone else. "Fuck!" I crack my neck. "What the bloody fuck am I going to do?"

There's silence in the room.

I glance at the faces of my friends, who seem to be digesting what I told them.

"Have you thought about approaching her, and asking her about it?" Damian ventures.

"I promised I'd stay away from her," I growl.

"Not that you're doing a good job of it," Weston snorts, "but seriously, the only way to clarify this situation is if you ask her."

"Have you all heard anything from your women?"

Sinner straightens. "You do realize I have other things to discuss with my wife, apart from your love life, or lack thereof?" His gaze narrows.

"Yeah, yeah." I crack my neck. "It was a thought." Fuck, if I'm not grasping at straws. Seriously? I'm asking my friends if they've heard of any gossip from their wives and girlfriends. Not that there isn't merit in gossip. After all, a whisper of a scandal could bring down a politician, but still, this is the absolute arse-end of things.

"Forget it," I snap.

He scowls, "And no, Summer hasn't mentioned anything to me. You're welcome."

I show him the bird.

He smirks. "You're definitely rattled, Beauchamp. You wouldn't resort to childish insults otherwise."

"Bugger off to whatever hole you came from," I mumble.

Sinner's smile grows wider. "Seems it's your turn to discover that tiny little thing inside of you —"

"You mean in his pants?" Damian smirks.

"Piss off," I snarl, and Damian laughs.

"As I was saying," Sinner quirks an eyebrow, "apparently, you don't have a choice but to strip yourself naked to the world."

"What, you mean literally?"

A few of the guys visibly shudder.

"No, you ass," Weston crows, "he means, we've all been there… Except for Father, here —" he nods at Edward, "we've had to face up to our deepest fears and come out the other side, before we could claim our women."

"Yeah, no idea what you're talking about," I growl.

"But you will," Sinner drawls.

I glance around the room as each of my dickwad friends nods sagely.

"Shit, this was a bad idea, calling you all here," I grumble. "Clearly, you have no constructive advice to offer."

"I do." Damian jerks his chin. "You need to talk this through with her."

"Hmm." I lean forward on the balls of my feet. "What do you think, Father?" I turn to Edward, "Should I speak with her?"

He drums his fingers on his thigh. "Loathe as I am to say this, you don't have a choice." He tilts his head. "The question is, will she hear you out long enough to have a conversation with you?"

52

Arpad

After that little huddle, the guys had taken off and I had drunk myself to sleep and woken up with a hangover which still knocks behind my eyes. Bloody hell. Gone are the days when I could drink an entire bottle of the hard stuff and bounce out of bed with a spring in my step. Time… It always catches up.

And apparently, so do my sins… It has to be the reason I am skulking up the sidewalk, ensuring I'm not too close to Karina.

She'd left her apartment, taken her car to King's Road and parked. Now, she's going in and out of shops, the number of bags she's carrying in her hands multiplying with each outlet she visits. Is she shopping for Christmas already? More likely, a wedding—her wedding. Fuck, what the hell am I thinking? She walks out of yet another shop, turns and the handbag under her arm slips from her grasp.

Only when my feet hit the ground do I realize that I am moving. I reach her, snatch up the bag from the pavement.

I hold it out to her, and she stares at me, oversized sunglasses perched on her nose. Her gorgeous hair flows around her shoulders.

And in her knee-length dress, she resembles a celebrity, all grace and poise.

She glances down at my hand, then back up at my face.

I raise the bag, move it closer to her, so she has no choice but to accept it.

"Thank you," she murmurs.

"You're welcome." I tilt my head.

Bloody hell, so this is what we've been reduced to—polite conversation?

She pivots and begins to slide up the street, her gait haughty, back straight, and that beautiful butt of hers wiggling in sultry promise with every step she takes in those fuck-me stilettos. Why do women dress up to go shopping, and in the most uncomfortable shoes ever? Don't most people shop online nowadays? Apparently, not her... Nope, Sparks always has that old world, don't-touch-me air about her, which is what had made me want to mess her up, right from the very start.

She pauses in front of a café, then walks inside. I follow.

The hostess leads her to a table by the window.

I step toward her, when the hostess stops me. "Good evening, Sir. Would you like a table?"

I glance past her at Karina. "I'm with her," I say.

The hostess looks between us, steps aside. I prowl over to Karina, then sink down onto the seat opposite her.

She stares at me through her oversized sunglasses. My fingers tingle to reach over and pluck them off her nose, but I resist. Instead, I reach for the bottle of water on the table and tip it into her glass.

"Drink," I mutter, "you need to stay hydrated."

"And you're supposed to stay away from me." She picks up the glass and raises it to her mouth. Her lips purse around the rim as she takes a sip. My cock instantly twitches. What the hell is wrong with me? I set my jaw, glare down at her. She swallows, then lowers the glass back to the table.

"And you and I both know you don't want that, Sparks."

She stiffens, then folds her hands in her lap. "What I want is moot right now."

"And why is that?"

"Your actions so far have convinced me you are not the one for me."

"And you know that's not true."

"It is," she tips up her chin, "that's why I am getting married."

"You're not serious." My heart begins to thud, my throat closes, and I lean forward in my chair. "You can't marry someone else."

"Is that your command?"

"And if it is?"

Her lips purse. "That's where you always go wrong, Ari. You think you can tell me what to do, and I'll obey?"

"You will," I snap. "You must. You know you want to, Sparks."

Her chin wobbles, then she glances away. "I've spent my life being torn apart by my heritage. I knew my family were part of the Bratva. I wanted no part of it, yet everywhere I turned, they were there. There was no escaping their influence, you know?"

"Is that why you didn't protest when I asked you to move to London?"

"That was part of it," she nods, "but not only."

My pulse rate speeds up. "What else?" I clear my throat, "What else prompted you to accept?"

"You mean, other than the fact that you and the rest of the Seven were clearly my biggest clients?" She pulls off her sunglasses and places them on the table. When she finally meets my gaze, the full impact of those golden eyes hits me in the chest.

Shit, what is wrong with me. Why hadn't I been up front with her about my affiliation with her family? What had I been worried about? My ego? Her judgement? Had I actually thought that I could coerce her into becoming my wife? This sassy, gorgeous, full-of-spirit woman who is my other half.

The breath whooshes out of me. Shit, that's what it is. I'd always known it and yet I hadn't accepted it… Not really. Not until this moment, when she holds my gaze and says, "I was falling for you, Ari. I'd felt the chemistry between us, you know that. Hell, then I got to know you, your past, your fetishes, and all of it cemented what I felt for you. But you spoiled it all."

My heart stutters. I want to open my mouth and talk to her, but I can't. All I can do is stare as she tips up her chin and says, "I can't forgive you or my family, for colluding against me."

"And I won't apologize for what I did." *What the hell are you saying? Why can't you simply swallow your bloody ego and tell her how you really feel, you wanker?*

She pales, then nods, "And I wouldn't have expected anything else from you."

"Fine," I growl.

"Fine." She grabs her sunglasses and plonks them back on her nose. She rises to her feet, reaches for her handbag, only to knock it off the table. I swoop down, grab it at the same time she does. Our fingertips brush and a shudder runs up my spine.

There's still time. Stop her. Stop her from leaving. Just apologize, you asshole.

She tugs on her bag and I release it.

She rises to her feet, tugs the strap over her shoulder, then grabs her shopping bags and brushes past me.

"Sparks." I call out to her, and she pauses.

She glances over her shoulder and through the lenses of her sunglasses her gaze widens. "What?" She swallows. "What is it."

"You'll make a wonderful bride."

Her lips firm, "Is that all you have to say to me?"

I blink. "Is there something else?"

"Yes," she snaps, "yes there is." She flounces over to me, plops her bags on the chair she vacated, then looks me up and down while shaking her head. In disgust? In disbelief? Before I can figure it out, she leans over, grabs the jug of water and upturns it on my head.

Around me, I hear gasps from the other tables.

"What the—?" I growl. "The hell is wrong with you?"

"The hell is wrong with you?" she hisses back. "You completely blind, neanderthal of a bastard."

"What—?" I gape. "What the hell did I do now?"

"Nothing. Everything." She stomps her foot, then slams the jug on the table, snatches her bags from the chair and stalks out.

53

Karina

That ass, that absolute wanker. That…that…jerkenstein. "Aargh." I grab
the bag of shopping and throw it across the room. It hits the wall,
bounces off, and the shoes I'd purchased burst out of their tissue wrapping. Shit, no man is worth damaging an expensive pair of stilettos. Not
even if he is the hottest, most desirable, six-feet five-inches, ripped like
Adonis, alphahole… Are they?

I'd been so sure that he would apologize. Five syllables. Three, if
he'd just say, "I'm sorry." Is that so hard for him? Am I wrong in
holding out until he says so? I twist my fingers together. Maybe it's
stupid that I'm holding out until he says so. I mean, what's the point of
going into a relationship with a man who doesn't realize what he's done
wrong? Things could only go downhill from there. If we are to enter
into any kind of relationship, it needs to be on an equal footing, with no
lies between us. Nothing to obscure how we feel for each other. And he
does feel…a lot for me… If only he'd, just once, come clean and admit it
to me.

I wrap the strands of my hair around my fingers. Guess there's no
choice then. I have to put the rest of the plan into action. Damn him, for

forcing my hand. I'd hoped the hint that I was getting married would be enough. That he'd see me through the shop window of the wedding boutique—of course, I knew he was there. I mean, just because I told the man back off... As if he would? As if he could! I would have been disappointed if he had. It's not in Arpad F'ing Beauchaump's nature to give up. And neither is it in mine.

I straighten, then walk over to the pair of shoes and lift them up. I pull them out of the wrapping, kick off the heels I am wearing, and slip into them. Instantly, I feel taller, more confident. Give a girl the right pair of shoes and she can conquer the world. Isn't it Marilyn Monroe who'd said that? And I am going to need every bit of faking it until I make it bravado to get through what I have planned. The girls are behind me. They'll help me out, for sure.

I only have to get through the wedding. That's all. I mean, two can play this game, right? I have to show him that he can't take me for granted. I have tried everything else possible, and now I have no choice but to take the final step.

The only way to tame an alphahole is to show him I'm not for sale. The only way to get him to take action is to show him I'm not available anymore. If he sees me on the arm of another man, surely, he'll drop all pretenses? I have to appeal to the caveman in him to come out and stake his claim. Damn him, but he hasn't left me any choice.

Isla is going to help me organize the wedding at the local city hall. The rest of the women are going to take their husbands into their confidence, and fingers crossed, they will be able to play along enough for Arpad to believe the story.

Now, the only thing left to do is to tell my family.

I pick up the phone and dial my father's number.

54

———————

Arpad

I've screwed this up. Clearly, I have. I begin to pace back and forth in the hotel room. Damn, why are the rooms so small? Despite this being the top hotel in the city, it feels like there isn't enough room to breathe here. I march to the window and try to pry open the pane. Of course, it's sealed tight, goddam it. I raise my fist, ready to punch my way through it, then stop. Fuck that.

I shrug out of my shirt, head toward the closet. I open the door, pull out the rope I'd folded into in a figure eight. I shake it out, then loop it around my palm, so it's fashioned into a whip. I raise my arm and that's when my phone rings. I glance from the rope to the phone, raise the whip again, and the phone rings once more. Ah, hell. I stalk to the side table, answer it.

"What?" I snap.

"Beauchamp?" Edward's voice echoes over the line, "You sound terrible."

"Wonder what gave you that impression?" I snort.

"Perhaps it's because you sound like someone destroyed your yacht."

"That would have been easier to stomach than—" I clamp my lips shut.

"Than?" He prompts me, "Go on, don't hold out now."

"Than finding out that she's definitely getting married."

He blows out a breath, "That's what I wanted to talk to you about. " I hear the sounds of vehicles in the background.

"Where are you?" I frown.

"On the road," he replies. "I'm going to dial in the other guys."

"Wait, don't," I growl.

"Too late." Saint's voice comes over the line. "Why the fuck aren't you on video man?"

"Because I don't want to see your ugly mugs?"

"You don't have a fucking choice." Damian comes on the line.

"Beauchamp, you pussy," Weston snorts across the phone line. "Activate your video, you tosser. Not that I want to see your pussy-whipped profile."

"Look who's talking." I growl, "The one who won't do a thing without consulting his wife."

There's silence, then Weston laughs, "Keep fooling yourself, you mofo. You are in the same boat as us, and by the way, it's called being collaborative, which is what you do in a partnership. As you are about to find out."

I activate my video and five different faces stare back from five different squares.

I groan, "Not again. I don't need an intervention. I don't."

"The man doth protest too much," Sinner drawls. "Gentlemen, one of you going to break the news to him?"

"I will," Edward offers. "She's getting married."

"I know that, Father."

"Tomorrow."

"What?" My jaw drops. A hot sensation stabs my chest. "Are you sure?"

"Yeah, man." Weston's voice sobers. "Amelie confirmed it."

"So did Julia," Damian interjects.

"And Victoria," Saint adds.

"Summer too." Sinner nods.

"Shit." I sit down on the bed with a thump, stare at the rope in my hand. It's true then. Of course, she'd told me, but honestly, I didn't think she would go through with it. How could she? How dare she do this?

"Where?" My voice cracks. I clear my throat. "Where is it taking place?"

"Islington City Hall, tomorrow, 9 am."

Shit. Fuck. What the hell am I going to do now? I stare at the rope in my hand.

"What are you going to do now?" Edward asks.

I disconnect the phone and toss it aside. It rings again, I pick it up and throw it against the wall. It bounces off and crashes to the floor. I jump up, then walk across the room and bring my heel down on it again and again. Fuck that.

I raise the rope fashioned into a whip and bring it down on my back. The pain slices up my spine, lights up my brain. *Focus, focus.* Some of the noise in my mind fades. I whip myself again and again. The tongue of the whip curls around me, hits my stomach, rips the flesh. Goosebumps pop on my skin. The blood rushes to my brain. Silence descends between my ears. My gaze narrows. I whip myself a fourth, a fifth time... I lose count of the number of times the rope assails my back. Sweat drips down my forehead, trails down my spine. The grooves etched on my back burn. Only when my shoulder screams in protest, do I stop. That's when I hear the hammering at the door.

"Arpad? Open up." Is that...? I recognize Edward's voice.

"If you don't open up, I'm going to call the concierge and get this door unlocked."

I blow out a breath, then fold the rope into an eight and place it in the closet. I pick up my shirt and shrug it on, then head for the door, just as it swings open.

A bellboy looks between us.

"Leave," I snap.

He pales, then backs away.

Edward frowns. "Still scaring the hired help, I see?"

"Still trying to play the empathy card, I see?"

Color flushes the Father's face. He firms his lips, then marches past me and into the room. He glances about the space. "What the fuck took you so long to get to the door."

I blink. Whoa, hold on. The Father used the F word?

When I don't answer, he turns on me, "What?"

"Um...you swore?"

"It happens," he grumbles, "I'll have to atone for it, of course, but fine."

I shake my head, "You okay, Ed?"

"Question is, are you?"

"I'm in stupendous shape." I snort. "Can't you see?"

"You look like you haven't slept in a few nights."

Welcome to my world.

"So?" I thrust out my jaw. "You here to preach?"

"No," he holds up his hands, "aren't I allowed to drop by to see my friend?"

"Who's that?" I glance around the space. "I don't see anyone here."

He groans, "Really? You going to play that card now?"

I blow out a breath. "You're right," I jerk my chin at the door, "I'd prefer it if you leave."

"I'm not going anywhere." Edward smiles.

"In which case..." I head for the door.

Edward draws in a breath.

I pause, turn to glare at him over my shoulder. "What?" I frown, "What is it."

"You been whipping yourself again?"

"You're not the only one who gets to indulge in his nightmares."

A nerve throbs at Edward's temple, then his expression relaxes. "I'll let that pass, for now."

He walks over and seats himself in a chair.

"The fuck are you doing, Father?" I growl over my shoulder.

"Making sure you don't hurt yourself."

"Too late." I'd already had my legs cut out from under me. My heart had been carved out too, but whatever.

"So, you're giving in to self-pity, I see?" He quirks an eyebrow.

I pause, then swivel around to face him. "The hell are you talking about?"

He looks me up and down. "You, my man. I'm talking about you."

"Don't put me in the same box as you, Father."

Color smears his cheeks. The skin around his lips tightens. Edward curls his fingers into fists, then draws in a breath. He rolls his shoulders, then seems to get control of his emotions. "I'll forgive you, again." He adds in a low voice, "I know how distraught you are."

"And how would you?" I glare at him. "You, who decided to divorce yourself from all emotions, while the rest of us battle our demons on a daily basis?"

"Is that what you think I did?" He tilts his head. "That I turned my back on all worldly matters?"

"Didn't you?"

"Being a priest is the hardest thing I've ever done." His lips twist. "Anything else would have been the easy way out for me, don't you see?"

"No," I frown, "I'm afraid, I don't."

"No matter." He draws in a breath. "Forget I said that."

"But—" I protest. It's rare for the Father to open up. Aside from that fucker Baron, he's the only one of us Seven, who, despite being with us, has rarely shared anything of his personal struggles with us. Which really makes it all worse, in a way. After all, he's been right here with us all these years, and yet, he's been closed off.

He folds his arms together, "Enough about me." He schools all emotion from his face. "What are you going to do now?"

"We were talking about you," I persist. "Why was becoming a priest the toughest decision you've ever made?"

"Now's not the time to discuss it."

"Then when?" I frown.

"When, the time is right."

"Which is?"

"Not now."

I blow out a breath, "You're bloody frustrating. You know that?"

"Says the man who's working himself into a tizzy over his future bride."

"She's not..." *Mine,* is what I want to say, but I can't. What the fuck is wrong with me? When did everything around me collapse to the point that I can't differentiate right from wrong and truth from fiction anymore?

I rub the back of my neck. "The hell am I going to do now?"

"We...are going to talk—"

I pale. "What? No, I am not in the mood for a sermon."

"Man to man." Edward scowls.

"Nor am I going to confess," I say in alarm.

He huffs, "As friends." He squeezes the bridge of his nose. "Why are the five of you so immature?"

"And Baron?"

He lowers his hand. "What about Baron?"

"I notice you didn't include him?"

"There's nothing to talk about. He escaped; good for him. The end."

"Hmm," I frown, "if you say so."

"I do." He firms his lips.

I open my mouth, and he holds up his finger.

I sigh, then hunch my shoulder. "Fine, fine," I grumble. "Have it your way."

"So..." he pivots and walks through to the living room of the suite. "What are you drinking?"

"We," I snap, "we are drinking."

"I don't indulge." He turns to face me over his shoulder. "You realize that, right?"

"Surely, a glass of whiskey is allowed?"

He nods, then pours amber liquid into two glasses. He turns and offers one to me.

I raise my glass, "Salut." I down it, top myself up again, throw that back as well.

"You trying to get drunk?"

"What do you think?" I chuckle.

"I think it's a bad idea. Not that it's going to stop you, but if you're going to do something tomorrow —"

"I'm not."

"You mean you're going to stand by and watch her get married to someone else?"

"She made her choice." I glance down into the depths of my glass. "I'm fine with it."

"Are you?"

I nod.

"So why are the knuckles of your hand white?"

I glance down, force myself to unclench my hands. I place the glass back on the bar. "There," I growl, "happy?"

"You're not thinking straight."

"And you are?"

He nods, "Most assuredly, I'm seeing clearer than you."

"So, what would you have me do? March in there and throw her over my shoulder and get her out of there?"

Silence.

I glance up to find his gaze boring into me.

"What?" I grumble. "You going to tell me what you are thinking?"

"You know what I'm going to say." A smile ghosts his lips.

"I can't read your mind, Father," I mutter. "You may as well spit out what you're thinking."

"You need to do what's right for you."

I stare at him. "That's all you have to tell me?"

He tilts his head. "That's all you need."

"What the hell?" I rub the back of my neck. "You are no help, at all."

"God helps those who helps themselves."

I slow blink. "Right, then," I roll my shoulders, "guess the only thing that's going to help me get through the night is drinking heavily."

55

Karina

"How do I look?" I glance at my reflection in the mirror. The simply-cut dress has a high lace neck, the pattern continuing down my arms to end just above my wrists. The front dips in a sweetheart neckline, only to cinch in at the waist, before flowing down to my feet. It's understated and elegant. Demure and sexy. While it's clearly a wedding gown, it's tasteful enough that I could wear it to a party. Not that I have any intention of doing so. I am getting married only once. At least, I have to believe that. He will come for me. He has to, right?

"Well?" I meet Isla's gaze in the mirror. "Why are you so quiet?"

"You look," she shakes her head, "you look—"

I twist my fingers in front of me. "Say it, already. It's all wrong, isn't it? Maybe I should have chosen another color?"

"You look incredible."

"Oh." I swallow, then stare at my flushed face in the mirror. Why the hell am I so nervous? "You sure?"

"If he doesn't lose his composure and sweep you off your feet when he sees you, I swear, I'll throttle him myself."

I laugh. "Join the queue. He can be such a stubborn dickhead, you know?" I draw in a breath. "That's assuming he shows up today."

"Of course, he will."

"I wish I could be that confident," I mutter.

"Since when have you, Ms. Self-assurance, herself, turned this doubtful?"

"Since..." Mr. Arpad f'ing Beauchamp came into my life. It's weird to think that, before him, I was ready to live life on my own terms, to have a child by myself, to think I didn't need anything or anyone else to complete me. Until I really got to know him. Does that make me any less independent? No.

Does it mean I am giving up all of my notions of making it on my own? No.

Does it mean I become less because I want him, want to lean on him? No.

For the first time in my life, I want someone to take care of me... I want to be with him, want him to be mine, want to have his child. My cheeks heat. Jesus, I've never felt like this about anyone else.

Is that why I'm here? Wearing a wedding gown, headed to City Hall, to get married, confident—or rather, not at all confident, right now—that he'll turn up. And if he doesn't? Well, then I'll know that he never did want me the way I want a man to want me. The way I want Arpad alphahole to want me. OMFG, I am doing my head in right now.

I squeeze my eyes shut. There's a touch on my shoulder, "You okay, doll?" Isla asks.

Yeah.

I'd called up my father and told him that I was marrying Arpad. Surprisingly, he'd told me I didn't have to do it. That they wouldn't cajole me into getting married again. But knowing my father… It's only a matter of time before he thrusts another man of his choosing at me.

I'd told him this is my decision, that I am going through with it. I'd invited him down to City Hall for the wedding, and though he'd discon-nected the phone without confirming, I hope that he'll be there, along with my brother.

Everything is set. Now I just have to go through with this.

I blow out a breath, then turn to her and paste a smile on my face. "Let's do this."

• • •

Half an hour later, our car pulls up in front of City Hall. Sinclair and Summer loaned me their car and chauffeur, for which I am grateful. Not to mention, Isla has pulled through, as always, orchestrating this wedding and the reception afterwards for me, in double quick time. Yeah, she is getting really good at it. What the hell is she going to do now that five of the Seven will be married? Hopefully.

I see the short flight of steps leading up to the imposing neo-classical façade of the building.

Isla turns to me, "I need to go ahead and see to the arrangements but Peter," she gestures to our driver, "he'll help you out." She gets out of the car.

I stay there, unable to move. What if he doesn't come? What if he doesn't show up?

Oh, god, this had been a bad idea... A very bad idea.

"Miss, are you okay?" Peter, asks.

"Yes," I clear my throat, "I think so."

"He'll be there, you know."

I blink, then turn to him. "Who are you talking about?"

"The man you are looking out for."

"Of course, he is." I square my shoulders. "He's waiting inside to marry me."

"I'm not talking about him."

"No?"

He shakes his head. "Mr. Sterling was seven when I came to work for him. I've seen him and the rest of the Seven grow up and turn into men who were lost until, one by one, they began to find their women. Each of them deserves a happy ending, as do you."

"Why are you telling me this?" I ask. "My happy ending is waiting in there for me."

"He'll come for you."

I laugh. "I don't know what you're talking about."

"Mr. Beauchamp," His smile grows. "He's the most stubborn of the lot. Comes from the French blood in him. He thinks he doesn't need anyone, that he can do this on his own. But he can't."

And neither can I, but I don't say that aloud.

"Like the others, he doesn't like admitting when he is wrong. Not unless he's about to lose the thing most important to him."

I stare at him. "You know of the plan?"

"Summer took me into her confidence."

I hunch my shoulders. "This was a stupid thing to do. What was I thinking? Or rather, not thinking. I had hoped he'd come to his senses and apologize to me... but he hasn't. And damn it, I guess I am as stubborn as him. God, we are match made in hell, the two of us. We'll never see eye to eye."

"You will. And when you finally do, it will be like no one and nothing else exists, just the two of you."

I blink away the sudden rush of tears. Shit, what is wrong with me? And I'm not even on any hormone injections.

"Thanks Peter," I mutter.

He nods, then gets out and comes around to open my door.

He offers me his hand and I allow him to help me out of the car.

I hear footsteps behind me. "There you are." Niko's voice reaches me.

I glance at him, "You came?"

"Of course, I came. My only sister is getting married, and you thought I wouldn't be here?"

More tears knock at the backs of my eyes. Shit, soon I am going to be blubbering, which is not good. I definitely don't want my mascara to run.

Peter places my hand in Niko's, then steps aside. Isla exits the building and walks toward us. "They're ready for you."

I take a deep breath, compose myself.

Niko turns to me. "You look beautiful," he bends down and kisses my cheek. "and I've never been prouder of you."

I swallow and he straightens to his full height.

"Shall we?" Niko asks.

56

Arpad

I wake up with a start, glance around, and find the room empty. Guess Edward must have left at some point. I'd been drinking; he hadn't. He'd had a glass of whiskey and nursed it through much of the evening. I must have passed out on the couch at some point. A thumping behind my eyes makes me groan.

I sit up and my stomach lurches. Shit, I can't be hungover. Am I hungover? I am never hungover. I rise to my feet and the world tilts. Sweat beads my palms. Bloody hell. I stumble toward the sink in the bathroom, grab a glass and hold it under the tap. I glug down the water, and my guts clench. I will not be sick, will not. I slap the glass back on the counter, take a breath, another.

I open the cabinet over the sink, grab the aspirin—yeah, it's the kind of hotel which caters to every need of its guests. I swallow two of the pills with water, then lurch back into the bedroom.

Sunlight filters in through the window.

Shit, what time is it? I check the watch on my wrist. It's 8.00 am. My heartbeat ratchets up.

In an hour, she'll be married. She'll belong to someone else.

Someone who will love her, who'll take care of her. Who'll never tie her up with ropes and fuck her. Someone who doesn't go chasing storms, putting his life at risk. Someone who'll have a nine-to-five job, come back to her every night, and give her the children she so badly wants. Shit. She's going to be someone else's wife, carry someone else's child.

Hell. I drag my fingers through my hair. How dare she do this? How dare she walk out on me without giving me another chance at...this, at being with her? At being the father of her child. I am the one who offered first, and she turned me down. What the hell is wrong with her?

I march into the bathroom, shower and get dressed. I grab my phone and check the time. 8.10 am. Shit, shit, shit.

I pocket the phone, grab my wallet and car claim ticket, and walk out. I am only going to drive by City Hall. It is enroute to St Katherine Docks where my yacht is moored. I am going to get on my boat, and get the hell out of here, and then not look back. I am going to find the next storm and sail my yacht straight through it. I'll get off on the adrenaline high, then come back to port and get laid. I'll do all that, then I'll get the hell out of this city. I'll return to LA, find the next hottest start-up to invest in. I'll do all that, and I'll be happy.

My stomach bottoms out.

Of course, I'll be bloody ecstatic to go back to my single ways.

No more stalking a sassy, curvy brunette who makes my cock hard, every time I think of her. More importantly, no more driving myself crazy every time she looks at another man. Or having a heart attack when she tries on a wedding dress after turning me down. Shit. I drag my fingers through my hair. I am losing it. Clearly, I'd been on my way to being pussy-whipped. Good thing she'd decided to marry someone else. She'd saved me from being ball-and-chained-up like those of the Seven who had tied the knot. Yeah, she'd done me a solid by deciding not to marry me. She'd saved me from turning into a boring, one-woman man—from turning into someone content with his life, his wife, his family... None of which I want, right? Shit... Shit... Sweat beads my forehead.

Why the hell is it so hot in here? Clearly, I have been on land for too long. I need to get out of here and back onto my yacht. Hell, this time I'll sail to the Caribbean, to the island I'd bought there and never been to... Because I'd been planning on taking her there for our honeymoon. Jesus H, get a grip, man.

Time to put the plan into action, and get the hell out of here. I'd had a lucky escape. Time to get out, while I still can.

I head down the corridor, then take the elevator to the reception of the hotel. I walk out the front door, toss my claim card over to the valet. He scampers off to get my car and I begin to pace up and down the sidewalk.

What the hell is wrong with me? Why can't I relax? *Do not look at your watch. Don't do it.* I glance at the dial of my wristwatch.

"What time is it?" a voice calls out.

I glance about and spot the homeless guy on the sidewalk. The same guy I'd seen in the alleyway near the boutique where she'd tried on her wedding dress.

I stalk toward him, "What the hell are you doing here?"

"It's a free country, last I checked, man." He smiles and his teeth gleam. Who the hell is this guy, who could afford such dental work?

"You following me, asshole?" I growl.

He chuckles. "Now, now, don't get ahead of yourself. I like to move around, that's all. Besides, I wanted to make sure you saw this."

"What?"

He holds up his phone, the screen face-up.

"Fuck that," I snort, " I don't want to see any of your porn."

"This is much more important." He waves his phone in my face.

I stare at the video playing on the screen and my heart twists. My guts knot. I see a vision in red. Damn it, she's wearing red. Is it because I'd told her that's the color that suits her the best? Of course, it is. She's wearing it to taunt me.

But hadn't she bought a white dress earlier at the boutique? No matter. She has her hair piled on top of her head and I take in the curve of her neck, the arch of her shoulders, the bouquet of white and pink flowers she holds between her fingers. I run my gaze down the curves of her body shown off by the dress, how the hem rises to show a flash of her legs as she steps inside a town car.

Peter, Summer and Sinclair's chauffeur, shuts the door behind her, then walks around to the driver's side.

Shit. My mouth dries. It's her, on the way to her wedding. She's about to get married and I am here holding my cock in my hands. Not literally, but you know what I mean.

"Hey, ol' chap. You okay?"

His voice seems to come from far away.

"You're not gonna faint or something, are you?"

"What?" I blink, then draw myself up to my full height, "You think I'm a pussy?"

"Yes."

I stare, "The fuck do you mean, asshole?"

"You're the one waiting for your valet to get your car while your girl walks away with another man."

"She's not..." Fuck, the word sticks in my throat. I force myself to say it. "Mine," I snarl. "She's fucking mine."

"Damn right," he nods, "you going to get her, or what?"

I squeeze my eyes shut. Fuck, fuck, fuck. How could I have messed this up so badly? How could I have not seen what was in front of me all this time?

I'd wanted her, decided she was for me. She is it for me. And yet, I'd let my ego come between us. I'd thought I was right all along, that I could get my way, no matter what. I'd forgotten how it is that a man treats a woman when he loves her. And fuck, if I don't love her. I love her more than I love myself, and fuck, if that isn't something.

And... holdonabloody second. How the hell did this guy get ahold of that video of my woman?

I snap my eyes open to find the space in front of me is empty. Huh? I glance about me and find the homeless guy hurrying away. The hair on the back of my neck rises.

Why the hell hadn't I thought of asking the question earlier? Had I been so shaken by what I'd seen that I'd forgotten basic common sense?

All of which doesn't answer the question: what the hell had he been doing watching her?

Why had he filmed her? How did he know I had checked into this hotel? Only the Seven know I'm here. How the hell had he found out? No way, would any of the Seven have told anyone else. So, who the hell is he? "Wait," I call out. He breaks into a run.

I spring forward, when the valet calls out, "Sir, your car is here."

I pause so suddenly that I almost stumble. Shit. I glance at my watch, 8.35am. Shit, no way, am I making it in time to stop the wedding, but I have to try. I glance up the sidewalk and spot the guy turning the corner. That will have to wait. For now, I have to go get my girl.

Turning, I race to my car and hop in.

I pull away from the curb, press down on the accelerator with such intensity that my Jag jumps forward. I tear around the corner, hit

Oxford Street and the inevitable traffic. I press down on my horn, swerve around the vehicle in front of me. The driver shows me the bird; I don't even bother to respond. I focus on finding breaks in the traffic, hit the next streetlight which, of course, turns red as I pull up. I hit the brakes, wait for the pedestrians to cross. Glance at my watch.

8.45am.

Hell. I am never going to make it in time. Sweat beads my brow and adrenaline laces my blood. As soon as the light changes, I hit the accelerator and the car jumps forward.

For the next ten minutes, I race through the streets of London. If I am too late, I will never forgive myself. If I allow her to become someone else's wife I... I will never be able to live through it. No, I have to get to her in time. I never lose, remember? I am going to reach her in time. I have to.

I navigate the roads, head closer to Islington City Hall. When I am only a few blocks away I hit a traffic jam. Bloody hell. Sweat trickles down my spine. I clutch the steering wheel with such force that my knuckles turn white. Come on, I am so close. I pound my fist on the steering wheel, peer through the windshield. Nothing seems to be moving. Shit, this isn't good. I am not going to make it. I shove the door open, spring out, then dodge around the vehicles.

The car in front rolls forward and a cacophony of horns sounds. Shit, I am going to get into so much trouble. But what-bloody-ever. Nothing is more important than getting to my woman in time. My heart begins to race. My pulse rate ratchets up. I increase my pace, reach the sidewalk and sprint forward. I reach the steps of City Hall, which is when I spot Sterling.

"Come to your senses finally?" He smirks.

I show him the bird, then race up the steps two at a time. What the hell is he doing out here, anyway?

I reach the top of the steps, when Saint shoves open the door for me. "About time," he grunts as I race past him.

Of course, all the Seven — except Baron — would be here to witness me being brought to my knees, but what the hell do I care? All that matters is that I get to her in time.

I race up the winding staircase inside, reach the first landing, where Weston smirks. "That way, ol' chap," he jerks his chin to the left. I race up the next flight of steps, then pause. Which way? Which way should I go?

Damian pushes away from the wall, heads to me, "You seem lost, my man."

"Shut your bloody trap," I pant. My chest heaves. Sweat trickles into my eyes and I wipe it away. "Which way?" I growl.

"Told ya, you'd come to your senses."

"Tell me, you tosser, or else."

He stabs his thumb to his right, and I take off. I race down the corridor, past the line of couples waiting, to the closed door at the end.

Nikolai stands at the doorway, folds his arms over his chest, "You can't go in."

"I have to," I choke out. "My...my...woman... My heart... My... Karina." I can barely get the words out. "She's inside."

His jaw firms. "If you think I am going to let you interrupt my sister's wedding, you are mistaken."

I glance at my watch. "Look," I show him the face of my watch, "it's only 8.57 am. It's not too late. She's not married yet. There's still time for me to stop this."

He shakes his head. "I can't let you in."

Anger thuds at my temples and adrenaline laces my blood,

"Get out of the way," I glare at him, "NOW."

The skin around his lips tightens. "You need to leave," he demands, "NOW."

"I'm not going anywhere." I raise my fist. "But if you don't move, things are about to become very ugly."

57

Karina

"What time is it?" I ask.

"The same as when you asked me two minutes ago," Isla mutters.

"That's two minutes since our last conversation." I scowl. "So, it's not the same time as when we last spoke, is it?"

"Fine, fine." She throws up her hands, then stares at the watch on her wrist. "It's 8.58 am."

"Shit." I hunch my shoulders. *He's not coming. He's not coming. I thought, for sure, he'd come. How am I going to face these people? How am I going to live my life without him?* I chew on my nail, and Isla leans forward and slaps my hand.

"Ow," I grimace. "What was that for?"

"You don't want to get married with bitten down nails, do you?"

"I don't want to get married, period," I mumble as I stare down at my hands. We're in a small room next to the registrar's office, and just off the hallway where the other couples are lining up for their turn. Don't ask me how, but Isla has arranged this private space for me. That woman is a genius when it comes to organizing events. Not that this is anywhere close to the weddings she's organized for the rest of the Seven. But then, nothing about this situation is ordinary, is it?

Not the fact that the women are here in the room—Summer, Julia, Amelie, Victoria and her bump, Sienna with her baby, even Ava, had turned up to lend me support. Well, I am going to need all of it, and more, considering the asshole still hasn't showed up.

I glance away from the window; it isn't going to help if I surgically attach myself to the frame and look out. Mr. Grumpy Pants isn't going to show up. I'd been stupid to think of this as a way to get him to recognize what he truly wants. Had I actually thought that I could get through to him? To strip away at his conceit, the barriers he'd thrown up against the world, and reveal himself to me—had I thought that I could accomplish that? I snort, I must have been dreaming.

I walk over to the mirror in the corner of the room, then begin to pull out the pins from my hair.

"What are you doing?" Isla asks in alarm. Behind me, I see the expressions on the faces of the other women, mirroring her concern. Shit, will I have to go through life remembering how he stood me up at the altar—? Well, technically, I had stood myself up, since this entire plan had been my grand idea. Bloody hell. "He's not coming," I growl, "no reason for me to put myself through this torture." I slap the pins down on the table in front of the mirror and my hair flows down to my shoulders. There, that's much better. I dig my fingers into my scalp and massage. A headache throbs at my temples. "This is all that asshole's doing," I mutter. "I should have cut my losses and left him. What is wrong with me, that I decided to come up with this grand idea?"

"Love?" Her lips curve up. "You're a romantic at heart, Karina."

"Tell that to my head, which insists that this is the craziest idea I've had since..." Since practicing my yoga stretches in his cabin and then falling asleep in his bed. I shake my head. I'd done that, all right. Stupid me... Why had I not wanted to leave his bedroom that day? Had something inside me wanted to stow away on his boat? Had my subconscious already chosen him to be the father of my child? Shit. I press my palm into my stomach. Speaking of, I'd gone into this hoping to get pregnant, only somewhere along the way, the dream had changed to being pregnant with his child, to having him in my life. I'd had to try one last time, didn't I? I'd had to give him one last chance to redeem himself.

"Since?" Her eyebrows quirk.

"Since... Nothing." I press my fingers together. "Was I wrong in what

I did? Should I have accepted his proposal and fallen into his arms? That would have made everything so much simpler."

"And allowed him to think he could take you for granted?" Summer walks up to stand next to me. "With the Seven, you need to stand your ground. They need to know that you won't hesitate to go toe-to-toe with them, that you are the kind of woman who'll rise to the challenge, every single time."

"You think so?" I bite down on my lower lip.

"I know so." Victoria walks up to stand behind me. "Do you think if I had simply given in to Saint, we'd have survived and made it this far?"

I meet her gaze in the mirror.

"It's only because I found it in me to stand up to him, that he took me seriously. It's only because I gave it back to him every time he decided to pull an alphahole stunt on me, that I got the man of my dreams."

"We make them better men." Julia draws abreast, next to Summer.

"They depend on us to bring out the empathetic side of them." Amelie glides over to join us. "Don't let their bluster fool you. These men have the softest of hearts, only they don't dare show it to the world. It's almost as if they want us in their lives so they have the permission to show their mushy side."

"Mushy side?" I twist my lips. "I don't think Arpad A'hole has anything soft about him."

"Oh, we know he's hard where it counts." Summer raises her eyebrows, as I choke.

"There, there," Isla slaps me on my back.

I cough, accept the glass of water that Julia hands me, then sip from it.

"It's what all that hardness is hiding from you that we want you to recognize," Summer adds.

"I am not sure I understand what you are trying to say?" I place the glass of water back on the counter.

"Don't give up yet," Summer urges.

"Yeah, about that. How long do I have left?"

Isla glances at her watch. "It's nine am."

My throat closes. "Clearly, if he hasn't come by now, then what's the point? He knows I'm getting married at nine... If he had wanted me at all, he'd have been here by now."

That's when I hear a commotion outside the door.

58

Arpad

I raise my fist, when my shoulder is gripped from behind. "What the hell?" I swing around and come face to face with Edward.

The Father's eyebrows are drawn down. "Calm down," he cautions, "it's not over yet."

"Of course, it is," I growl. "She's in there getting married, and you're asking me to calm down?"

I twist my torso to get away, and the Father tightens his grip. Anger flares at my nerve-endings and my vision narrows. "Let go of me, Edward."

"Will you listen to me?"

"Back the hell away from me."

"I will, if you calm down and listen to me first."

"Why the hell should I?" I snap. "When everything I want is in there and you're preventing me from going in."

"For once in your fucking life, will you stop to think before rushing into yet another storm?" Edward's voice thunders around the place.

Silence descends. A beat. Another. I firm my lips, glare at Edward, who glares right back. And that cuts through the noise in my head. The

Father, angry, on the verge of losing his temper. Whoa, okay. I've never seen that happen before. At least, not since Edward returned from his stint to wherever he'd gone, and declared that he was going to become a priest.

Then, Edward jerks his chin, "Breathe, Arpad."

He releases me and I stumble back. "Why the hell should I?" I swallow. "When my heart, my love..." A ball of emotion blocks my throat. "My life..." Something hot stabs at my chest. Jesus, what the hell is wrong with me? Am I actually going to lose my composure, here in front of everyone?

"She's...everything to me," I whisper, "you understand that, don't you?"

He nods, "I do, but does she? Have you told her what you just told me?"

"It's too late... Too late now."

"It isn't." A ghost of a smile kicks up his lips.

"What the hell do you mean?"

That's when the door to the side flies open. A vision in red stands silhouetted against the light. I blink. She takes a step forward and out of the light. Her dark hair flows about her shoulders, her color is high on her cheeks, and her eyes are bright with emotion—with unshed tears? She stands there, chest heaving.

My beauty, my heart, my love.

"Karina?" I whisper, as Edward steps aside.

She stares at me as if she can't believe what she's seeing. In truth, neither can I. "Aren't you supposed to be—" I stab my thumb over my shoulder, at the closed double doors behind me, "in there."

"And you're supposed to have been here by nine am."

Warmth flushes my face. Shit. What, now I'm embarrassed? The next thing you know, I'll be saying please and thank you in every sentence.

"I'm... I'm sorry?" My neck heats. Did I just say that? I said that.

"About time," she murmurs, then walks forward and links her hand through mine.

I glance down at our joined hands, then at her face.

She tilts her head. "They're waiting for us."

"Who's waiting for us?" My heart begins to hammer; my pulse rate ratchets up.

She jerks her chin toward the double doors. I turn as they open.

Inside, I see chairs set up on either side of an aisle, at the end of which, a man in a suit stands beaming at us, with his hands folded in front of him.

"Huh?" I blink. "Is that the registrar who is going to conduct the marriage ceremony? Are we..." I turn to her, "but weren't you...?"

"Going to marry someone else?"

I nod.

"You actually believed I could do that?"

"No," I shake my head, "I didn't want to... But I knew I'd behaved like a complete ass—"

"—a wanker," she interrupts me. "You behaved like a complete tosser."

"That too," I agree. "I deserve all the names you called me."

"Is that an apology?" She frowns. "Because it's a pretty shitty one."

I can't stop the chuckle that bubbles up. This woman... She is going to make my life really bloody interesting as hell. I sink down onto one knee, place her hand between both of mine.

"I'm sorry, Karina. Sorry I took you for granted. Sorry I manipulated your life so you could be near me. Sorry I colluded with your family behind your back. Sorry that I...didn't come right out and tell you that I love you, that I want to be with you, that you are the only woman I want to spend my life with, the only one I want to wake up next to every morning, the only one I want to hold in my arms, and say I do to. You are the only one, Sparks, who means more to me than anything in the world, even myself. If I'd lost you, I wouldn't have been able to live anymore, I—"

She places her finger on my lips. "Don't," she swallows, "don't say that. If anything had happened to you, I wouldn't have been able to live with myself."

"Live with me instead. Be my wife. Marry me, Sparks."

Her face splits apart in a wide smile, "Yes."

Claps break out; there's cheering. I glance around to see Isla and the rest of the women crowding at the doorway. The men, cluster behind them.

A younger girl I don't recognize joins the women. "Oh, your babies are going to be soo beautiful."

Next to me, Edward stiffens. I shoot him a sideways glance to find him staring at her. Interesting.

Summer wraps her arm around the girl and pulls her close. "Never change, Ava," she grins, "your romantic heart is what sets you apart from the rest."

Niko guides me and Karina, to the side as the rest of the group file into the room. Saint wraps his arm around Victoria, Sinner pulls Summer to his side, Weston hugs Amelie, and Damian bends down to kiss Julia's cheek. Ava takes a seat in front. Edward stays by the door, his gaze still on her.

Niko turns to me, "You passed my earlier test, doesn't mean you're off the hook. You'd better take care of her, or I'll blow your brains out." He jerks his chin at me, then retreats to the side.

I take both of Karina's hands in mine as I peruse her features, "What do you say, Sparks? You ready to get started on that baby making plan?"

59

Karina

"I thought you'd never ask," I whisper.

He rises to his feet and I tilt my head back, all the way back, as he towers over me. Shit, has he always been this big, this tall, this huge? Enough for his shoulders to block out the sight of everything else.

He rakes his gaze over my face and a flash of heat trails down my spine. He leans in close enough for the tips of his shoes to brush my stilettos, then bends his head until his face is right above mine. "There's still a chance for you to leave," he mutters. "Still a chance for you to save yourself from me."

"And if I don't?" I whisper. "What if I don't want that? What if I want everything you can give me?"

"What if you can't take it?" His gaze narrows. "What if I hurt you?"

"Promise me you will?" I allow my lips to curl into a smile and his nostrils flare.

His shoulders flex, and he tucks my hand into his. "I should have known you'll always have an answer." His mouth twists. "What am I going to do with you, Sparks?"

"The same thing that I am going to do with you?" I smile at him.

"Love me, hold me, touch me, caress me, fight with me, make up with me, take care of me, never let me go."

"Never." He brings my palm to his lips and kisses my knuckles. "You're stuck with me, Sparks."

"Hey, you guys, shouldn't you get a move on?" Edward jerks his chin toward the room in front of us. "The registrar's waiting."

"I'd rather you marry us." Arpad holds my hand as we approach him. "It's tradition, after all."

"Maybe some traditions are meant to be broken?" Edward's features take on an odd look. "Perhaps, the more things change, the more they remain the same, know what I mean?"

"No," I shake my head, "not really."

"Edward means, why not have the registrar marry us, so he has a chance to enjoy the wedding? Not that he doesn't enjoy it when he's conducting the ceremony," Arpad adds. "Am I right, Father?"

Edward nods, "Also, and not that this would matter, but just so you are aware, it's your name that's on the license."

"It is?" Arpad scowls then turns to me, "So you were sure all along that I'd turn up?"

"I'd hoped." I half smile at him. "I had nothing to lose right?"

"And the white dress at the boutique?" He rubs his jaw, "I could have sworn I saw you purchase a white wedding dress."

"White huh?" I can't stop the smile from curving my lips, "How did you know that?"

He presses his lips together. "You knew I was keeping an eye on you?"

I nod.

"You knew that I couldn't keep away from you?"

I smile wider.

He scowls and I can't stop the giggle that wells up from my throat.

"Bloody hell, Sparks," He rubs the back of his neck, "you really were one step ahead of me all this time."

"I tried." I say trying and failing to sound gleeful.

His gaze intensifies. He peruses my features, "What would you have done if I hadn't turned up?"

"But you did." I peer up at him from under my eyelashes.

"Were you that confident that I'd show?" he murmurs.

"Yes." I glance down, then back at him, "No, I wasn't. But I had nothing to lose, right? I had to put things in motion, then pray every-thing worked out."

"You have a devious mind, almost wife."

"I learned from the best, almost husband."

I lick my lips and he lowers his head to mine, the intent to kiss me clear.

Edward clears his throat just then, and I frown up at him.

"You'll have plenty of time for that later." He chuckles, "Besides the registrar is waiting."

He moves to the side as Nikolai steps up. "I'm walking my sister down the aisle."

He glares at Niko, "If you think I'm letting go of her for one minute now that I've found her again —"

"Ari," I nudge him, "behave."

He glances down at me. "You want him to walk you down the aisle?"

"He's my brother."

Arpad searches my features, then nods. He places my hand in Niko's outstretched one, then turns to me again. "I'll see you soon, babe."

After Arpad walks into the room, Edward shuts the doors behind them.

Isla hands my bridal bouquet over to me. She walks around to stand between us and the door, then turns, "You ready, Karina?"

I nod, grip my brother's arm. This is it. I am doing it now.

She pushes open the door and walks forward. We wait until she reaches the end of the short aisle. She slips into a chair by the front row, then it's our turn.

Niko places his wide palm over mine. "You look beautiful, Kaykay." He smiles down at me. "You know Dad would have made it, except it's too risky for him to be seen in the open."

I nod. "I am glad you are here."

Then we're walking forward, down the aisle. I glance around at the faces of my friends, my made family, who are as important, if not more so, than my blood family. A tingle runs up my back. I glance up and my gaze connects with his blue-grey ones, and the rest of the room fades. I am aware of putting one foot in front of the other, of covering the distance between us, of stopping in front of him, of Niko placing my hand back where it belongs, in his wide warm one.

He twines his fingers with mine, the warmth in his eyes setting shivers of anticipation, of something else, excitement, contentment, all of it intertwined into a ball of happiness; of being exactly where I want to be in that moment; of seeing my entire future stretched out in front of me; of reaching forward and grabbing it and holding on and allowing it to sweep me away until there is no me, no him... There is only us.

"I do." His lips form the words. His eyes crinkle. He slips his hand into his pocket and pulls out a ring.

He reaches for my left hand when I realize I am still clutching the bouquet. Oh! I glance around, and Ava jumps up. "Here, I'll take it." She closes the distance between us and I hand the bouquet over to her before turning back to my bridegroom.

Arpad takes my left hand and slides the ring onto my finger—a band of plain gold, with a single blue sapphire embedded in it. The metal is worn and instantly warms my skin.

"It's grandmama's," he says, "she wanted you to have it."

Tears prick my eyes as I hold onto his hands. Then I'm raising my gaze to his.

"I do too," I whisper, as a teardrop slides down my cheek.

"You may now kiss the bride." Barely has the registrar spoken, when we both move. I raise my head, he swoops down, and we meet some-where in the middle.

EPILOGUE

Karina

I glance across the bedroom of Arpad's yacht. After the wedding, we'd spent the rest of the morning at a very boozy brunch with the Seven and their women at the Michelin starred restaurant of the Dorchester Hotel. It is the hottest restaurant in London and Saint had shut it down for our wedding reception. Imagine that.

Nothing should surprise me. Not after the life I've led so far. Not after the excesses that I've known the Bratva to indulge in... But the Seven... They are so matter-of-fact about the position they occupy on the food chain... Sometimes it takes my breath away; and that's saying something. And... Okay, it isn't about the money.

When I'd left my family behind in LA, I'd turned my back on the kind of extremes that money brings with it... I'd wanted to carve out my own life, create my own career, my own family. I'd been ready to go so far as to have a child on my own and bring him or her up by myself so I didn't have to depend on anyone else. Then Arpad happened.

It's not just his good looks, or his more dominant than anyone else personality, or the fact that he'd do anything for the Seven, or how he'd been with his grandmother, caring and protective and so authentic...that had appealed to me.

Okay, maybe it was all of that... And that space inside of him... That hurt, that anger against the world he carries inside and which resonates with the part of me that still blames the universe for taking my mother away from me when I was barely an adult.

Maybe I see him as much of a challenge as he sees me as a provocation.

Maybe, on some level, I see him as someone who is strong enough to dominate me; someone who can claim me and rule over me with a firm hand; someone who will take away the onus to choose, the anxiety of making decisions... Something I'd never known I craved until I met him.

My husband who prowls over to where I stand.

The boozy brunch had gotten progressively boozier and noisier, with the rest of the Seven and their women not able to keep their hands off each other as well.

In the middle of it all, Ari had grabbed my hand, and pulled me to my feet. Good thing I'd had the foresight to change out of my wedding dress at some point during the morning, for he'd literally whisked me off to his car and driven us over to his yacht, where he intended to consummate our marriage. He'd also told me that we were setting sail for Malta and then Greece for our honeymoon. As for clothes and my things? He'd produced our packed suitcases from the boot of the car. Someone had been busy shooting off text messages to get everything organized during the course of the morning. Something I swear I hadn't noticed.

Now he pauses in front of me and peers into my face. "There's one more thing I need to do." He slips his hand into his pocket, brings out a short piece of rope.

He presses the rope into the palm of my hand. "I want you to have it," he says. "I want you to have it when you think you're ready to use it on me."

"On you?" I blink. "You want me to use it on you?"

He nods.

"But..." I swallow, "you hate being tied up."

He glances down at the rope, then back at me, "Apparently, it depends on the person who's doing it."

"Oh." I wrap the length of rope around my palm, allowing the rest of it to trail to the floor.

It's the same rope that he'd used that first time he'd restrained me.

The late afternoon sunlight slants through the window of the cabin, and highlights the reddish gold sparks woven through the cord.

He backs away and I follow his progress as he saunters over to the bed. He sits down, kicks his legs out in front of him. His thighs are powerful columns of strength and his stance is wide enough for my attention to stray right to his crotch. The fabric of his pants tented there indicates that he's already aroused. It's something I have yet to get used to, for the man has the stamina of someone who can push himself to the limits and recover quickly enough to start all over again.

I lick my lips and his gaze narrows. I walk over to stand in front of him, weave the piece of rope about my palm. He tips his chin up, trains those flinty grey-blue eyes on me. My stomach trembles and my heart begins to race. Oh, hell, one glance from him and I'm already a goner. How the hell am I going to do this?

I let the rope slither to the ground, then reach forward and push the jacket down his shoulders. He shrugs it off, holds my gaze as I unbutton his shirt. My fingers graze his skin and he hisses. His blue gaze deepens, until his irises seem almost black. Oh, wow, that's never happened before. Is he turned on? His jaw tics and a vein throbs at his temple... Ah, okay, he's more frustrated. "Is it tough to hand over control, for even this small amount of time?"

He bares his teeth, "What do you think, wife?"

I swallow. *Wife.* Jesus, will I ever get used to him calling me wife?

"I think..." I finish the task of unbuttoning his shirt, then shove it down his shoulders. The material catches around the tense bulge of his biceps, and I tug it down. He flicks the shirt away, places his hands on his thighs.

His shoulder muscles knot, his chest planes ripple, and the tendons of his neck stand out in relief. I rake my gaze down the expanse of his beautiful torso, the concave stomach, the pants that ride low on his hips. My pulse begins to thud and my heartbeat ratchets up. I am this close to throwing myself at him, wrapping myself around him, and straddling him, and riding against the rough fabric of his jeans until I come.

"You were saying?" The alphahole smirks, knowing full-well that I can barely string together a complete sentence right now.

"I think..." I mumble, "that I should bind you up while I still have my faculties about me.

He holds up his hands, his expression innocent, and damn, if that doesn't make me suspicious. Arpad f'ing Beauchamp, offering himself up, all meek and tame... Nah, he's up to something. But what?

"Put your hands behind you," I order.

His smile widens.

"I mean it." I scowl, "Come on, Arpad, you promised you'd comply."

He hesitates, then obliges. He folds his arms behind his back, thrusts out his chest. Corrugated ripples of muscles stretch his torso, and my fingers itch to rake my nails down that gleaming expanse. Sweat beads my brow and my toes curl. Damn it, why am I holding back? I lean down, run my tongue around one erect male nipple.

A groan rumbles up his chest. I drag my nails across the hardened nub of his other nipple and his body jolts.

"Fuck me, what the hell are you trying to do, Sparks?"

"I'm getting to know my husband's body, you mind?"

He stiffens, then a chuckle rolls up his throat. "I don't mind at all, darling. In fact," he leans back, allowing me more space, "I insist you not stop until you get to know every part of me as well as yourself."

My heart thuds against my ribcage and a melting sensation coils in my chest. Suddenly, I want to feel myself naked and plastered to every inch of him.

I reach down, lower the zipper of his pants, and there's only Arpad. Hell. I stare at his engorged length that springs free and stands upright against his stomach.

"Fuck me."

"If you don't get on with it, that's exactly what I'm going to do," he growls.

I swallow, and tug on his pants. He lifts his hips, allows me to pull off his pants. I straighten, unable to take my gaze off his thick cock. Its head almost purple with the intensity of his arousal, beads of precum lace the slit on the crown. My mouth waters and my chest hurts. The flesh between my legs aches with so much need that my legs tremble. I bend, grab the rope, then straddle him, one knee on each side of his waist. He tips up his head, his blue eyes stalking my every move as I reach around and begin to wind the rope around the arms he still has folded behind him. With every move, my still clothed breasts brush his chest. The heat of his body seems to intensify; the strength of his domi-nance pushes into my chest, pins me down as I manage to loop around his wrists, once, twice, a few more times. I knot the rope, tug to secure it again and again. My twists are nowhere as neat as how he'd bound me —I can't even see what I'm doing—but it will have to do.

I lean back, perch on his lap, then glance up into his face.

"Done?" He lifts an eyebrow.

"I'm just getting started." I push back a little more, then reach between us to grip his pulsing shaft.

His breath catches and a shudder rolls under his skin as I massage him from base to tip, and again. I don't take my gaze off of his face as his features twist, as his breathing grows heavier, and as his chest muscles ripple and flex, like there's an animal somewhere inside waiting to break lose.

I slide one hand lower to cup his heavy balls and he throws his head back and growls. The sound is so primitive, so feral, liquid heat slides from between my legs.

Sweat beads his forehead; his jaw hardens as he lowers his head. "You're fuckin' killing me, Sparks."

A vein throbs at his temples and the skin around his eyes tightens. Color smears his cheeks and my nipples tighten until they are almost painful to bear.

I rise up on my knees, reach under my dress to push my panties aside, then I position myself over his swollen dick and sink down.

Arpad

She impales herself on my cock, and fuck me, but the sensation of her pussy clenching my length as she sinks down on me, until I am completely wrapped in her melting heat, is the single most perfect moment of my life. I am not a spiritual person, but surely, the white light that flashes behind my eyes right now is as close to oneness as I'm going to get, right?

I gaze into her upturned face and the sight of her flushed features, her parted lips, her tits bouncing under her dress as she begins to ride me...is an image that will be etched into my memory forever.

She digs her fingers into my shoulders, clenches her inner muscles around my thickness. She squeezes her thighs around the outside of mine and rotates her hips.

Heat blasts up my spine. My groin hardens, my cock lengthens inside her, and damn it, but I've had enough. I piston my hips upward, and slam into her, even as I begin to work at the rope she's bound around my wrists.

She gasps aloud, lowers her chin and stares at me from under heavy eyelids. "Ohmigod," she moans, "oh, Ari, oh my—"

I chuckle, "Love it when I render you speechless, baby."

She leans in close enough for our eyelashes to tangle. "You said you'd let me take the lead," she pouts.

"I said," I thrust up and into her with enough force for her entire body to jolt, "that I'd let you restrain me, and I have. And now I'm going to fuck you with my hands tied behind my back. I'm going to tear into your pretty little pussy until your clothes tear."

"Oh my." Her pupils dilate, her lips tremble, she clamps her melting core around my length, and goosebumps rise on my skin. My vision narrows, my pores pop, and all of my senses hone in on her.

"Hold on, baby."

She digs her fingernails into my skin with enough pressure to draw blood, and hell, if that doesn't turn me on further.

I pump up and into her, again and again. With every impact she moans, whimpers, then throws her head back and wheezes, "I'm going to—"

"Come all over my dick, Sparks. Come for me."

With a low, keening cry, she arches her spine back and shatters.

She slumps into me, and instantly, I move. I yank free of my restraints, flip her over on her back and peer down at her. I reach for her panties, tear them off of her, and she gasps. She opens her eyelids, holds my gaze as I hook my fingers into the neckline of her dress and tug. The fabric tears down the center and she half screams, "Ari, what the fuck? I love this dress."

"And I love you more than anything else. I'll buy you enough dresses to fill up this yacht, hell, to fill up an entire apartment, if you want."

"I don't need that, you crazy man." She reaches up to wind her arms around my neck. "I only want you in my arms, your dick inside me, your tongue worshipping me, your legs entwined with mine as you bring me to orgasm."

"I knew it," I shake my head, "I've created a sex maniac."

"Only for your body, your lips, your mouth, your beautiful cock which, if you don't put it inside me right this moment, I'll—"

I surge forward and enter her in one long, smooth stroke.

"A...Ah..." she stutters. Her eyes roll back in her head.

"You were saying?" I chuckle.

"Hmm, what?" She clenches her inner muscles around my shaft, and bloody hell, my thighs spasm and my groin hardens. I bring her leg up and around my waist, then plant my elbows on each side of her shoulders. I piston my hips forward and plunge into her with enough force that her body moves up the bed.

I swipe my palm up her other leg and coax her to wind it around me, then grip her hips, to pin her in place.

Bending my face close to hers, I close my mouth over hers. I slide my tongue in between her lips, suck on her mouth, coax her to open herself to me completely. Then I propel my hips forward and slide into her, again and again, until the tension at the base of my spine tightens.

Under me, her body shudders. She wraps her arms and legs around me, plasters those beautiful breasts against me, then rocks up and into me, receiving all of me, finally arching against me.

I tear my mouth from hers, stare into her face, "Look at me, baby."

She cracks open her lids and her golden eyes blaze at me. This woman... She owns me, possesses me. Nothing I do will ever be enough to show her what she means to me.

"Sparks." I swallow, then brush my lips against hers, "Come with me, darling."

I pull back, then slide into her, bottoming out, hitting that spot inside of her which I know drives her wild.

Her entire body seems to hum, then she bends her spine and shatters against me. Her tight core clamps around my length and the tautness in my groin vibrates out, growing bigger, wider. The reverberations engulf me, rock me, my balls draw up, and with a groan, I empty myself inside of her. I slump down onto my elbows, lower my head and nuzzle that spot at the side of her throat where her scent is the most concentrated.

"You okay, baby?" I kiss her soft, dewy skin.

She hums.

"You sure?"

She nods her head.

Her shoulders shudder, she bites down on her lower lip, and a tear runs down from the corner of her eyes.

My heart stutters and a hot sensation stabs at my ribcage. "Sparks?" I roll over, pull her onto my chest, and cradle her. "Shh, what's wrong, sweetheart?"

"You," she hiccups, "you are what's wrong."

I stiffen, caress her spine, rub soothing circles across her back, down the curve of her hips. "Explain that to me, darling."

"You, with all of your endearments and your perfect cock, and your ability to fuck me until I come, every time. Do you know how wrong that is?"

"Huh?" I frown. "You'll have to explain that further, babe."

She pulls back in the circle of my arms and I loosen my grip, enough for her to crawl up until her face is directly over mine.

She gazes into my eyes with such intensity that heat sears the back of my neck. "What is it?" I mutter. "You can tell me anything, you know?"

She nods.

"Anything at all," I prompt, "I'll set the world on fire. Hell, I'll give up sailing if you ask." I wince. "Okay, maybe not that."

She chuckles, then bumps her fist against my shoulder, "A child," she mumbles, "I want you to get me pregnant, Ari. I want your child, our child, a child that has the best of you and me, and maybe some of the not good parts too. Sometimes, I want to hold a baby in my arms so much that it feels real, it feels as if I can see her, hold her, sense her, smell her fresh innocence. I can visualize her, imagine her, see her grow up to be the most amazing person in the world ever. Know what I mean?"

I swallow down the ball of emotion that blocks my throat. I bring her close, curl her into me, "I know, babe, I want that too."

She buries her nose in my chest and inhales. I can't stop the smile that curves my lips. "I'm so sorry for not trying my best to impregnate you the first time around. I didn't stick to my end of the bargain. I may have a small problem with letting go of control."

"You don't say," she snorts. "You're just a dominant, obnoxious alphahole, you know that?"

"I can't make excuses for that; it's what I am." I lower my head and press a kiss to the top of her head. "It's also why you can't resist me."

"Oh?"

"Yep," I hook my finger under her chin, raise her head so she meets my gaze, "But I'm going to do everything in my power to make you happy, starting with getting you pregnant."

"Promise?"

"Promise."

Don't miss Arpad and Karina's bonus scene set nine months later. Claim your FREE bonus scene HERE.

EPILOGUE 2

Ava

*"Each blossom still blooms in its field; each child still clutches your hand; each
friend still lingers in your heart. And that…is where time goes."*

I glance at the words I've scrawled out in my diary.

My heart stutters. The hair on my forearms rises. Time. Why am I so
obsessed with time? I am only nineteen; I have my entire life in front of
me. So why do I often ponder how fast time goes by? How it can all be
over in a matter of minutes… Blink, and it's gone. A mother playing with
her son as an infant one second; the next, he's all grown up and she's
shooting a movie with him as her subject. The son, who is the mirror
image of her first and only love, the man she fell for, her soulmate…who
turned out not to be. And now she has him… The son, who is the image
of the father. *Stop it…* All these thoughts that meld and flow and turn
my brain to mush. Even *Twilight* was more cheerful than this.

I hear a splash from the pool, and glance around from my perch on
the chair in the far corner of the pool area. I am at my friend Summer's
townhouse in Primrose Hill. It's February and freezing in London.
Which is why I had grabbed my book and my blanket, then crawled
over to the far end of the pool area. I'd hidden behind the wide trunk of
the oak-tree, then settled down to write.

People hate the cold. Me? I thrive on it. Darkness is my friend, my
companion. It clothes me, hides me from the sight of the world, like this
blanket that I've wrapped around myself. If I look down, I can see the
slope of Primrose Hill fall away below, the grass an undulating carpet
that stretches down to the canal. This early in the day, it is quiet, except
for a few joggers… And the man who'd dived into the pool and is now
swimming laps.

From my hiding place, I can see his massive shoulders flex as he cuts
through the water. He propels forward, leaving ripples in his wake. He's
moving so fast, he's almost a blur as his powerful arms slice through the
water. He hits one end of the swimming pool, then pushes away and
begins to swim toward the other side. He zips forward, flings out an
arm, thrusts the other back so his body shoots ahead. He lunges
onward, keeps going until he hits the other edge of the pool, then turns
back. I watch as he does five more laps of the pool… Hell, is he training

for a triathlon or something? My entire body hurts, thinking of the punishment he's putting himself through. What the hell is he trying to prove anyway?

He hits the edge of the pool, throws his arms over the rim and holds on. Then he presses his hands down on the ground, hauls himself up. He pitches his leg up and over. The corded muscles of his thigh tauten as he raises himself up and over the side. Water streams down from his sculpted chest, the cut planes of his back, and pours down the sides of his thighs. He raises his arms, throws back his head and stretches. For a second, he stands poised. The first rays of the sun hit his skin, and he seems to sparkle. My throat dries. All of my nerve endings pop. Moisture pools in my core. A shiver runs down my spine.

He turns, giving me a full-frontal view and I draw in a breath. I saw him at my friend Karina's wedding, a few weeks ago. Only difference, he had more clothes on…and he wasn't this wet. *Nor was I—ha!* Nor did he have his thick hair slicked back to outline the contours of his scalp. Nor did the hollows under his cheekbones seem this prominent. I trace my gaze down his hooked nose to his thin upper lip, made all the more pronounced by his full lower lip, which seems soft, pouty enough for me to sink my teeth into and suck. My belly clenches. My core softens. I squeeze my thighs together, watch as he moves toward the deckchair and picks up a towel. He drags it down his massive chest, across that ripped stomach, down the crotch of his black swimsuit, which outline what he's packing. I bite down on the inside of my cheek. Is that man packing or what?

Is he some kind of athlete? He has that strength and confidence that comes with someone who works a physical profession. Or else, he trains a lot. As evidenced by this morning's work out.

He loops the towel around his neck, straightens, then meets my gaze.

I pull back. "Shit, shit, shit." *Did he see me? Of course, he spotted me.* He seems like the kind of man who wouldn't miss a thing in his surroundings.

Go on, get out there and wave at him or something. Tell him 'Hi.'

"Hi." I wiggle my fingers in the air in his general direction, too embarrassed to look that way again.

"Hello, there." A gruff voice sounds above me and I yelp. My heart pounds in my chest as I glance up, straight at eye-level with his gorgeous crotch—now covered by his pants. He'd managed to pull those on before heading over, apparently. Not that it does anything to hide, but rather, reveals the gargantuan proportions of whatever it is that it encloses.

Jeez, get your mind out of the gutter, bitch.

I raise my gaze, and hell, if the view doesn't get even more serious. Dense muscles, packed one on top of the other, moving, slipping, sliding as he draws in a breath. An intricate design inches over one shoulder, and damn, if I don't want to jump up and peek around to find out how it continues across his back.

He folds his arms across his chest and his biceps bulge.

Heat sears my blood. My thighs clench.

I tilt my head back, and further back. The sun chooses that moment to shine on him again, shadowing his features. This guy is a sun trap; that's for sure. The golden glow folds about him, caresses him, so sparks of amber flare in the air around him. I blink, and his face comes into view. Dark close-cropped hair slicked back from the water. His eyes are golden...amber with a hint of black in their depths. Like he has secrets which he holds close to his chest. Thick eyelashes that sweep down over high cheekbones you could cut yourself on. I curl my fingers into fists and my nails dig into my flesh.

A scar mars the expanse of his left cheek, and somehow that only heightens how perfect the rest of his face is.

"You okay?" He tilts his head.

"Of course." My voice cracks and I clear my throat. "Why wouldn't I be?"

"You seem like you saw something...unexpected?"

"Uh, you're not a vampire, are you?"

He blinks, then chuckles. A full-throated, deep reverberation that sucker-punches me in the gut. My thighs tremble. My toes curl. I watch as those full lips of his quirk.

"I'm Edward." He holds out his hand.

"Wha—" I gape, "you're kidding me, right?"

He frowns. "Excuse me?"

"Your...your name," I choke out. "It can't be Edward."

"I am not following..." His cultured tone carries a note of warning, which I ignore.

"I mean, you can't be called Edward. Who put you up to this? Was it Isla?" Only she knows about my slightly stalkerish obsession with Edward, from Twilight, and surely, she wouldn't tell the others, right?

"Ah." The wrinkles on his forehead dissipate. "You're Isla's friend?"

I hold out my hand, "Ava."

"Ava?" He frowns.

He touches my hand and the rest of the words dry in my throat. Goosebumps flare on my skin. His gaze widens and the planes of his chest twitch. Did he feel that shock of the impact as well? I try to pull back my hand but he holds onto it.

"Why are you hiding, Eve?"

"I'm not," I scowl. "and that's not my name."

"It suits you better," he tilts his head, "and you haven't answered my question yet."

"Which one?"

"What are you doing here?"

"I came here to write," I bite the inside of my cheek, "only... I heard the splashing in the pool and I turned around and spotted you swimming.

"And you watched?" His lips curl in a hint of a smirk.

I glance away. "I, uh, may have peeked a bit."

"Did you like what you saw?"

I jerk my head in his direction, to find him watching me closely. His expression is one of curiosity, like I am some kind of lab specimen whose responses he is clocking in a clinical way. The hair on the back of my neck rises. I want to glance away, break the connection with this man, but I can't. My pulse rate ratchets up. Despite the chill in the morning, my palms begin to sweat. I clear my gaze, force the words out, "Wh....why Eve?"

"You know why." He peruses my features. "And you haven't answered the question."

"Do I?" My heart begins to race. "And what question?"

"You know the answer to both." He folds his arms across his chest and his impressive biceps bulge. Heat blooms between my legs and I resist the urge to rub my thighs together.

"I'm not sure what you're referring to," I say stiffly, "and no, I don't find you attractive."

His grin widens, and the impact of that smile... Oh, my. His teeth sparkle against the tan of his skin, his features brighten, the charisma pours off of him, and honestly, I can't glance away. I take in the gleam in his eyes, the hair on his forehand drying and already curling a little.

I blink. "Aren't you cold?"

The breeze picks up, and a strand of hair whips across my face.

He releases my hand, only to lean down and push the hair aside. Goosebumps pop on my skin. My stomach trembles and my heart begins to race. I watch as his gaze holds mine, as the pupils of his eyes dilate. His nostrils flare, and he straightens. "I'd better be going. Sinclair's expecting me for breakfast."

"Oh, that's right. Me too." I'd promised Summer I'd join them for breakfast. I jump up, and the movement brings me close to him. The heat of his body slams into my chest and my throat dries. I stare up at him, as he glares down his nose. Something like anger steals across his features, before he schools all expression from his face. A strange sensation grips my chest. I draw in a breath and the oxygen rushes to my head. Shit, when had I forgotten to breathe? He steps back, and the cold air rushes in. I shiver.

He pivots, walking toward the pool house. I take in the tattoo of the snake that crawls diagonally across his back. Whoa! That's one mean-ass tattoo. It's as spectacular as it is unexpected against the much paler skin of his back. The forked tongue of the snake is thick in girth, and within it are etched tribal signs that I can't decipher. The edge of it flows over his shoulder, which is what I must have seen earlier. The scales on the snake are patterned in color and the triangular head has slitted eyes which seem to follow me as I jump to my feet, then tug the blanket around me, hold my book close and follow.

"Hold on," I protest, "your legs are too long."

He slows his pace and I catch up.

"So, you are a friend of Sinclair's?"

He nods.

"You're one of the Seven, aren't you?" I peer up into his face, "I saw you at Arpad and Karina's wedding."

His jaw hardens. Now what did I say for him to seem angry?

"Surely, you remember?" I mutter. "Didn't you notice me?"

"I don't notice every girl who crosses my path."

I blink, then pause my steps, "Now, that's not fair. I could have sworn that you saw me there. Besides, I am not a girl."

He pulls forward, and I run to catch up. "Did you hear what I said?" I demand. "I am not a—"

"Girl." He stops so quickly that I bump into him. The scent of chlorine, and under that, the fresh-cut grass scent of him teases my nostrils. I draw in a breath, filling my lungs with his earthy essence. Moisture pools in my center and my nerve-endings seem to fire all at once. Why the hell does he have to smell so utterly delectable?

He pivots to face me and the heat of his body seems to turn up a notch. Does this man have a furnace under his skin, or what?

He looks me up and down. "What are you then?" he asks.

"What—" I blink.

"You said you are not a girl, so what are you?"

I tip up my chin. "A woman." I square my shoulders. "I am a woman."

"And I..." He squares his shoulders, "I am sworn to celibacy."

*To find out what happens next, read Billionaire's Sins **HERE***

Binge read the Big Bad Billionaire Series

US

UK

All markets

Start the series with Sinclair & Summer's story here

Read Saint & Victoria's story here

Read Weston & Amelie's story here

Read Damian & Julia's story here

Read an excerpt from mafia king

Karma

"Morn came and went—and came, and brought no day..."

Tears prick the back of my eyes. Goddamn Byron. Crept up on me when I am at my weakest. Not that I am a poetry addict, by any measure, but words are my jam.

The one consolation I have, that when everything else in the world is wrong, I can turn to them, and they'll be there, friendly steady, waiting with open arms. And this particular poem had laced my blood, crawled into my gut when I'd first read it. Darkness had folded into me like an insidious snake that raises its head when I least expect it. Like now. I'd managed to give my bodyguard the slip and veered off my usual running route to reach *Waterlow Park*.

I look out on the still sleeping city of London, from the grassy slope of the expanse. Somewhere out there the Mafia was hunting me, apparently.

I purse my lips, close my eyes. Silence. The rustle of the wind between the leaves, the faint tinkle of the water from the nearby spring.

I could be the last person on this planet, alone, unsung, bound for the grave.

Ugh! Stop. Right there. I drag the back of my hand across my nose. Try it again, focus, get the words out, one after the other, like the steps of my sorry life.

"Morn came and went—and came, and brought no day..." My voice breaks. "Bloody, asinine, hell." I dig my fingers into the grass and grab a handful and fling it out. Again. From the top. I open my eyes, focus on a spot in the distance.

"Morn came and went—and came, and...."

"...brought no day."

I whip my head around. His profile fills my line of sight. Dark hair combed back by a ruthless hand that booked no measure.

My throat dries.

Hooked nose, thin upper lip, a fleshy lower lip, that hints at hidden desires. Heat. Lust. The sensuous scrape of that whiskered jaw over my innermost places. Across my inner thigh, reaching toward that core of me that throbs, clenches, melts to feel the stab of his tongue, the thrust of his hardness as he impales me, takes me, makes me his.

"Of this their desolation; and all hearts
Were chill'd into a selfish prayer for light.."

Sweat beads my palm; the hairs on my nape rise. "Who are you?"

He stares ahead, his lips moving,

"Forests were set on fire—but hour by hour
They fell and faded—and the crackling trunks
Extinguish'd with a crash—and all was black."

I swallow, squeeze my thighs together. Moisture gathers in my core. How can I be wet by the mere cadence of this stranger's voice?

I spring up to my feet.

"Sit down."

His voice is unhurried, lazy even, his spine erect. The cut of his black jacket stretches across the width of his massive shoulders. His hair... I was mistaken. There are strands of dark gold woven between the darkness that pours down to brush the nape of his neck. My fingers tingle. My scalp itches.

I take in a breath and my lungs burn.

This man, he's sucked all the oxygen in this open space, as if he owns it, the master of all he surveys. The master of me. My death. My life. A shiver ladders its way up my spine. *Get away, get away now, while you still can.*

I take a step back.

"I won't ask again."

Ask. Command. Force me to do as he wants. He'll have me on my back, bent over, on the side, over him, under him, he'll surround me, overwhelm me, pin me down with the force of his personality. His charisma, his larger-than-life essence that will crush everything else out of me and I... I'll love it.

"No."

"Yes."

A fact. A statement of intent, spoken aloud. So true. So real. Too real. Too much. Too fast. All of my nightmares... my dreams come to life. Everything I've wanted is here in front of me. I'll die a thousand deaths before he'll be done with me... and then, will I be reborn? For him. For me. For myself. I live first and foremost to be the woman I am... am meant to be.

"You want to run?"

No.

No.

I nod my head.

He turns his head and all of the breath leaves my lungs. Blue eyes, cerulean, dark like the morning skies, deep like the nighttime, hidden corners, secrets that I don't dare uncover. He'll destroy me, have my heart, and break it so casually.

My throat burns. A boiling sensation squeezes my chest.

"Go then, my beauty, fly. You have until I count to five. If I catch you, you are mine."

"If you don't?"

"Then I'll come after you, stalk your every living moment, possess your nightmares, and steal you away in the dead of midnight, and then..."

I draw in a shuddering breath; liquid heat drips from between my legs. "Then?" I whisper.

"Then, I'll ensure you'll never belong to anyone else, you'll never see the light of day again, for your every breath, your every waking second, your thoughts, your actions... and all of your words, every single last one, will belong to me." He peels back his lips, and his teeth glint in the first rays of the morning light. "Only me." He straightens to his feet, and rises, and rises.

He is massive. A beast. A monster who always gets his way. My guts churn. My toes curl. Something primal inside me insists I hold my own. I cannot give in to him. Cannot let him win whatever this is. I need to stake my ground in some form. *Say something. Anything. Show him you're not afraid of him.*

"Why?" I tilt my head back, all the way back. "Why are you doing this?"

He tilts his head, his ears almost canine in the way they are silhouetted against his profile.

"Is it because you can? Is it a… a..." I blink, "a debt of some kind?"

He stills.

"My father. This is about how he betrayed the Mafia, right? You're one of them?"

All expression is wiped clean of his face, and I know then I am right. My past… Why does it always catch up with me? *You can run, but you can never hide.*

"Tick-tock, Beauty." He angles his body and his shoulders shut out the sight of the sun, the dawn skies, the horizon, the city in the distance, the whisper of the grass, the trees, the rustle of the leaves... All of it fades, and leaves me and him. Us. *Run.*

"Five." He jerks his chin. Straightens the cuffs of his sleeves.

My knees wobble.

"Four."

My heart hammers in my chest. I should go. Leave. But my feet are welded to this earth. This piece of land where we first met. What am I, but a speck in the larger scheme of things? To be hurt. To be forgotten. To be brought to the edge of climax and taken without an ounce of retribution. To be punished... by him.

"Three." He thrusts out his chest, widens his stance, every muscle in his body relaxed. "Two."

I swallow. The pulse beats at my temples. My blood thrums.

"One."

Michael

"Go."

She pivots and races down the slope. The fabric of her dress streams behind her, scarlet in the blue morning. Her scent, lushly feminine with silver moonflowers, clings to my nose, then recedes. I reach forward, thrust out my chin, sniff the air, but there's only the green scent of dawn. She stumbles and I jump forward. Pause when she straightens. *Wait. Wait. Give her a lead. Let her think she has almost escaped, that she's gotten the better of me… As if.* I clench my fists at my sides, force myself to relax. *Wait. Wait.* She reaches the bottom of the incline, turns. I surge forward. One foot in front of the other, my heels dig into the grassy surface as mud flies up, clinging to the edges of my £4000 Italian pants. Like I care? Plenty more where that came from. An entire walk-in closet full of tailor-made clothes, to suit every occasion, with every possible accessory needed by a man in my position to impress… everything, except the one thing that I have coveted from the first time I had laid eyes on her. Sitting there on the grassy slope, unshed tears in her eyes, and reciting… Byron? For hell's sake. Of all the poet's in the world, she had to choose the Lord of Darkness.

I huff. All a ploy. Clearly, she'd known I was sitting near her… No, not possible. I had walked toward her and she hadn't stirred, hadn't been aware. Yeah, I am that good. I've been known to slice a man from ear to ear while he was awake and fully aware. Alive one second, dead the next. That's how it is in my world. You want it, you take it. And I… I want her.

I increase my pace, eat up the distance between myself and the girl… that's all she is. A slip of a thing, a slim blur of motion. Beauty in hiding. A diamond in the rough, waiting for me to get my hands on her, polish her, show her what it means to be… dead. She is dead. That's why I am here.

Her skirts flash behind her, exposing a creamy length of thigh. My groin hardens; my legs wobble. I lurch over a bump in the ground. The hell? I right myself, leap forward, inching closer, closer. She reaches a curve in the path, disappears out of sight. My heart hammers in my chest. I will not lose her, will not. *Here, Beauty, come to Daddy.* The wind whistles past my ears. I pump my legs, lengthen my strides, turn the corner. There's no one there, huh?

My heart hammers, the blood pounds at my wrists and my temples, and adrenaline thrums through my veins. I slow down, come to a stop. Scan the clearing.

The hairs on my forearms prickle. She's here. Not far. Where? *Where is she?* I prowl across to the edge of the clearing, under the tree with its spreading branches. *When I get my hands on you, Beauty, I'll spread your legs like the pages of a poem. Dip into your honeyed sweetness, like a quill into an inkwell, drag my aching shaft across that melting weeping entrance.* My balls throb. My groin tightens. The crack of a branch above shivers across my stretched nerve endings. Instinctively, I swoop forward, hold out my arms. A blur of red, dark blonde hair, skirt swept up in a gust of breeze. She drops into my arms and I close my grasp around the trembling, squirming mass of precious humanity. I cradle her close to my chest, heart beating thud-thud-thud, overwhelming any other thought.

Mine. All mine. The hell is wrong with me? She wriggles her little body, and her curves slide across my forearms. My shoulders bunch, my fingers tingle. She kicks out with her legs and arches her back. Her breasts thrust up, the nipples outlined against the fabric of her jogging vest. *She'd dared come out dressed like that…? In that scrap of fabric that barely covered her luscious flesh?*

"Let me go." She whips her head toward me, her hair flowing around her shoulders, across her face. She blows it out of the way. "You monster, get away from me."

Anger drums at the backs of my eyes; desire tugs at my groin. The scent of her is sheer torture, something that I had dreamed of in the wee hours of twilight when dusk turned into night. She's not real. Not the woman I think she is. She is my downfall. My sweet poison. The bitter medicine I must imbibe to cure the ills that plague my company.

"Fine." I lower my arms and she tumbles to the floor, hits the ground butt first.

"How dare you?" She huffs out a breath, her hair messily arranged across her face.

I shove my hands into the pockets of my fitted pants, knees slightly bent, legs apart. Tip my chin down and watch her as she sprawls at my feet.

"You… dropped me?" She makes a sound deep in her throat.

So damn adorable.

"Your wish is my command." I quirk my lips.

"You don't mean it."

"You're right." I lean my weight forward on the balls of my feet and she flinches.

"What… what do you want?"

"You."

She pales. "You want to… rob me? I have nothing of value. I'm not carrying anything… except." She reaches for her pocket.

"Don't." I growl.

"It's only my phone."

"So you say, hmm?"

"You can…" She swallows, "you can trust me."

I chuckle.

"I mean, it's not like I can deck you with a phone or anything, right?"

I glare at her and she swallows. "Fine… you… you take it."

Interesting.

"Hands behind your neck."

She hesitates.

"Now."

She instantly folds her arms at the elbows, cradles the back of her head with her palms.

I lean down and every muscle in her body tenses. Good. She's wary. She should be. She should have been alert enough to have run as soon as she sensed my presence. But she hadn't. And I'd delayed what was meant to happen long enough.

I pull the gun from my pocket, hold it to her temple. "Goodbye Beauty."

TO FIND OUT WHAT HAPPENS NEXT READ KARMA AND MICHAEL BYRON'S STORY **HERE**

CLAIM YOUR FREE CONTEMPORARY ROMANCE BOOK. CLICK HERE

CLAIM YOUR FREE PARANORMAL ROMANCE BOOK HERE

MORE BOOKS BY L. STEELE

JOIN MY NEWSLETTER

FOLLOW ME ON **AMAZON**

FOLLOW ME ON BOOKBUB

FOLLOW ON GOODREADS

FOLLOW ME ON TIKTOK

FOLLOW MY PINTEREST BOARDS

FOLLOW ME ON **FB**

FOLLOW ME ON INSTAGRAM

JOIN MY SECRET FACEBOOK READER GROUP; I AM DYING TO MEET **YOU!**

FOLLOW ME ON TWITTER

READ MY BOOKS **HERE**

FREE BOOKS

 Created with Vellum